MR. PUZZLE

Super Collection!

by Chris "Elio" Eliopoulos

capstone
young readers

MR. PUZZLE

Super Collection!

Ashley C. Andersen Zantop - PUBLISHER
Donald Lemke - EDITOR
Michael Dahl - EDITORIAL DIRECTOR
Brann Garvey - SENIOR DESIGNER
Heather Kindseth - CREATIVE DIRECTOR
Bob Lentz - ART DIRECTOR

Mr. Puzzle Super Collection! is published by
Capstone Young Readers
1710 Roe Crest Drive
North Mankato, Minnesota 56003
www.capstoneyoungreaders.com

Cataloging-in-Publication Data is available
on the Library of Congress website.

ISBN (paperback): 978-1-62370-035-5

Printed in China by Nordica.
1213/CA21302224
112013   007892R

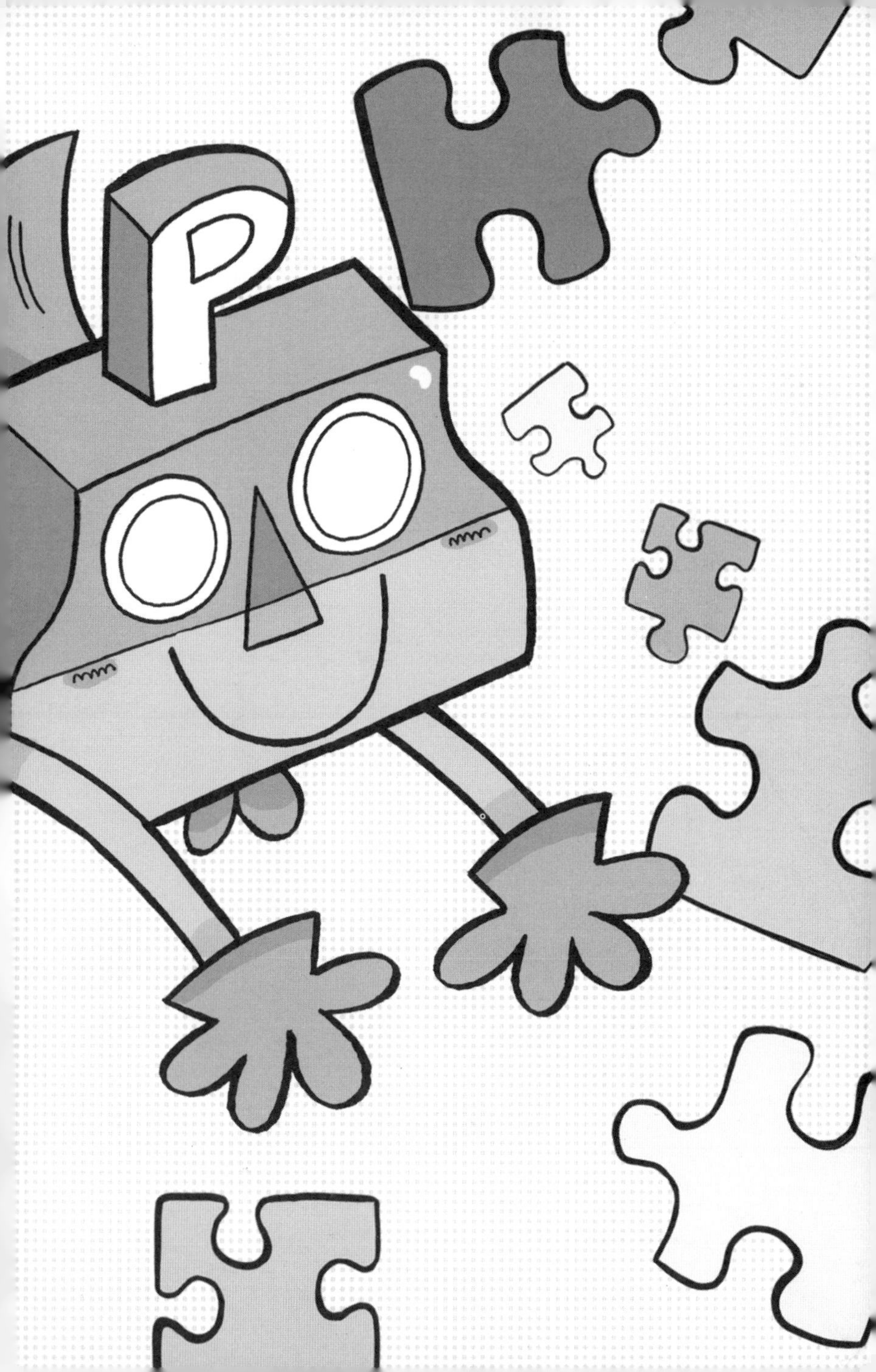
P

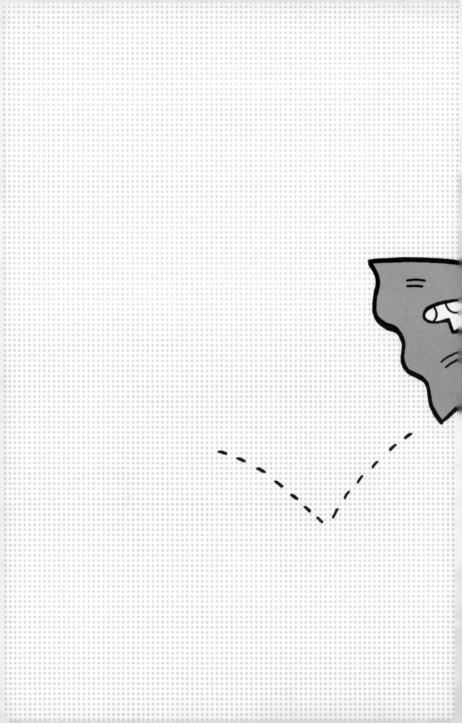

MR. PUZZLE

A Perfect Fit

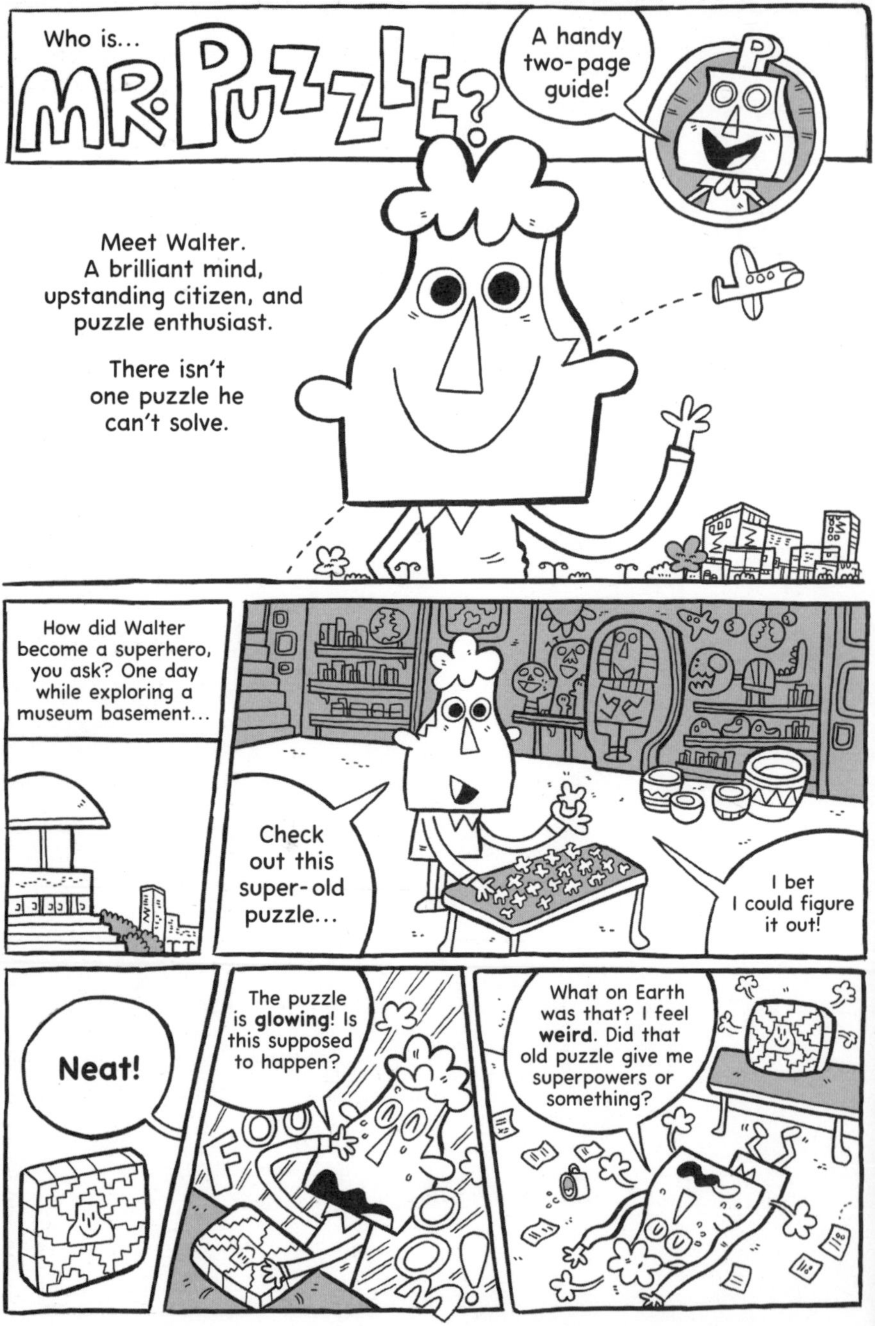
Who is...
MR. PUZZLE?
A handy two-page guide!
Meet Walter. A brilliant mind, upstanding citizen, and puzzle enthusiast.
There isn't one puzzle he can't solve.
How did Walter become a superhero, you ask? One day while exploring a museum basement...
Check out this super-old puzzle...
I bet I could figure it out!
Neat!
The puzzle is **glowing**! Is this supposed to happen?
FOOOOM!
What on Earth was that? I feel **weird**. Did that old puzzle give me superpowers or something?

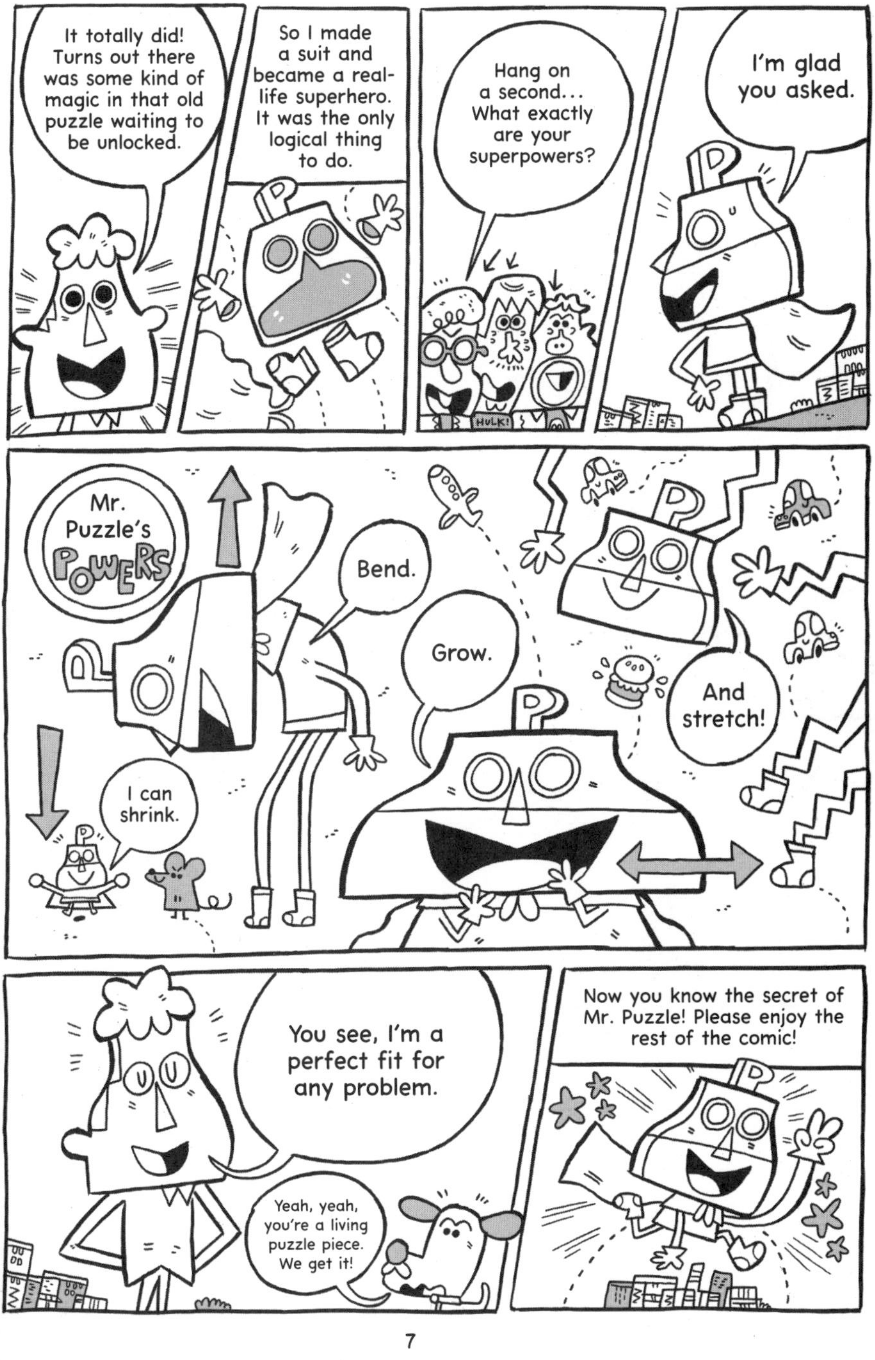
It totally did! Turns out there was some kind of magic in that old puzzle waiting to be unlocked.
So I made a suit and became a real-life superhero. It was the only logical thing to do.
Hang on a second... What exactly are your superpowers?
HULK!
I'm glad you asked.
Mr. Puzzle's POWERS
Bend.
Grow.
And stretch!
I can shrink.
You see, I'm a perfect fit for any problem.
Yeah, yeah, you're a living puzzle piece. We get it!
Now you know the secret of Mr. Puzzle! Please enjoy the rest of the comic!

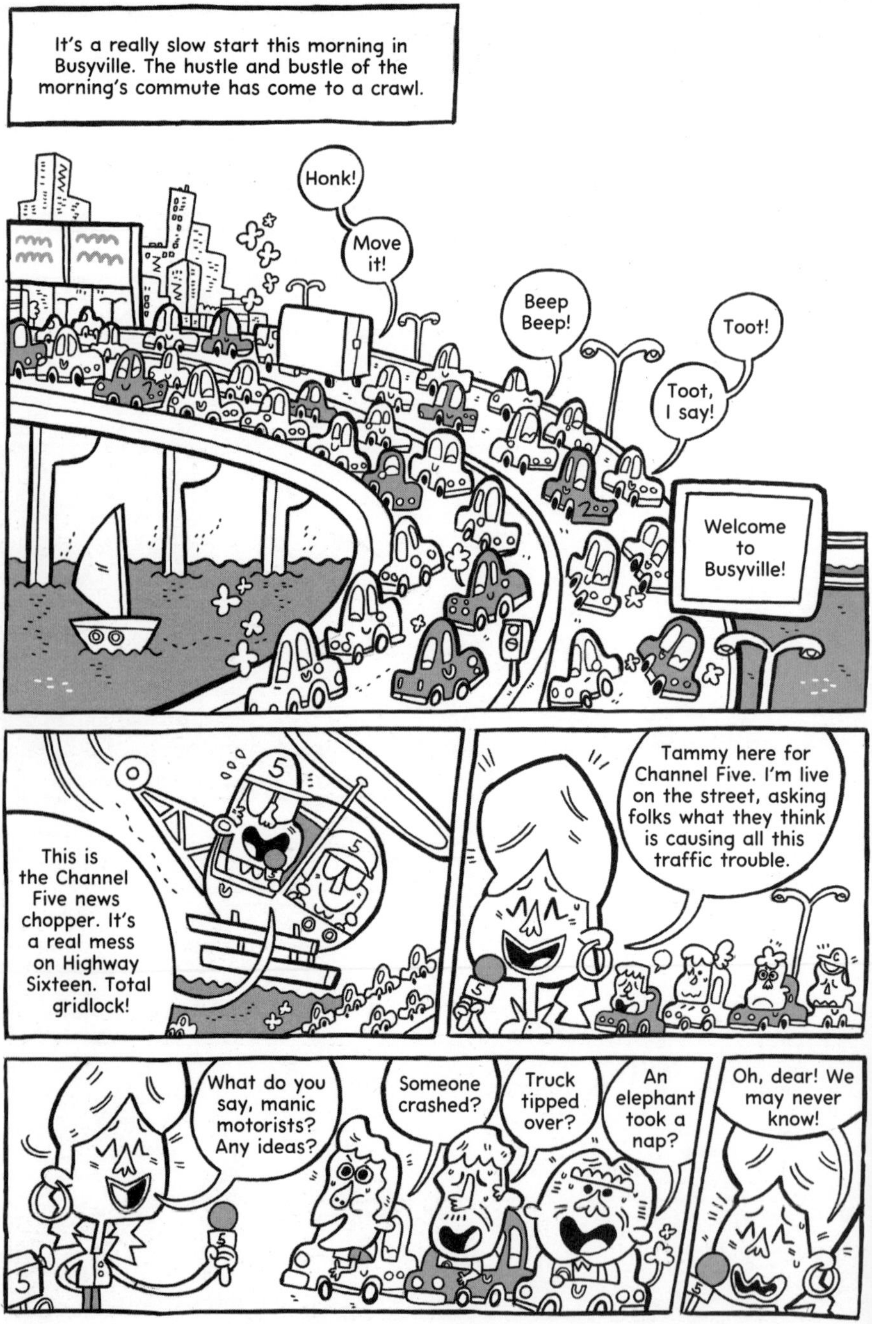
It's a really slow start this morning in Busyville. The hustle and bustle of the morning's commute has come to a crawl.
Honk!
Move it!
Beep Beep!
Toot!
Toot, I say!
Welcome to Busyville!
This is the Channel Five news chopper. It's a real mess on Highway Sixteen. Total gridlock!
Tammy here for Channel Five. I'm live on the street, asking folks what they think is causing all this traffic trouble.
What do you say, manic motorists? Any ideas?
Someone crashed?
Truck tipped over?
An elephant took a nap?
Oh, dear! We may never know!

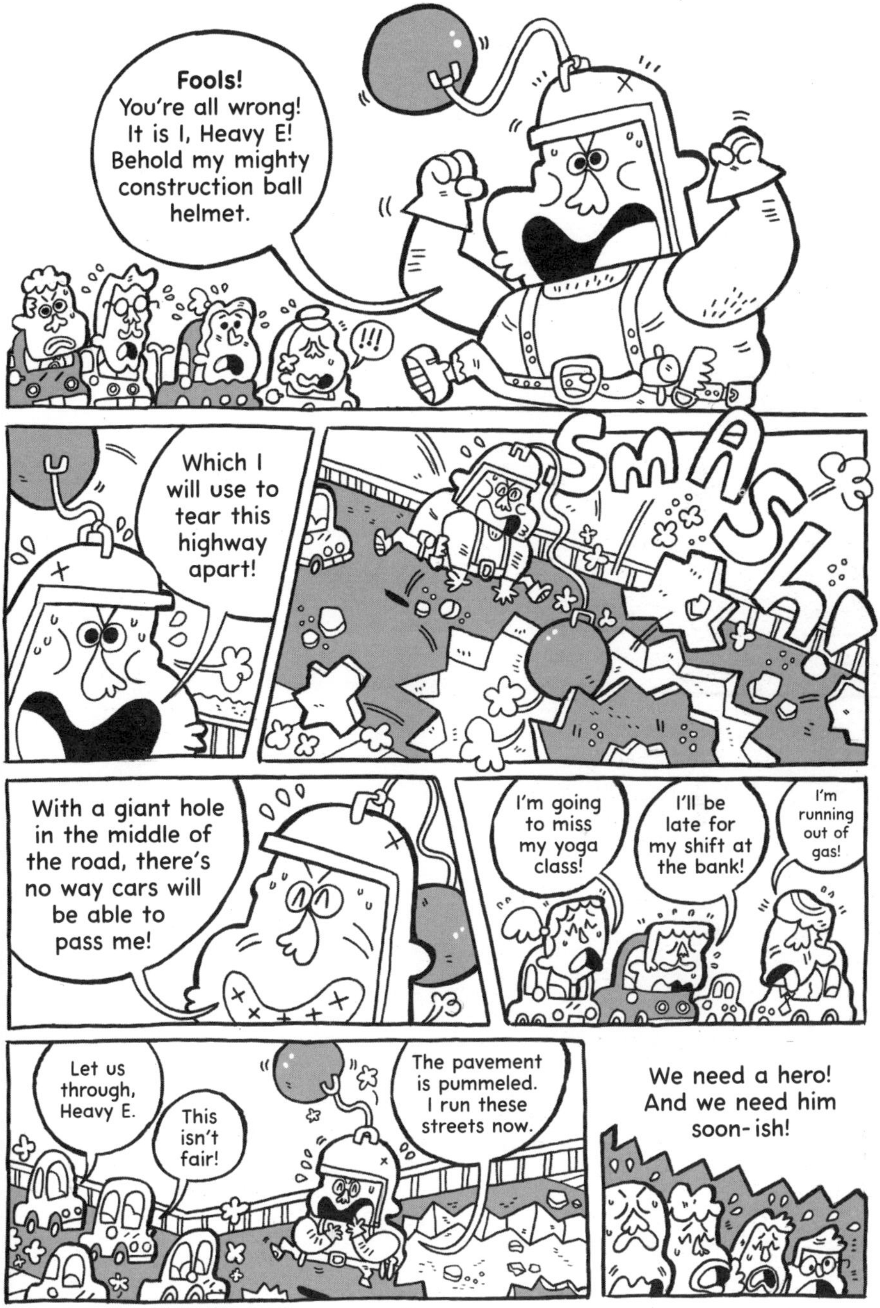

Fools!
You're all wrong! It is I, Heavy E! Behold my mighty construction ball helmet.
!!!
Which I will use to tear this highway apart!
SMASH
With a giant hole in the middle of the road, there's no way cars will be able to pass me!
I'm going to miss my yoga class!
I'll be late for my shift at the bank!
I'm running out of gas!
Let us through, Heavy E.
This isn't fair!
The pavement is pummeled. I run these streets now.
We need a hero! And we need him soon-ish!

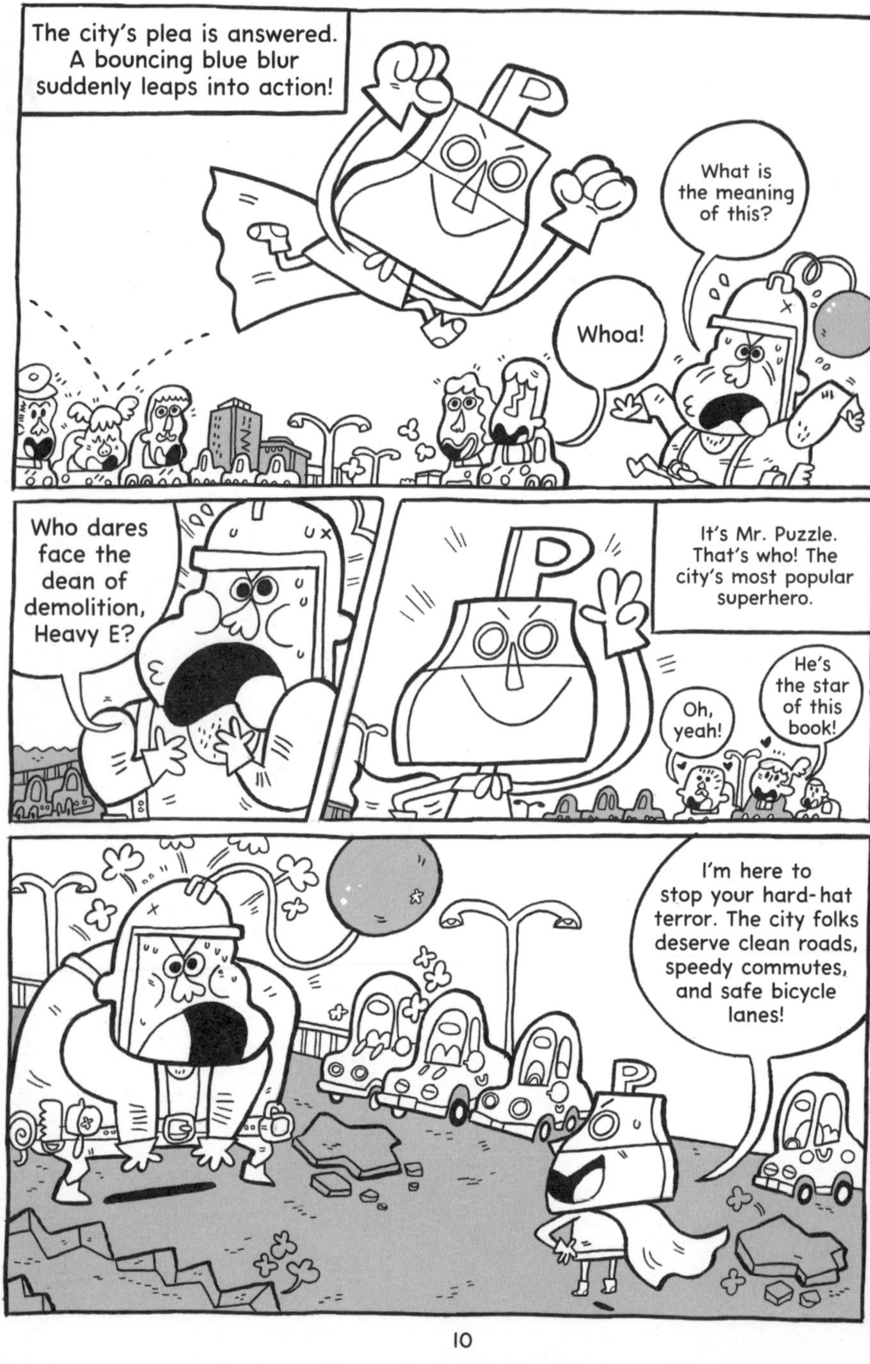
The city's plea is answered. A bouncing blue blur suddenly leaps into action!
What is the meaning of this?
Whoa!
Who dares face the dean of demolition, Heavy E?
It's Mr. Puzzle. That's who! The city's most popular superhero.
Oh, yeah!
He's the star of this book!
I'm here to stop your hard-hat terror. The city folks deserve clean roads, speedy commutes, and safe bicycle lanes!

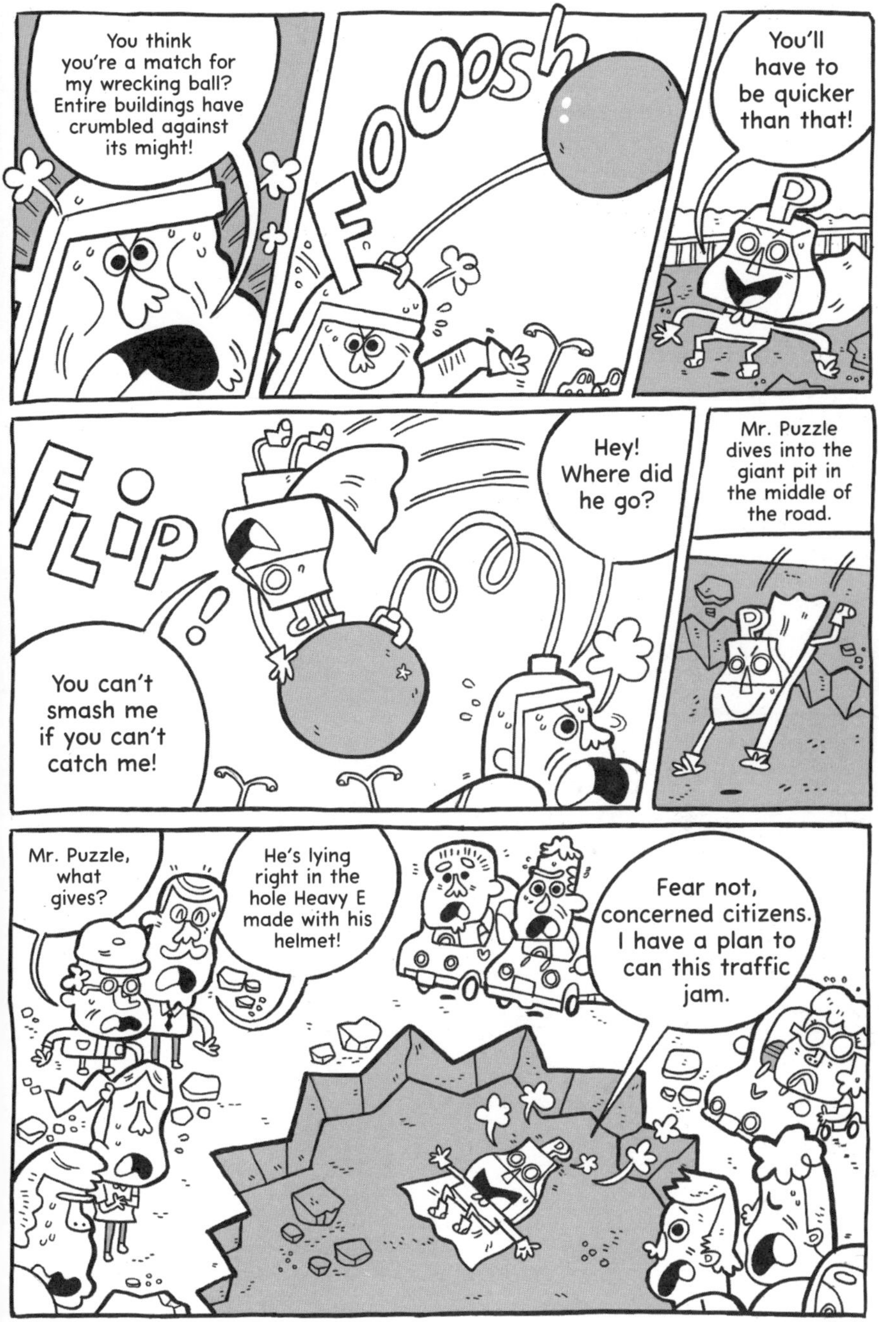
You think you're a match for my wrecking ball? Entire buildings have crumbled against its might!
FOOOOSH
F
You'll have to be quicker than that!
FLIP
!
You can't smash me if you can't catch me!
Hey! Where did he go?
Mr. Puzzle dives into the giant pit in the middle of the road.
Mr. Puzzle, what gives?
He's lying right in the hole Heavy E made with his helmet!
Fear not, concerned citizens. I have a plan to can this traffic jam.

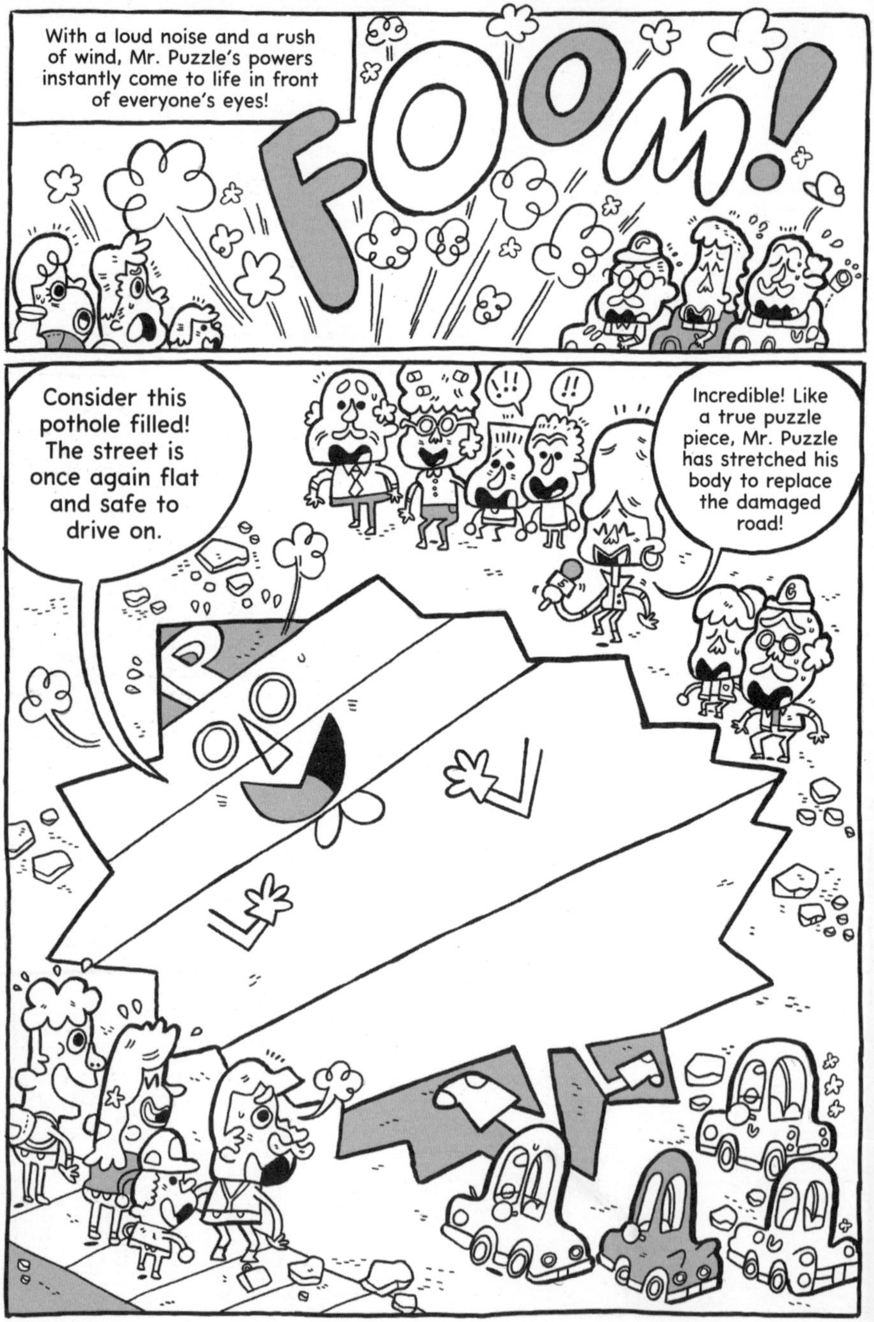
With a loud noise and a rush of wind, Mr. Puzzle's powers instantly come to life in front of everyone's eyes!
FOOM!
Consider this pothole filled! The street is once again flat and safe to drive on.
!!!
!!
Incredible! Like a true puzzle piece, Mr. Puzzle has stretched his body to replace the damaged road!

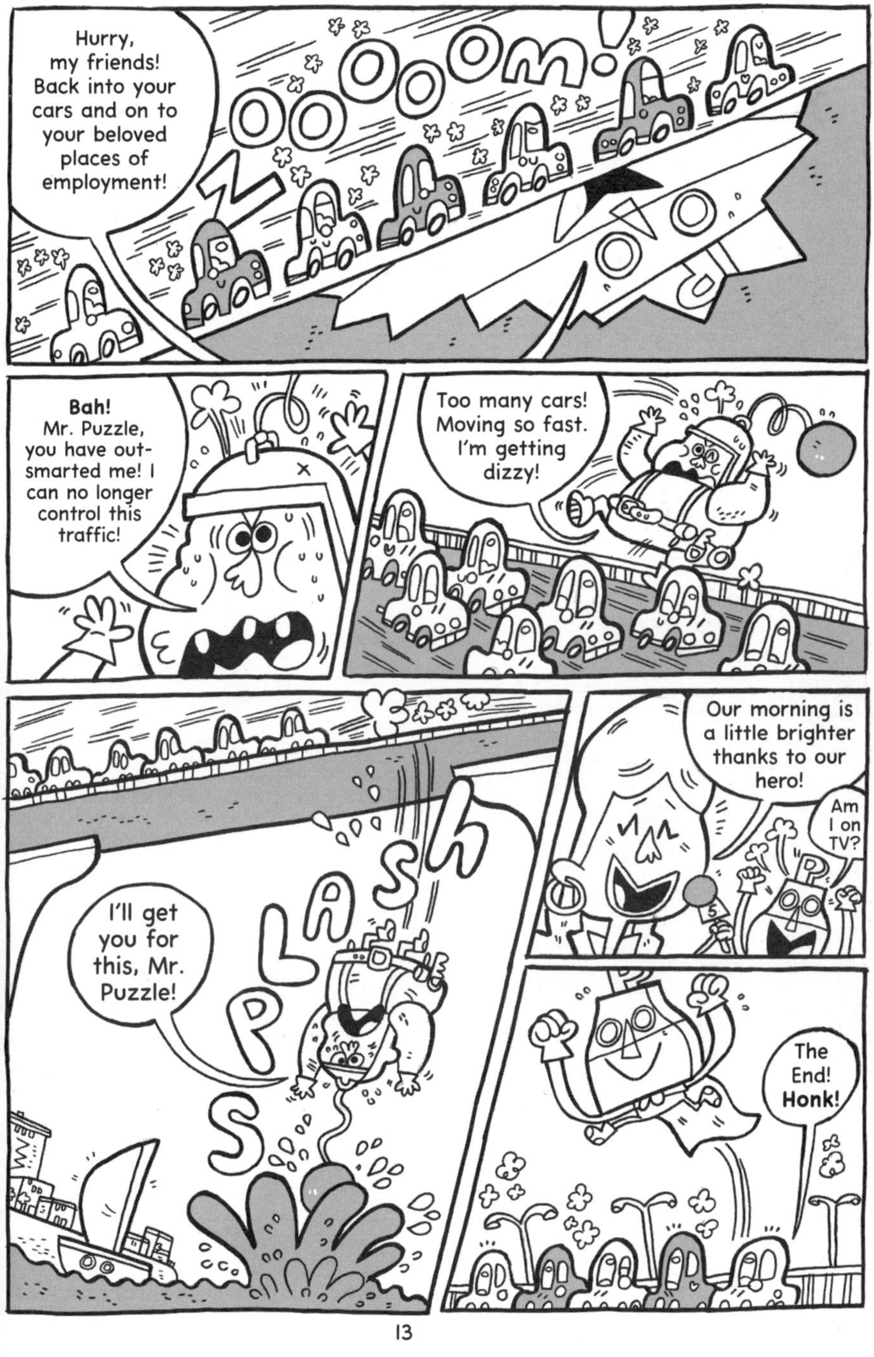

Hurry, my friends! Back into your cars and on to your beloved places of employment!
ZOOOOOM!
Bah! Mr. Puzzle, you have outsmarted me! I can no longer control this traffic!
Too many cars! Moving so fast. I'm getting dizzy!
SPLASh
I'll get you for this, Mr. Puzzle!
Our morning is a little brighter thanks to our hero!
Am I on TV?
The End! Honk!

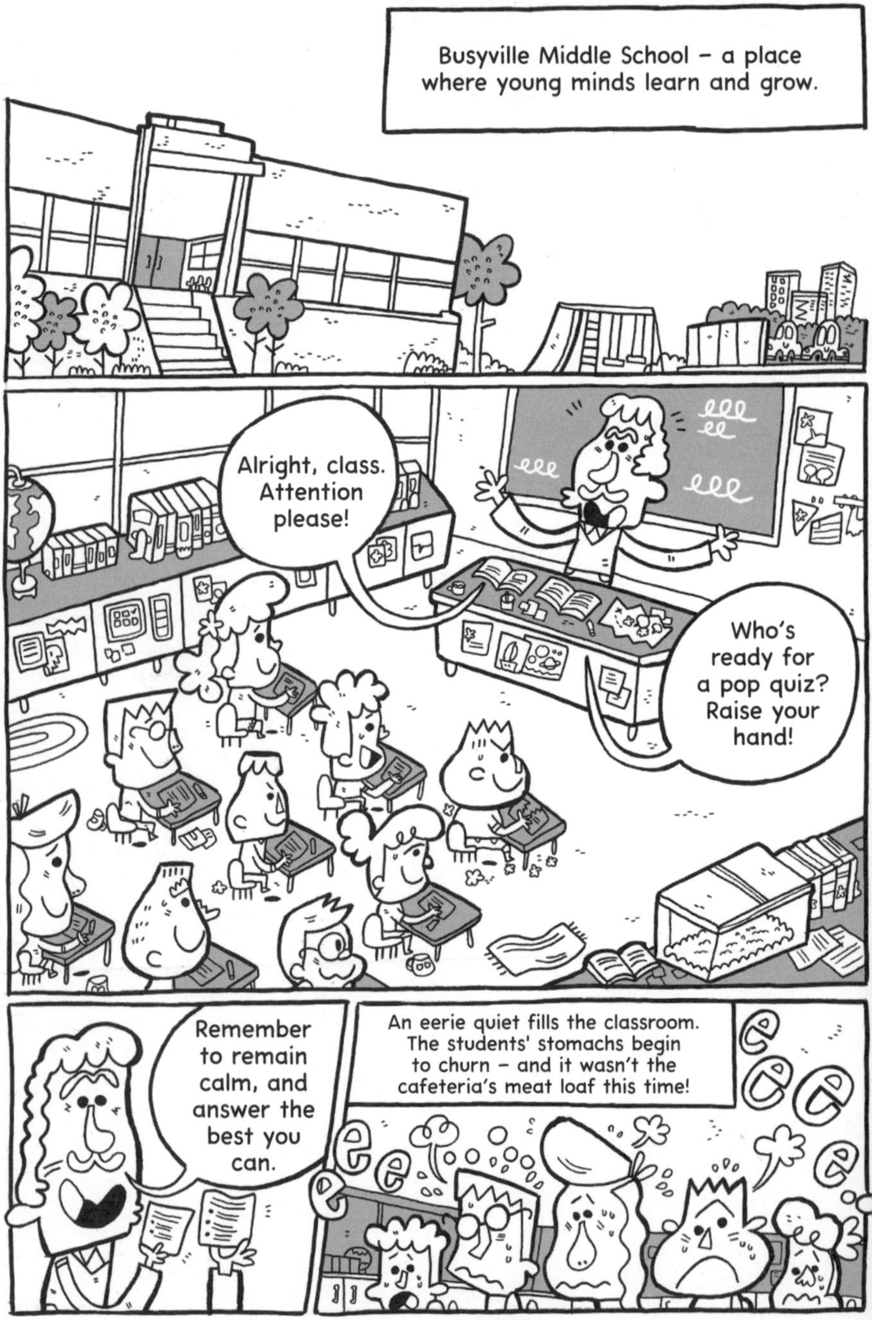
Busyville Middle School – a place where young minds learn and grow.
Alright, class. Attention please!
Who's ready for a pop quiz? Raise your hand!
Remember to remain calm, and answer the best you can.
An eerie quiet fills the classroom. The students' stomachs begin to churn – and it wasn't the cafeteria's meat loaf this time!

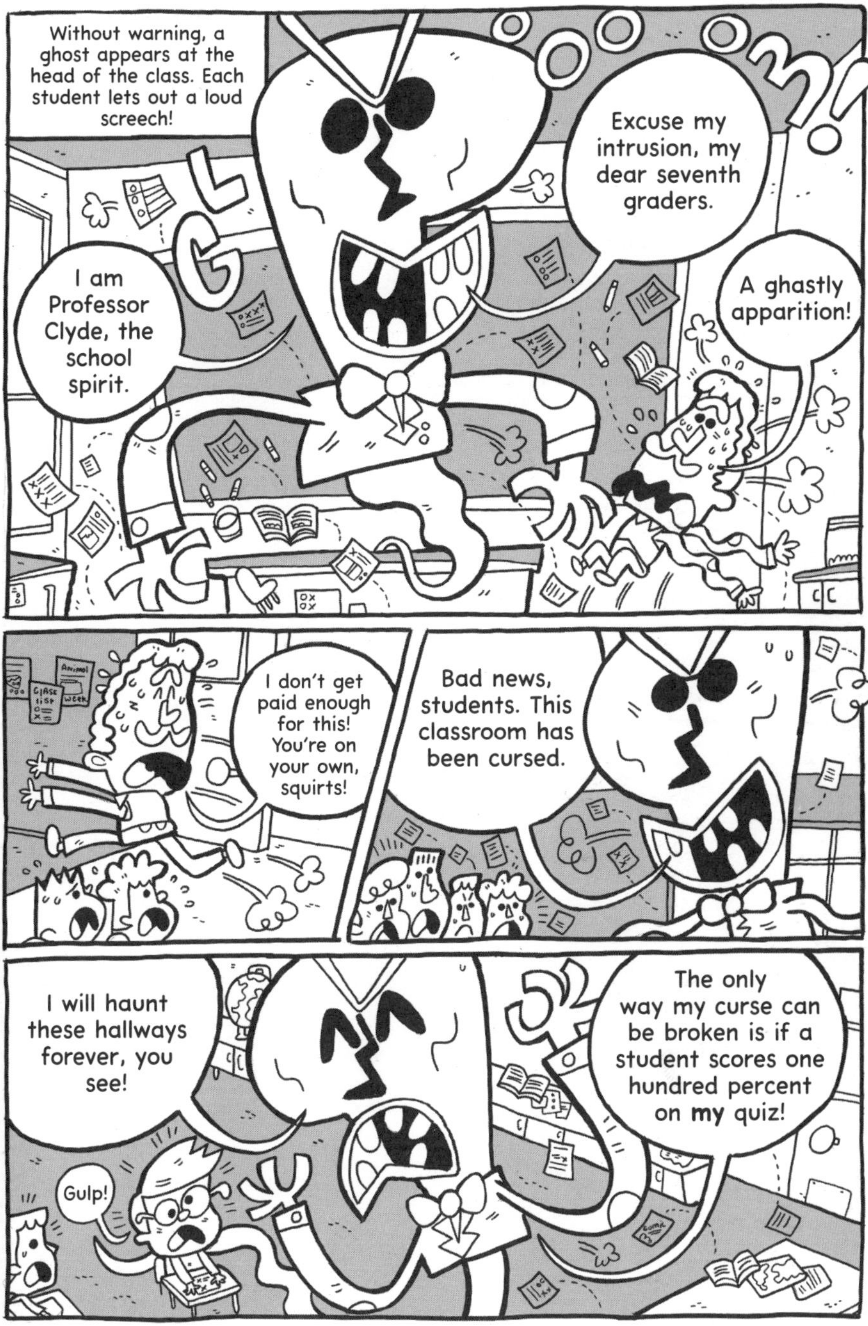

Without warning, a ghost appears at the head of the class. Each student lets out a loud screech!
OOOOM!
GL
Excuse my intrusion, my dear seventh graders.
I am Professor Clyde, the school spirit.
A ghastly apparition!
I don't get paid enough for this! You're on your own, squirts!
Bad news, students. This classroom has been cursed.
I will haunt these hallways forever, you see!
The only way my curse can be broken is if a student scores one hundred percent on **my** quiz!
Gulp!

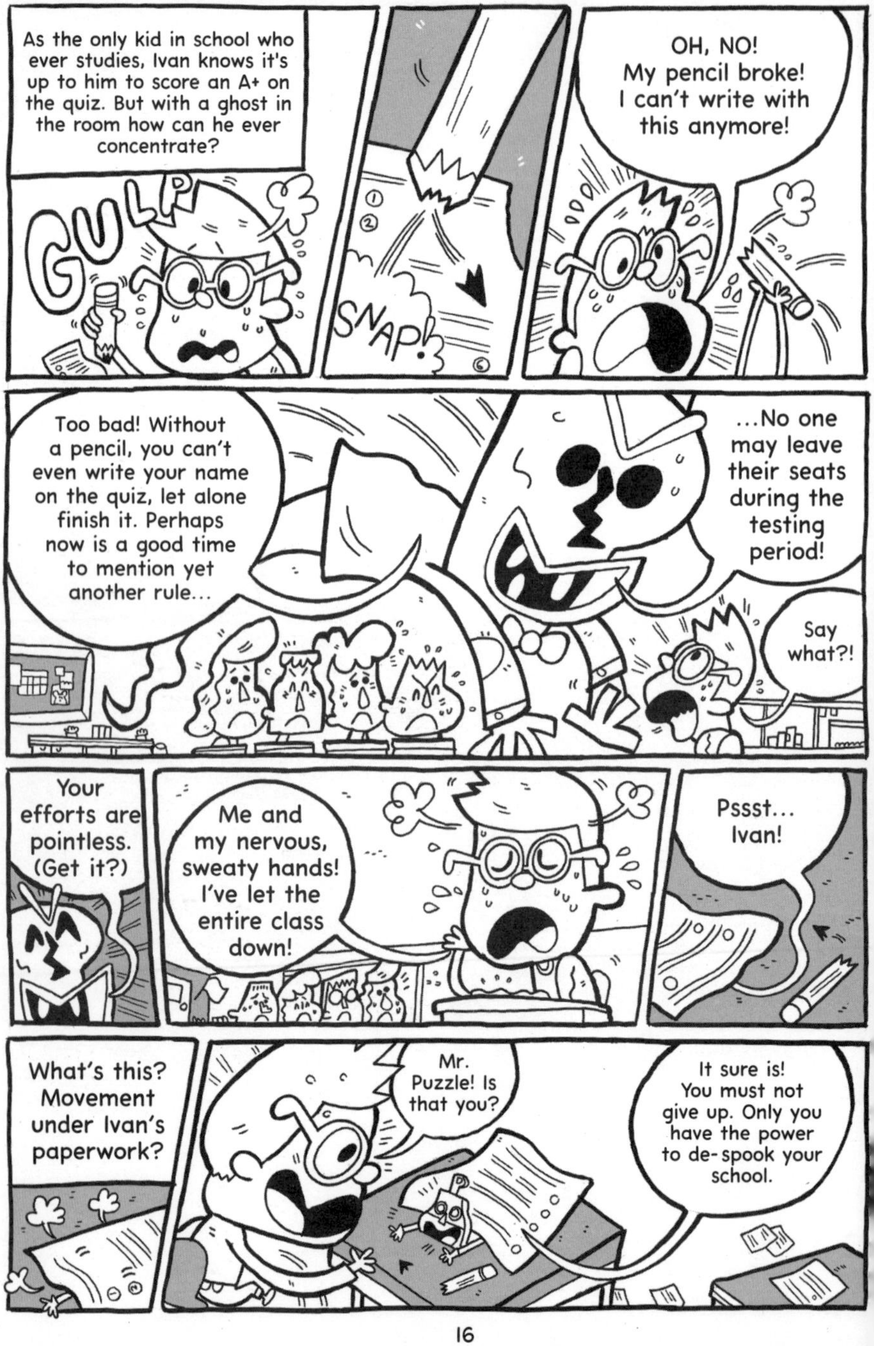
As the only kid in school who ever studies, Ivan knows it's up to him to score an A+ on the quiz. But with a ghost in the room how can he ever concentrate?
GULP
SNAP!
OH, NO! My pencil broke! I can't write with this anymore!
Too bad! Without a pencil, you can't even write your name on the quiz, let alone finish it. Perhaps now is a good time to mention yet another rule...
...No one may leave their seats during the testing period!
Say what?!
Your efforts are pointless. (Get it?)
Me and my nervous, sweaty hands! I've let the entire class down!
Pssst... Ivan!
What's this? Movement under Ivan's paperwork?
Mr. Puzzle! Is that you?
It sure is! You must not give up. Only you have the power to de-spook your school.

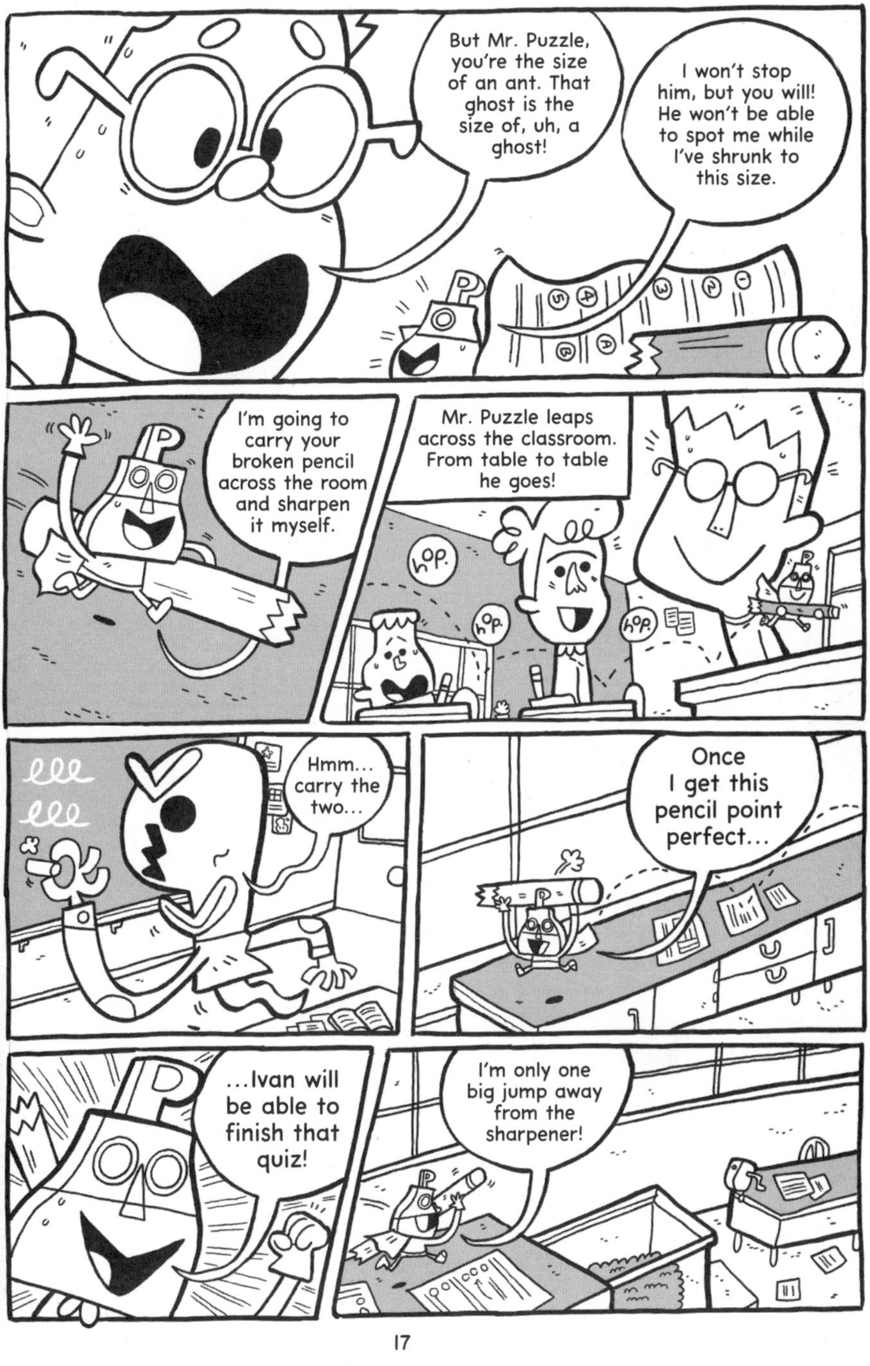
But Mr. Puzzle, you're the size of an ant. That ghost is the size of, uh, a ghost!
I won't stop him, but you will! He won't be able to spot me while I've shrunk to this size.
I'm going to carry your broken pencil across the room and sharpen it myself.
Mr. Puzzle leaps across the classroom. From table to table he goes!
hop.
hop.
hop.
Hmm... carry the two...
Once I get this pencil point perfect...
...Ivan will be able to finish that quiz!
I'm only one big jump away from the sharpener!

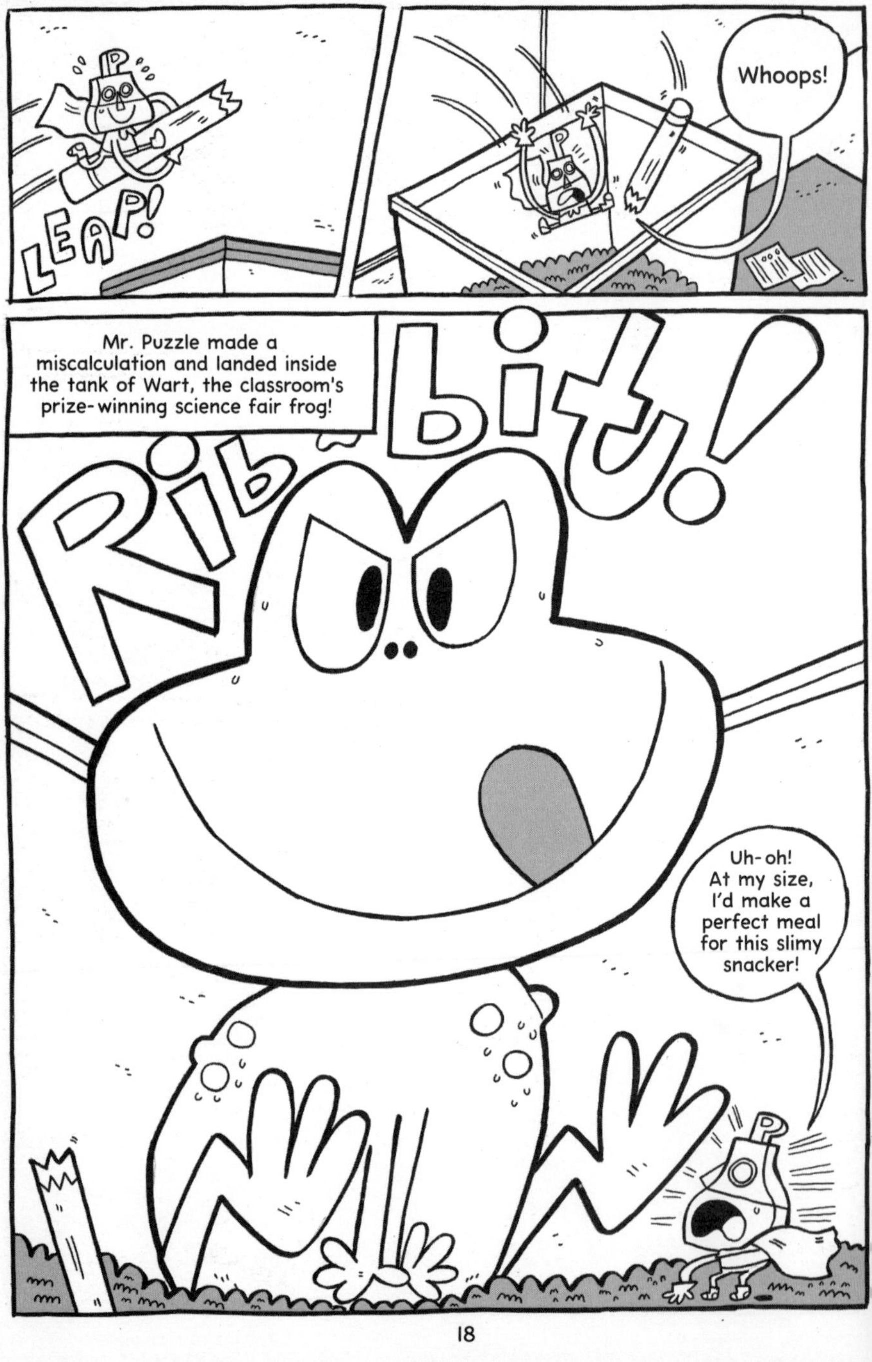
LEAP!
Whoops!
Mr. Puzzle made a miscalculation and landed inside the tank of Wart, the classroom's prize-winning science fair frog!
Rib-bit!
Uh-oh! At my size, I'd make a perfect meal for this slimy snacker!

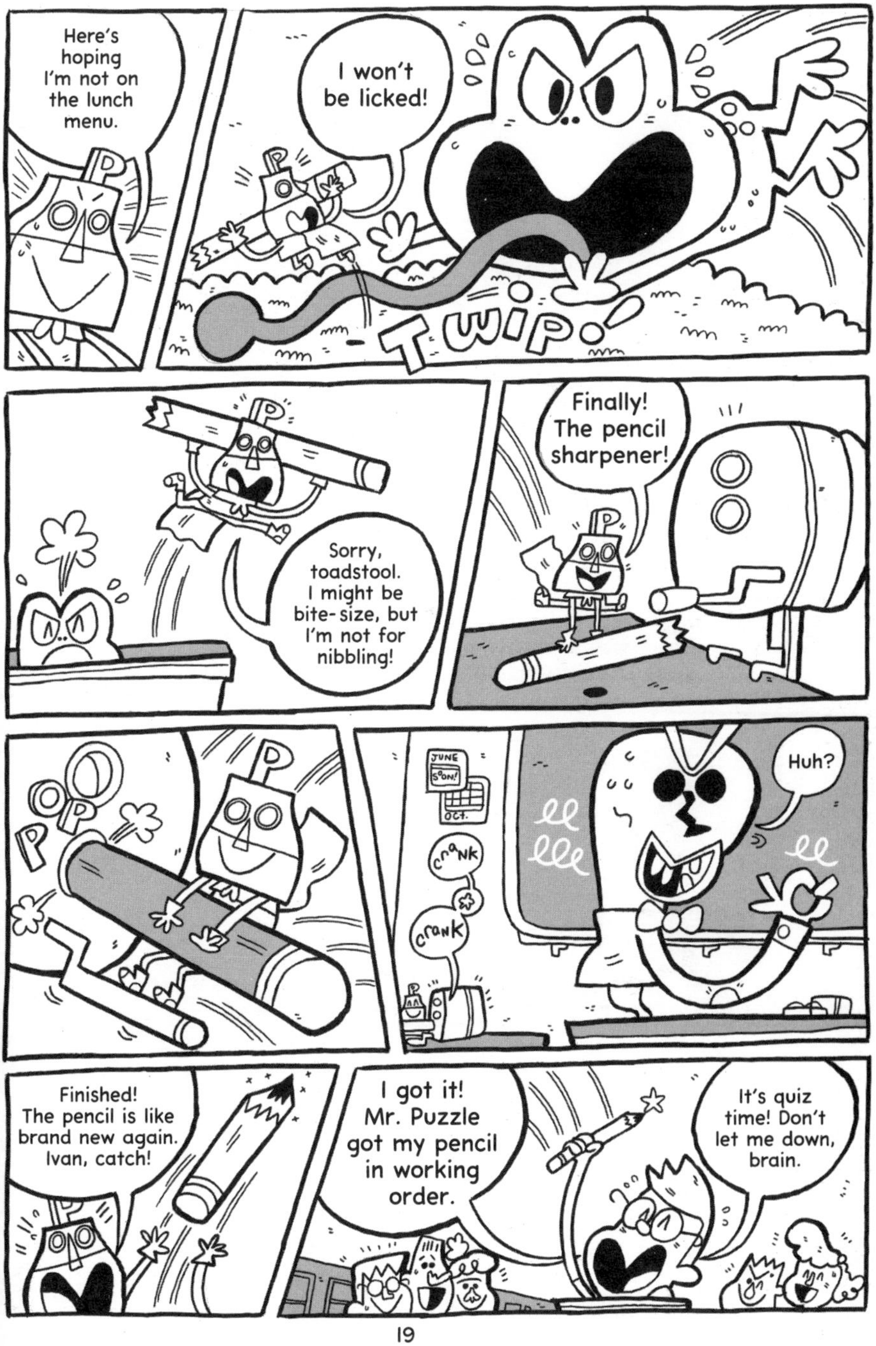
Here's hoping I'm not on the lunch menu.
I won't be licked!
TWIP!
Sorry, toadstool. I might be bite-size, but I'm not for nibbling!
Finally! The pencil sharpener!
POP
JUNE
SOON!
OCT.
crank
crank
Huh?
Finished! The pencil is like brand new again. Ivan, catch!
I got it! Mr. Puzzle got my pencil in working order.
It's quiz time! Don't let me down, brain.

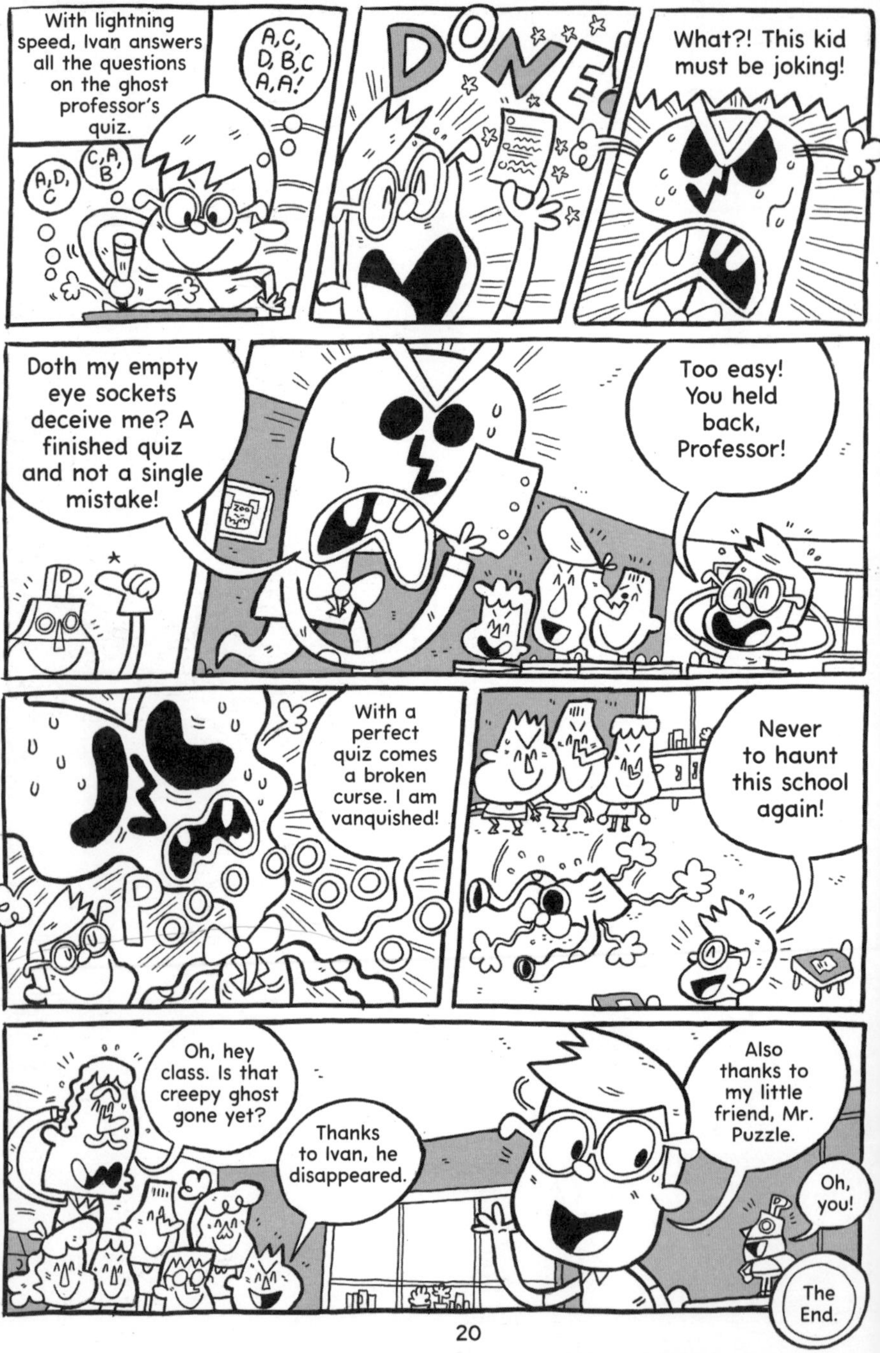
With lightning speed, Ivan answers all the questions on the ghost professor's quiz.
A,C, D, B,C A,A!
A,D, C
C,A, B
DONE!
What?! This kid must be joking!
Doth my empty eye sockets deceive me? A finished quiz and not a single mistake!
Too easy! You held back, Professor!
ZOO
With a perfect quiz comes a broken curse. I am vanquished!
Never to haunt this school again!
Oh, hey class. Is that creepy ghost gone yet?
Thanks to Ivan, he disappeared.
Also thanks to my little friend, Mr. Puzzle.
Oh, you!
The End.

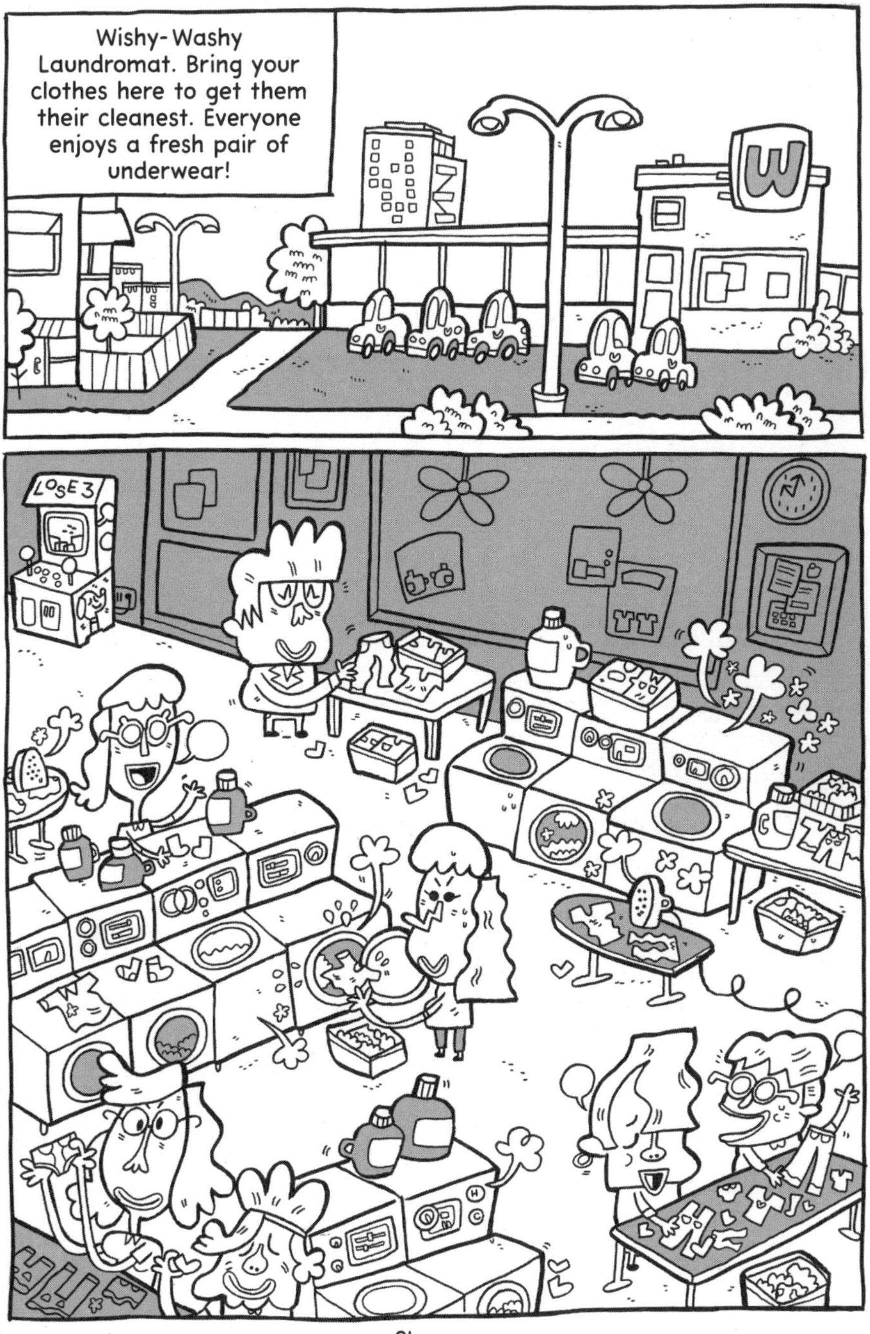
Wishy-Washy Laundromat. Bring your clothes here to get them their cleanest. Everyone enjoys a fresh pair of underwear!
LOSE 3

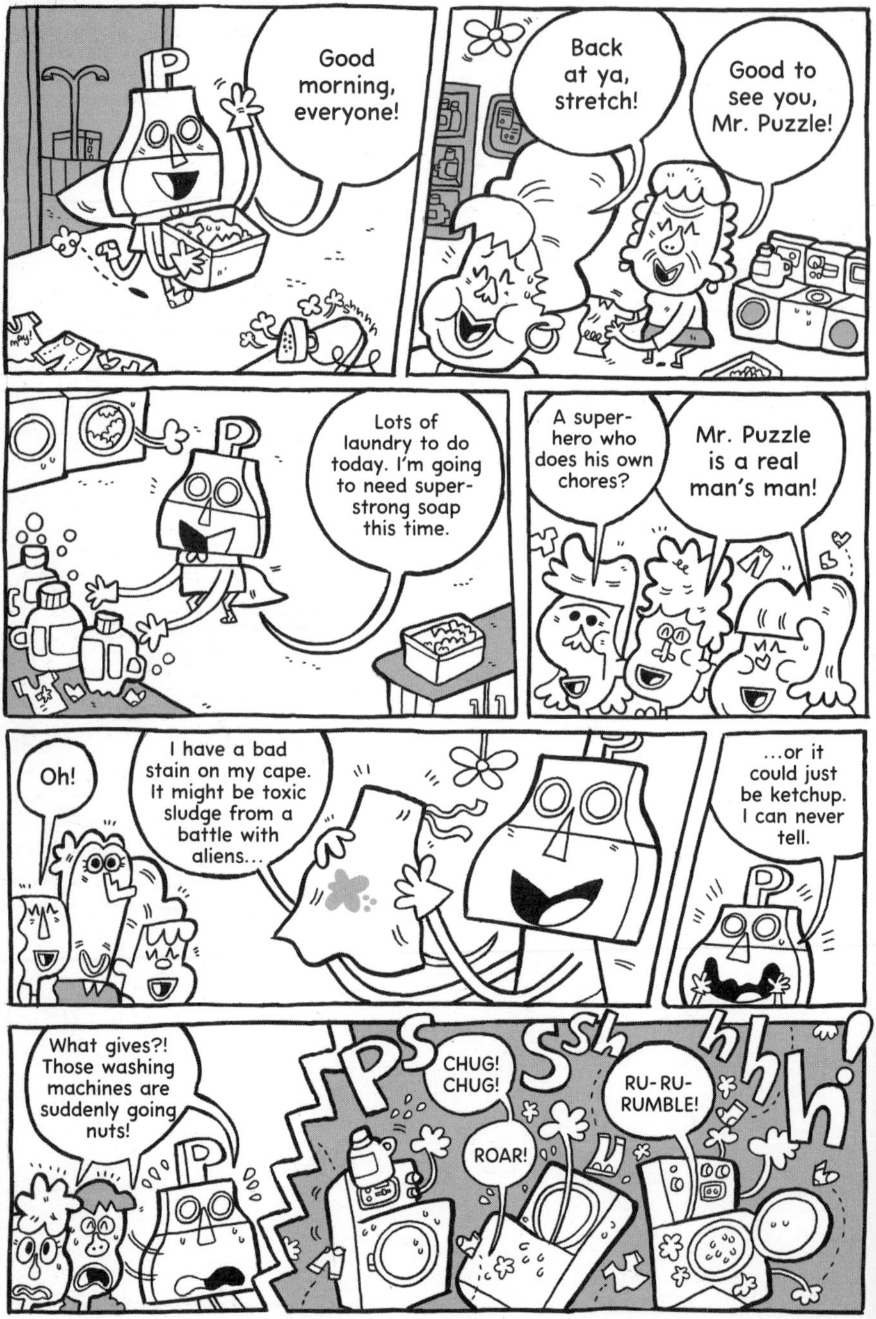
Good morning, everyone!
Back at ya, stretch!
Good to see you, Mr. Puzzle!
Lots of laundry to do today. I'm going to need super-strong soap this time.
A super-hero who does his own chores?
Mr. Puzzle is a real man's man!
Oh!
I have a bad stain on my cape. It might be toxic sludge from a battle with aliens...
...or it could just be ketchup. I can never tell.
What gives?! Those washing machines are suddenly going nuts!
PSSShhhh!
CHUG! CHUG!
ROAR!
RU-RU-RUMBLE!

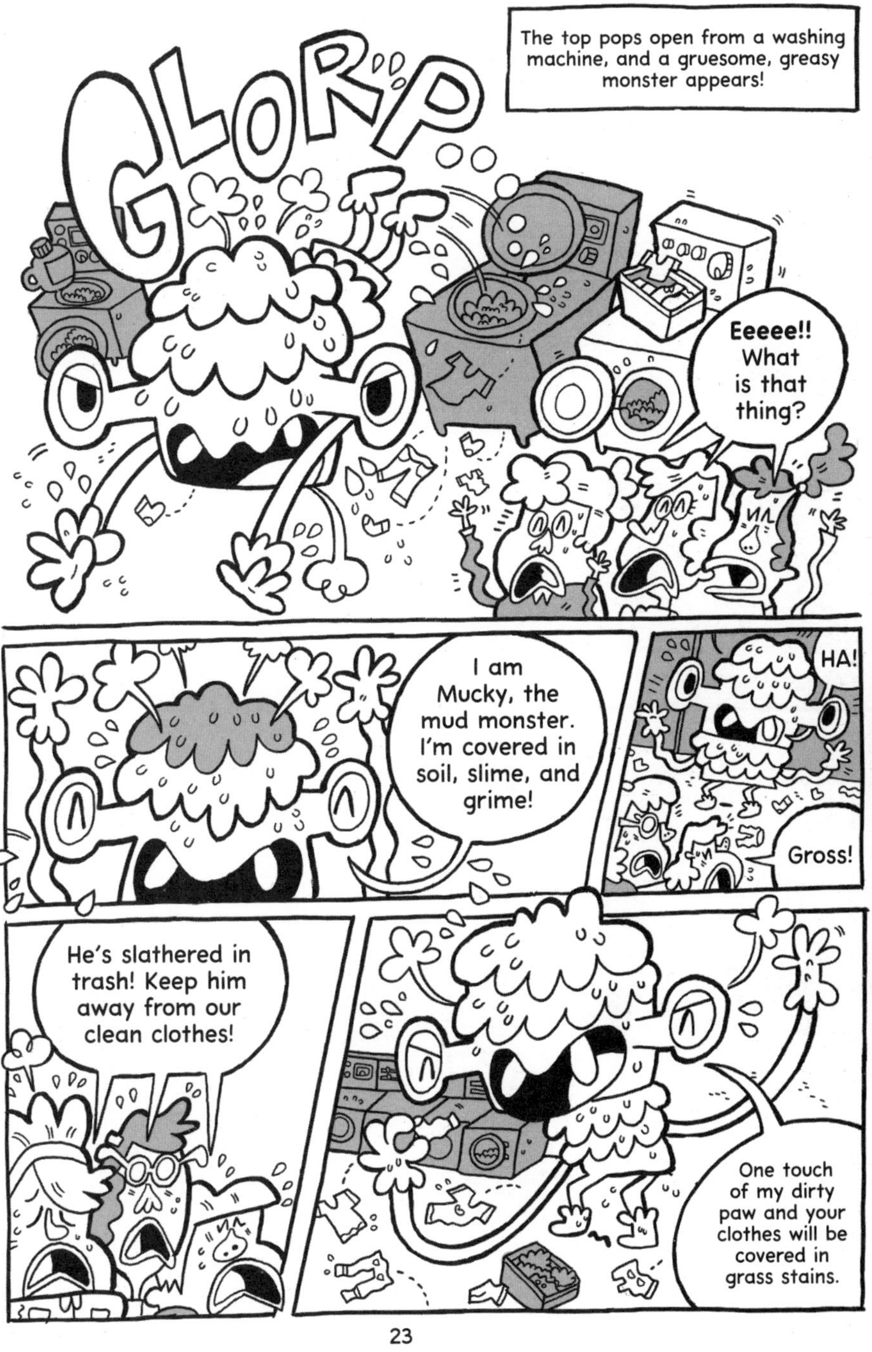
The top pops open from a washing machine, and a gruesome, greasy monster appears!
GLORP
Eeeee!! What is that thing?
I am Mucky, the mud monster. I'm covered in soil, slime, and grime!
HA!
Gross!
He's slathered in trash! Keep him away from our clean clothes!
One touch of my dirty paw and your clothes will be covered in grass stains.

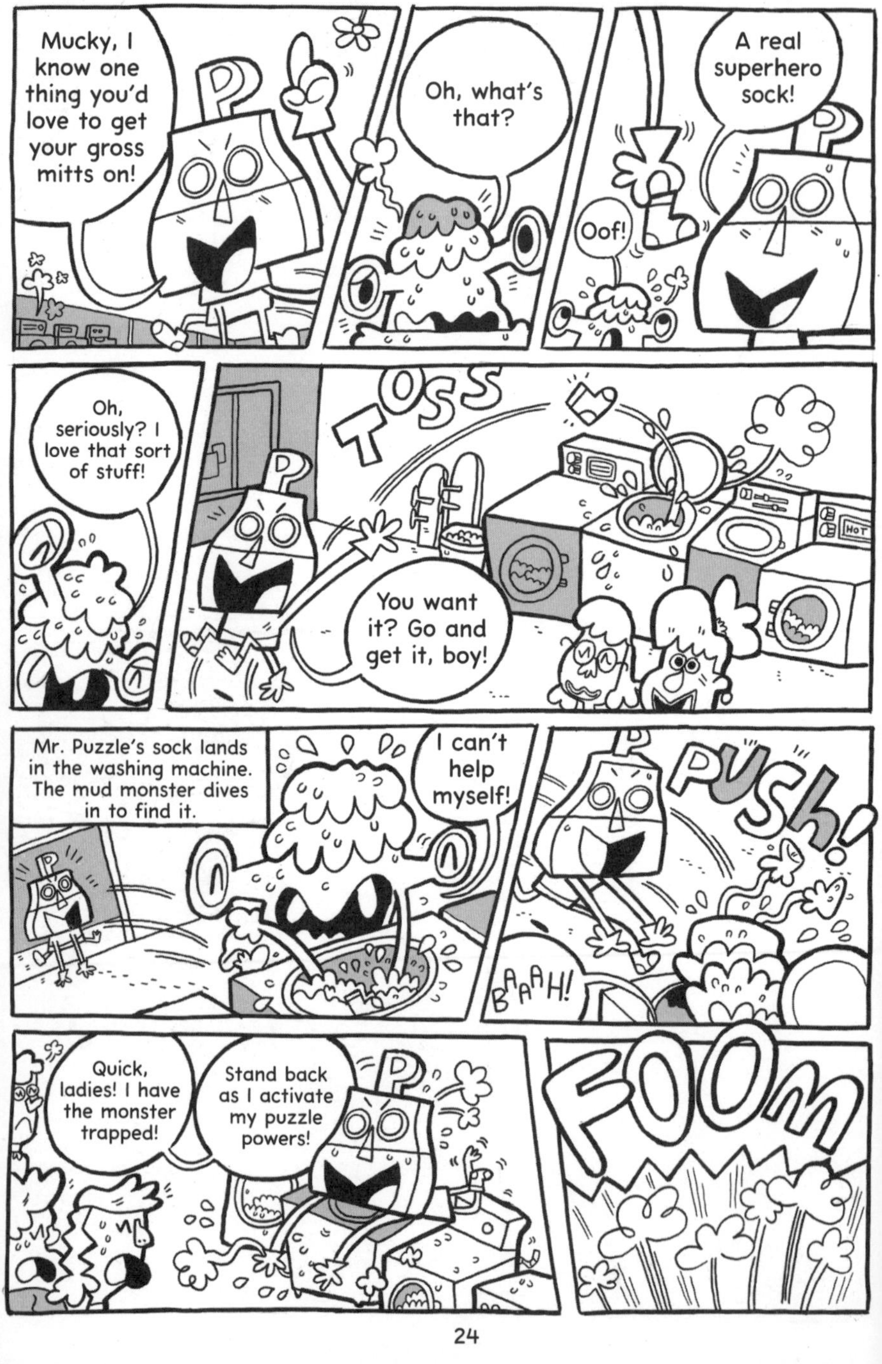
Mucky, I know one thing you'd love to get your gross mitts on!
Oh, what's that?
A real superhero sock!
Oof!
Oh, seriously? I love that sort of stuff!
TOSS
You want it? Go and get it, boy!
HOT
Mr. Puzzle's sock lands in the washing machine. The mud monster dives in to find it.
I can't help myself!
PUSH!
BAAAH!
Quick, ladies! I have the monster trapped!
Stand back as I activate my puzzle powers!
FOOM

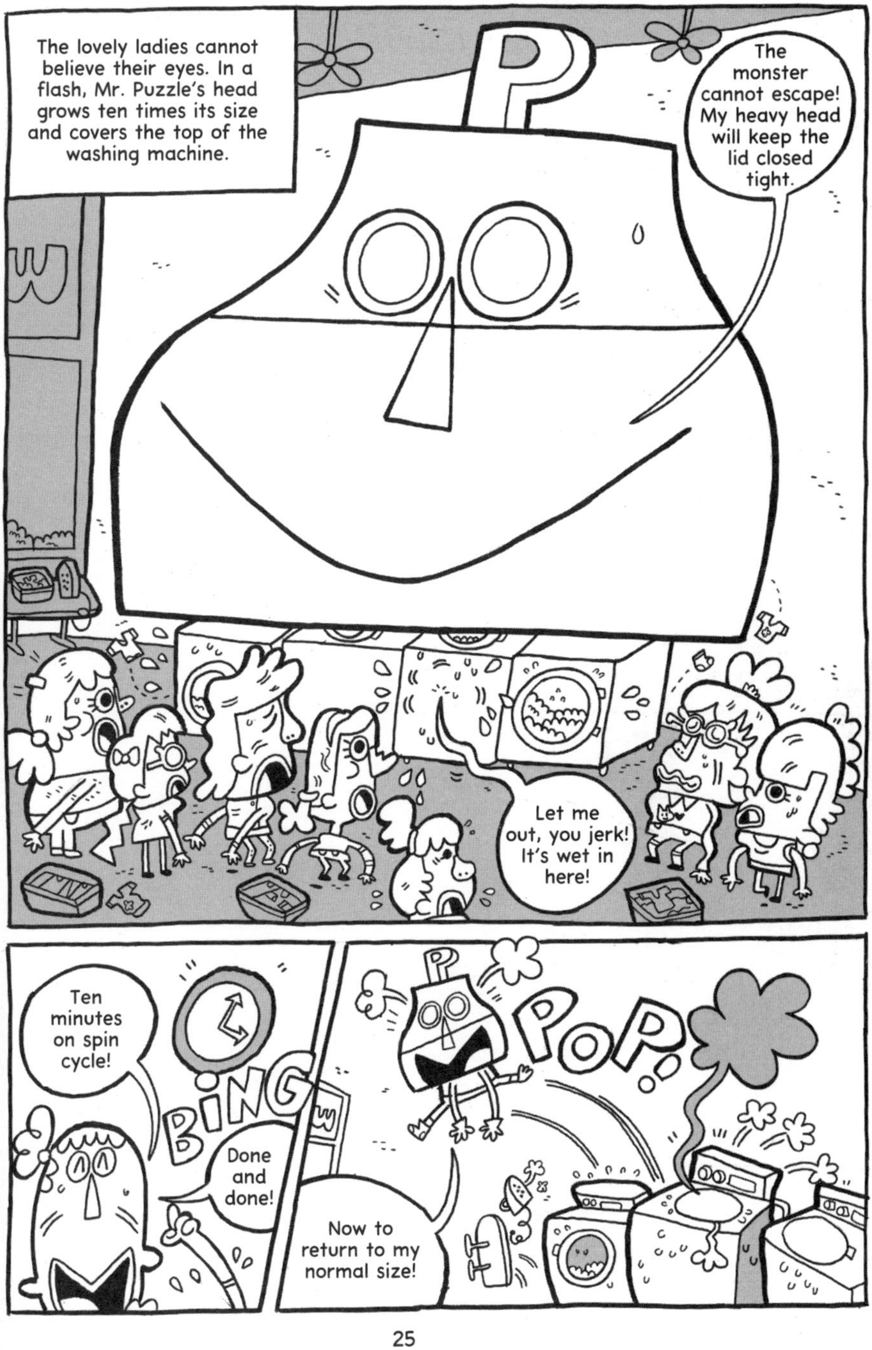

The lovely ladies cannot believe their eyes. In a flash, Mr. Puzzle's head grows ten times its size and covers the top of the washing machine.
The monster cannot escape! My heavy head will keep the lid closed tight.
Let me out, you jerk! It's wet in here!
Ten minutes on spin cycle!
BING
Done and done!
POP!
Now to return to my normal size!

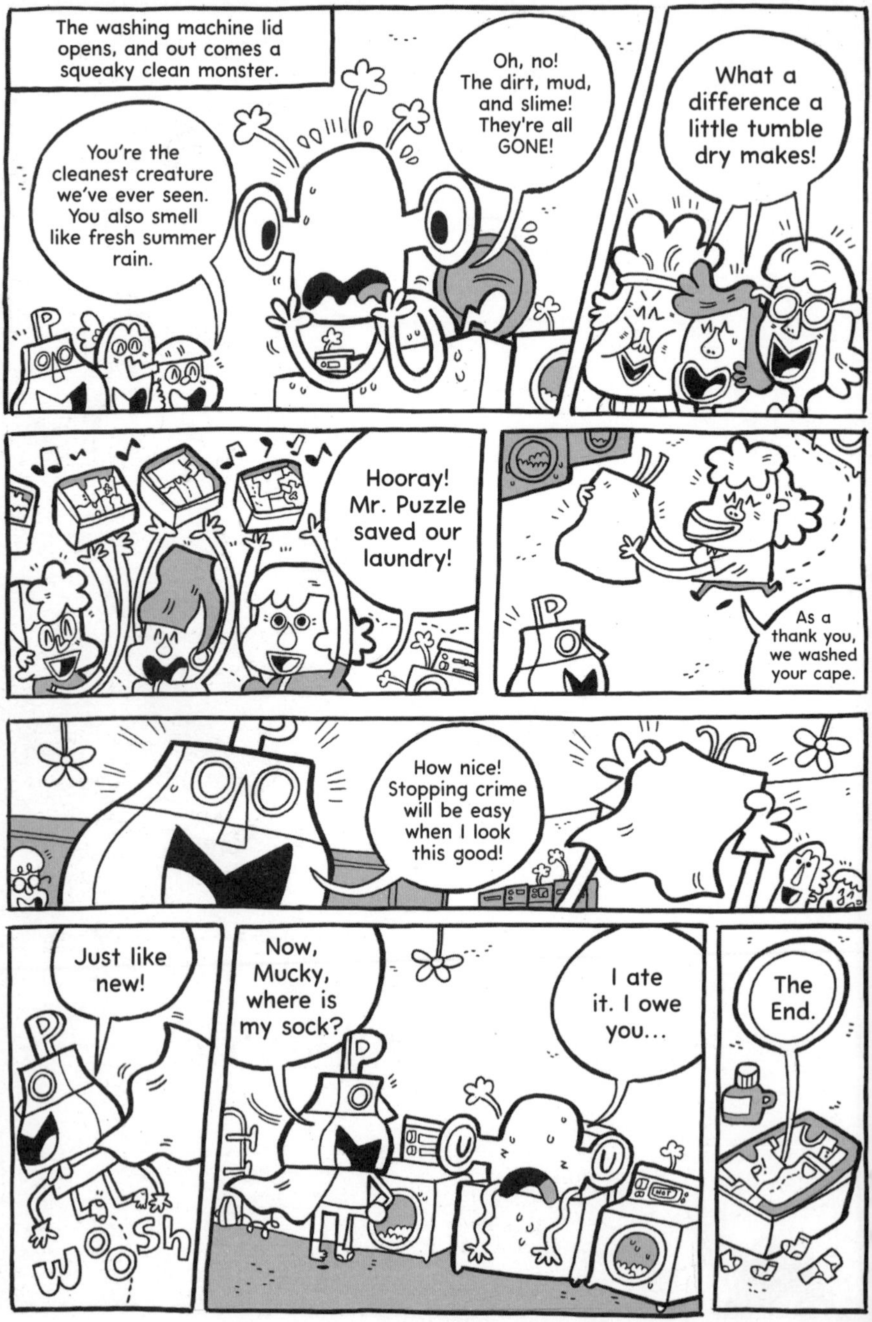
The washing machine lid opens, and out comes a squeaky clean monster.
You're the cleanest creature we've ever seen. You also smell like fresh summer rain.
Oh, no! The dirt, mud, and slime! They're all GONE!
What a difference a little tumble dry makes!
Hooray! Mr. Puzzle saved our laundry!
As a thank you, we washed your cape.
How nice! Stopping crime will be easy when I look this good!
Just like new!
WOOSH
Now, Mucky, where is my sock?
I ate it. I owe you...
The End.

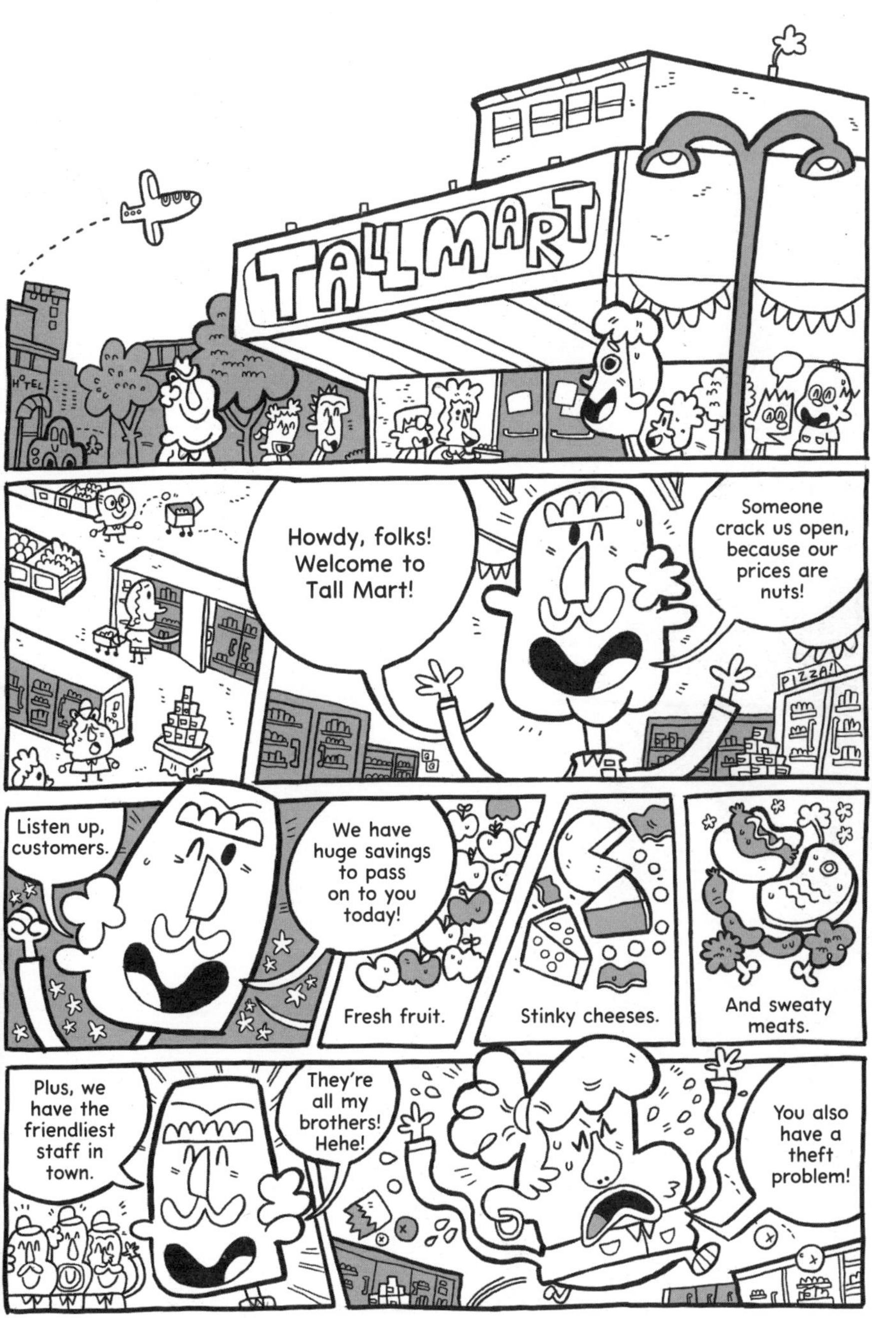
TALLMART
HOTEL
PIZZA!
Howdy, folks! Welcome to Tall Mart!
Someone crack us open, because our prices are nuts!
Listen up, customers.
We have huge savings to pass on to you today!
Fresh fruit.
Stinky cheeses.
And sweaty meats.
Plus, we have the friendliest staff in town.
They're all my brothers! Hehe!
You also have a theft problem!

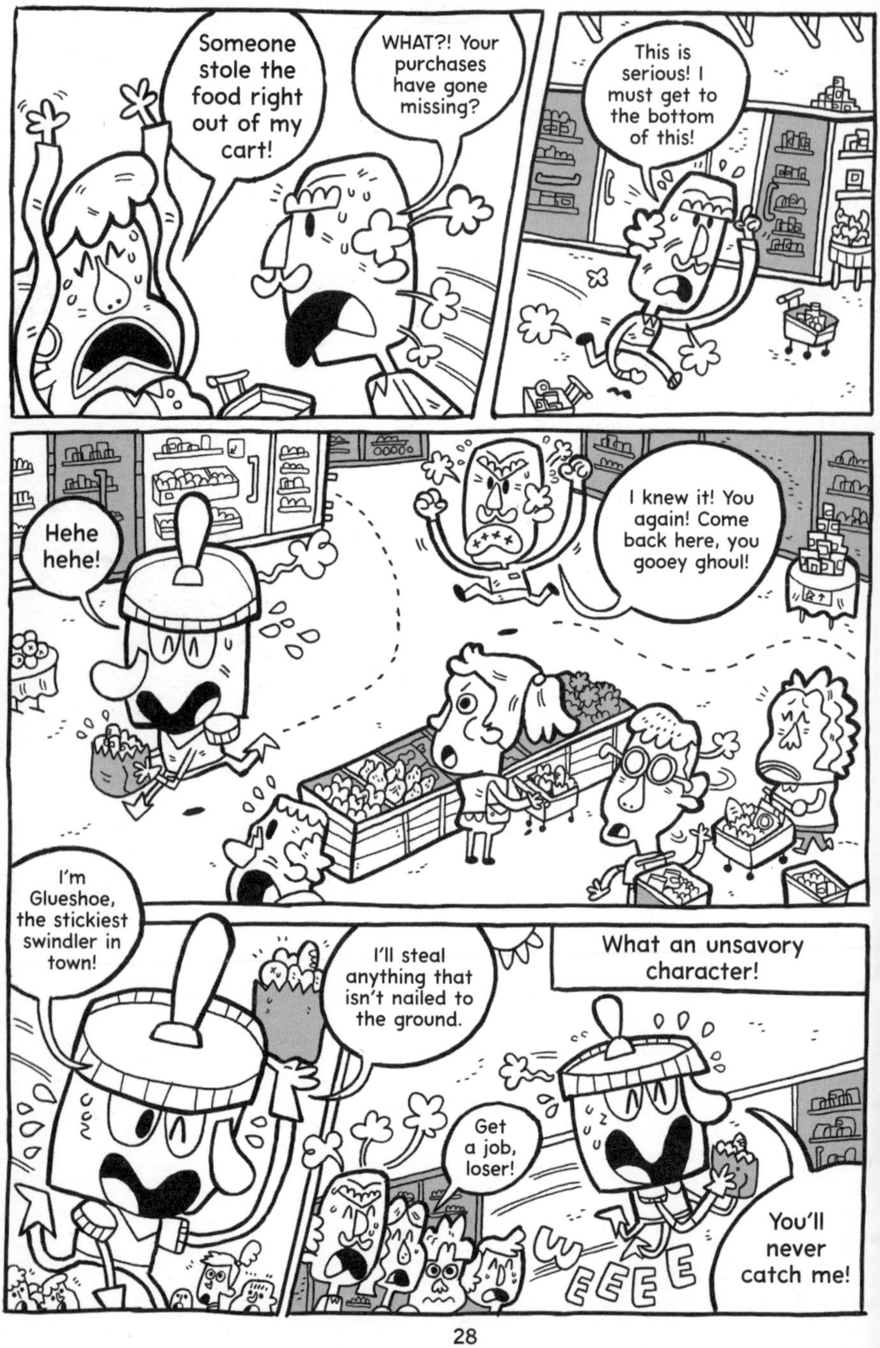
Someone stole the food right out of my cart!
WHAT?! Your purchases have gone missing?
This is serious! I must get to the bottom of this!
Hehe hehe!
I knew it! You again! Come back here, you gooey ghoul!
I'm Glueshoe, the stickiest swindler in town!
I'll steal anything that isn't nailed to the ground.
What an unsavory character!
Get a job, loser!
WEEEE
You'll never catch me!

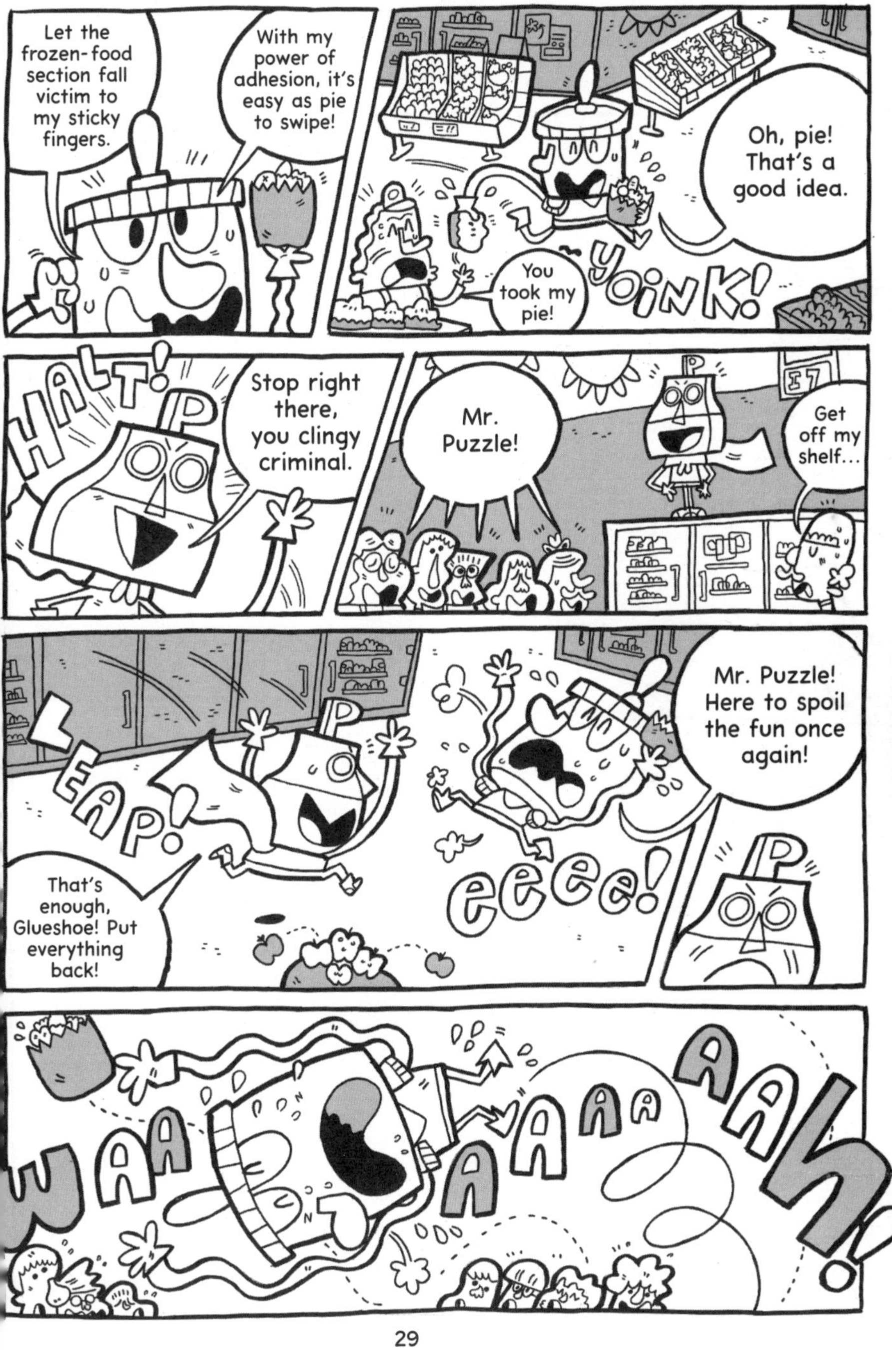
Let the frozen-food section fall victim to my sticky fingers.
With my power of adhesion, it's easy as pie to swipe!
You took my pie!
YOINK!
Oh, pie! That's a good idea.
HALT!
Stop right there, you clingy criminal.
Mr. Puzzle!
Get off my shelf...
LEAP!
That's enough, Glueshoe! Put everything back!
eeee!
Mr. Puzzle! Here to spoil the fun once again!
WAAAAAAAAAAH!!

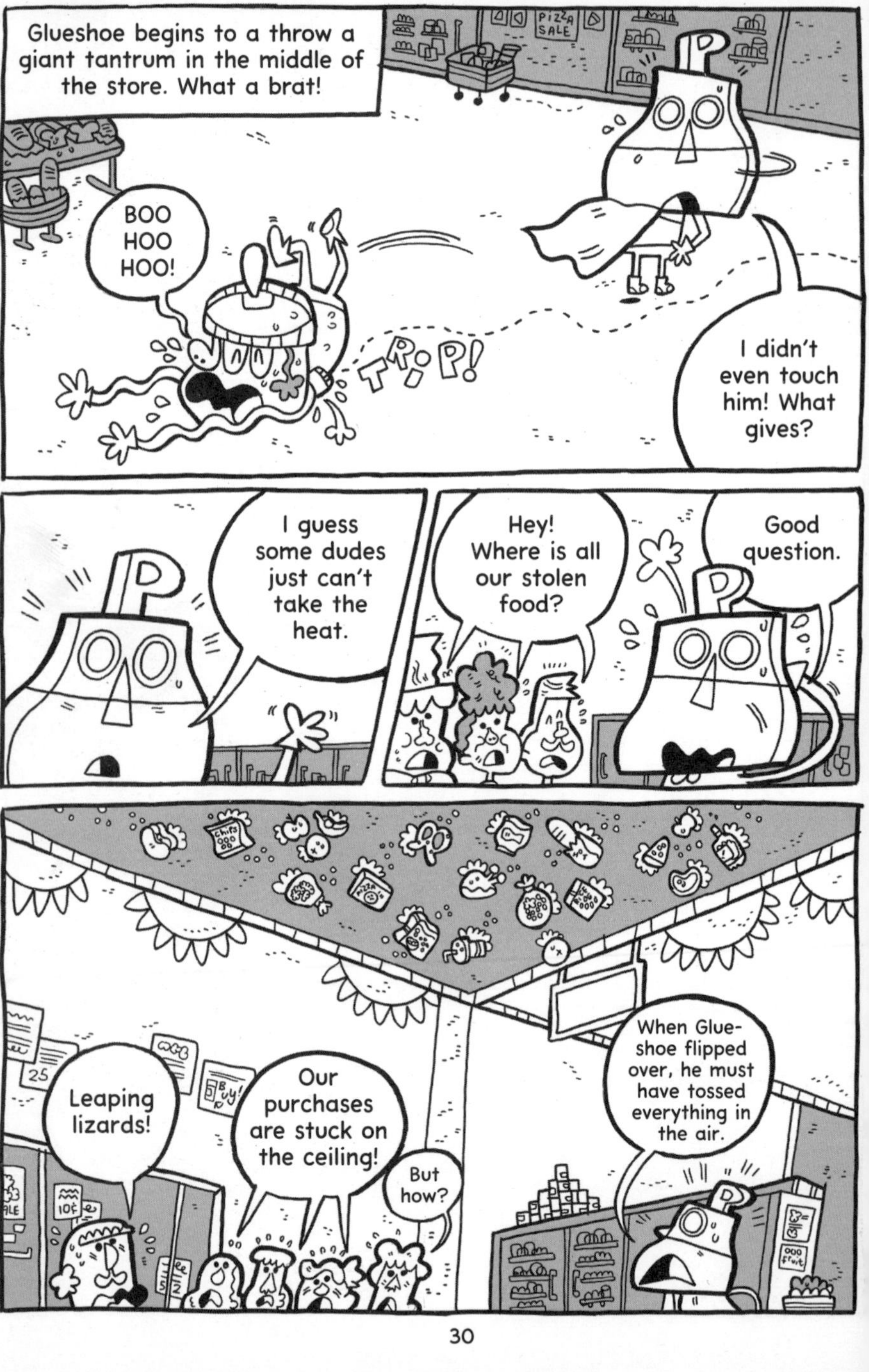

Glueshoe begins to a throw a giant tantrum in the middle of the store. What a brat!
PIZZA SALE
BOO HOO HOO!
TRIP!
I didn't even touch him! What gives?
I guess some dudes just can't take the heat.
Hey! Where is all our stolen food?
Good question.
chips
Leaping lizards!
Our purchases are stuck on the ceiling!
But how?
When Glueshoe flipped over, he must have tossed everything in the air.

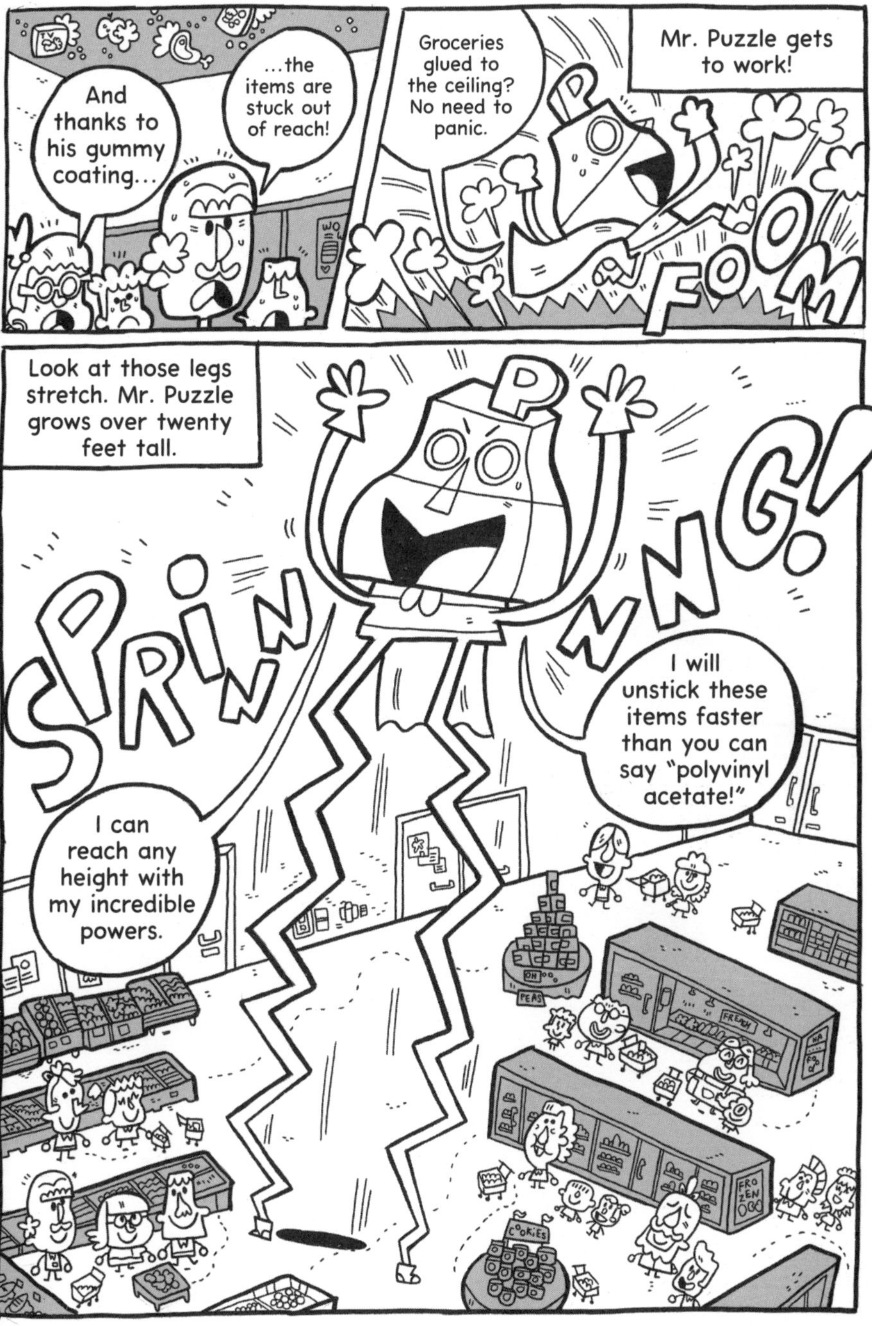

And thanks to his gummy coating...
...the items are stuck out of reach!
Groceries glued to the ceiling? No need to panic.
Mr. Puzzle gets to work!
FOOM
Look at those legs stretch. Mr. Puzzle grows over twenty feet tall.
SPRINNNNNG!
I will unstick these items faster than you can say "polyvinyl acetate!"
I can reach any height with my incredible powers.
PEAS
FRESH
FROZEN
COOKIES

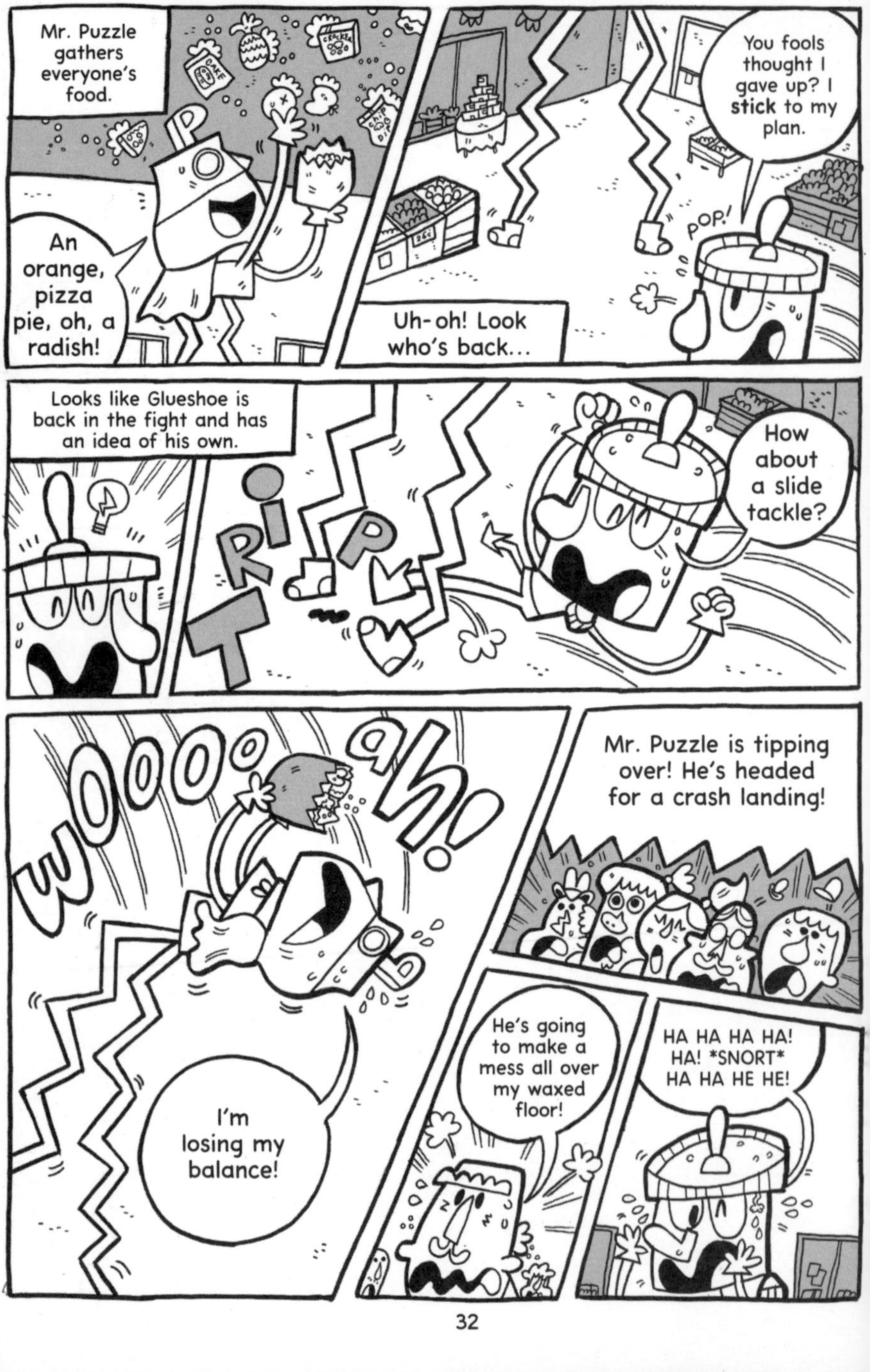

Mr. Puzzle gathers everyone's food.
CAKE
CRACKER
CHIP DIP
An orange, pizza pie, oh, a radish!
Uh-oh! Look who's back...
You fools thought I gave up? I **stick** to my plan.
POP!
25¢
Looks like Glueshoe is back in the fight and has an idea of his own.
TRIP
How about a slide tackle?
WOOOOah!
I'm losing my balance!
Mr. Puzzle is tipping over! He's headed for a crash landing!
He's going to make a mess all over my waxed floor!
HA HA HA HA! HA! *SNORT* HA HA HE HE!

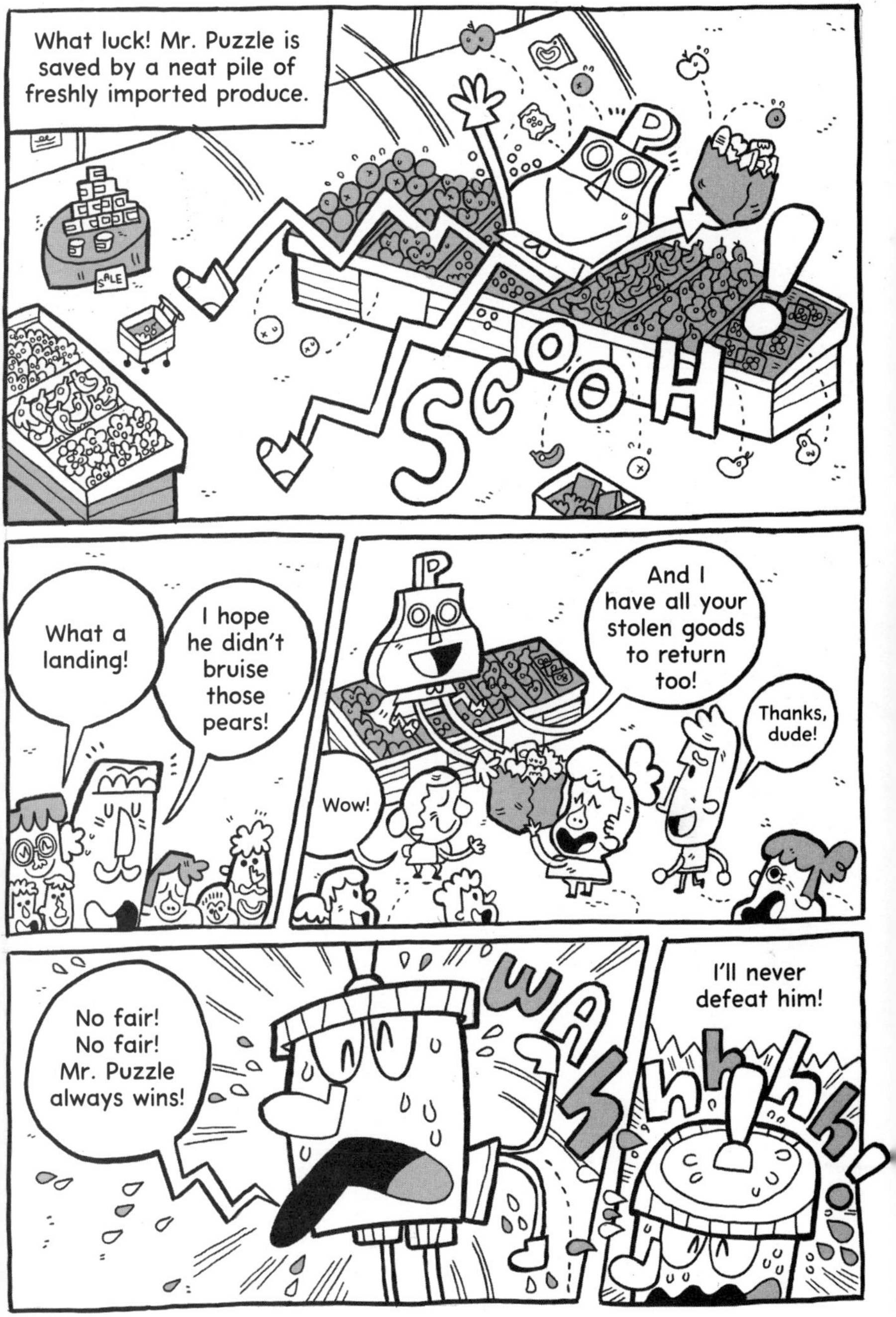
What luck! Mr. Puzzle is saved by a neat pile of freshly imported produce.
SCOOH!
What a landing!
I hope he didn't bruise those pears!
And I have all your stolen goods to return too!
Thanks, dude!
Wow!
No fair! No fair! Mr. Puzzle always wins!
WAAHhhhh!
I'll never defeat him!

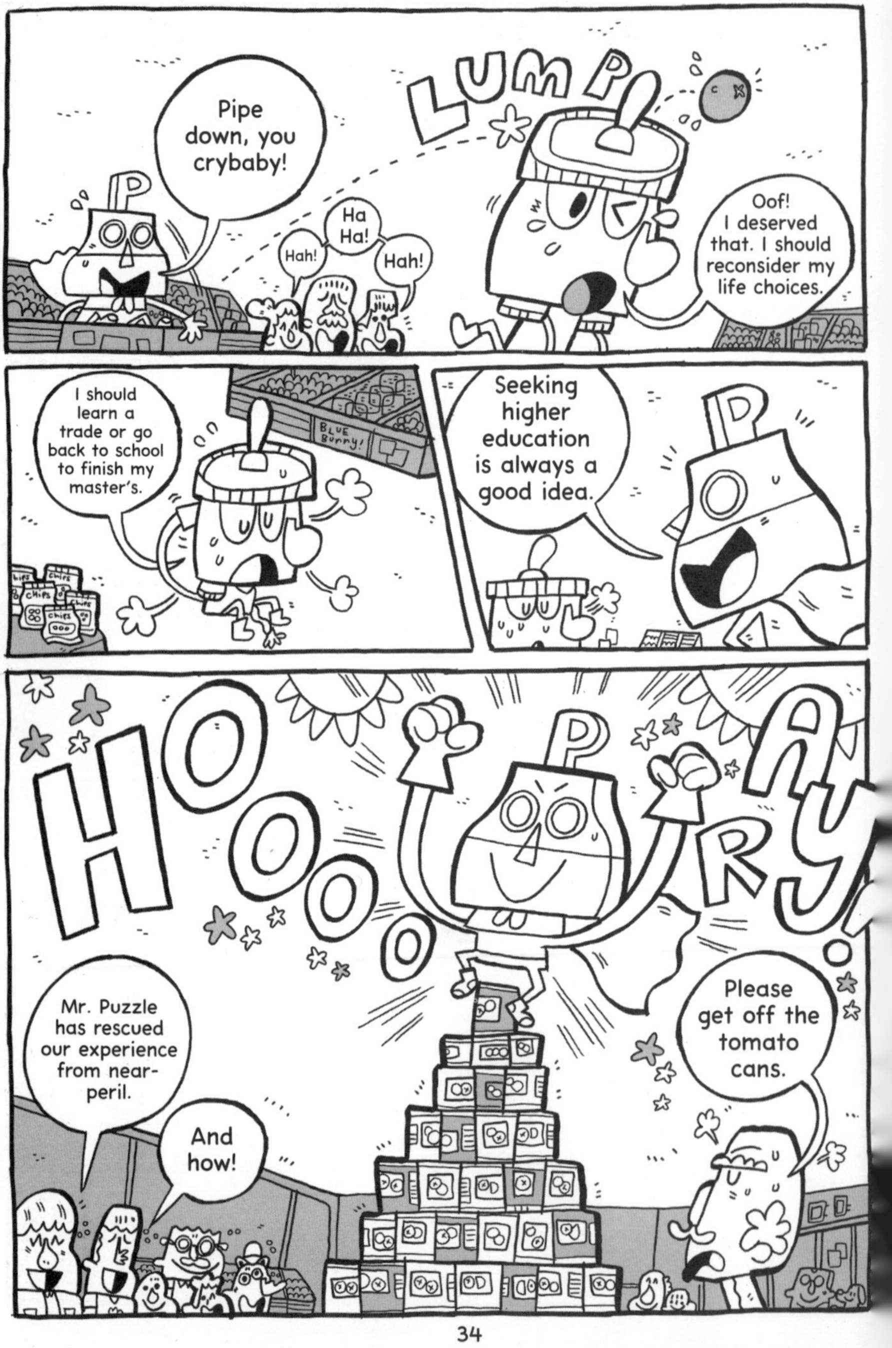
Pipe down, you crybaby!
LUMP!
Hah!
Ha Ha!
Hah!
Oof! I deserved that. I should reconsider my life choices.
I should learn a trade or go back to school to finish my master's.
BLUE Bunny!
CHIPS
Seeking higher education is always a good idea.
HOOOOOOORAY!
Mr. Puzzle has rescued our experience from near-peril.
And how!
Please get off the tomato cans.

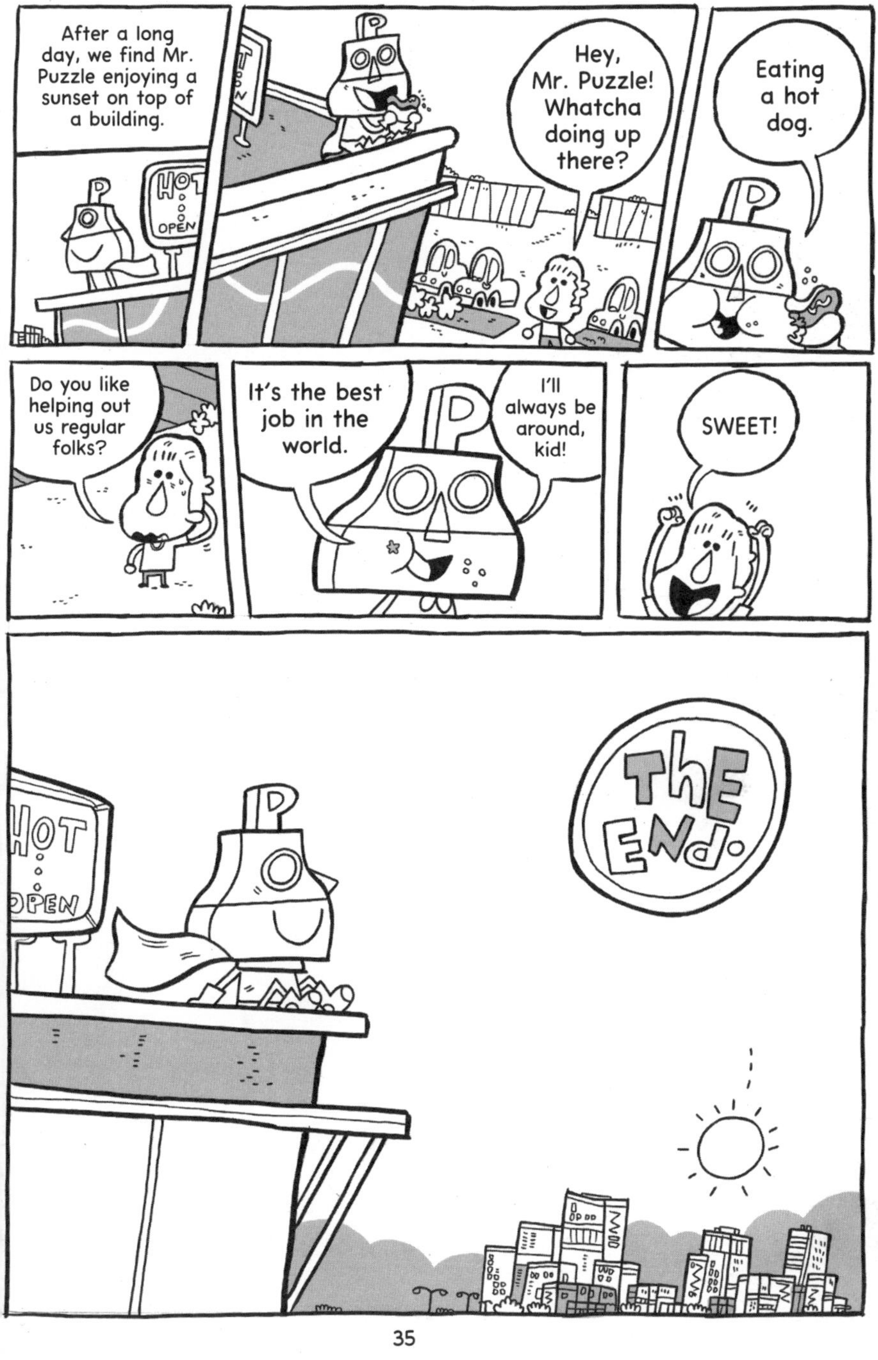
After a long day, we find Mr. Puzzle enjoying a sunset on top of a building.
HOT
OPEN
Hey, Mr. Puzzle! Whatcha doing up there?
Eating a hot dog.
Do you like helping out us regular folks?
It's the best job in the world.
I'll always be around, kid!
SWEET!
HOT
OPEN
THE END

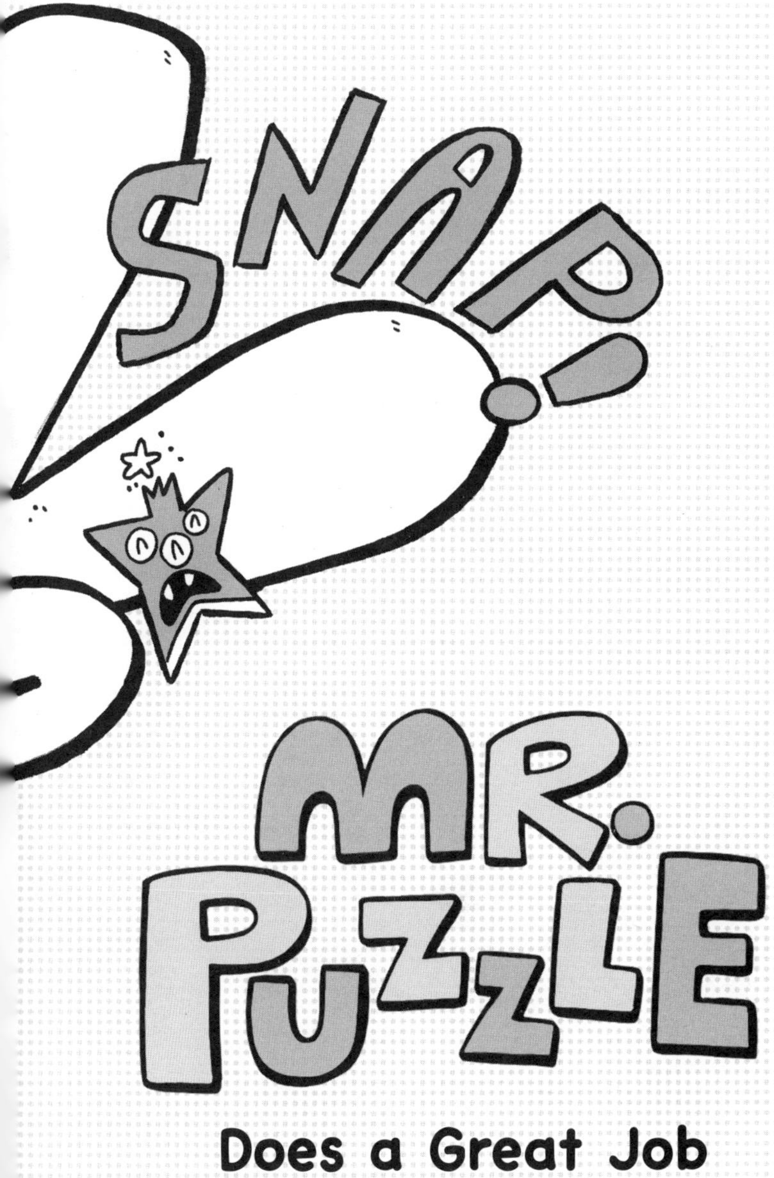
SNAP!

MR. PUZZLE

Does a Great Job

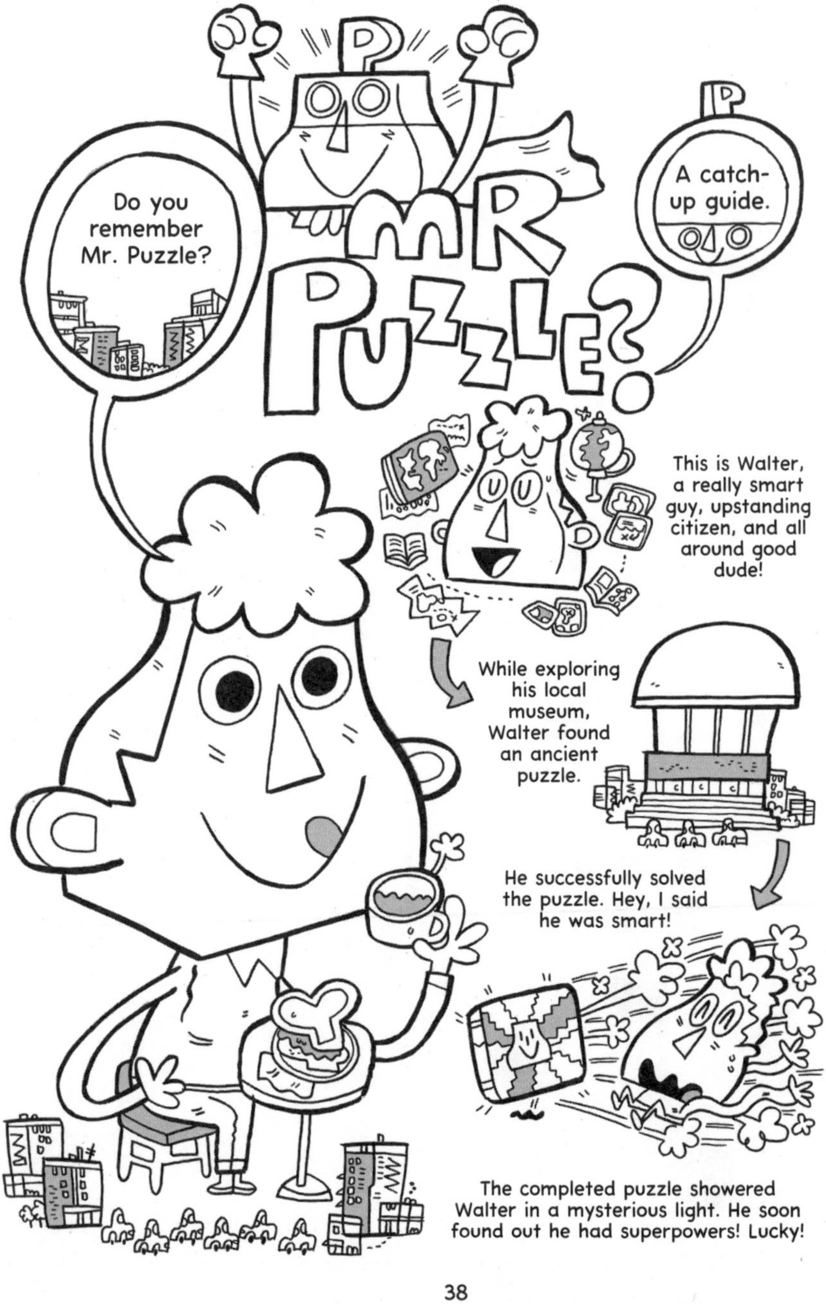

Do you remember Mr. Puzzle?
MR PUZZLE?
A catch-up guide.
This is Walter, a really smart guy, upstanding citizen, and all around good dude!
While exploring his local museum, Walter found an ancient puzzle.
He successfully solved the puzzle. Hey, I said he was smart!
The completed puzzle showered Walter in a mysterious light. He soon found out he had superpowers! Lucky!

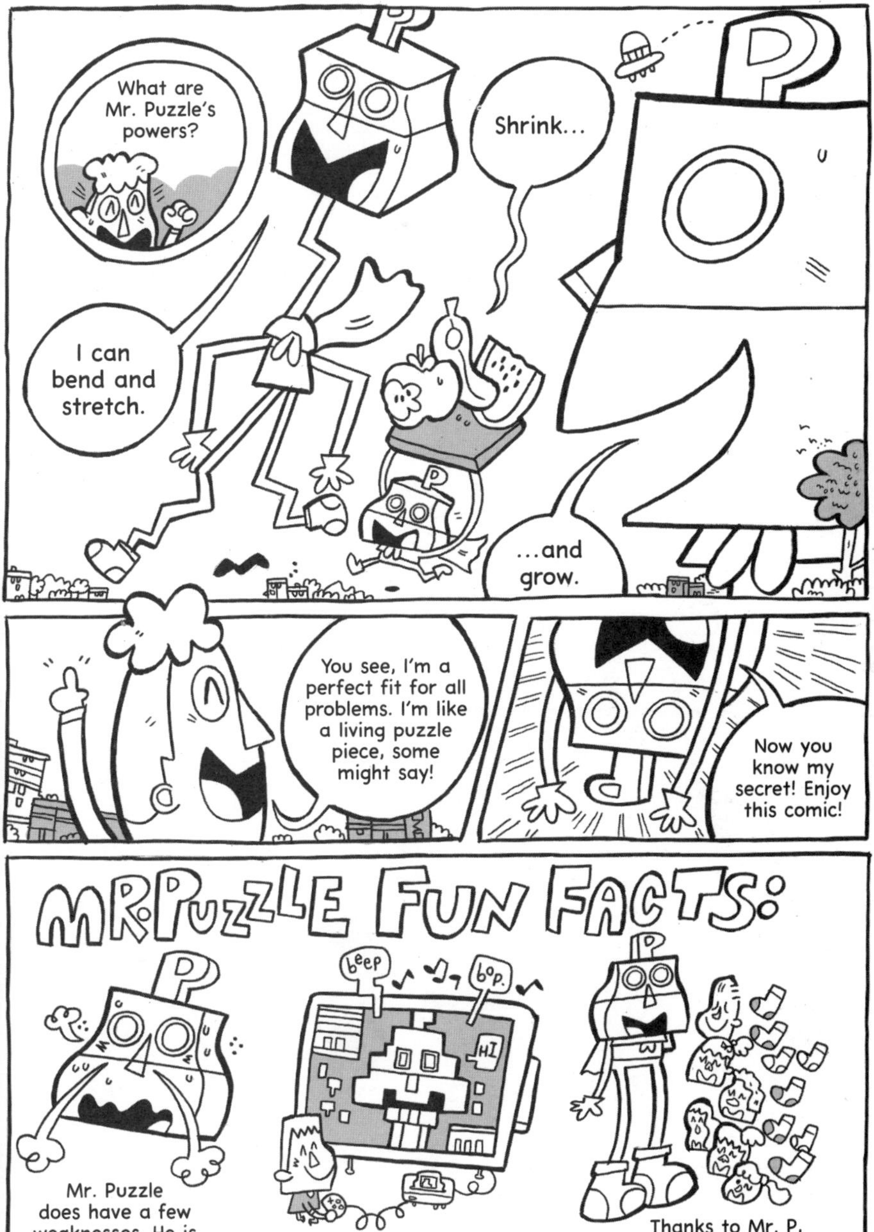
What are Mr. Puzzle's powers?
I can bend and stretch.
Shrink...
...and grow.
You see, I'm a perfect fit for all problems. I'm like a living puzzle piece, some might say!
Now you know my secret! Enjoy this comic!
MR. PUZZLE FUN FACTS:
beep
bop.
HI
Mr. Puzzle does have a few weaknesses. He is allergic to dust, mold, and some types of seasonal pollens.
Mr. Puzzle: The Video Game is currently the highest selling action/adventure game today.
Thanks to Mr. P, socks have become the new fashion statement. Everyone is wearing them!

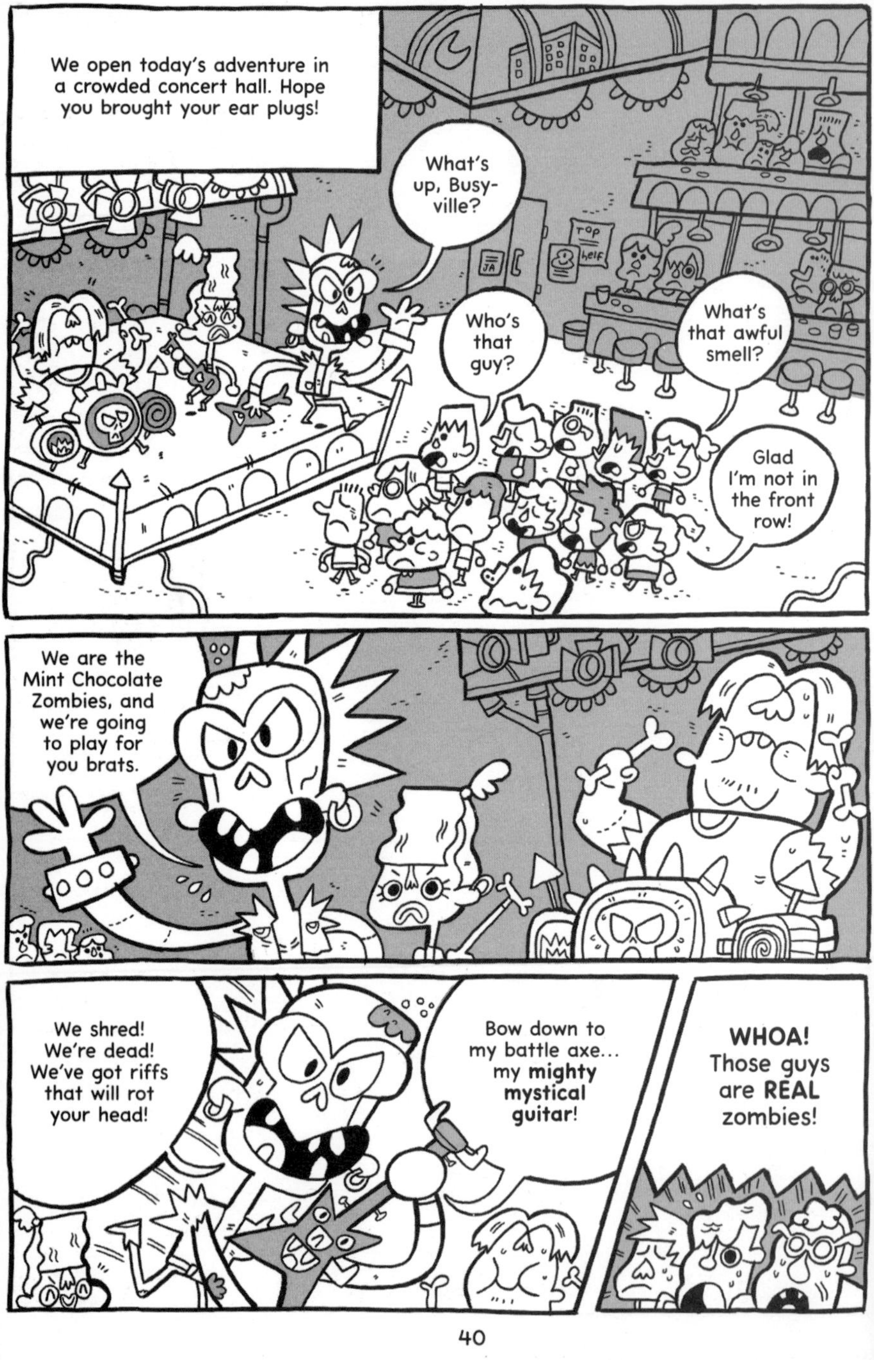
We open today's adventure in a crowded concert hall. Hope you brought your ear plugs!
What's up, Busy-ville?
Who's that guy?
What's that awful smell?
Glad I'm not in the front row!
We are the Mint Chocolate Zombies, and we're going to play for you brats.
We shred! We're dead! We've got riffs that will rot your head!
Bow down to my battle axe... my **mighty mystical guitar**!
WHOA! Those guys are **REAL** zombies!

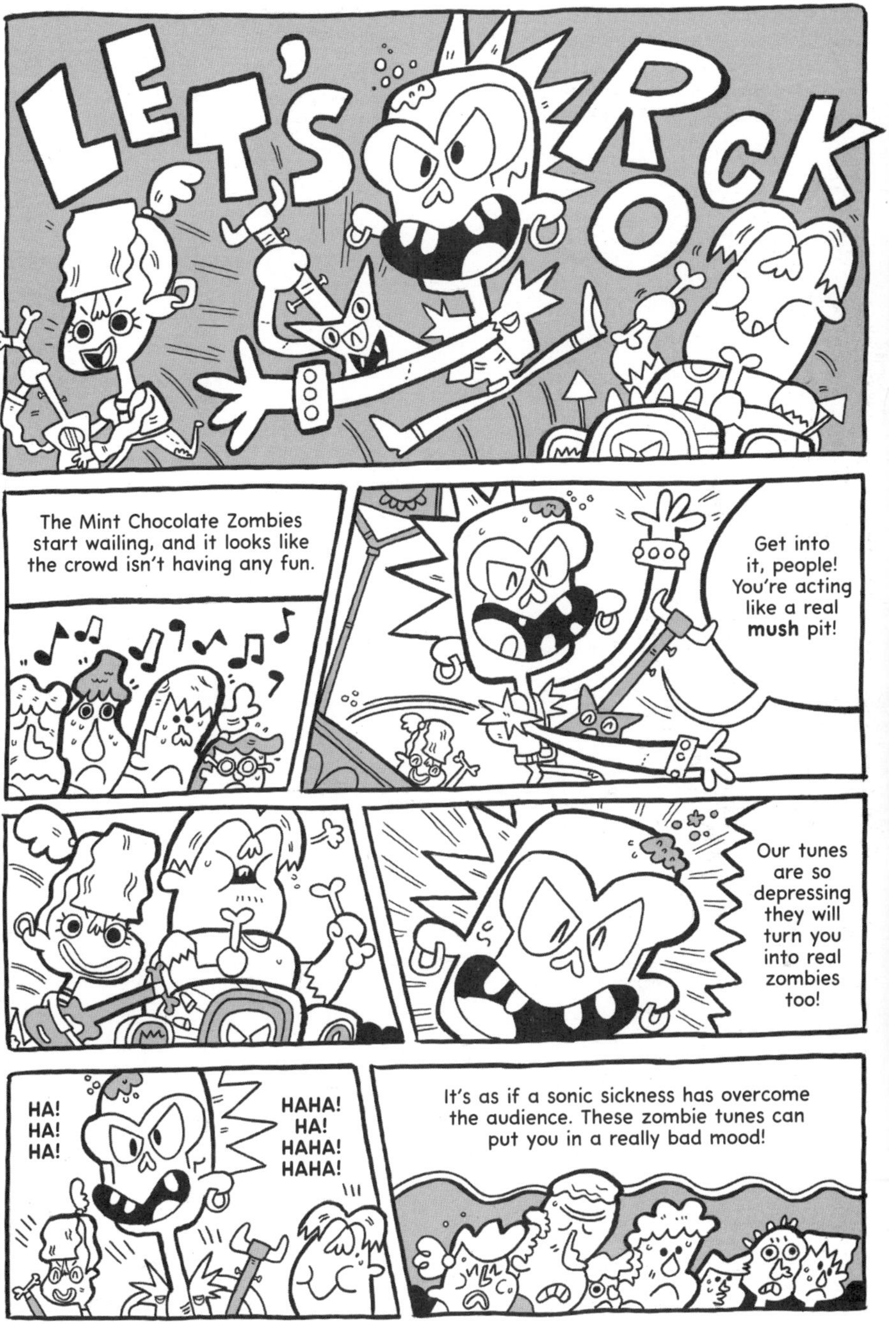
LET'S ROCK
The Mint Chocolate Zombies start wailing, and it looks like the crowd isn't having any fun.
Get into it, people! You're acting like a real **mush** pit!
Our tunes are so depressing they will turn you into real zombies too!
HA! HA! HA!
HAHA! HA! HAHA! HAHA!
It's as if a sonic sickness has overcome the audience. These zombie tunes can put you in a really bad mood!

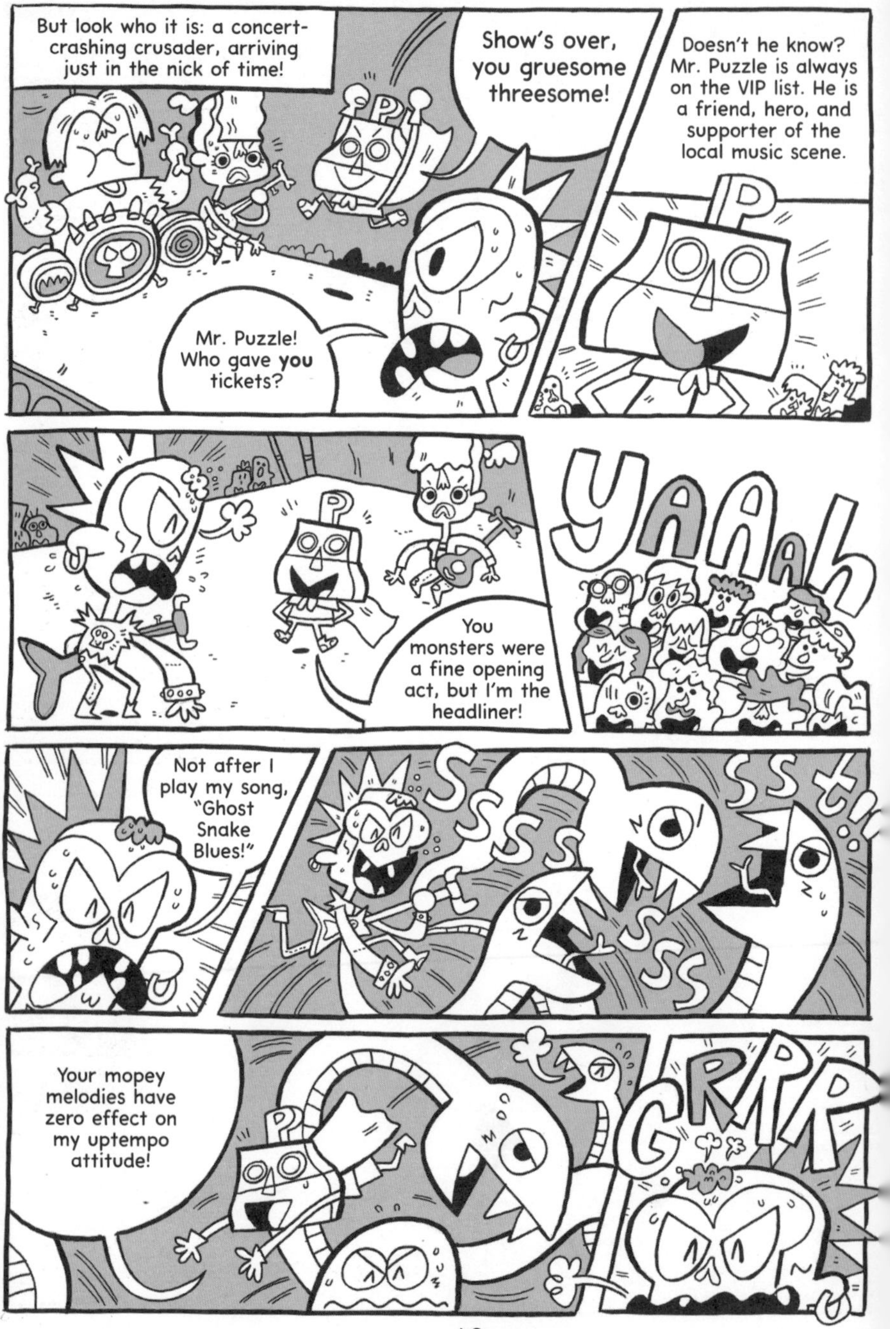

But look who it is: a concert-crashing crusader, arriving just in the nick of time!
Show's over, you gruesome threesome!
Mr. Puzzle! Who gave **you** tickets?
Doesn't he know? Mr. Puzzle is always on the VIP list. He is a friend, hero, and supporter of the local music scene.
You monsters were a fine opening act, but I'm the headliner!
YAAAh
Not after I play my song, "Ghost Snake Blues!"
SSSSSS
SSSSSt!
Your mopey melodies have zero effect on my uptempo attitude!
GRRR

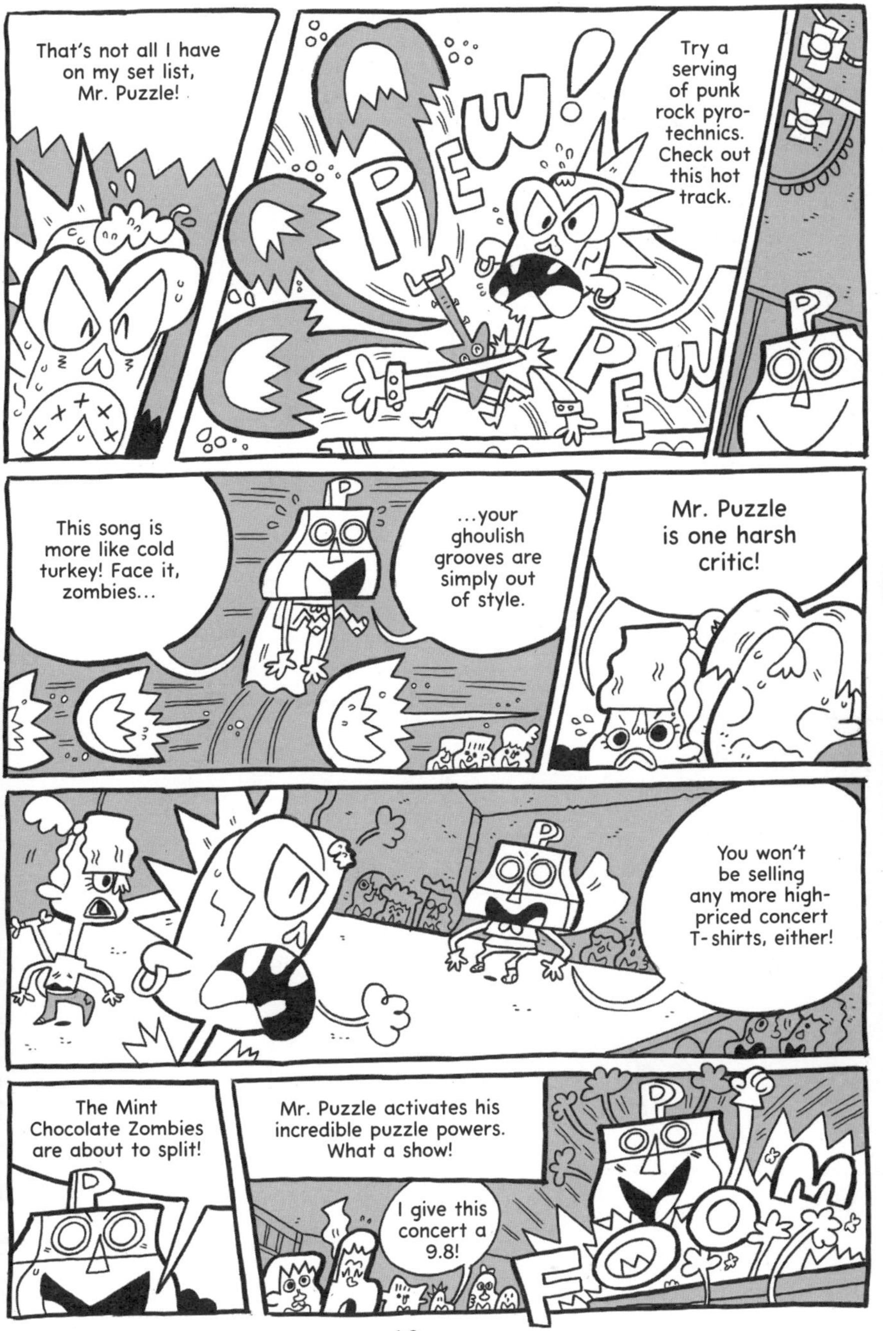
That's not all I have on my set list, Mr. Puzzle!
PEW!
Try a serving of punk rock pyro-technics. Check out this hot track.
PEW
This song is more like cold turkey! Face it, zombies...
...your ghoulish grooves are simply out of style.
Mr. Puzzle is one harsh critic!
You won't be selling any more high-priced concert T-shirts, either!
The Mint Chocolate Zombies are about to split!
Mr. Puzzle activates his incredible puzzle powers. What a show!
I give this concert a 9.8!
FOOOM

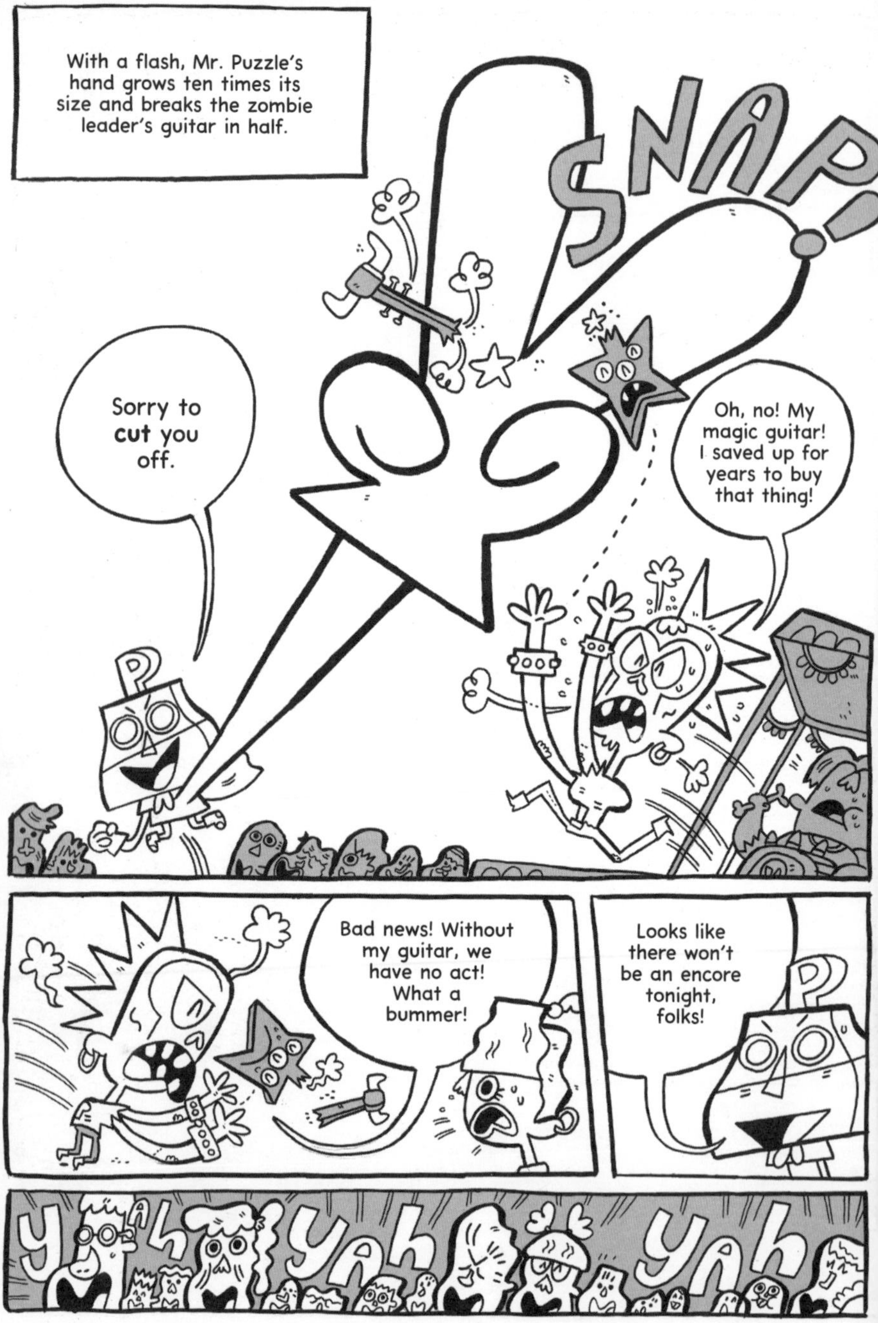
With a flash, Mr. Puzzle's hand grows ten times its size and breaks the zombie leader's guitar in half.
SNAP!
Sorry to **cut** you off.
Oh, no! My magic guitar! I saved up for years to buy that thing!
Bad news! Without my guitar, we have no act! What a bummer!
Looks like there won't be an encore tonight, folks!
yah yah yah

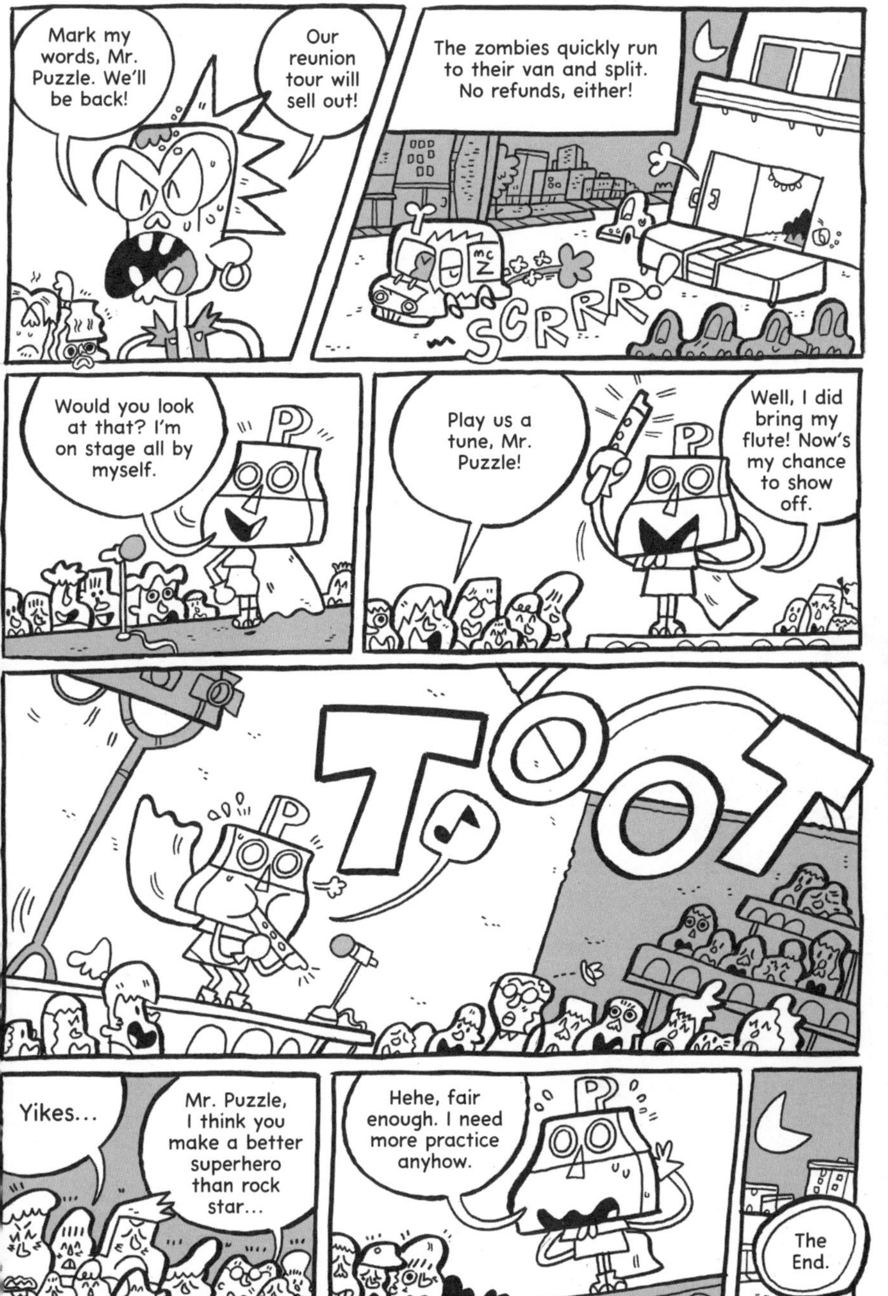
Mark my words, Mr. Puzzle. We'll be back!
Our reunion tour will sell out!
The zombies quickly run to their van and split. No refunds, either!
SCRRR!
Would you look at that? I'm on stage all by myself.
Play us a tune, Mr. Puzzle!
Well, I did bring my flute! Now's my chance to show off.
TOOT
Yikes...
Mr. Puzzle, I think you make a better superhero than rock star...
Hehe, fair enough. I need more practice anyhow.
The End.

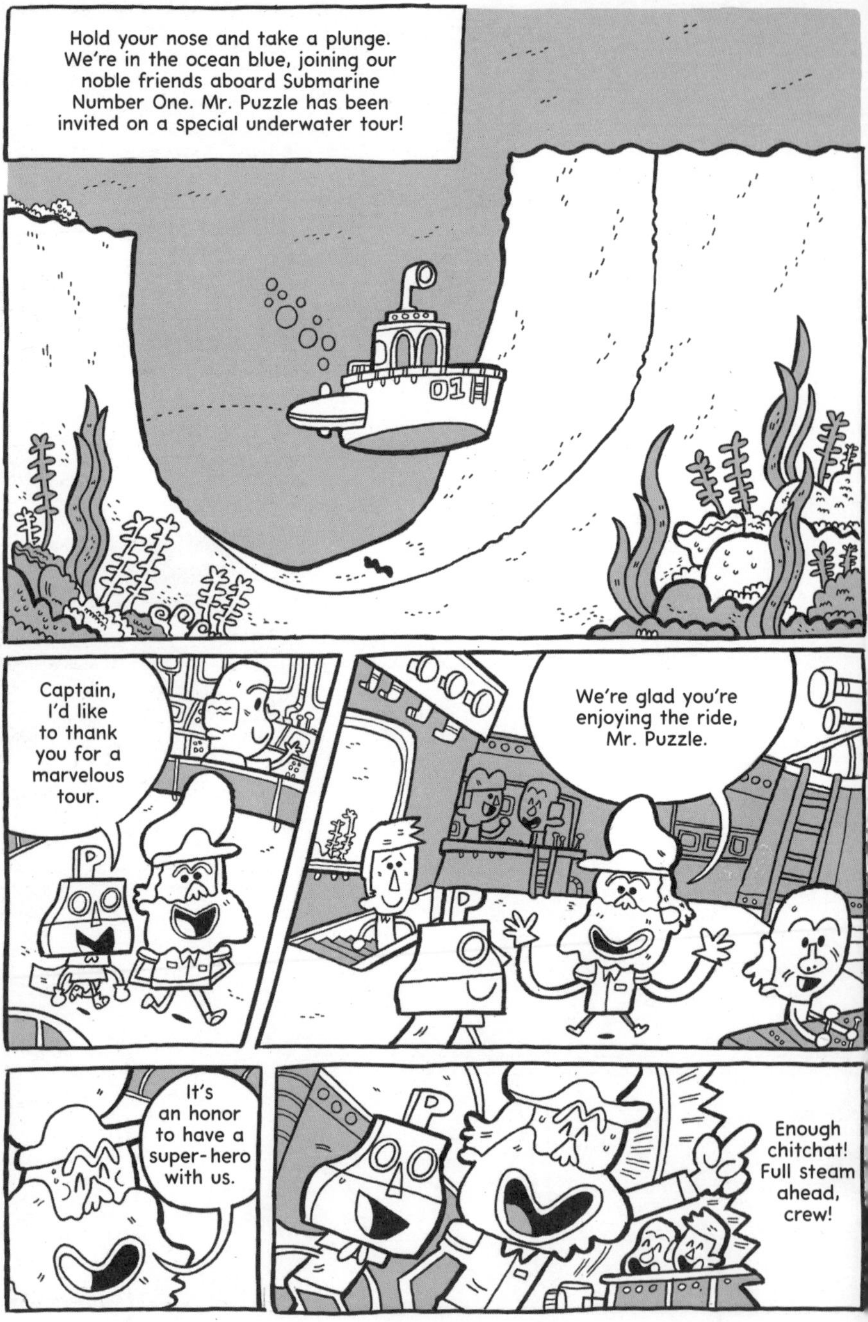
Hold your nose and take a plunge. We're in the ocean blue, joining our noble friends aboard Submarine Number One. Mr. Puzzle has been invited on a special underwater tour!
01
Captain, I'd like to thank you for a marvelous tour.
P
We're glad you're enjoying the ride, Mr. Puzzle.
P
It's an honor to have a super-hero with us.
P
Enough chitchat! Full steam ahead, crew!

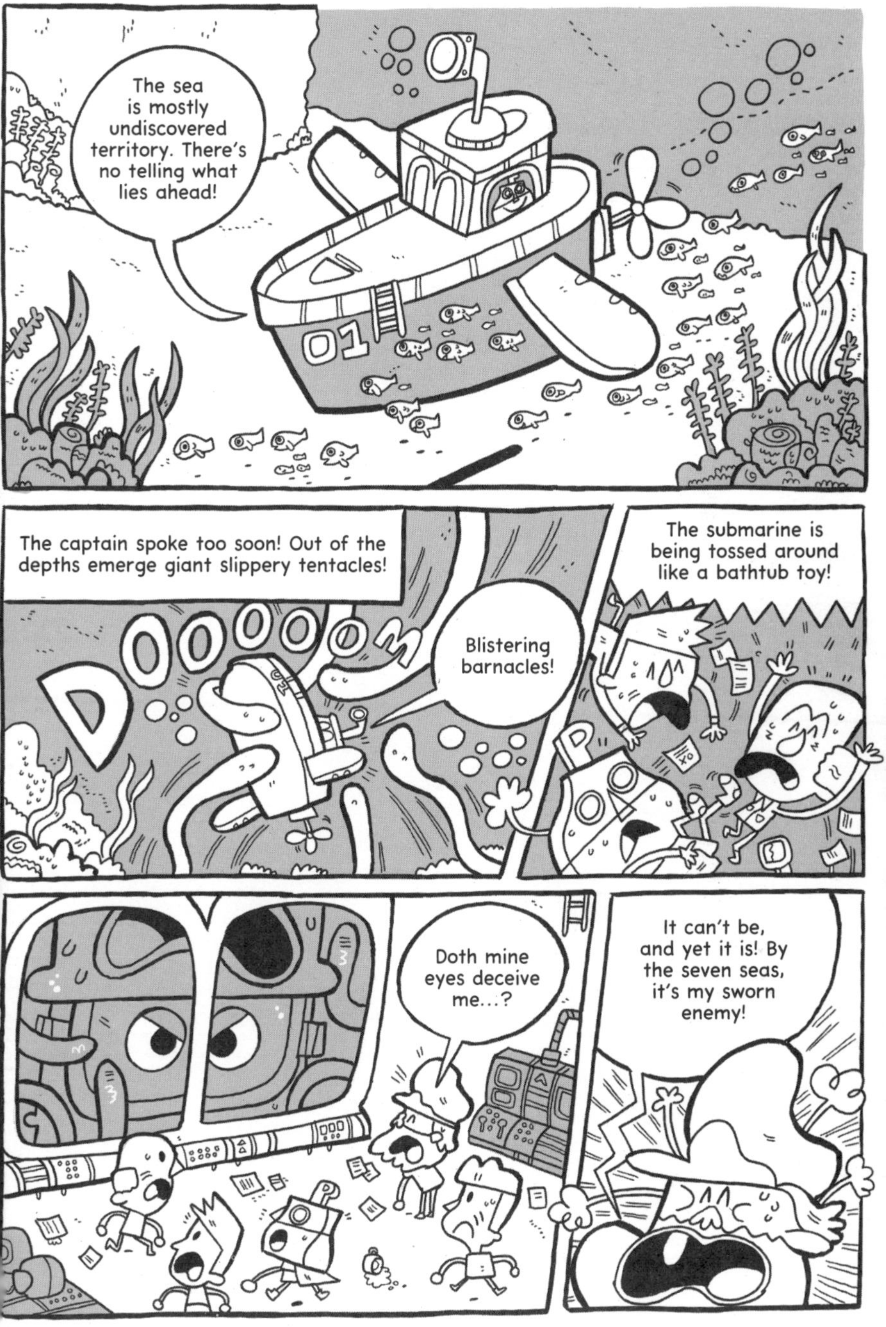

The sea is mostly undiscovered territory. There's no telling what lies ahead!
The captain spoke too soon! Out of the depths emerge giant slippery tentacles!
DOOOOOOM
Blistering barnacles!
The submarine is being tossed around like a bathtub toy!
Doth mine eyes deceive me...?
It can't be, and yet it is! By the seven seas, it's my sworn enemy!

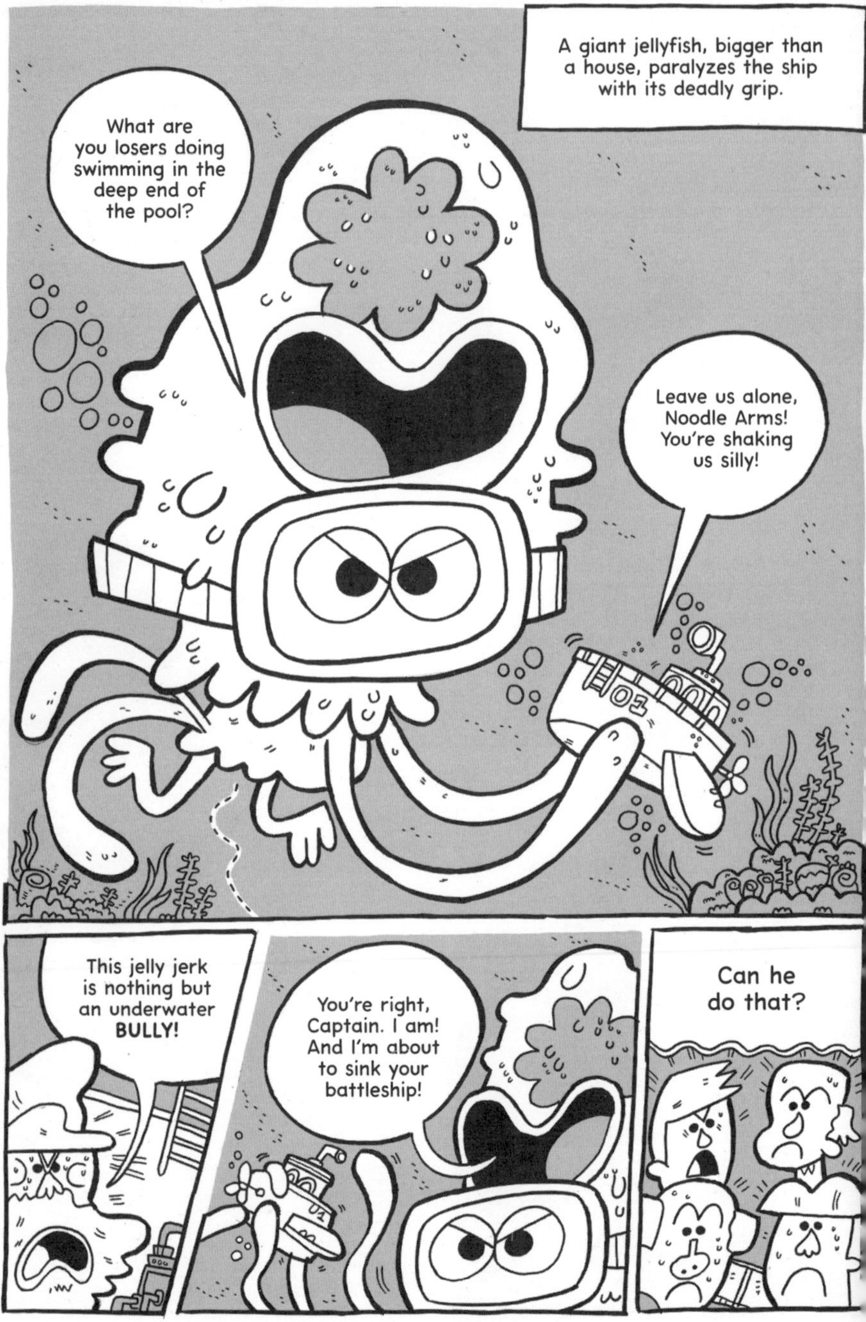
A giant jellyfish, bigger than a house, paralyzes the ship with its deadly grip.
What are you losers doing swimming in the deep end of the pool?
Leave us alone, Noodle Arms! You're shaking us silly!
01
This jelly jerk is nothing but an underwater **BULLY!**
You're right, Captain. I am! And I'm about to sink your battleship!
Can he do that?

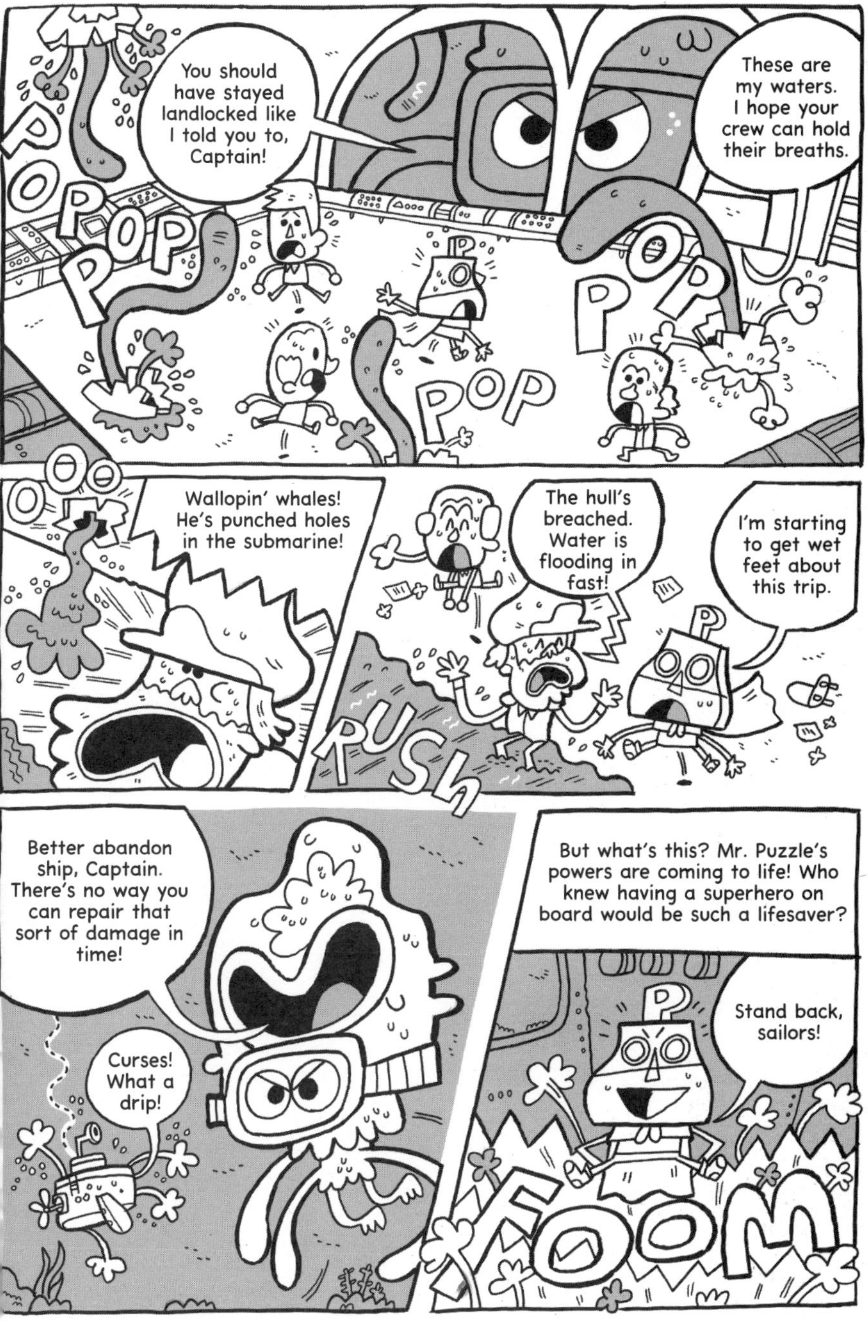

You should have stayed landlocked like I told you to, Captain!
These are my waters. I hope your crew can hold their breaths.
POP
POP
POP
POP
POP
POP
OOO
Wallopin' whales! He's punched holes in the submarine!
The hull's breached. Water is flooding in fast!
I'm starting to get wet feet about this trip.
RUSH
Better abandon ship, Captain. There's no way you can repair that sort of damage in time!
Curses! What a drip!
But what's this? Mr. Puzzle's powers are coming to life! Who knew having a superhero on board would be such a lifesaver?
Stand back, sailors!
FOOM

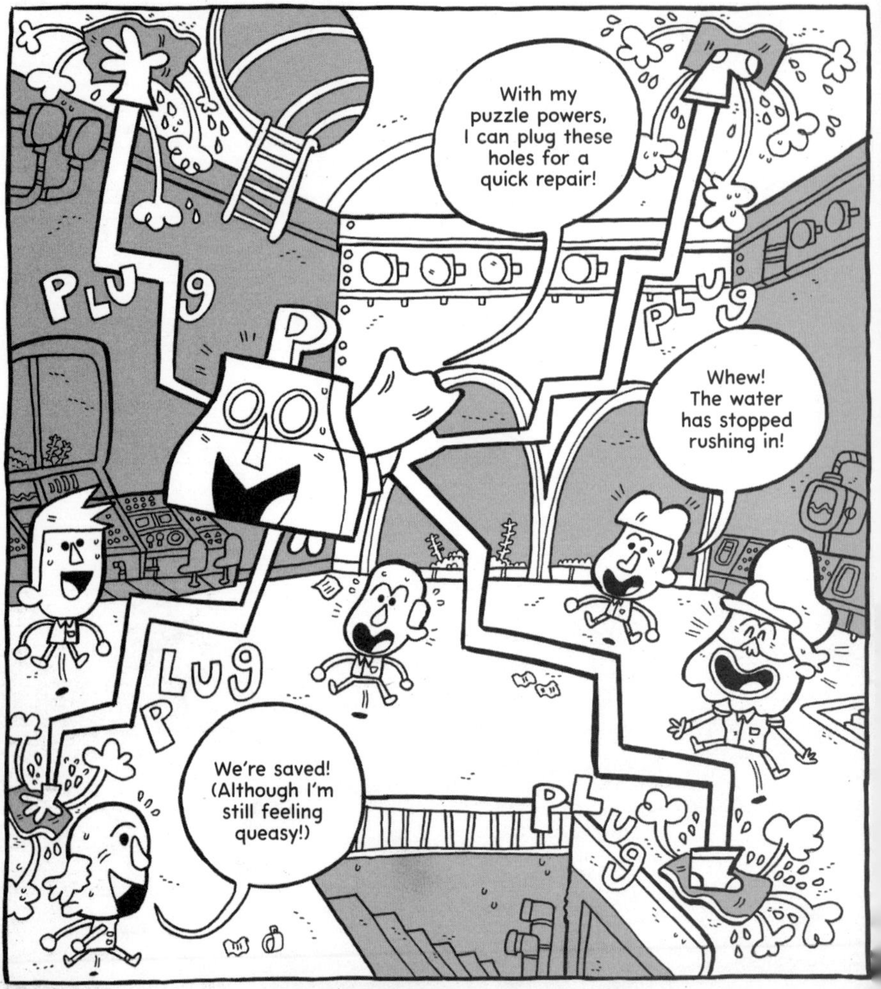
With my puzzle powers, I can plug these holes for a quick repair!
PLUG
PLUG
Whew! The water has stopped rushing in!
PLUG
We're saved! (Although I'm still feeling queasy!)
PLUG

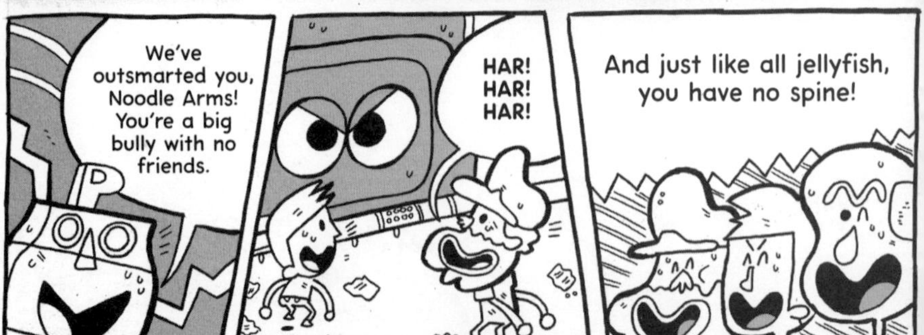
We've outsmarted you, Noodle Arms! You're a big bully with no friends.
HAR! HAR! HAR!
And just like all jellyfish, you have no spine!

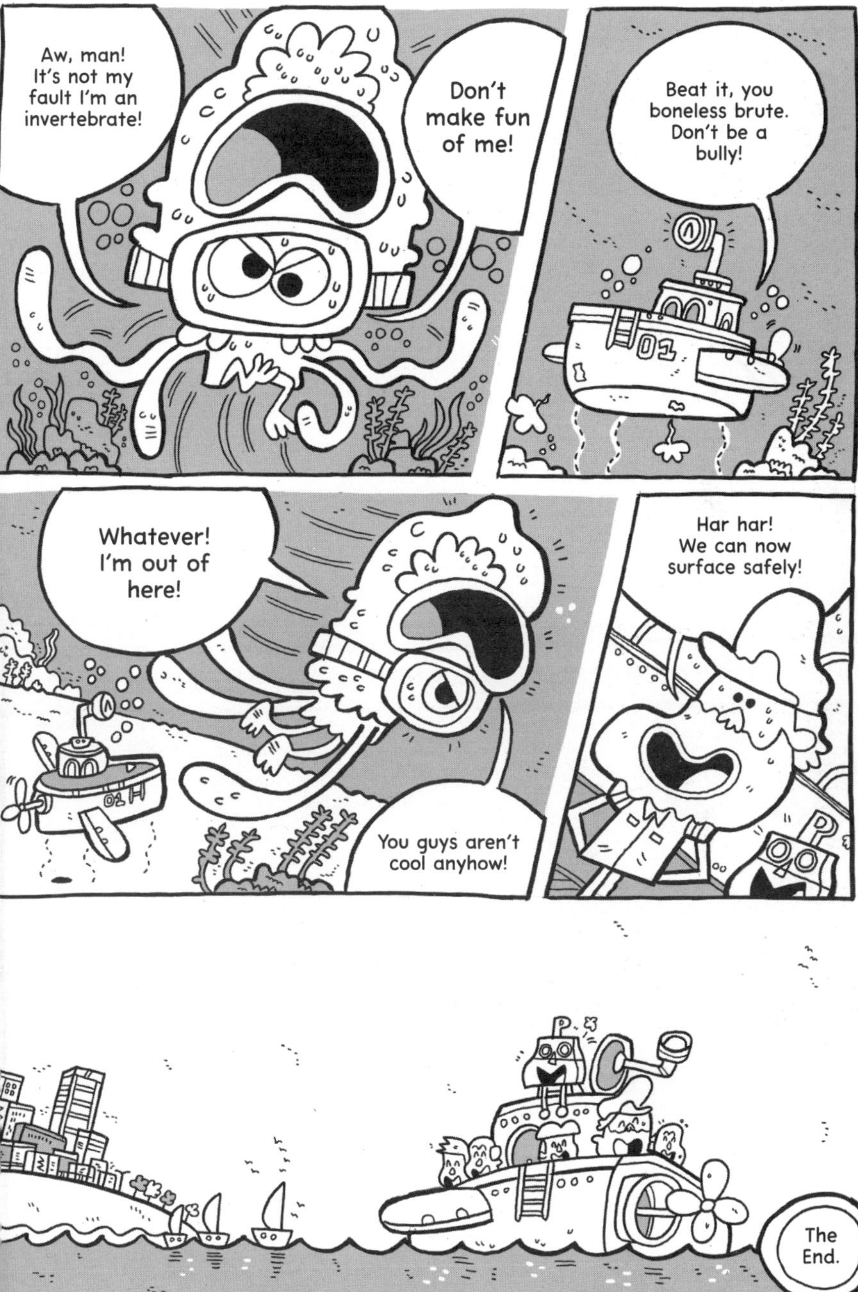
Aw, man! It's not my fault I'm an invertebrate!
Don't make fun of me!
Beat it, you boneless brute. Don't be a bully!
Whatever! I'm out of here!
You guys aren't cool anyhow!
Har har! We can now surface safely!
The End.

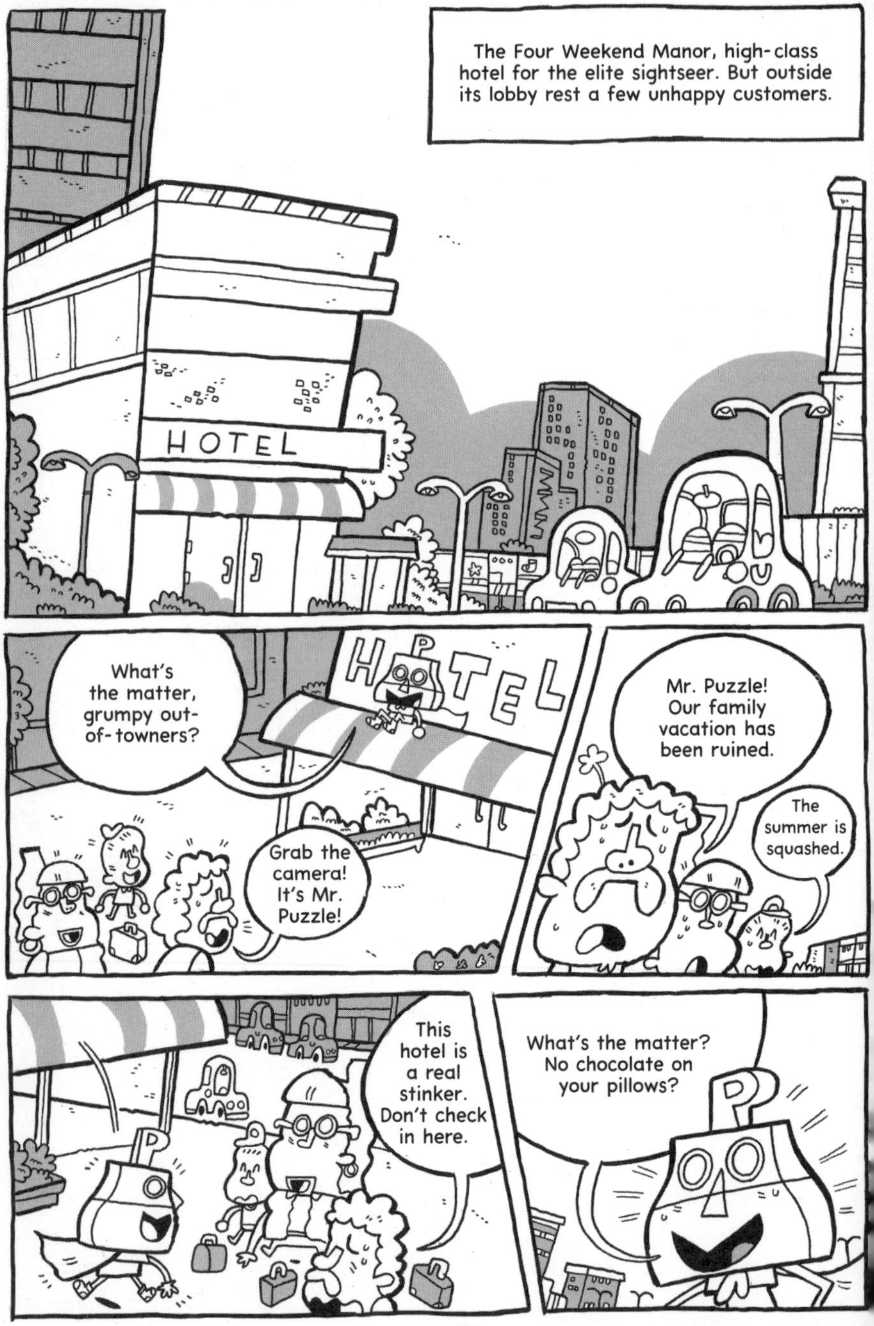
The Four Weekend Manor, high-class hotel for the elite sightseer. But outside its lobby rest a few unhappy customers.
HOTEL
What's the matter, grumpy out-of-towners?
Grab the camera! It's Mr. Puzzle!
Mr. Puzzle! Our family vacation has been ruined.
The summer is squashed.
This hotel is a real stinker. Don't check in here.
What's the matter? No chocolate on your pillows?

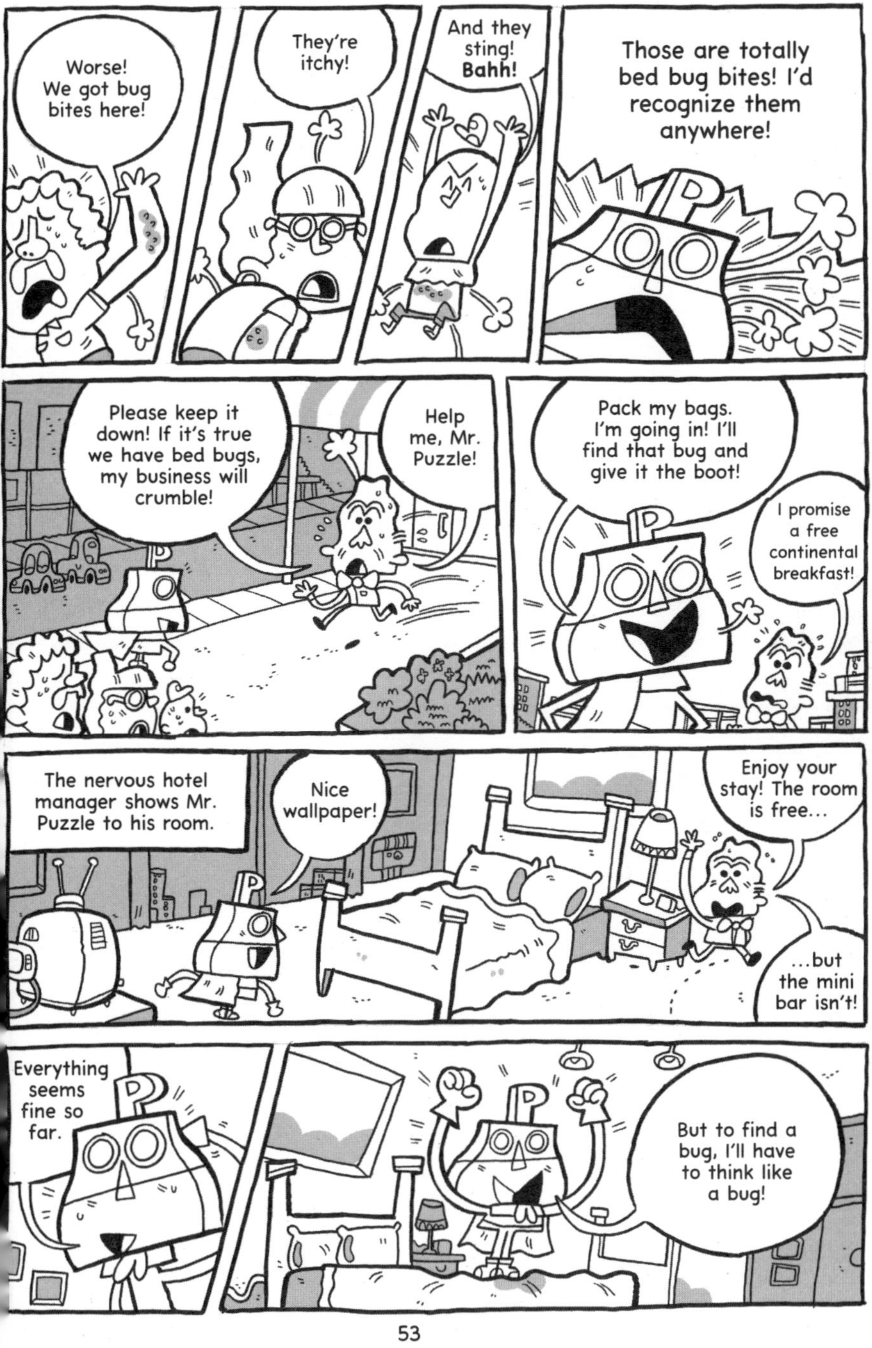

Worse! We got bug bites here!
They're itchy!
And they sting! **Bahh!**
Those are totally bed bug bites! I'd recognize them anywhere!
Please keep it down! If it's true we have bed bugs, my business will crumble!
Help me, Mr. Puzzle!
Pack my bags. I'm going in! I'll find that bug and give it the boot!
I promise a free continental breakfast!
The nervous hotel manager shows Mr. Puzzle to his room.
Nice wallpaper!
Enjoy your stay! The room is free...
...but the mini bar isn't!
Everything seems fine so far.
But to find a bug, I'll have to think like a bug!

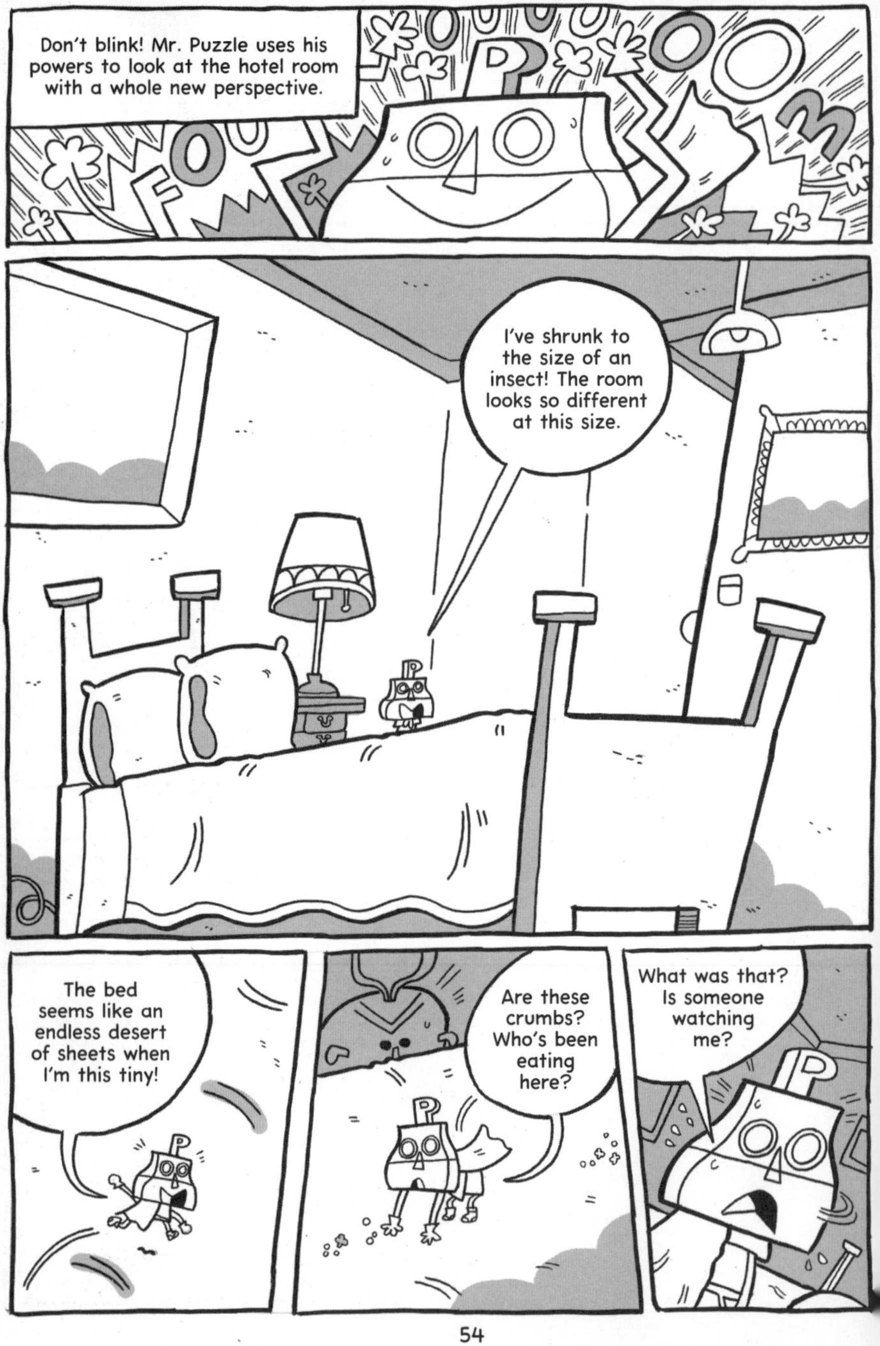
Don't blink! Mr. Puzzle uses his powers to look at the hotel room with a whole new perspective.
FOOOOOOOOM
I've shrunk to the size of an insect! The room looks so different at this size.
The bed seems like an endless desert of sheets when I'm this tiny!
Are these crumbs? Who's been eating here?
What was that? Is someone watching me?

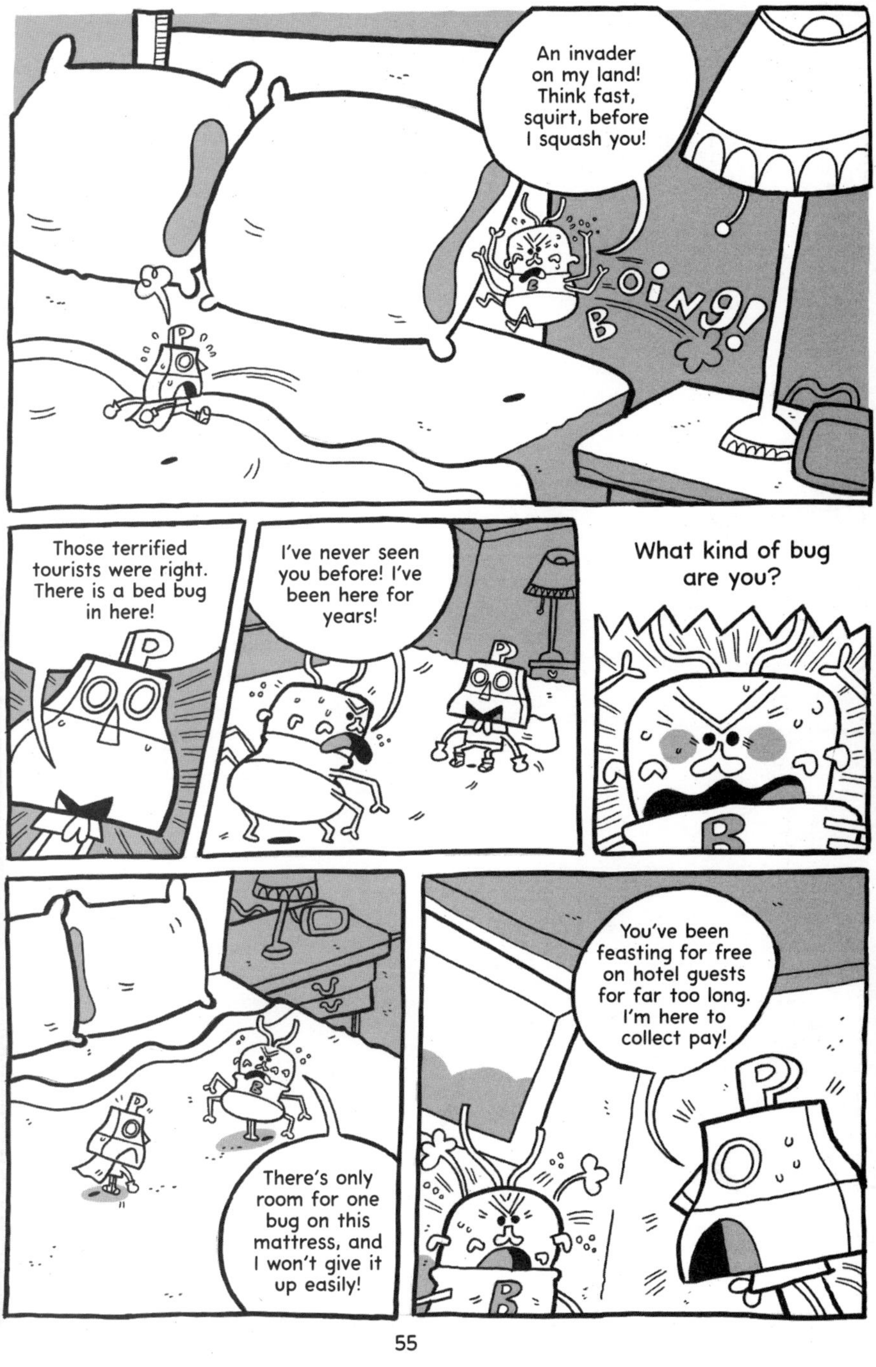
An invader on my land! Think fast, squirt, before I squash you!
BOING!
Those terrified tourists were right. There is a bed bug in here!
I've never seen you before! I've been here for years!
What kind of bug are you?
There's only room for one bug on this mattress, and I won't give it up easily!
You've been feasting for free on hotel guests for far too long. I'm here to collect pay!

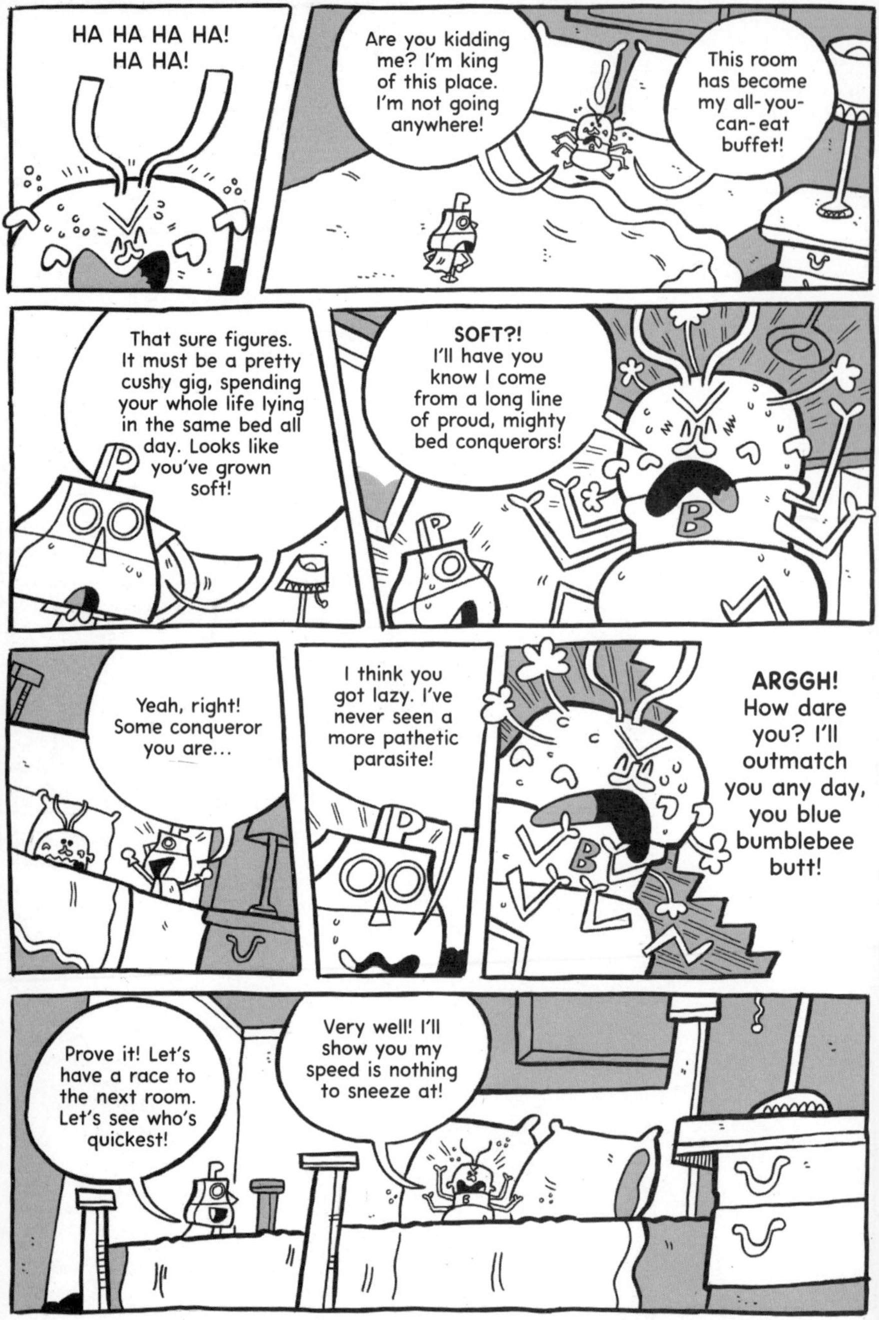
HA HA HA HA! HA HA!
Are you kidding me? I'm king of this place. I'm not going anywhere!
This room has become my all-you-can-eat buffet!
That sure figures. It must be a pretty cushy gig, spending your whole life lying in the same bed all day. Looks like you've grown soft!
SOFT?! I'll have you know I come from a long line of proud, mighty bed conquerors!
Yeah, right! Some conqueror you are...
I think you got lazy. I've never seen a more pathetic parasite!
ARGGH! How dare you? I'll outmatch you any day, you blue bumblebee butt!
Prove it! Let's have a race to the next room. Let's see who's quickest!
Very well! I'll show you my speed is nothing to sneeze at!

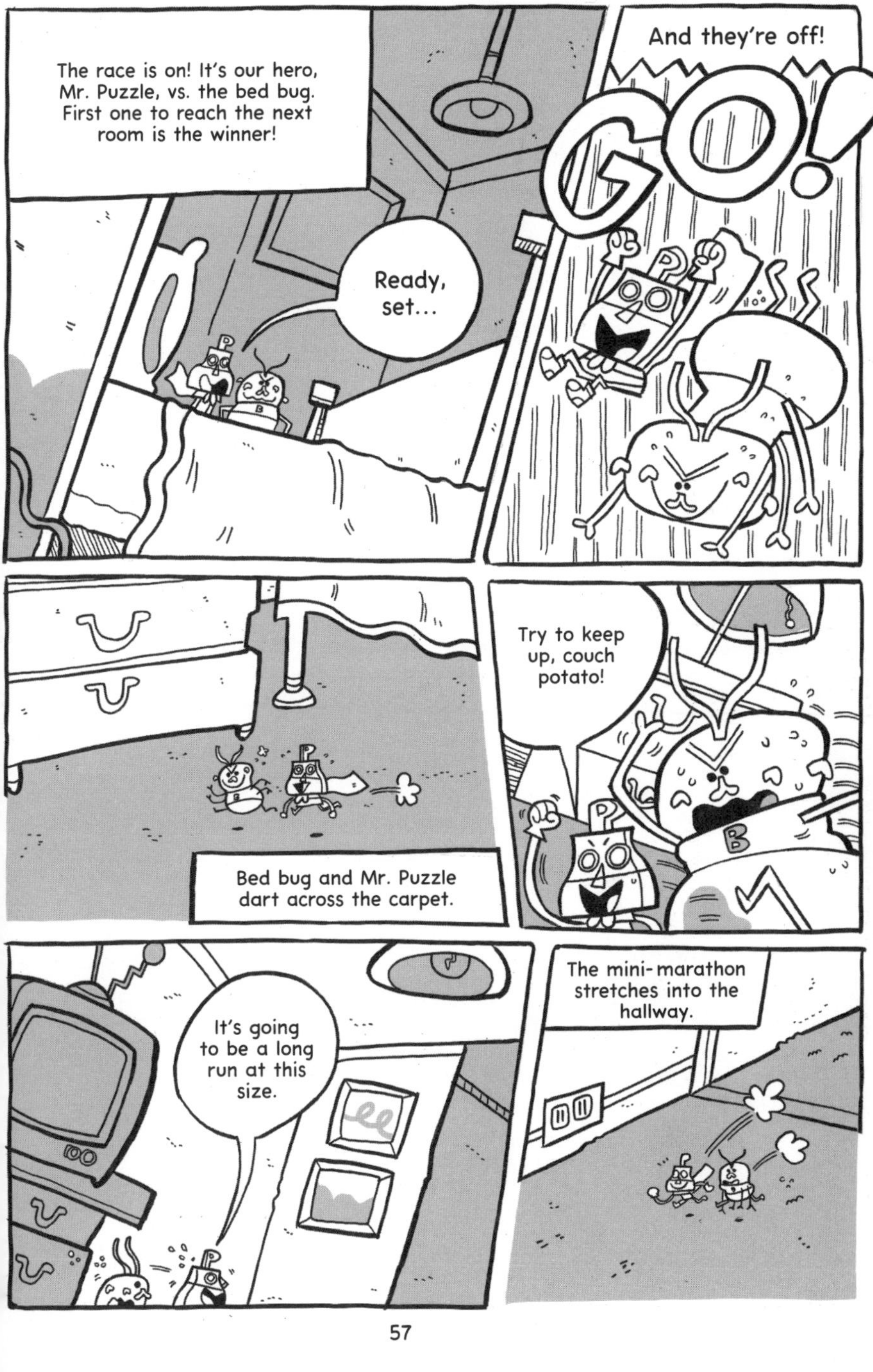
The race is on! It's our hero, Mr. Puzzle, vs. the bed bug. First one to reach the next room is the winner!
Ready, set...
And they're off!
GO!
Try to keep up, couch potato!
Bed bug and Mr. Puzzle dart across the carpet.
It's going to be a long run at this size.
The mini-marathon stretches into the hallway.

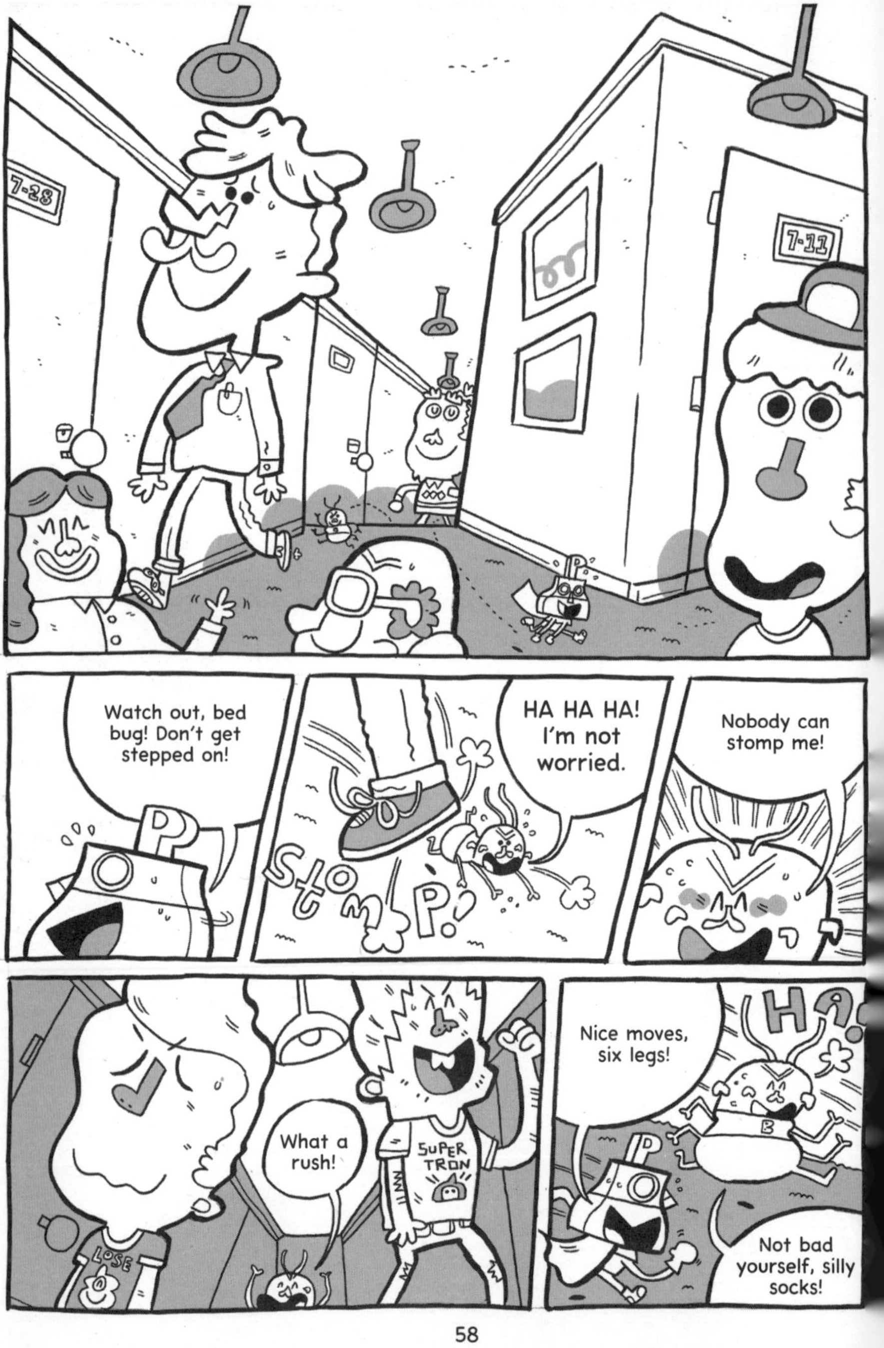

7-28
7-11
Watch out, bed bug! Don't get stepped on!
HA HA HA! I'm not worried.
STOMP!
Nobody can stomp me!
LOSE
What a rush!
SUPER TRON
Nice moves, six legs!
HA
Not bad yourself, silly socks!

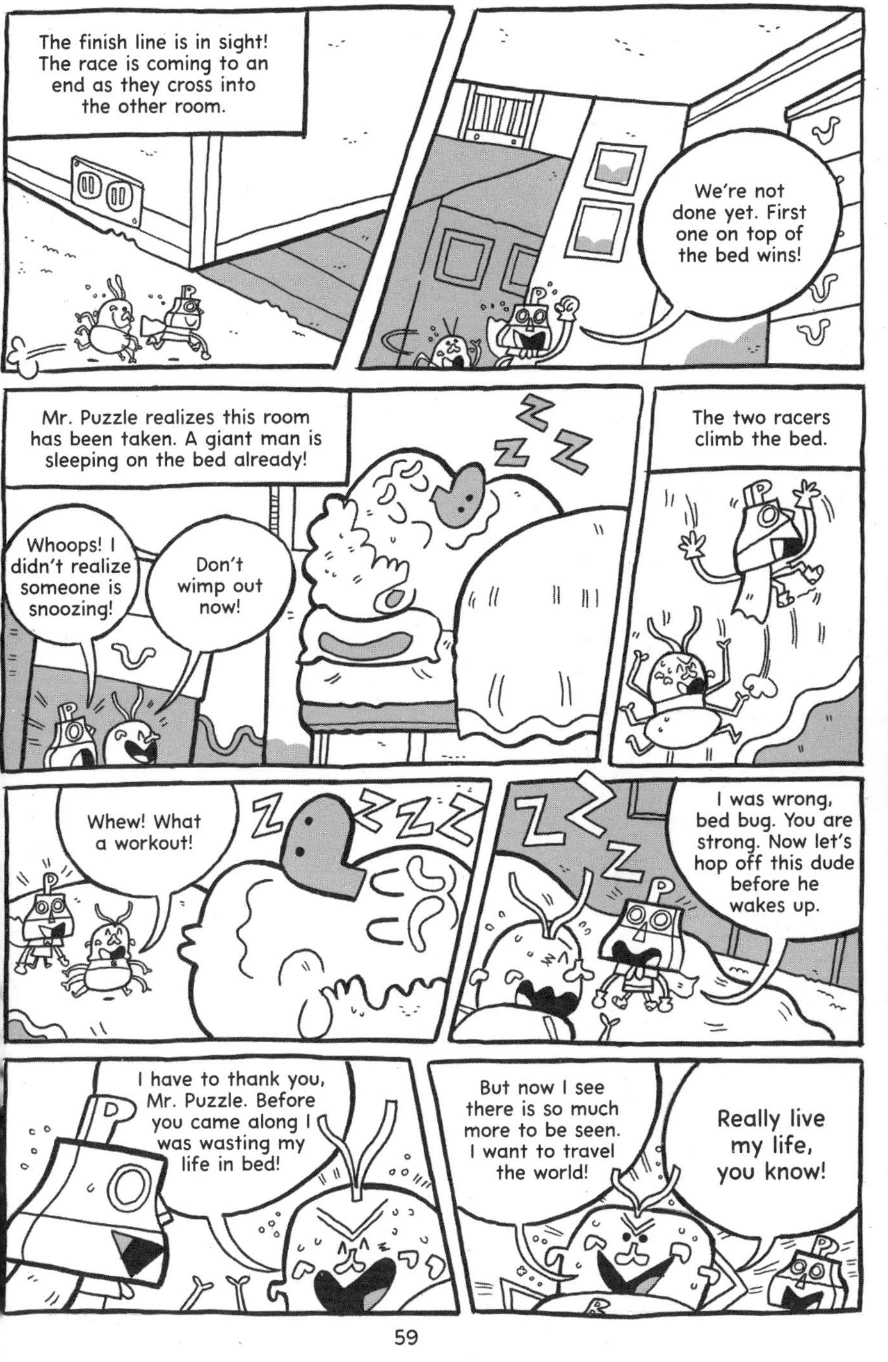
The finish line is in sight! The race is coming to an end as they cross into the other room.
We're not done yet. First one on top of the bed wins!
Mr. Puzzle realizes this room has been taken. A giant man is sleeping on the bed already!
Whoops! I didn't realize someone is snoozing!
Don't wimp out now!
The two racers climb the bed.
Whew! What a workout!
I was wrong, bed bug. You are strong. Now let's hop off this dude before he wakes up.
I have to thank you, Mr. Puzzle. Before you came along I was wasting my life in bed!
But now I see there is so much more to be seen. I want to travel the world!
Really live my life, you know!

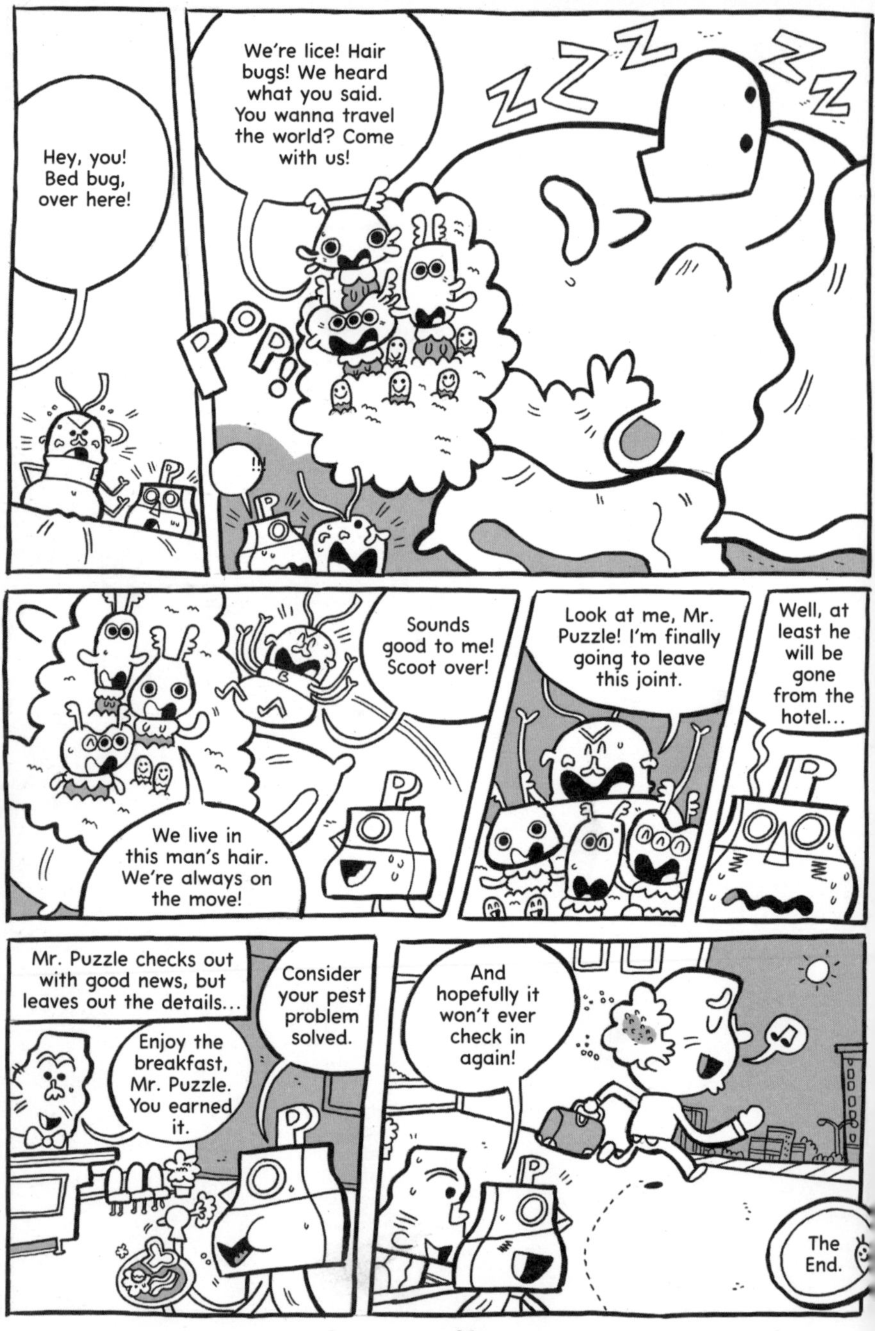
Hey, you! Bed bug, over here!
We're lice! Hair bugs! We heard what you said. You wanna travel the world? Come with us!
ZZZZZ
POP!
Sounds good to me! Scoot over!
We live in this man's hair. We're always on the move!
Look at me, Mr. Puzzle! I'm finally going to leave this joint.
Well, at least he will be gone from the hotel...
Mr. Puzzle checks out with good news, but leaves out the details...
Enjoy the breakfast, Mr. Puzzle. You earned it.
Consider your pest problem solved.
And hopefully it won't ever check in again!
The End.

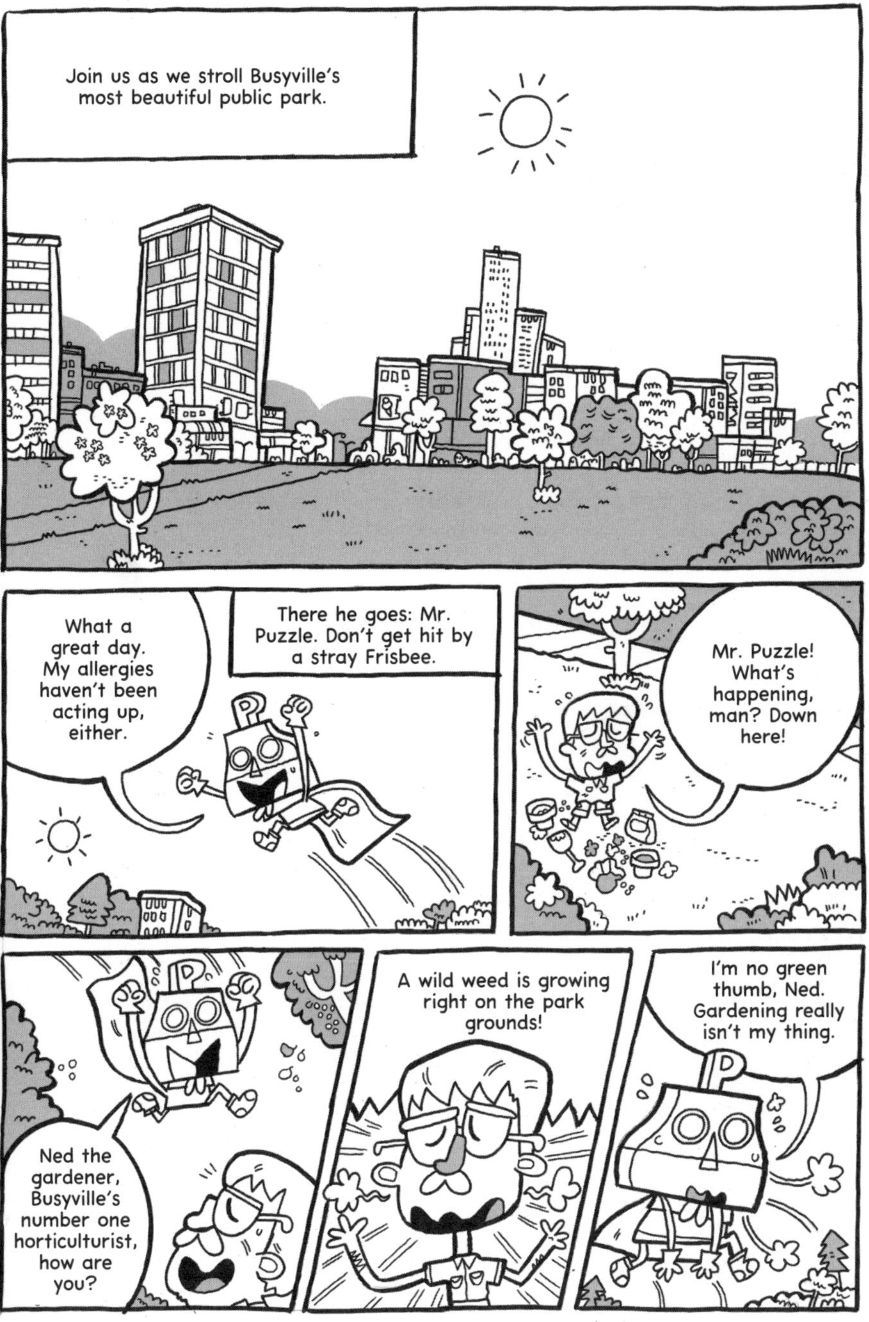
Join us as we stroll Busyville's most beautiful public park.
What a great day. My allergies haven't been acting up, either.
There he goes: Mr. Puzzle. Don't get hit by a stray Frisbee.
Mr. Puzzle! What's happening, man? Down here!
Ned the gardener, Busyville's number one horticulturist, how are you?
A wild weed is growing right on the park grounds!
I'm no green thumb, Ned. Gardening really isn't my thing.

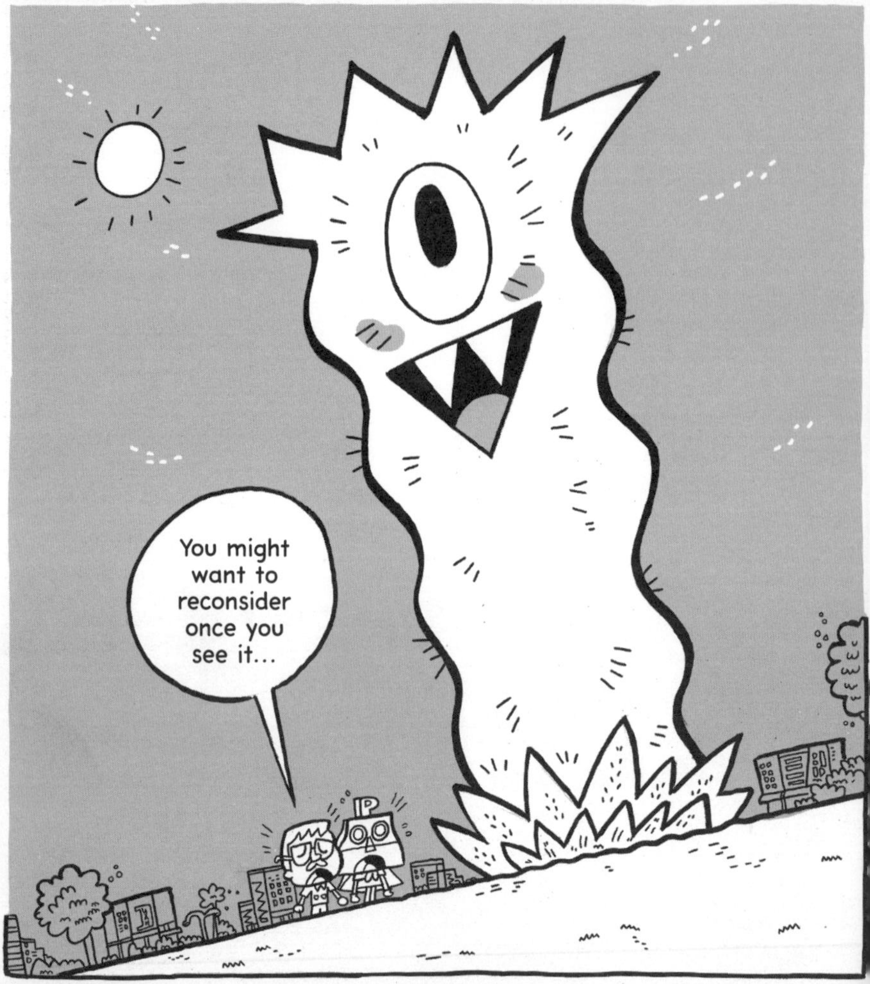
You might want to reconsider once you see it...
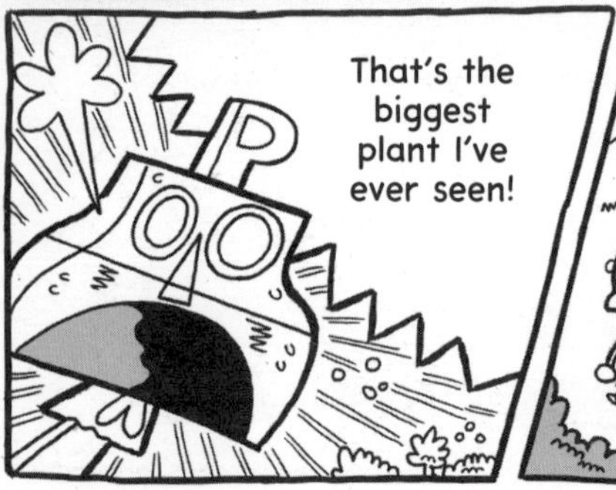
That's the biggest plant I've ever seen!
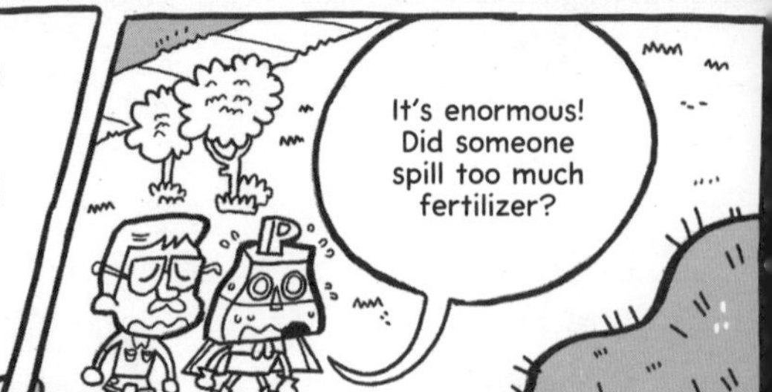
It's enormous! Did someone spill too much fertilizer?

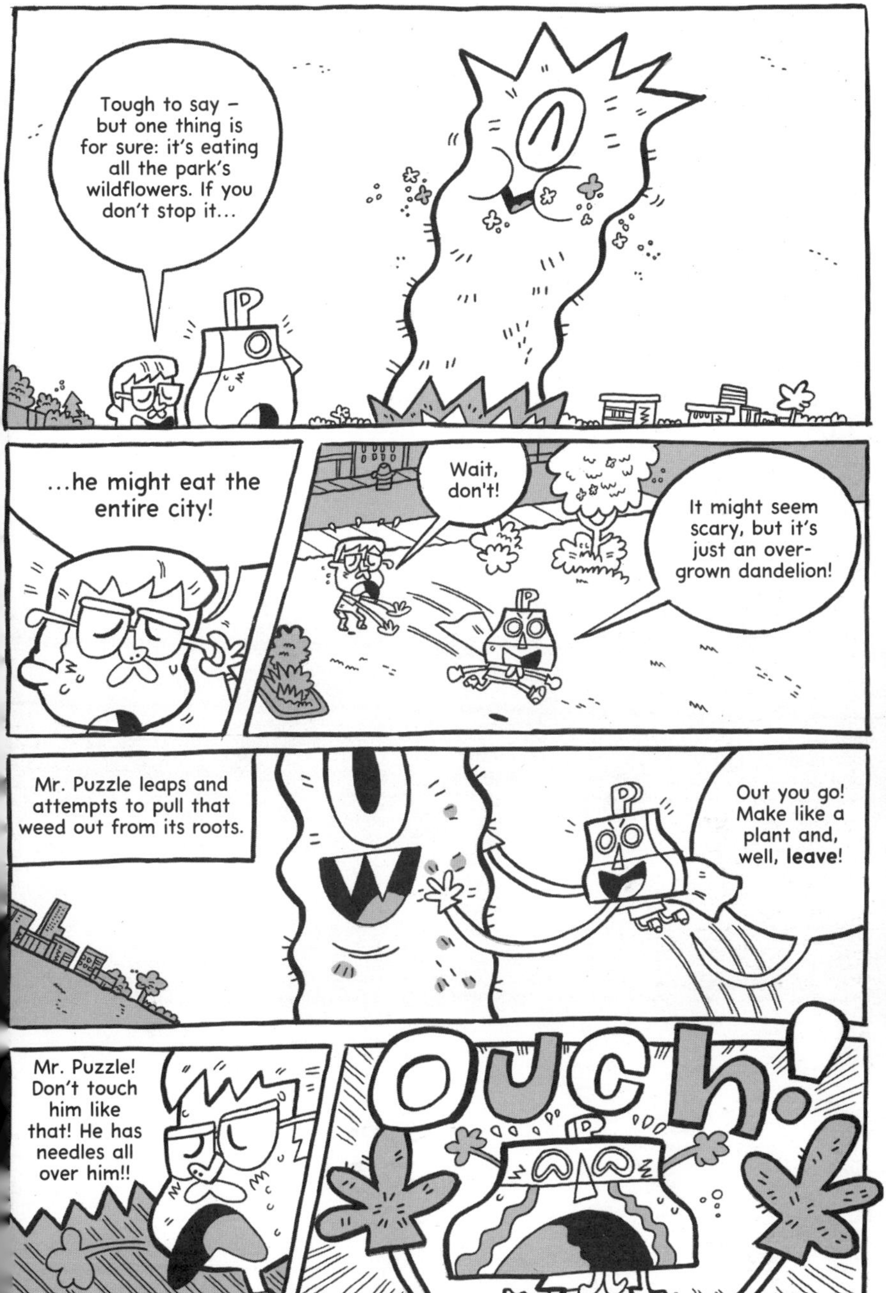

Tough to say – but one thing is for sure: it's eating all the park's wildflowers. If you don't stop it...
...he might eat the entire city!
Wait, don't!
It might seem scary, but it's just an over-grown dandelion!
Mr. Puzzle leaps and attempts to pull that weed out from its roots.
Out you go! Make like a plant and, well, **leave**!
Mr. Puzzle! Don't touch him like that! He has needles all over him!!
Ouch!

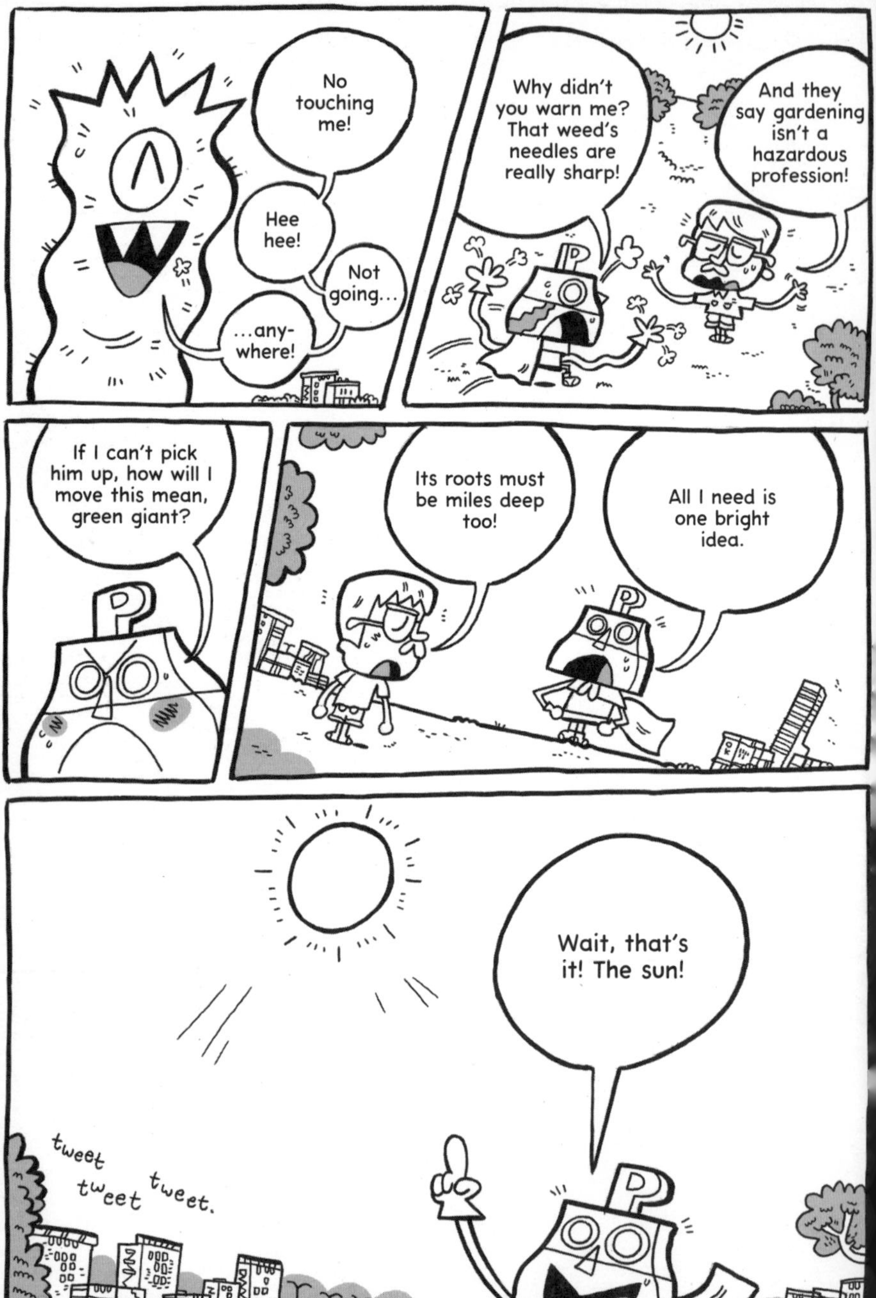
No touching me!
Hee hee!
Not going...
...any-where!
Why didn't you warn me? That weed's needles are really sharp!
And they say gardening isn't a hazardous profession!
If I can't pick him up, how will I move this mean, green giant?
Its roots must be miles deep too!
All I need is one bright idea.
Wait, that's it! The sun!
tweet
tweet tweet.

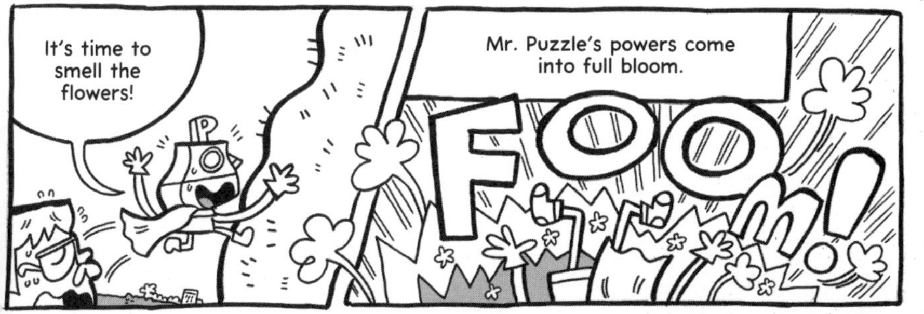
It's time to smell the flowers!
Mr. Puzzle's powers come into full bloom.
FOOOM!

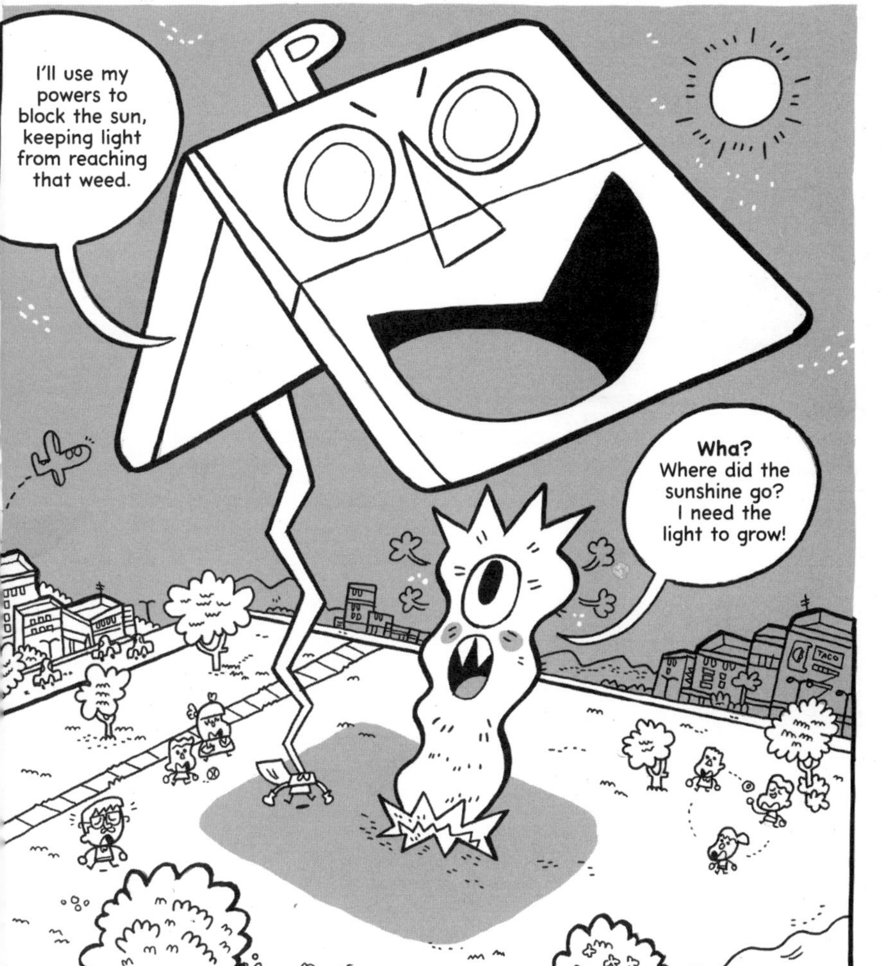
I'll use my powers to block the sun, keeping light from reaching that weed.
Wha? Where did the sunshine go? I need the light to grow!
TACO

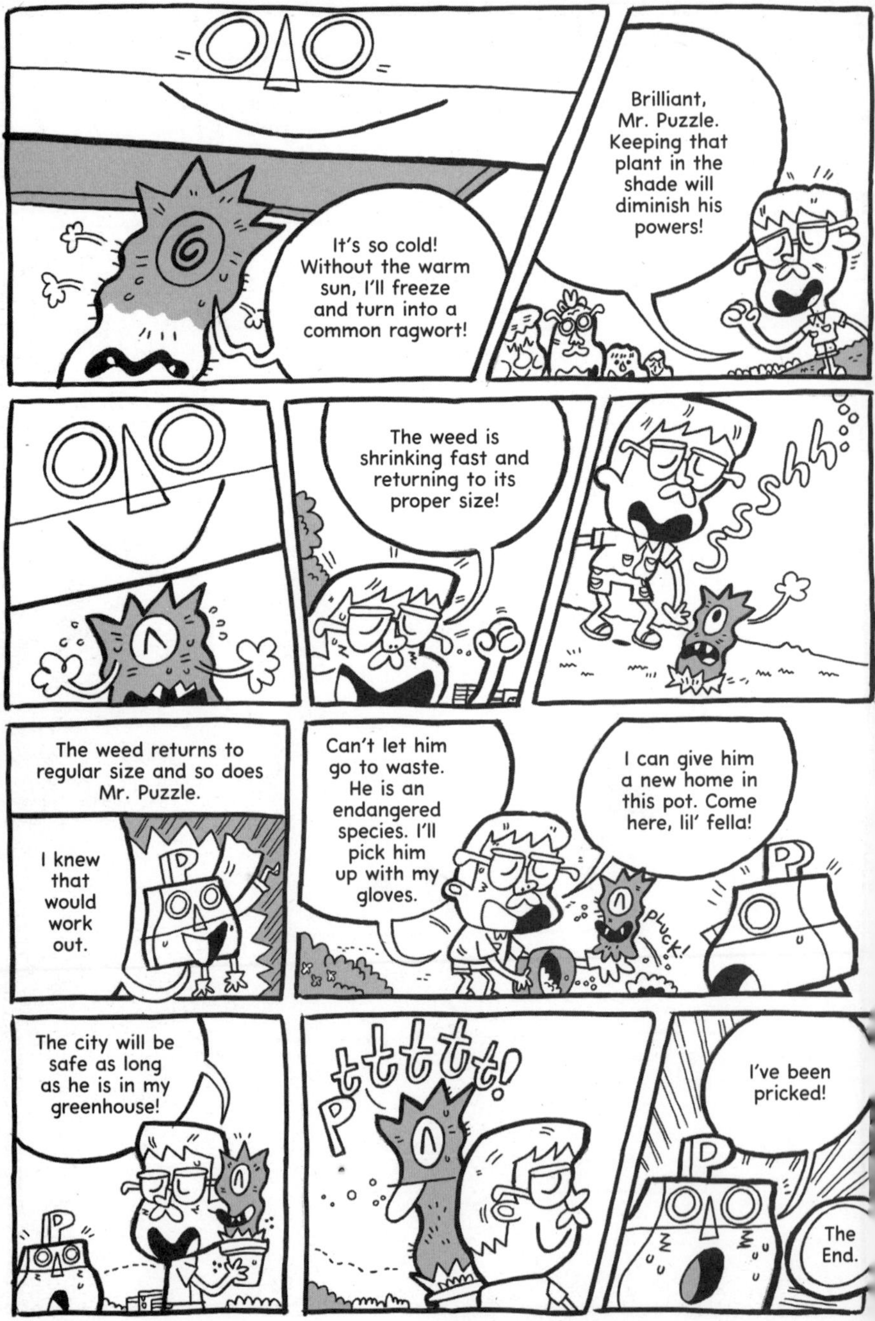
It's so cold! Without the warm sun, I'll freeze and turn into a common ragwort!
Brilliant, Mr. Puzzle. Keeping that plant in the shade will diminish his powers!
The weed is shrinking fast and returning to its proper size!
ssshh
The weed returns to regular size and so does Mr. Puzzle.
I knew that would work out.
Can't let him go to waste. He is an endangered species. I'll pick him up with my gloves.
I can give him a new home in this pot. Come here, lil' fella!
PLUCK!
The city will be safe as long as he is in my greenhouse!
Ptttttt!
I've been pricked!
The End.

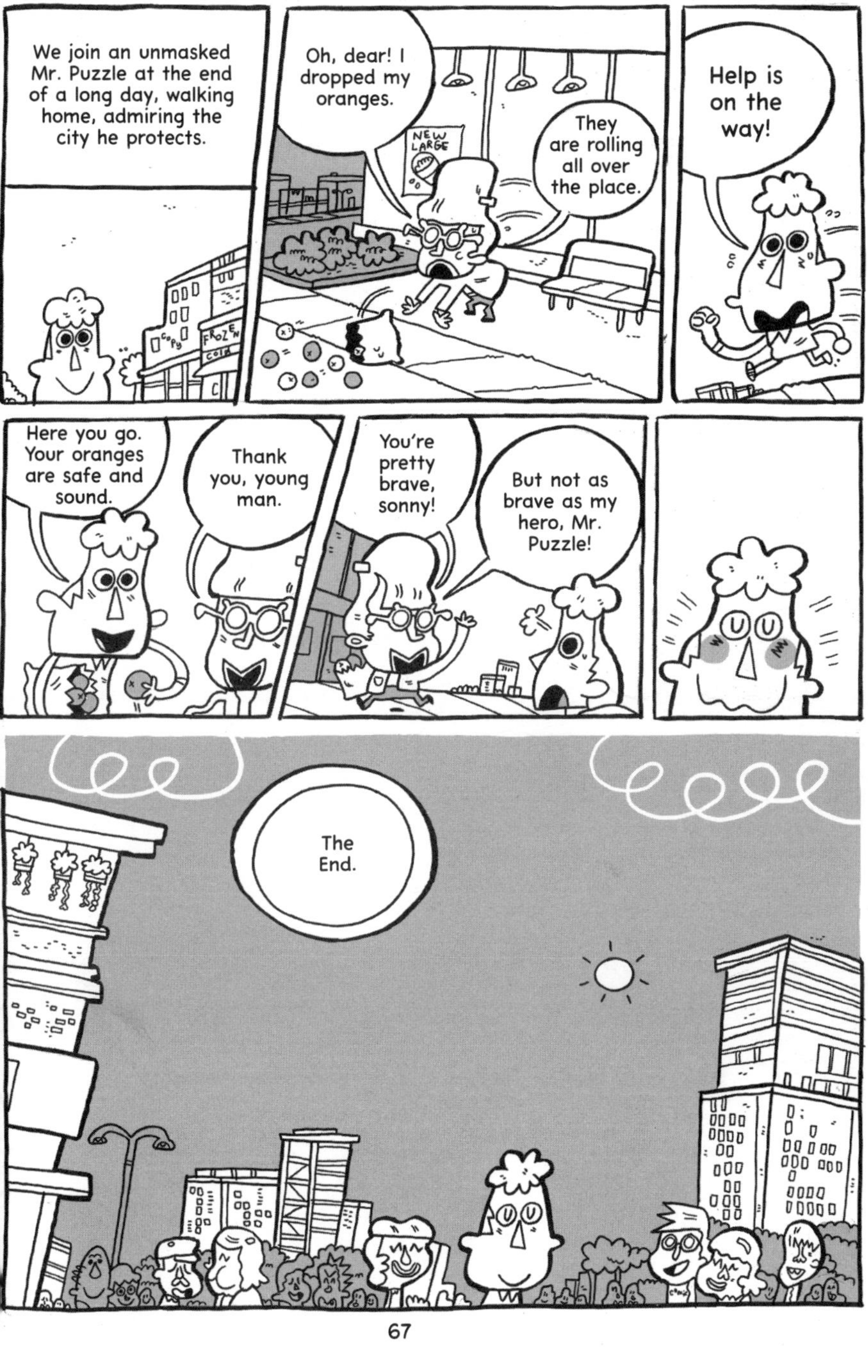
We join an unmasked Mr. Puzzle at the end of a long day, walking home, admiring the city he protects.
Oh, dear! I dropped my oranges.
They are rolling all over the place.
Help is on the way!
Here you go. Your oranges are safe and sound.
Thank you, young man.
You're pretty brave, sonny!
But not as brave as my hero, Mr. Puzzle!
The End.

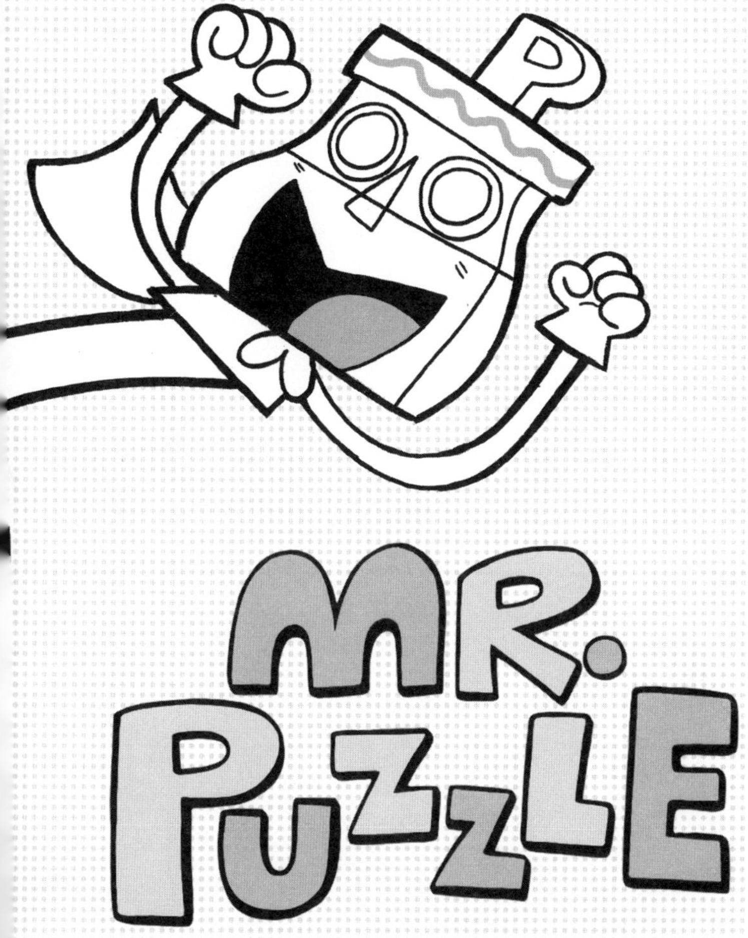

MR. PUZZLE

No Instructions Needed

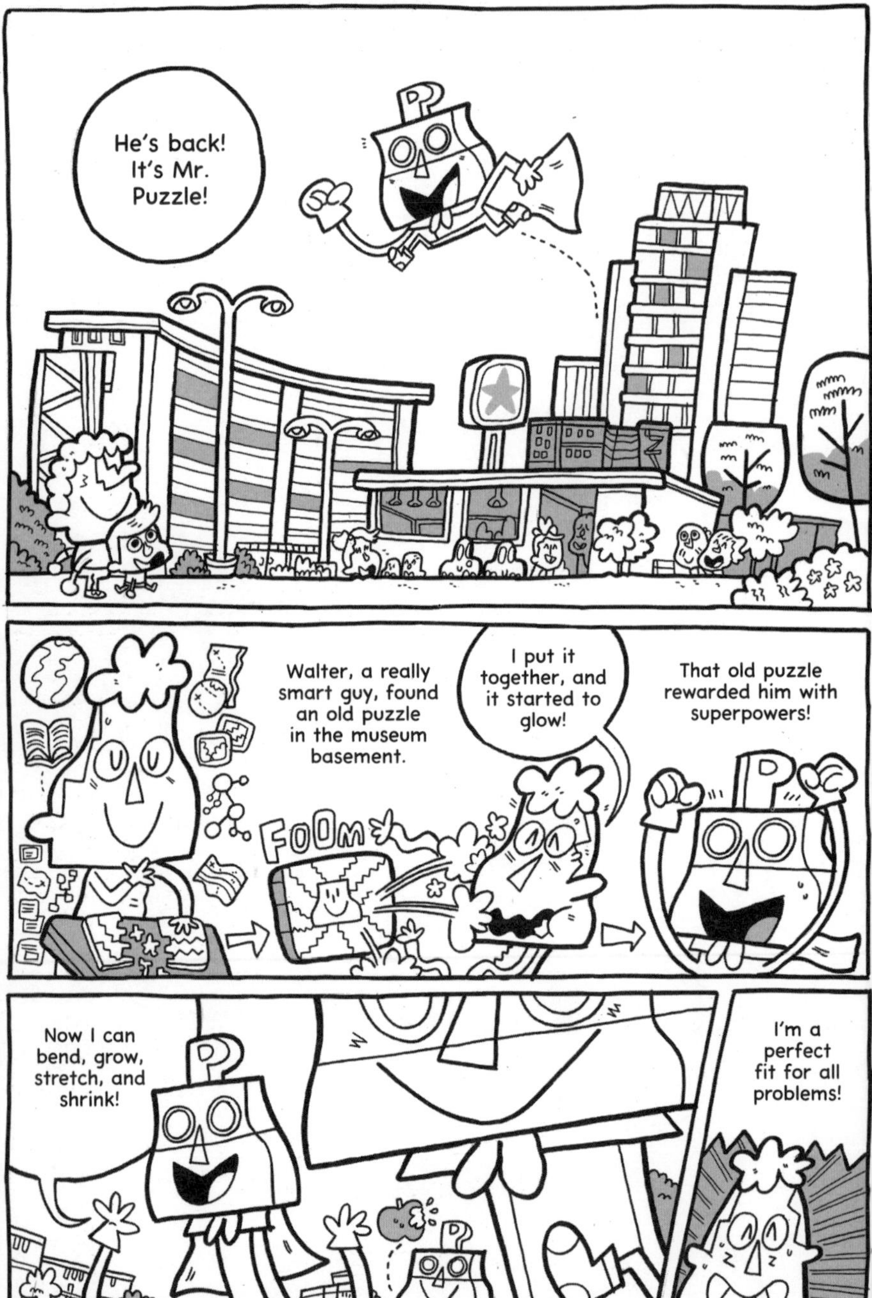
He's back! It's Mr. Puzzle!
Walter, a really smart guy, found an old puzzle in the museum basement.
FOOM
I put it together, and it started to glow!
That old puzzle rewarded him with superpowers!
Now I can bend, grow, stretch, and shrink!
I'm a perfect fit for all problems!

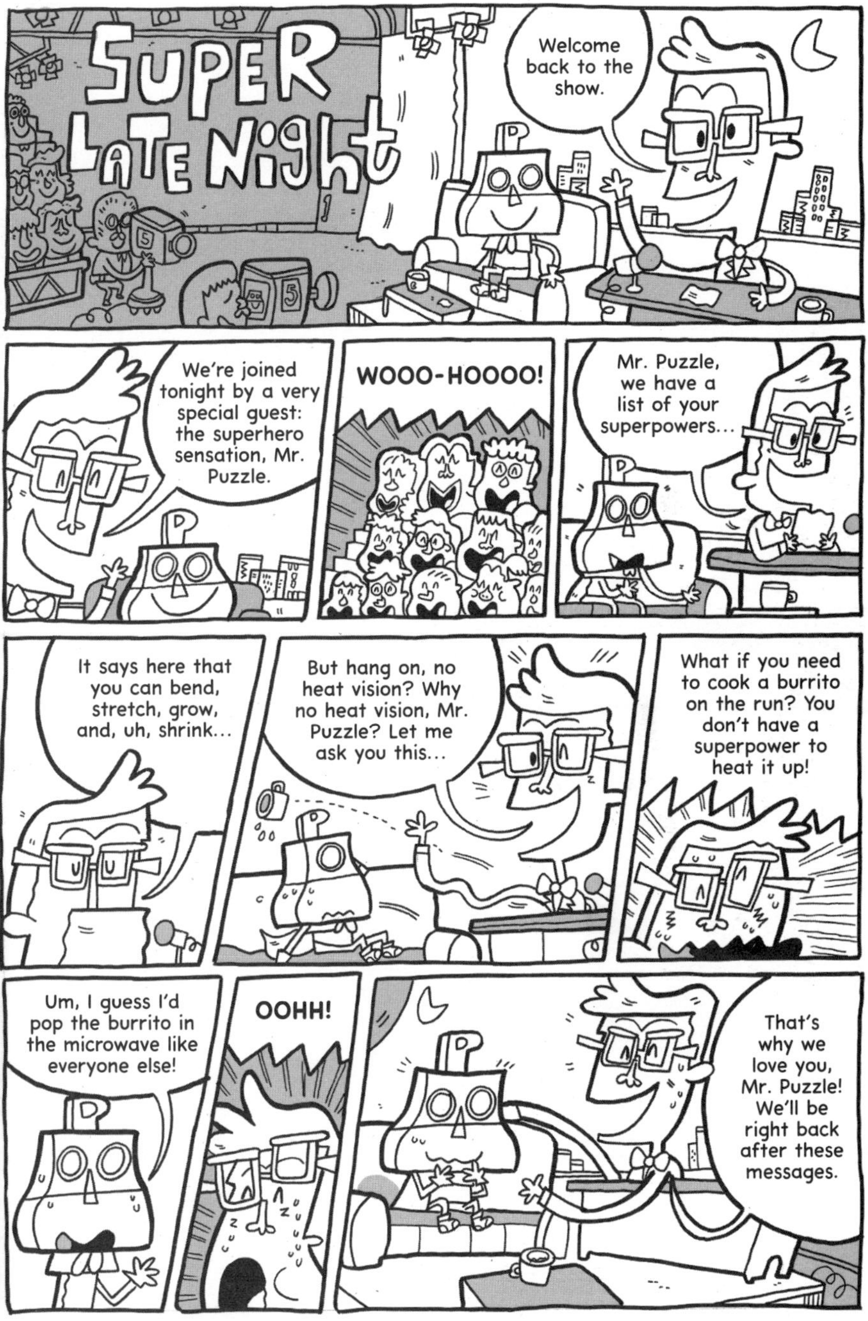
SUPER LATE NIGHT
Welcome back to the show.
We're joined tonight by a very special guest: the superhero sensation, Mr. Puzzle.
WOOO-HOOOO!
Mr. Puzzle, we have a list of your superpowers...
It says here that you can bend, stretch, grow, and, uh, shrink...
But hang on, no heat vision? Why no heat vision, Mr. Puzzle? Let me ask you this...
What if you need to cook a burrito on the run? You don't have a superpower to heat it up!
Um, I guess I'd pop the burrito in the microwave like everyone else!
OOHH!
That's why we love you, Mr. Puzzle! We'll be right back after these messages.

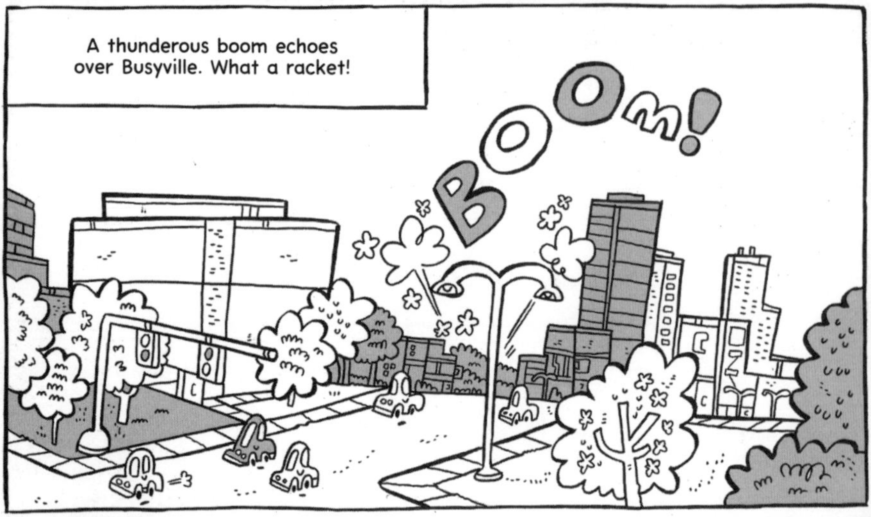
A thunderous boom echoes over Busyville. What a racket!
BOOOm!

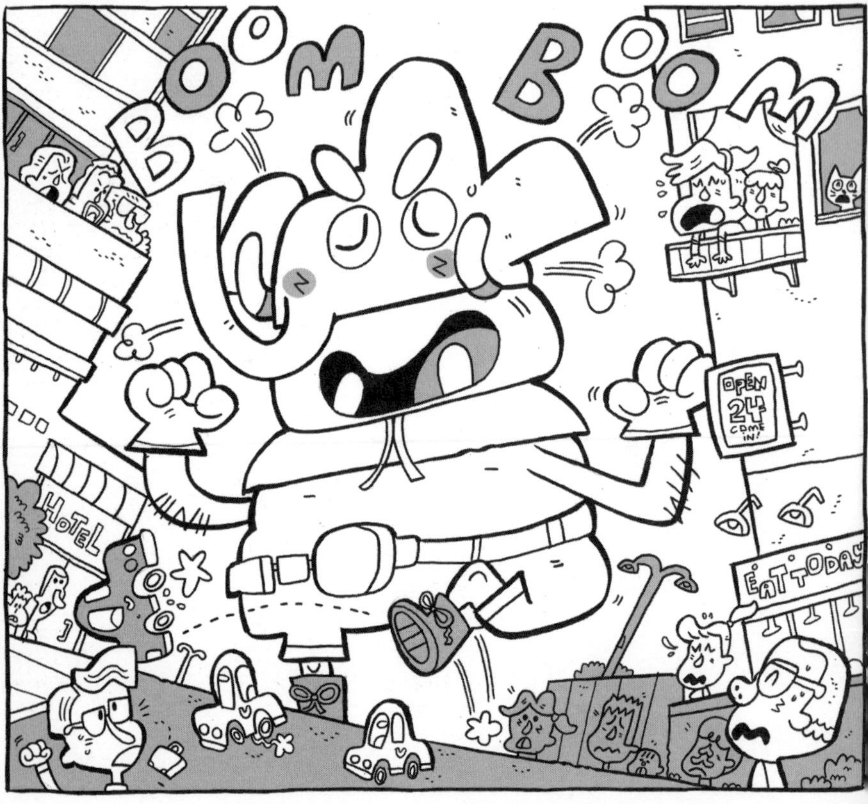
BOOM BOOOM
OPEN 24 COME IN!
HOTEL
EAT TODAY

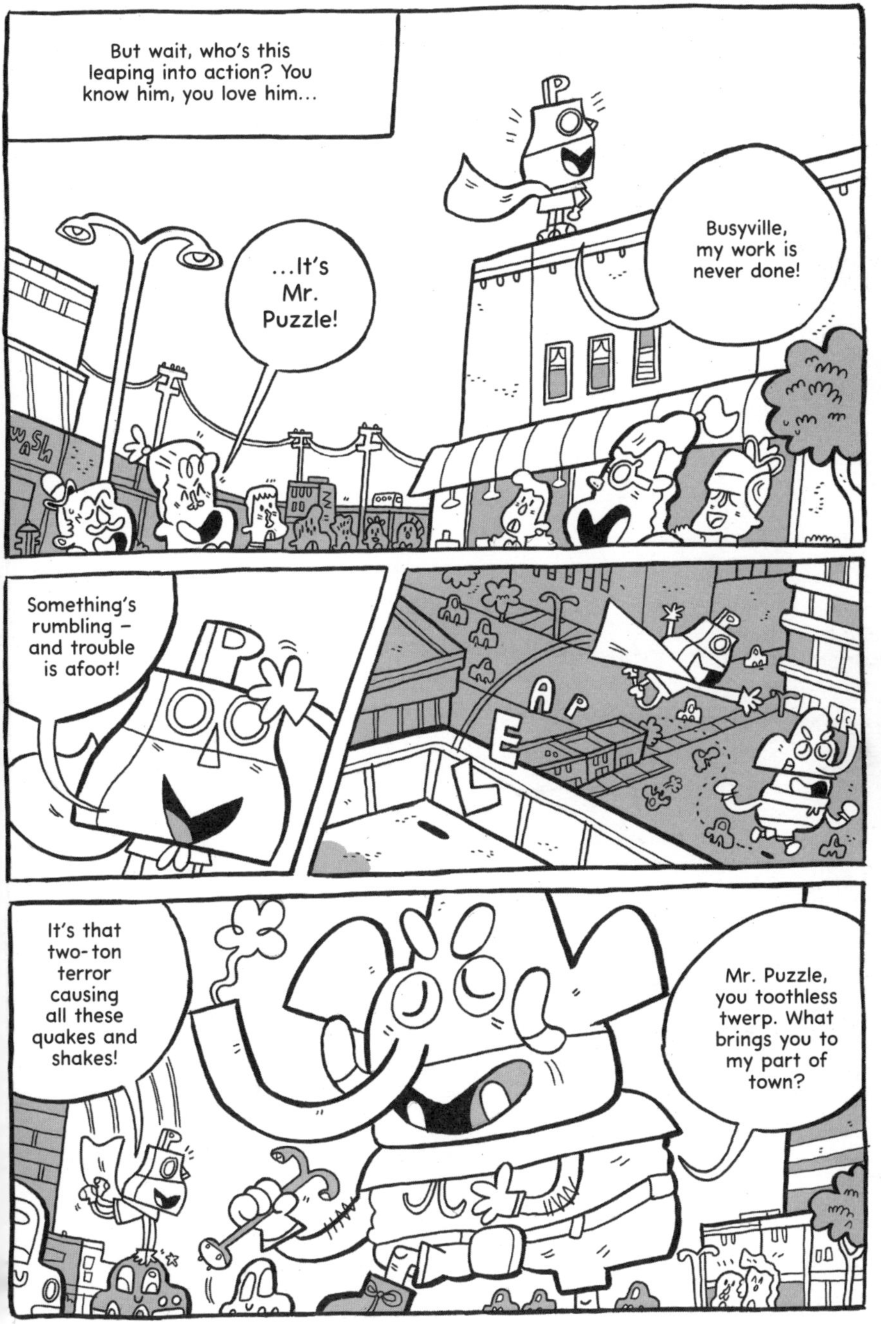
But wait, who's this leaping into action? You know him, you love him...
...It's Mr. Puzzle!
Busyville, my work is never done!
WaSh
Something's rumbling – and trouble is afoot!
It's that two-ton terror causing all these quakes and shakes!
Mr. Puzzle, you toothless twerp. What brings you to my part of town?

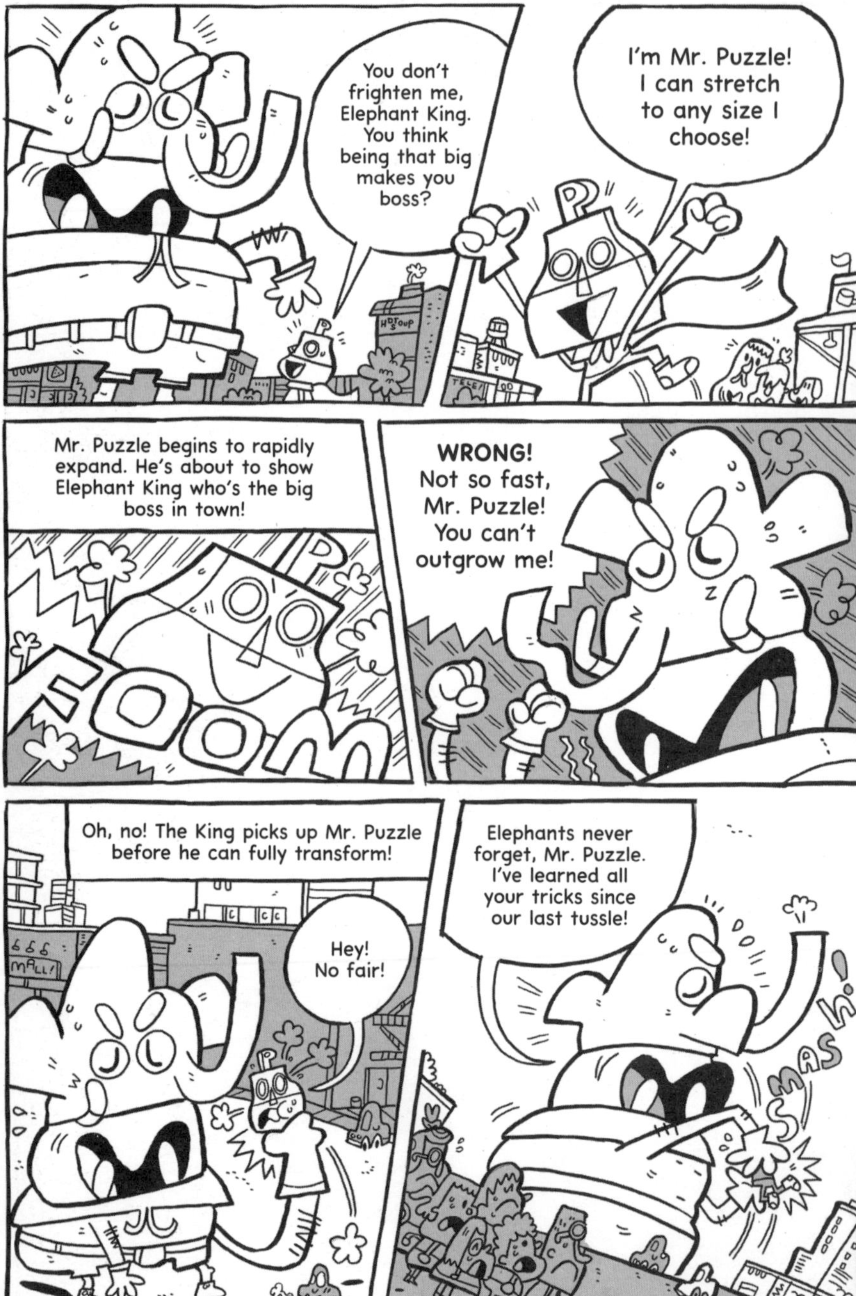
You don't frighten me, Elephant King. You think being that big makes you boss?
I'm Mr. Puzzle! I can stretch to any size I choose!
Mr. Puzzle begins to rapidly expand. He's about to show Elephant King who's the big boss in town!
FOOM
WRONG! Not so fast, Mr. Puzzle! You can't outgrow me!
Oh, no! The King picks up Mr. Puzzle before he can fully transform!
Hey! No fair!
Elephants never forget, Mr. Puzzle. I've learned all your tricks since our last tussle!
SMASH!

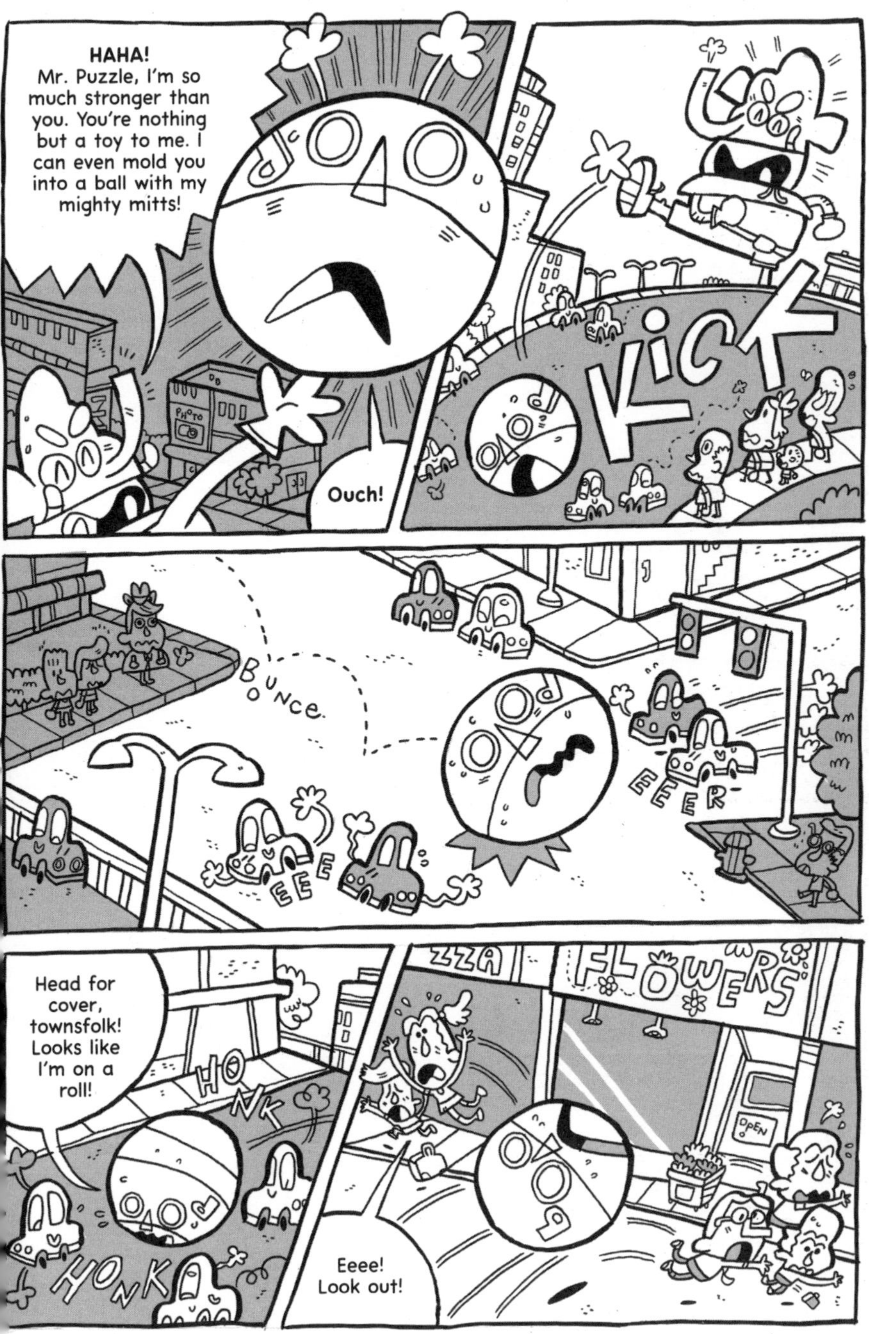
HAHA!
Mr. Puzzle, I'm so much stronger than you. You're nothing but a toy to me. I can even mold you into a ball with my mighty mitts!
Ouch!
KICK
BOUNCE
EEE
EEER
Head for cover, townsfolk! Looks like I'm on a roll!
HONK
HONK
FLOWERS
OPEN
Eeee! Look out!

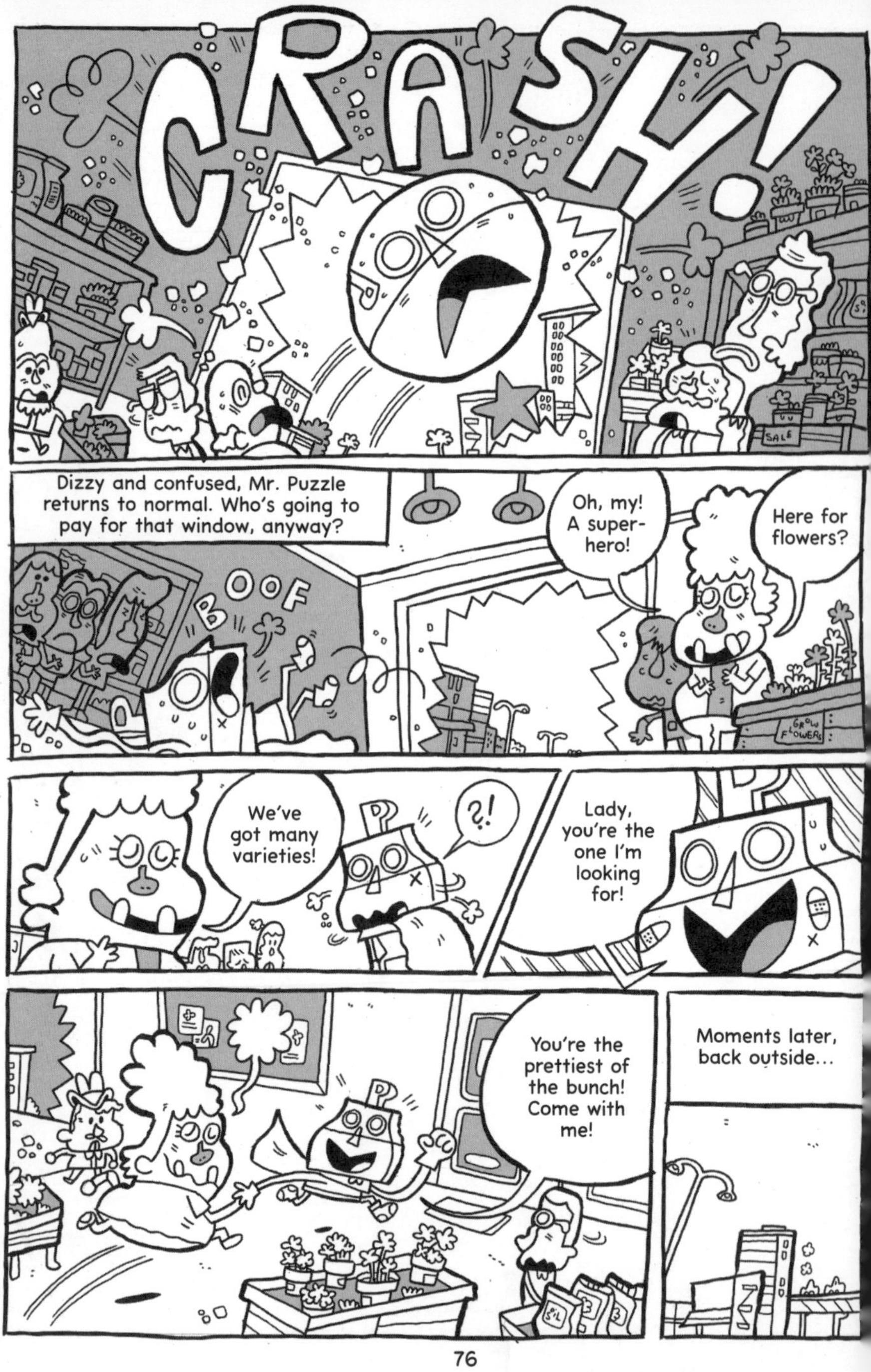

CRASH!
Dizzy and confused, Mr. Puzzle returns to normal. Who's going to pay for that window, anyway?
BOOF
Oh, my! A super-hero!
Here for flowers?
GROW FLOWERS
We've got many varieties!
?!
Lady, you're the one I'm looking for!
You're the prettiest of the bunch! Come with me!
Moments later, back outside...

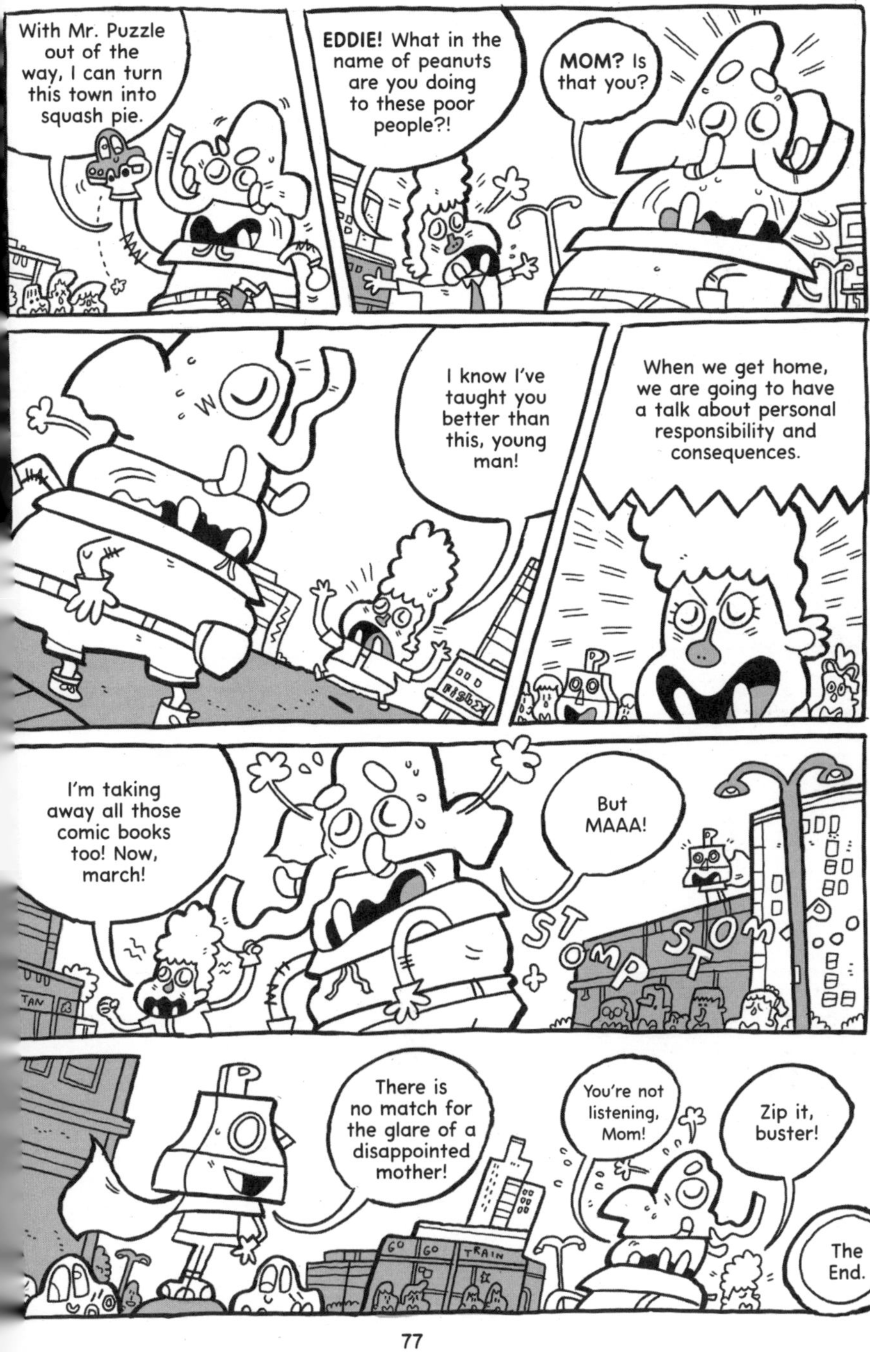
With Mr. Puzzle out of the way, I can turn this town into squash pie.
EDDIE! What in the name of peanuts are you doing to these poor people?!
MOM? Is that you?
I know I've taught you better than this, young man!
When we get home, we are going to have a talk about personal responsibility and consequences.
I'm taking away all those comic books too! Now, march!
But MAAA!
STOMP STOMP STOMP
There is no match for the glare of a disappointed mother!
You're not listening, Mom!
Zip it, buster!
The End.

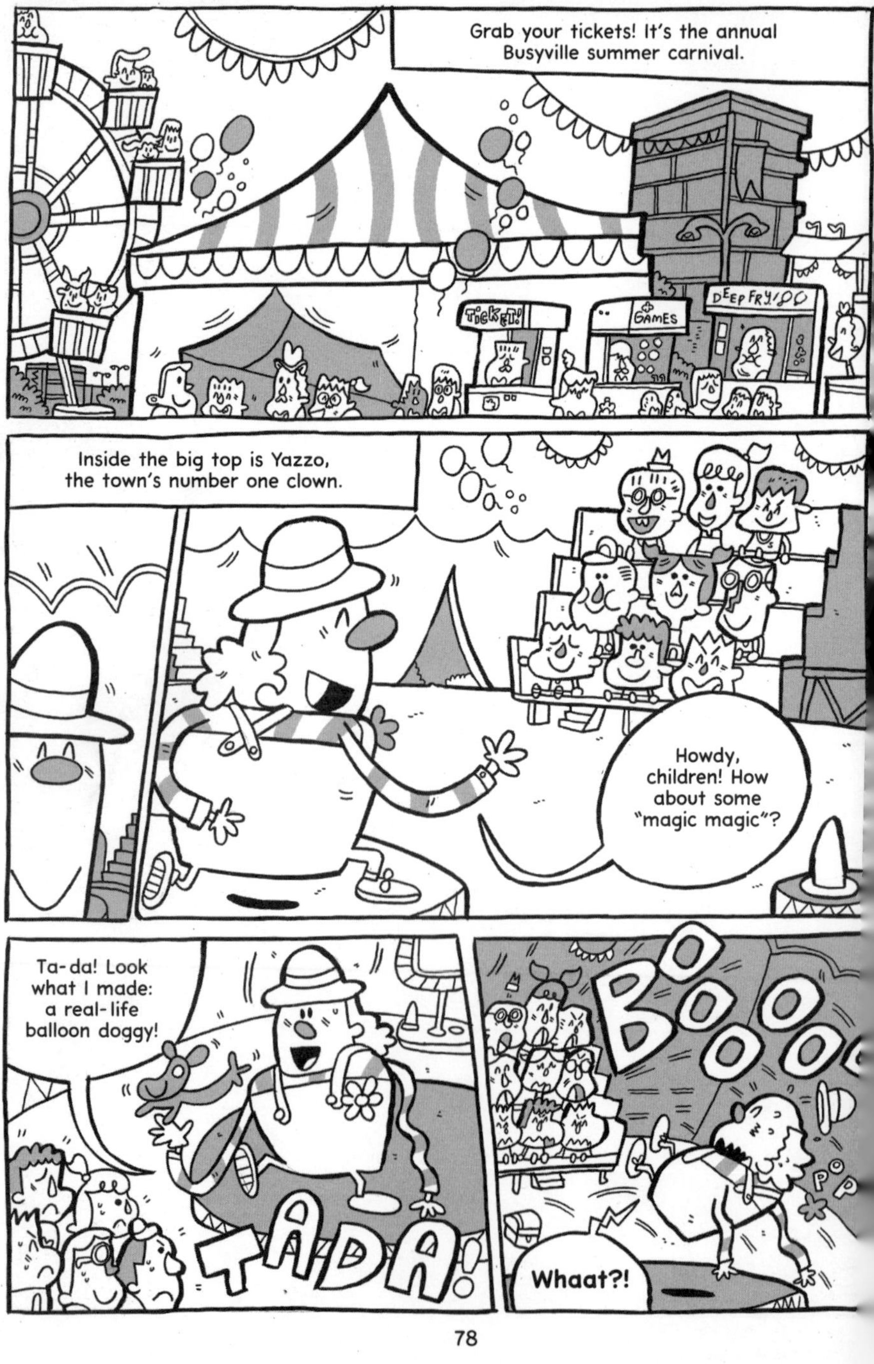
Grab your tickets! It's the annual Busyville summer carnival.
TICKET!
GAMES
DEEP FRY!
Inside the big top is Yazzo, the town's number one clown.
Howdy, children! How about some "magic magic"?
Ta-da! Look what I made: a real-life balloon doggy!
TADA!
BOOOOO
POP
Whaat?!

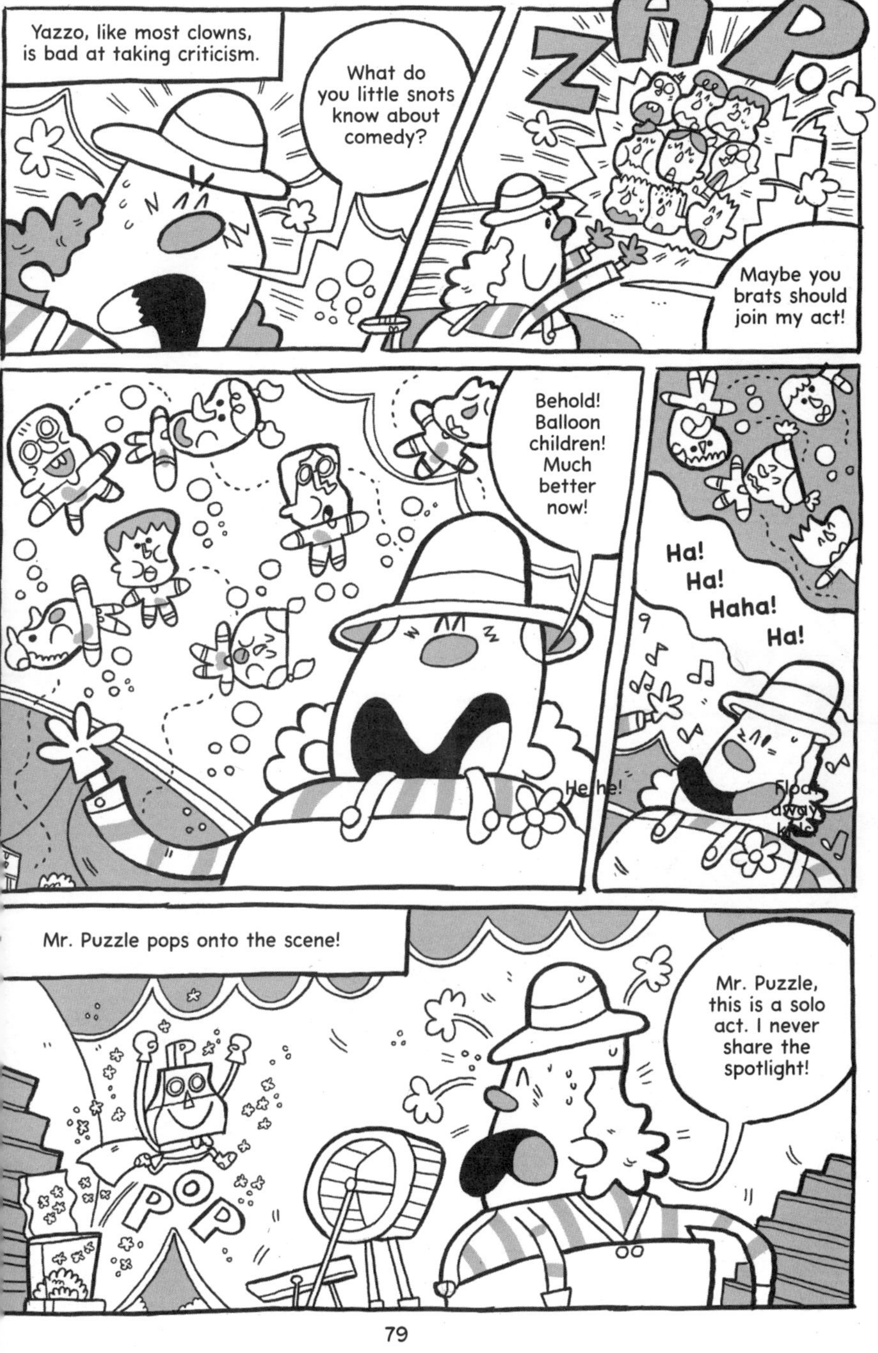
Yazzo, like most clowns, is bad at taking criticism.
What do you little snots know about comedy?
ZAP
Maybe you brats should join my act!
Behold! Balloon children! Much better now!
Ha! Ha! Haha! Ha!
He he!
Mr. Puzzle pops onto the scene!
Mr. Puzzle, this is a solo act. I never share the spotlight!
POP

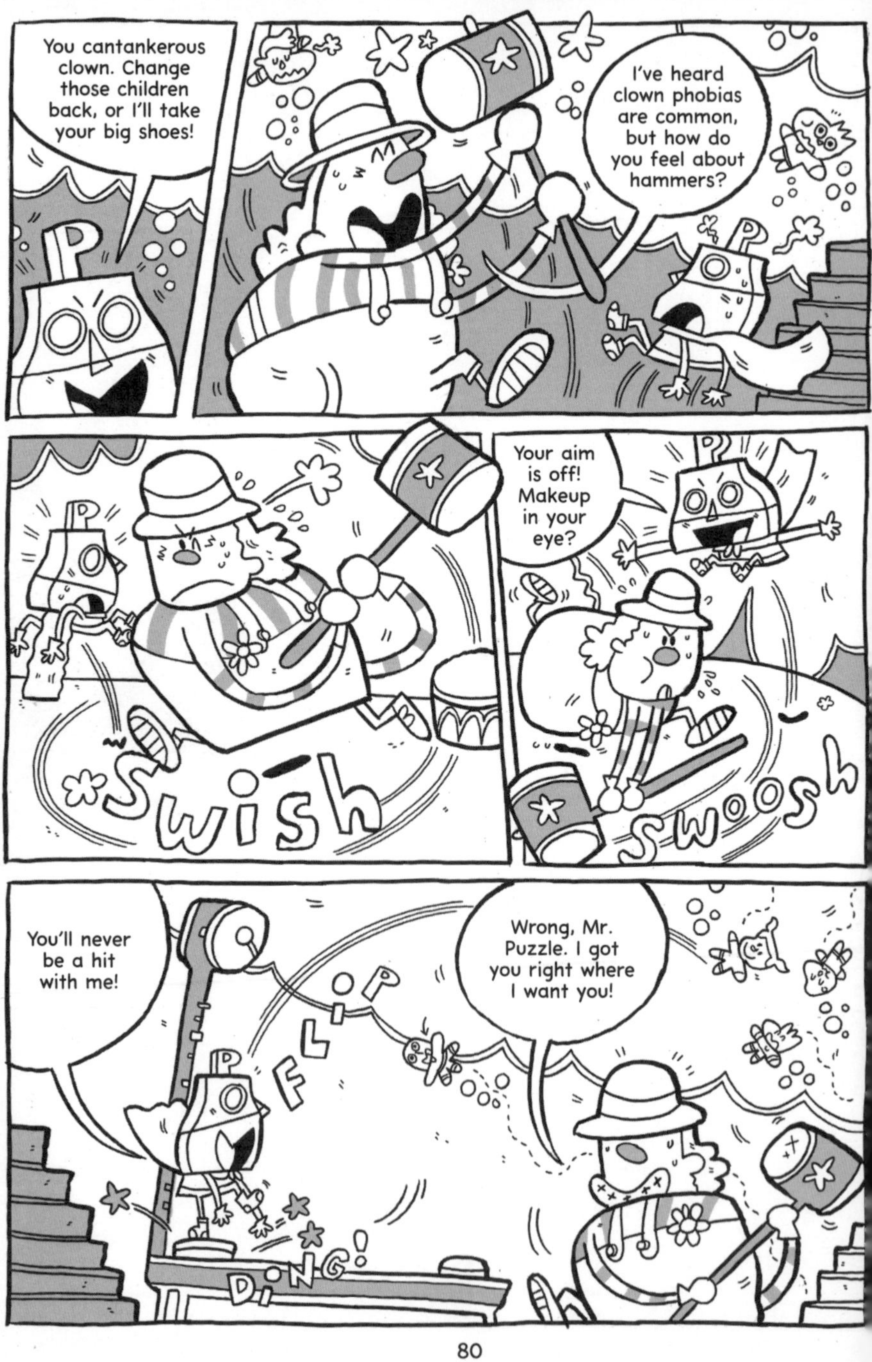
You cantankerous clown. Change those children back, or I'll take your big shoes!
I've heard clown phobias are common, but how do you feel about hammers?
SWISH
Your aim is off! Makeup in your eye?
SWOOSH
You'll never be a hit with me!
FLIP
Wrong, Mr. Puzzle. I got you right where I want you!
DING!

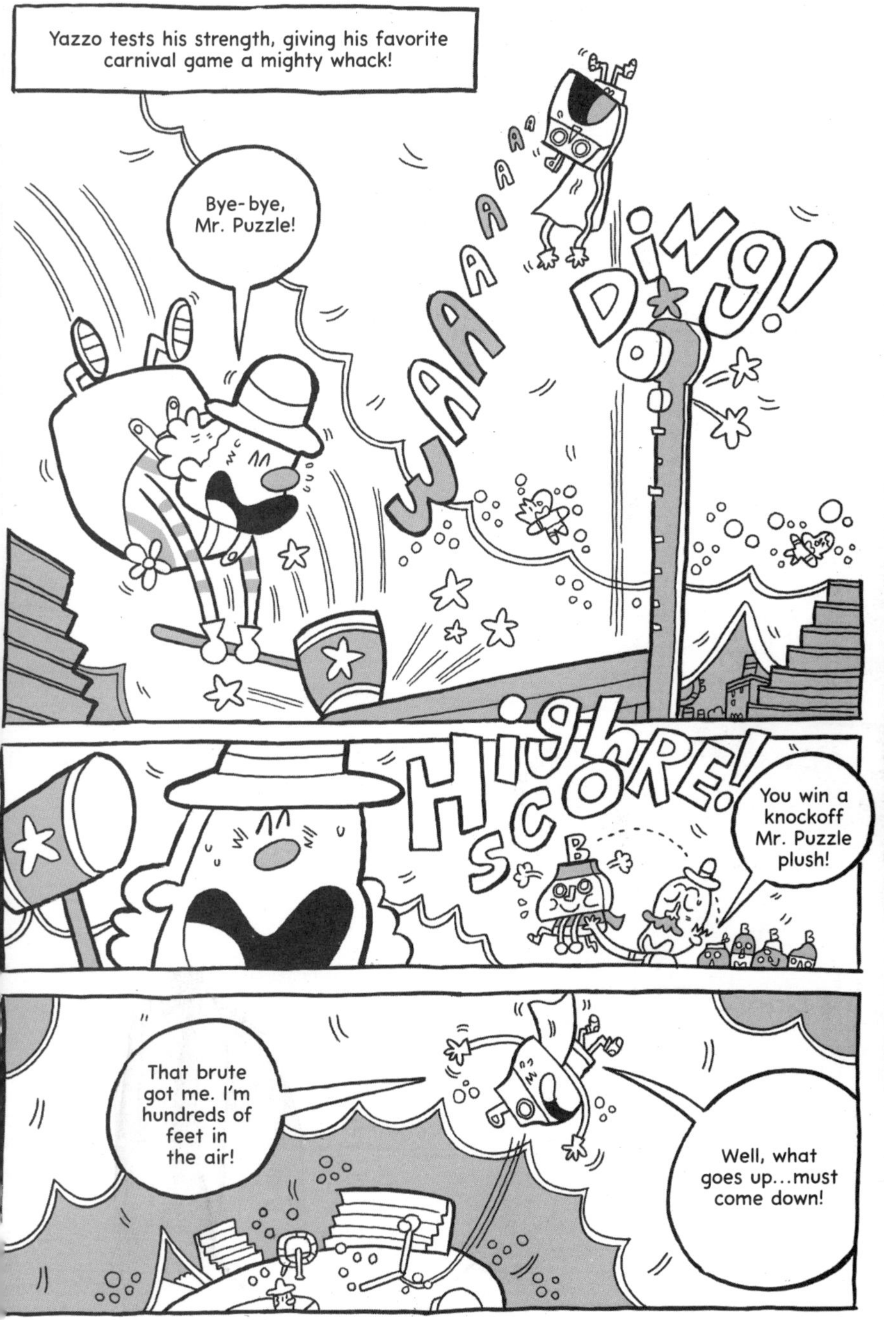
Yazzo tests his strength, giving his favorite carnival game a mighty whack!
Bye-bye, Mr. Puzzle!
WAAAAAAA
DING!
HIGH SCORE!
You win a knockoff Mr. Puzzle plush!
That brute got me. I'm hundreds of feet in the air!
Well, what goes up...must come down!

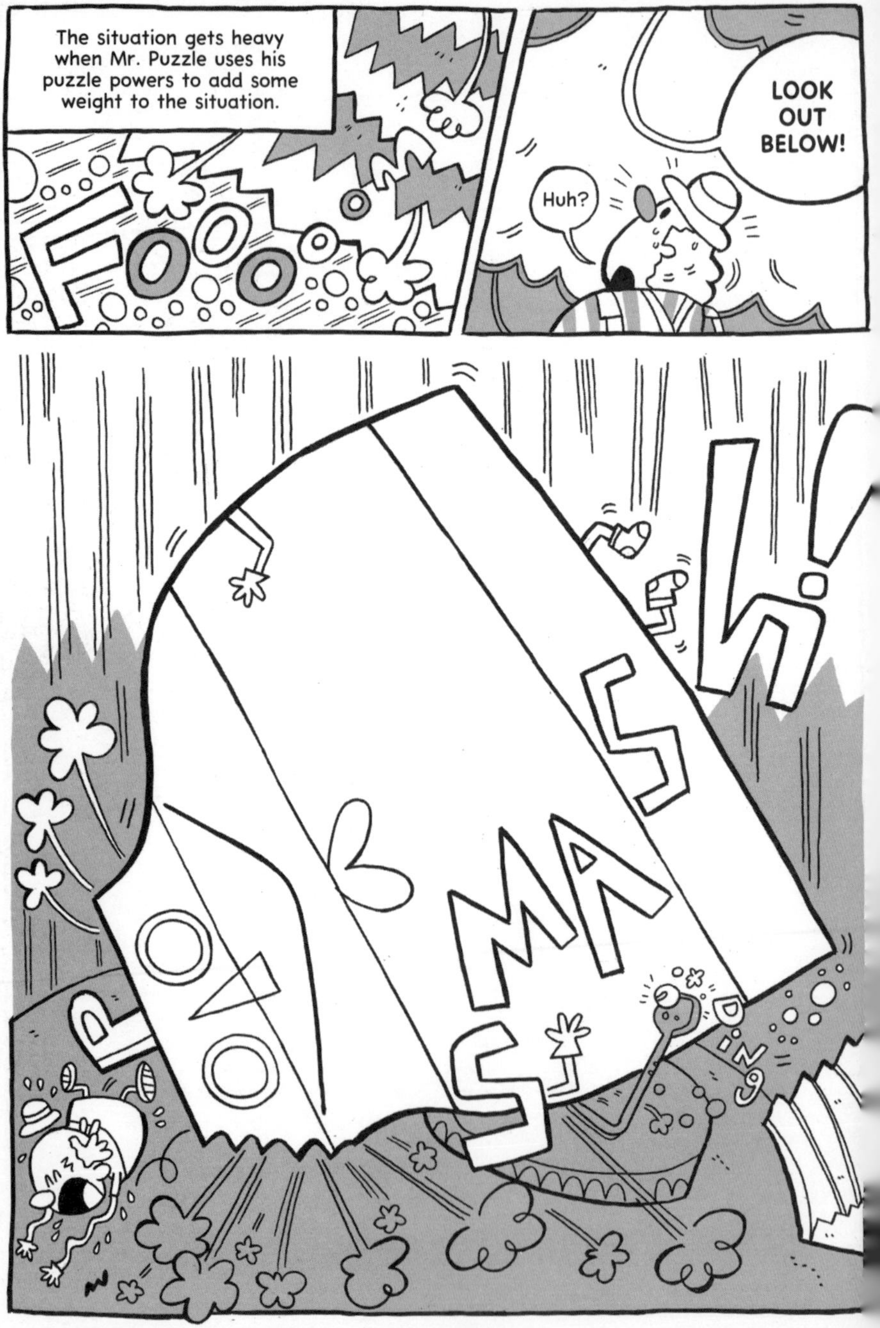
The situation gets heavy when Mr. Puzzle uses his puzzle powers to add some weight to the situation.
FOOOOM
LOOK OUT BELOW!
Huh?
SMASH!
DING

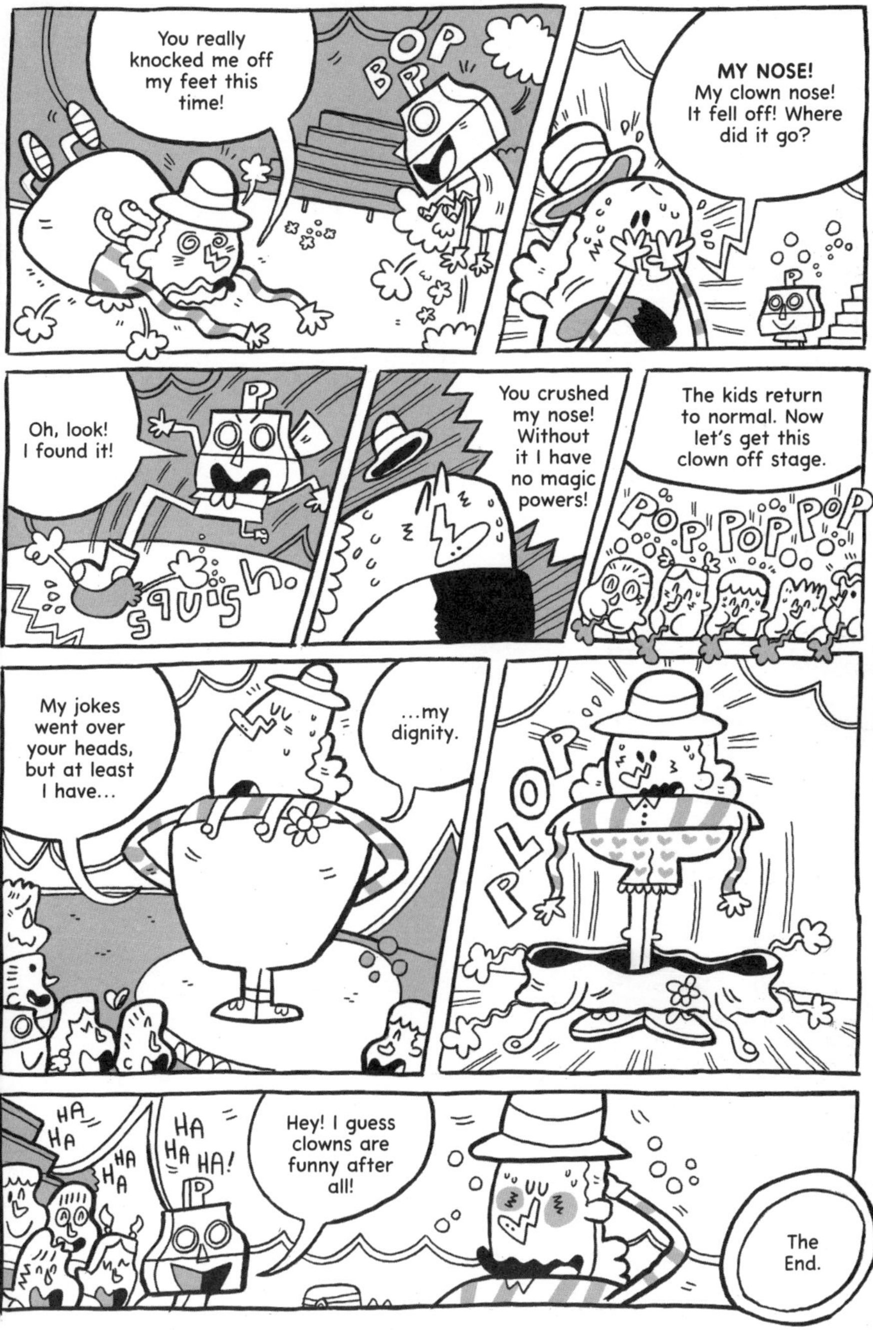
You really knocked me off my feet this time!
BOP
MY NOSE! My clown nose! It fell off! Where did it go?
Oh, look! I found it!
squish
You crushed my nose! Without it I have no magic powers!
The kids return to normal. Now let's get this clown off stage.
POP POP POP
My jokes went over your heads, but at least I have...
...my dignity.
PLOP
HA HA
HA HA
HA HA HA!
Hey! I guess clowns are funny after all!
The End.

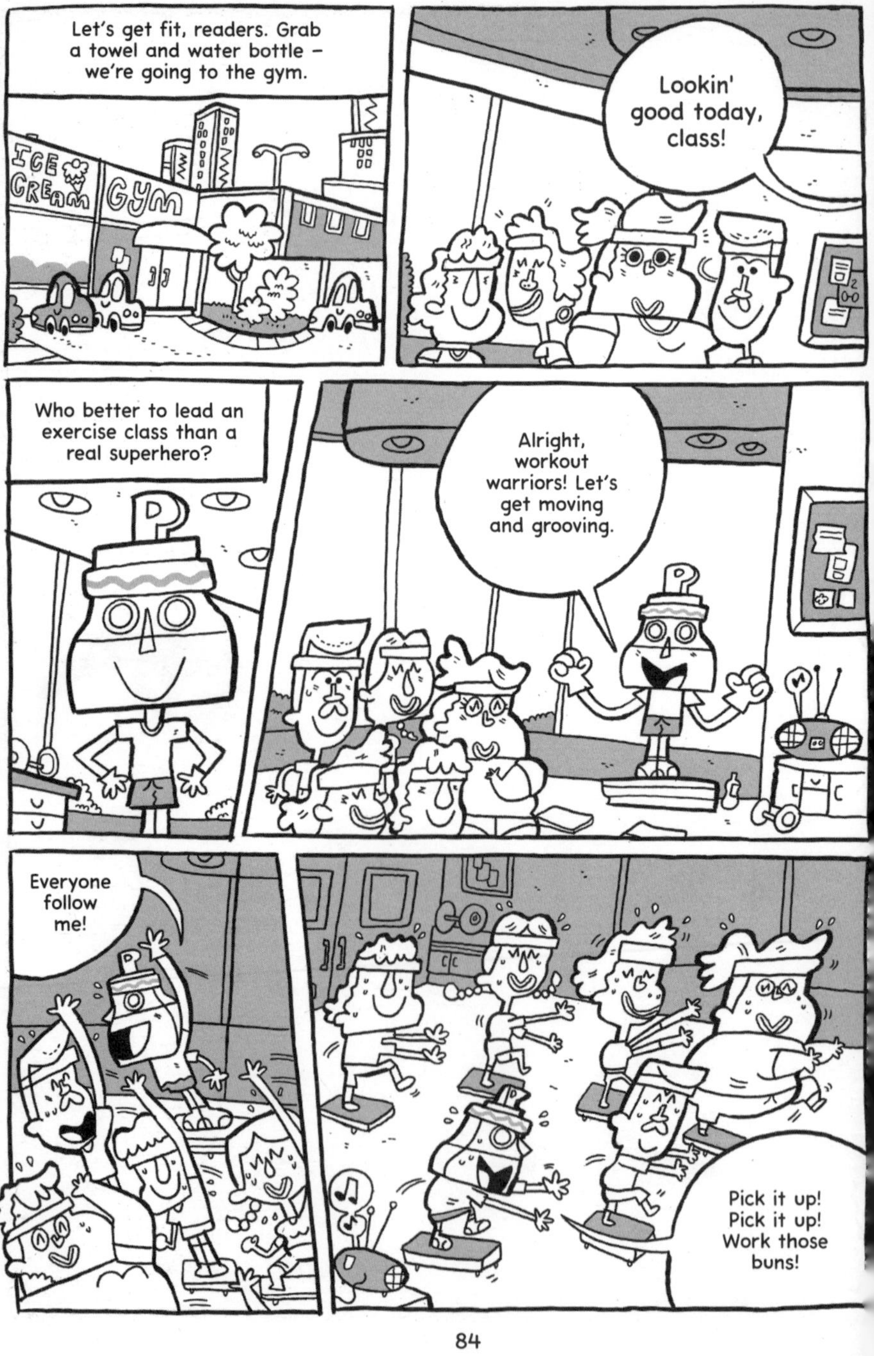
Let's get fit, readers. Grab a towel and water bottle – we're going to the gym.
ICE CREAM
GYM
Lookin' good today, class!
Who better to lead an exercise class than a real superhero?
Alright, workout warriors! Let's get moving and grooving.
Everyone follow me!
Pick it up! Pick it up! Work those buns!

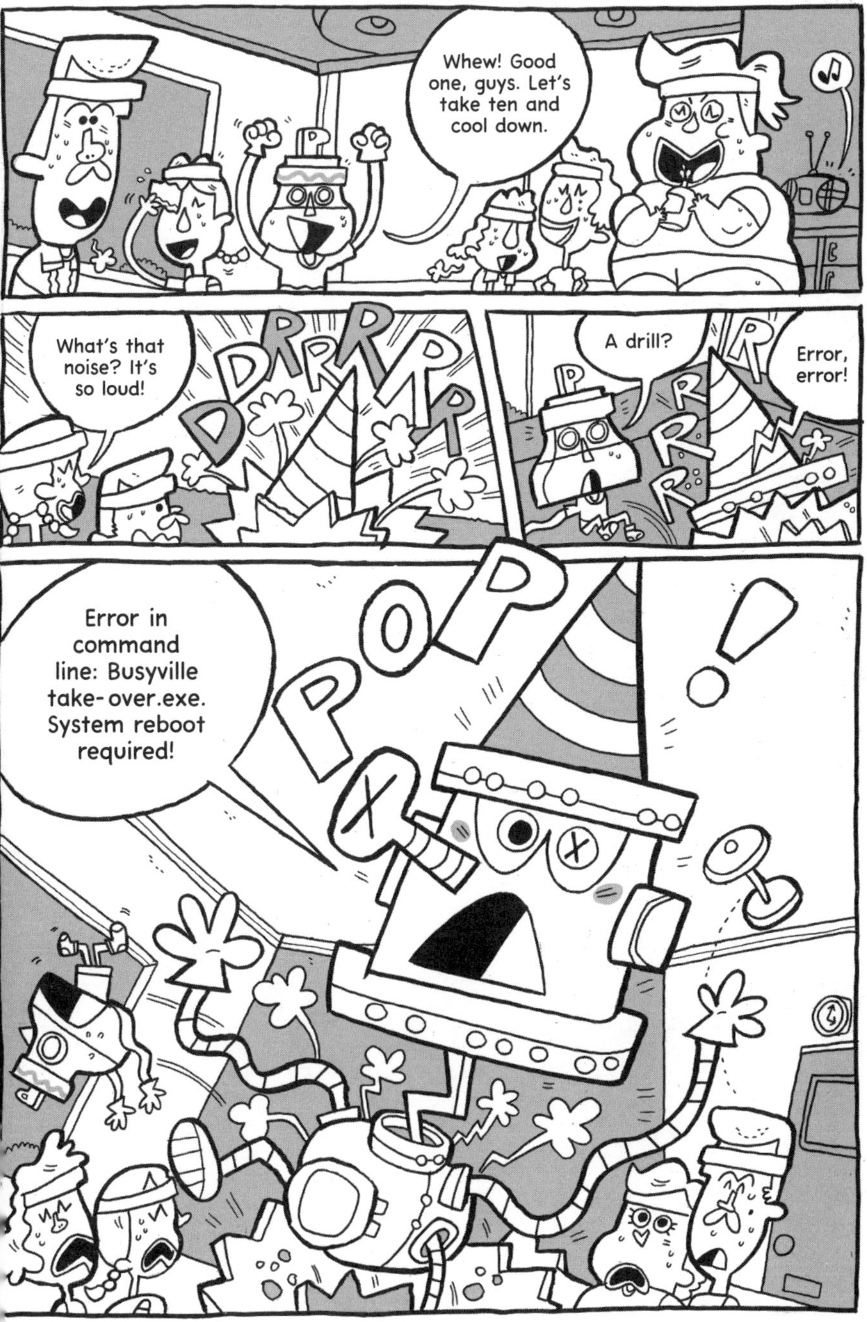
Whew! Good one, guys. Let's take ten and cool down.
What's that noise? It's so loud!
DRRRRR
A drill?
Error, error!
RRRR
Error in command line: Busyville take-over.exe. System reboot required!
POP!

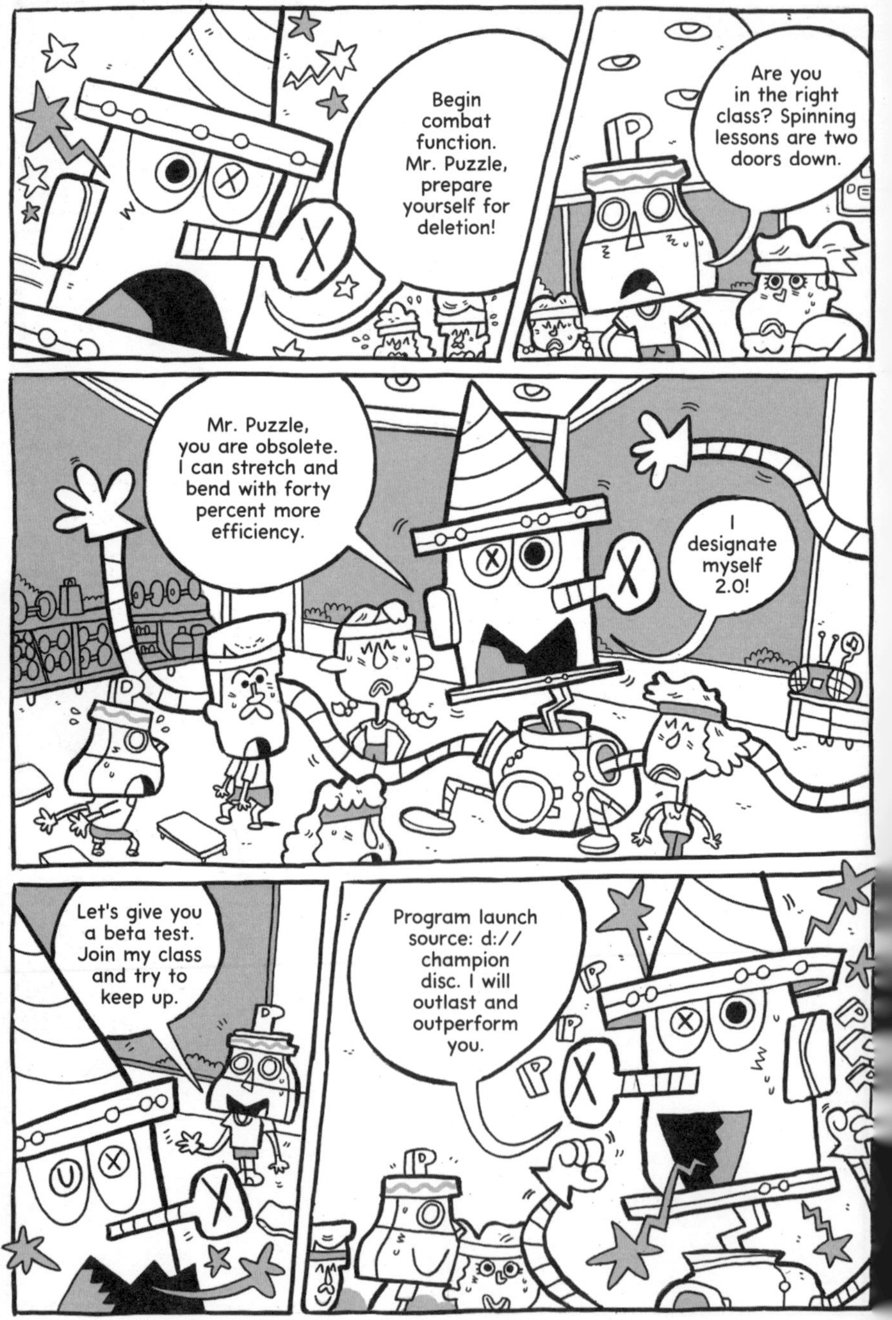

Begin combat function. Mr. Puzzle, prepare yourself for deletion!
Are you in the right class? Spinning lessons are two doors down.
Mr. Puzzle, you are obsolete. I can stretch and bend with forty percent more efficiency.
I designate myself 2.0!
Let's give you a beta test. Join my class and try to keep up.
Program launch source: d:// champion disc. I will outlast and outperform you.

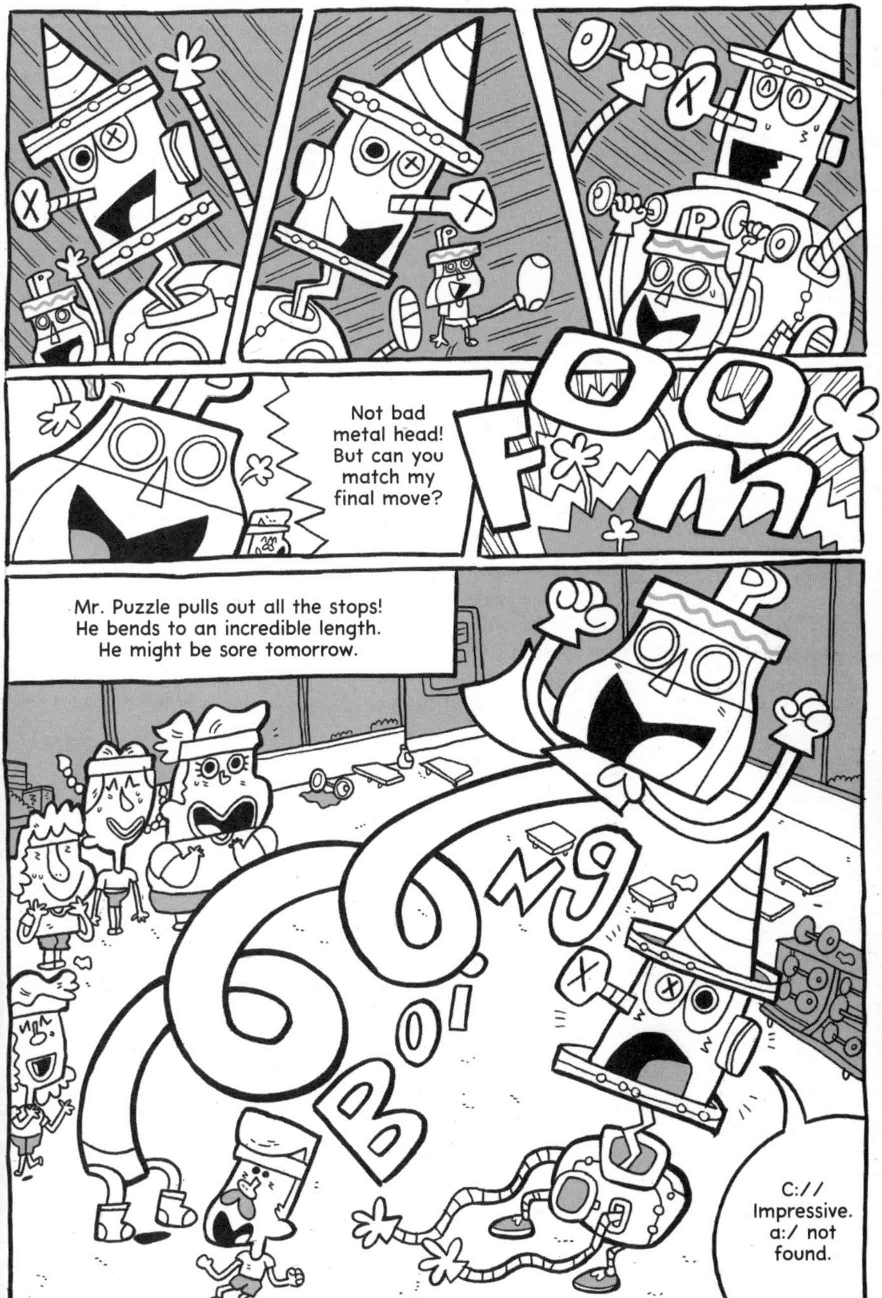
Not bad metal head! But can you match my final move?
FOOM
Mr. Puzzle pulls out all the stops! He bends to an incredible length. He might be sore tomorrow.
BOIOING
C:// Impressive. a:/ not found.

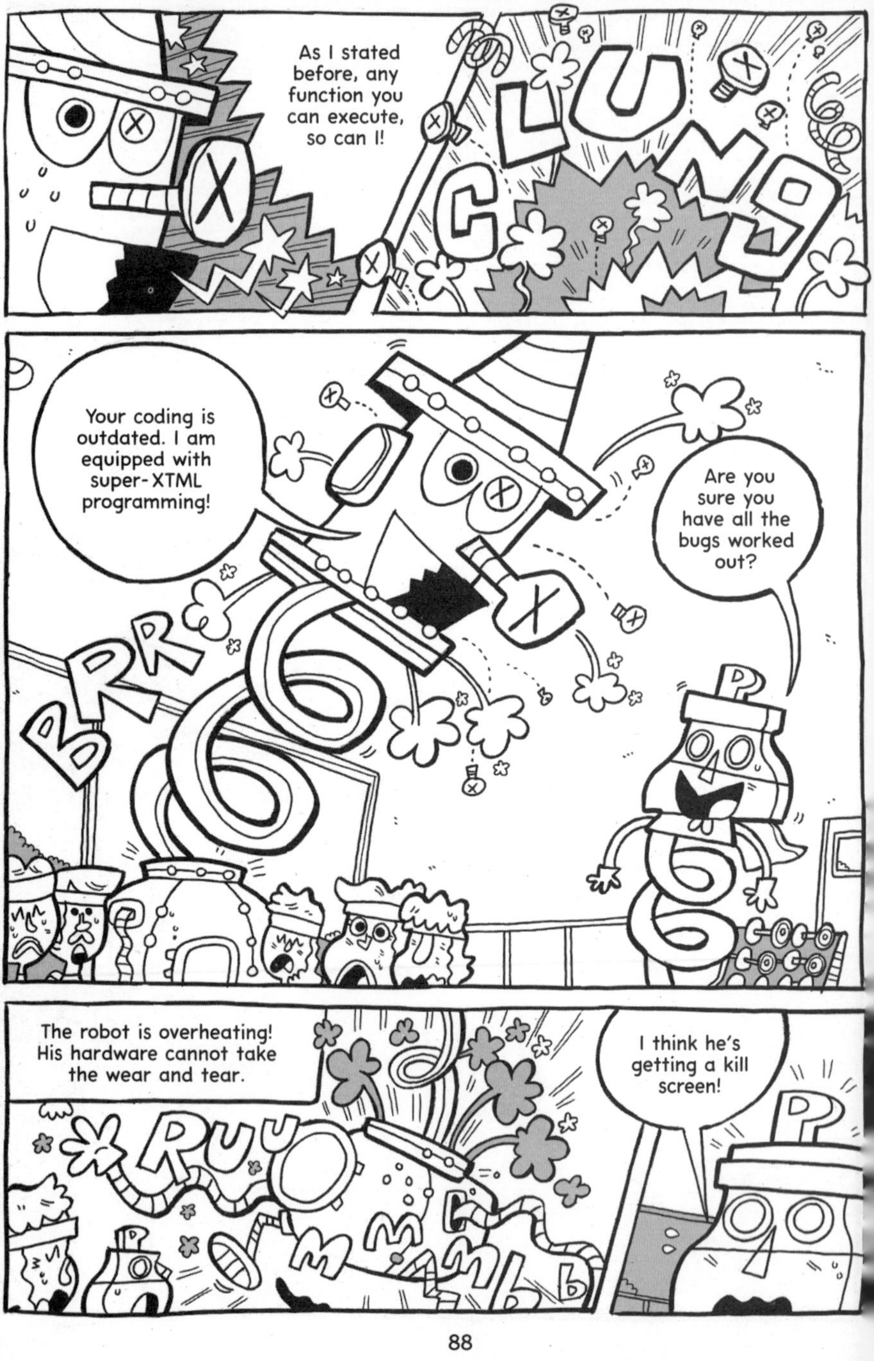

As I stated before, any function you can execute, so can I!
CLUNG
Your coding is outdated. I am equipped with super-XTML programming!
Are you sure you have all the bugs worked out?
BRR
The robot is overheating! His hardware cannot take the wear and tear.
I think he's getting a kill screen!
RUU

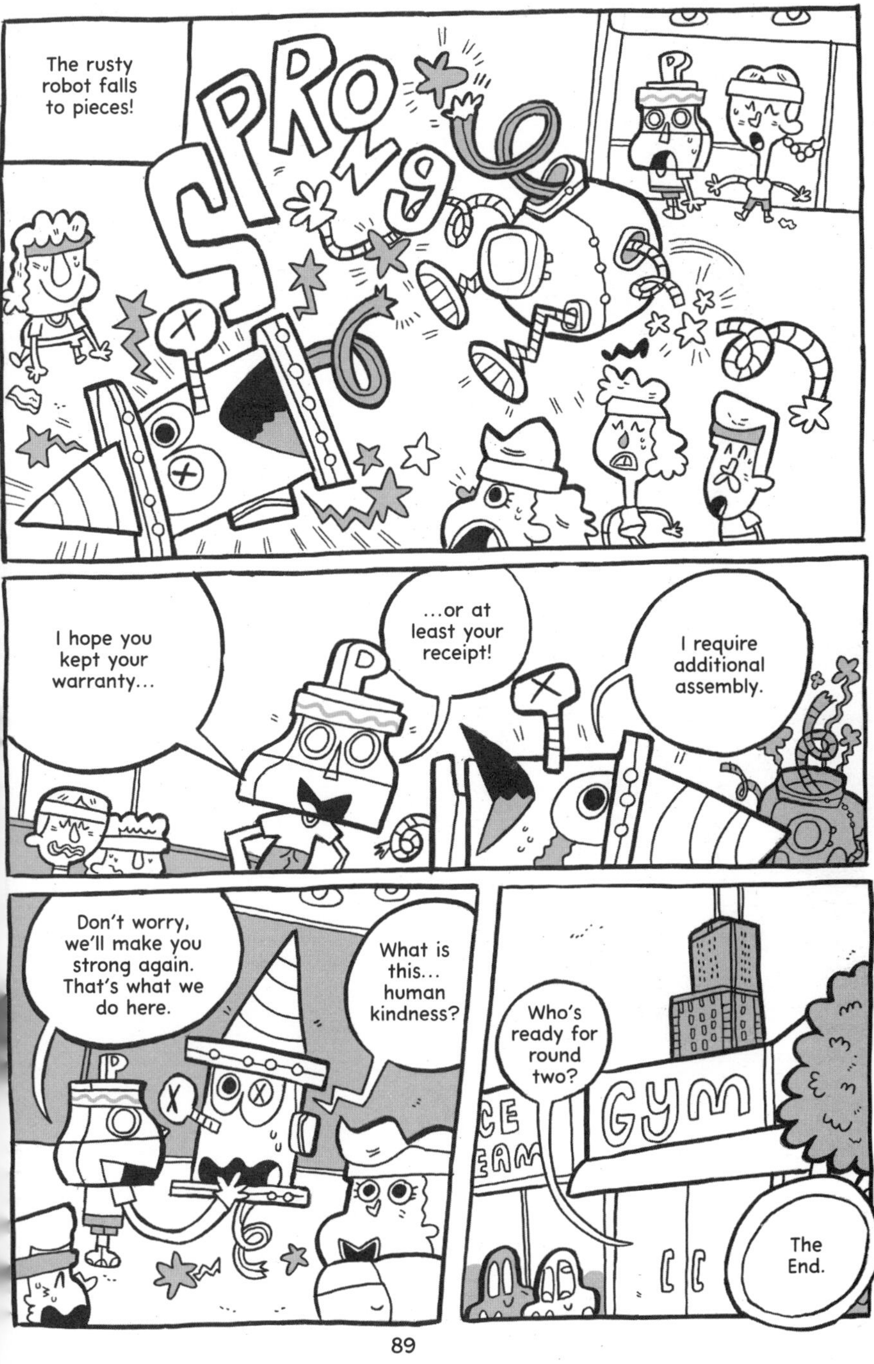

The rusty robot falls to pieces!
SPRONG
I hope you kept your warranty...
...or at least your receipt!
I require additional assembly.
Don't worry, we'll make you strong again. That's what we do here.
What is this... human kindness?
Who's ready for round two?
GYM
The End.

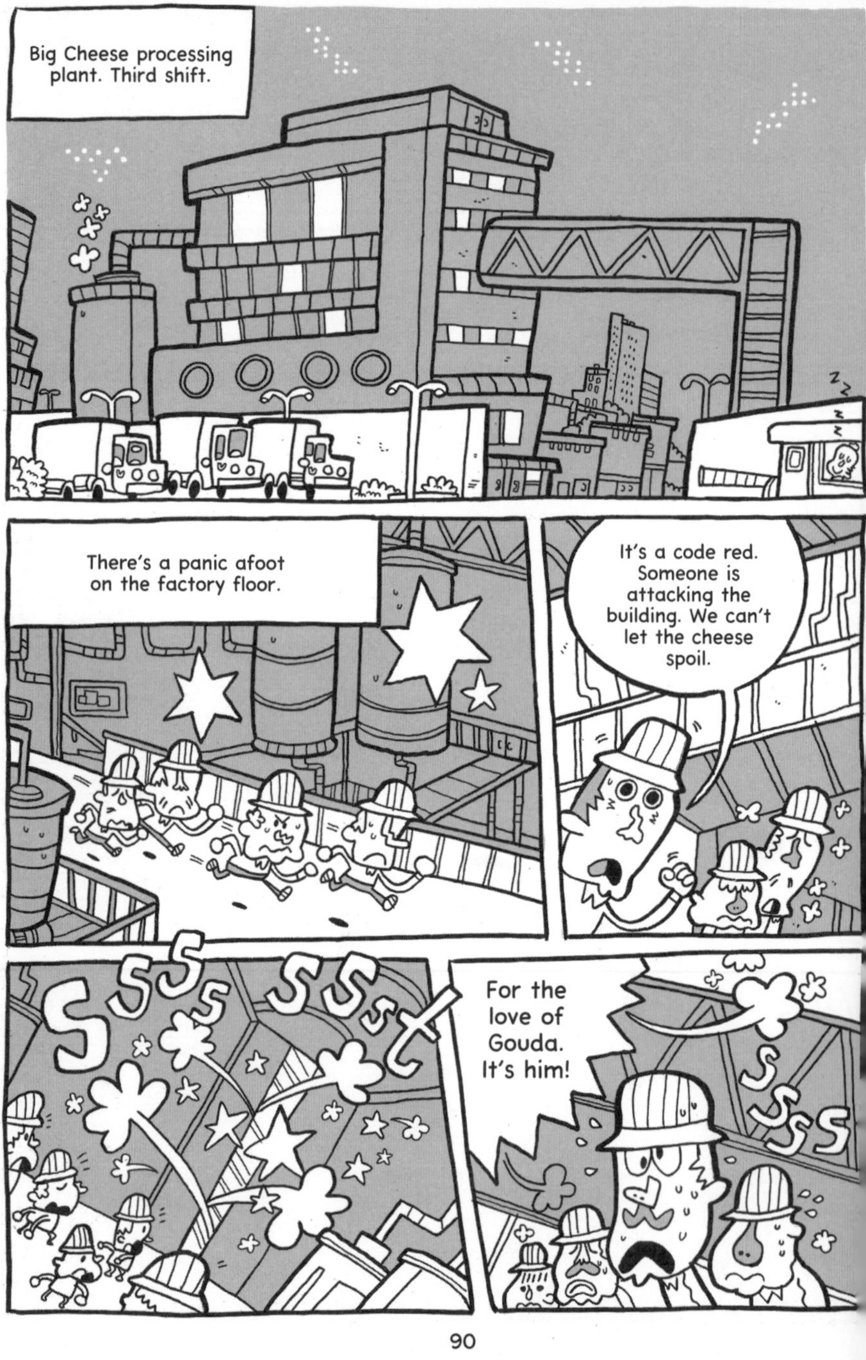
Big Cheese processing plant. Third shift.
There's a panic afoot on the factory floor.
It's a code red. Someone is attacking the building. We can't let the cheese spoil.
SSSSSSSSSt
For the love of Gouda. It's him!
SSSS

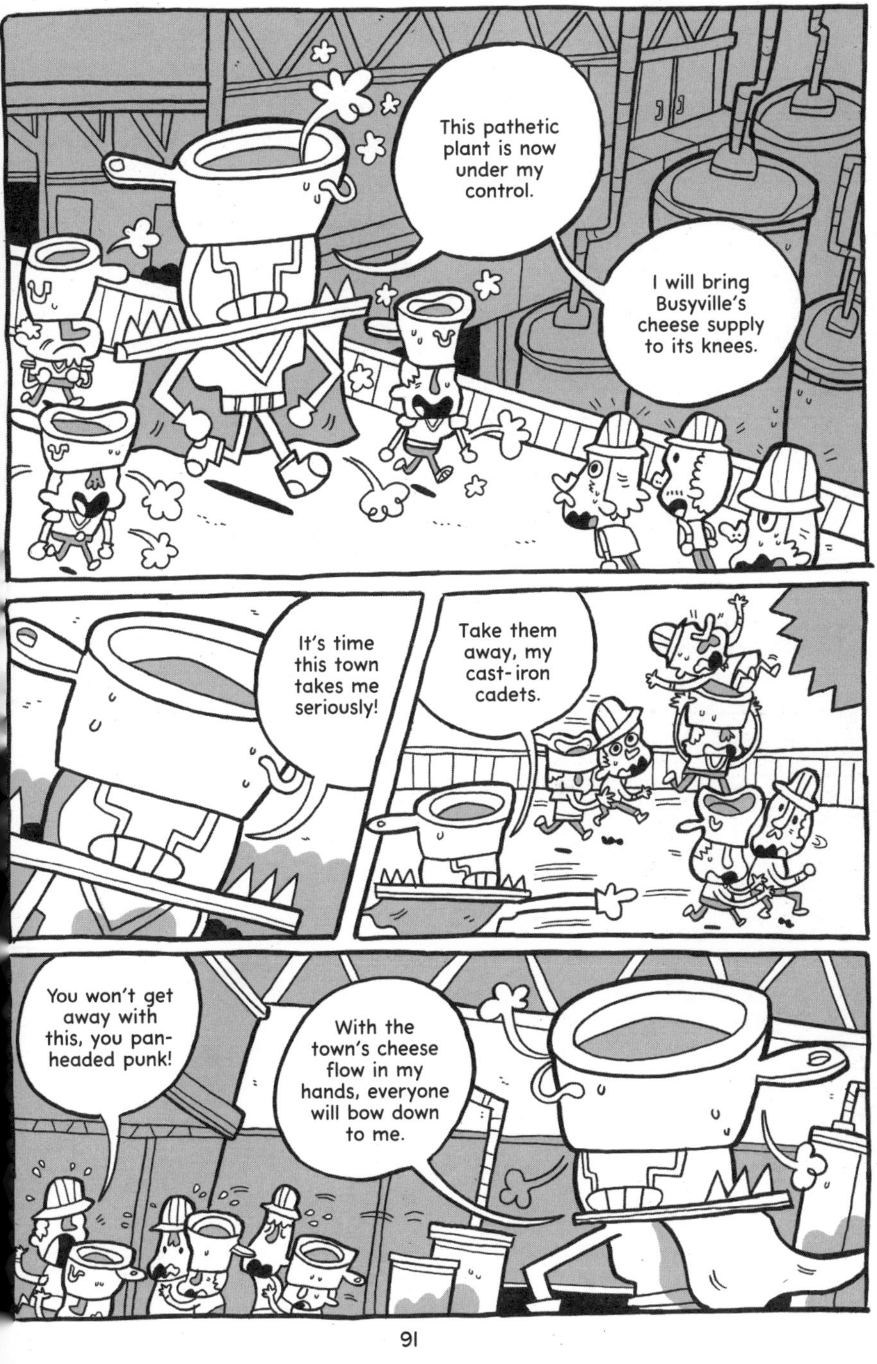
This pathetic plant is now under my control.
I will bring Busyville's cheese supply to its knees.
It's time this town takes me seriously!
Take them away, my cast-iron cadets.
You won't get away with this, you pan-headed punk!
With the town's cheese flow in my hands, everyone will bow down to me.

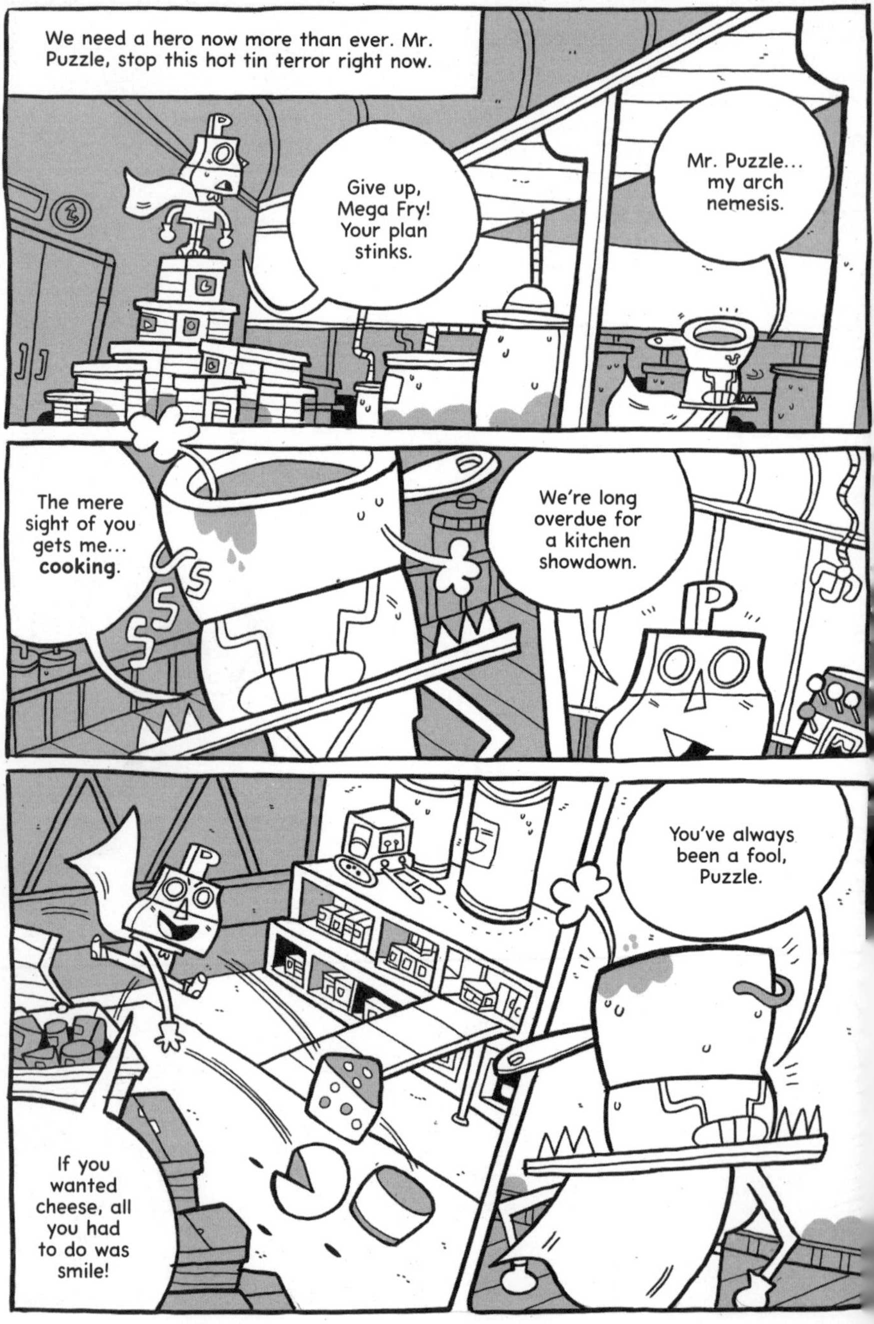
We need a hero now more than ever. Mr. Puzzle, stop this hot tin terror right now.
Give up, Mega Fry! Your plan stinks.
Mr. Puzzle... my arch nemesis.
The mere sight of you gets me... **cooking**.
We're long overdue for a kitchen showdown.
If you wanted cheese, all you had to do was smile!
You've always been a fool, Puzzle.

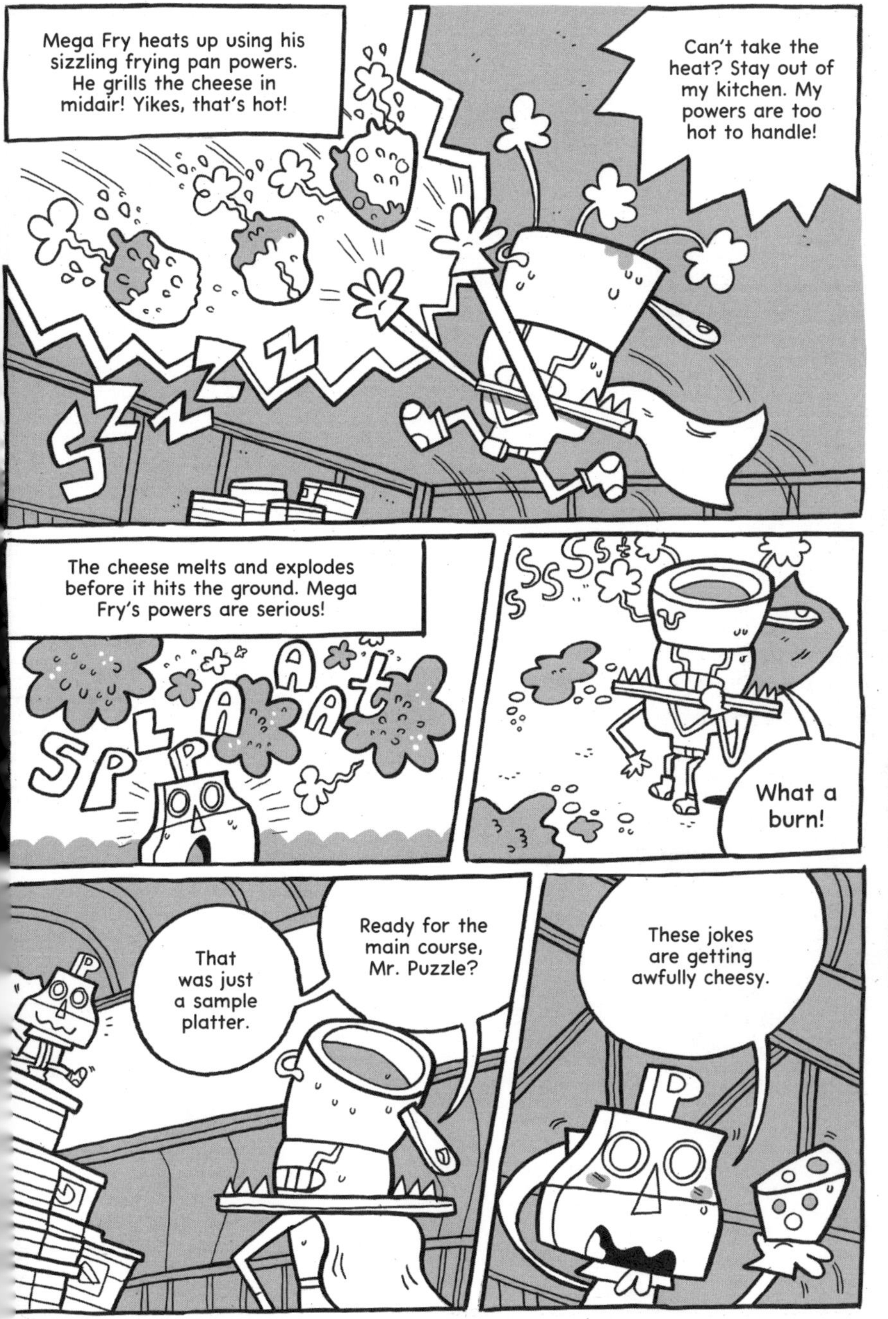

Mega Fry heats up using his sizzling frying pan powers. He grills the cheese in midair! Yikes, that's hot!
Can't take the heat? Stay out of my kitchen. My powers are too hot to handle!
SSZZZZ
The cheese melts and explodes before it hits the ground. Mega Fry's powers are serious!
SPLPAAAt
What a burn!
That was just a sample platter.
Ready for the main course, Mr. Puzzle?
These jokes are getting awfully cheesy.

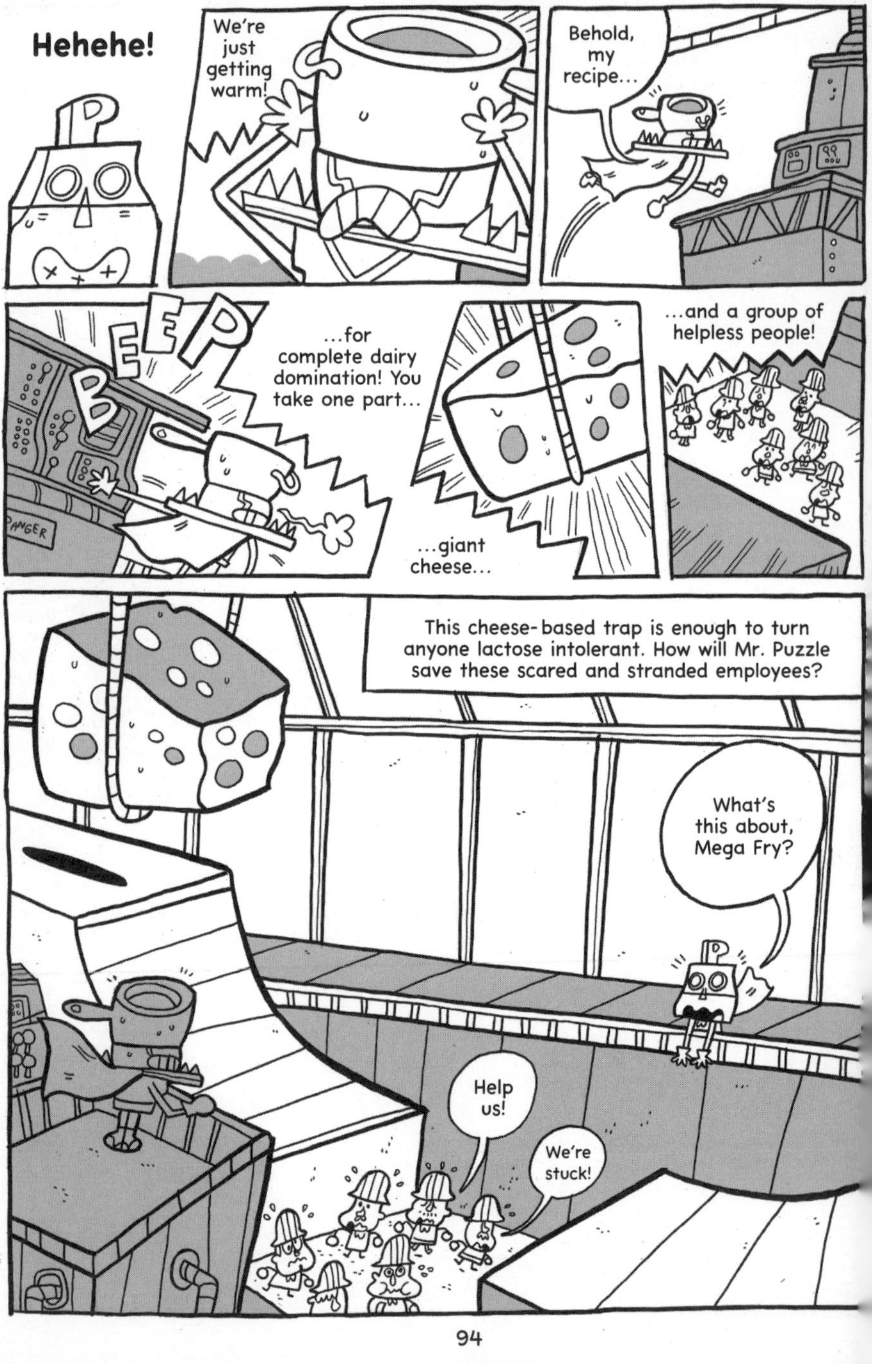
Hehehe!
We're just getting warm!
Behold, my recipe...
BEEP
...for complete dairy domination! You take one part...
DANGER
...giant cheese...
...and a group of helpless people!
This cheese-based trap is enough to turn anyone lactose intolerant. How will Mr. Puzzle save these scared and stranded employees?
What's this about, Mega Fry?
Help us!
We're stuck!

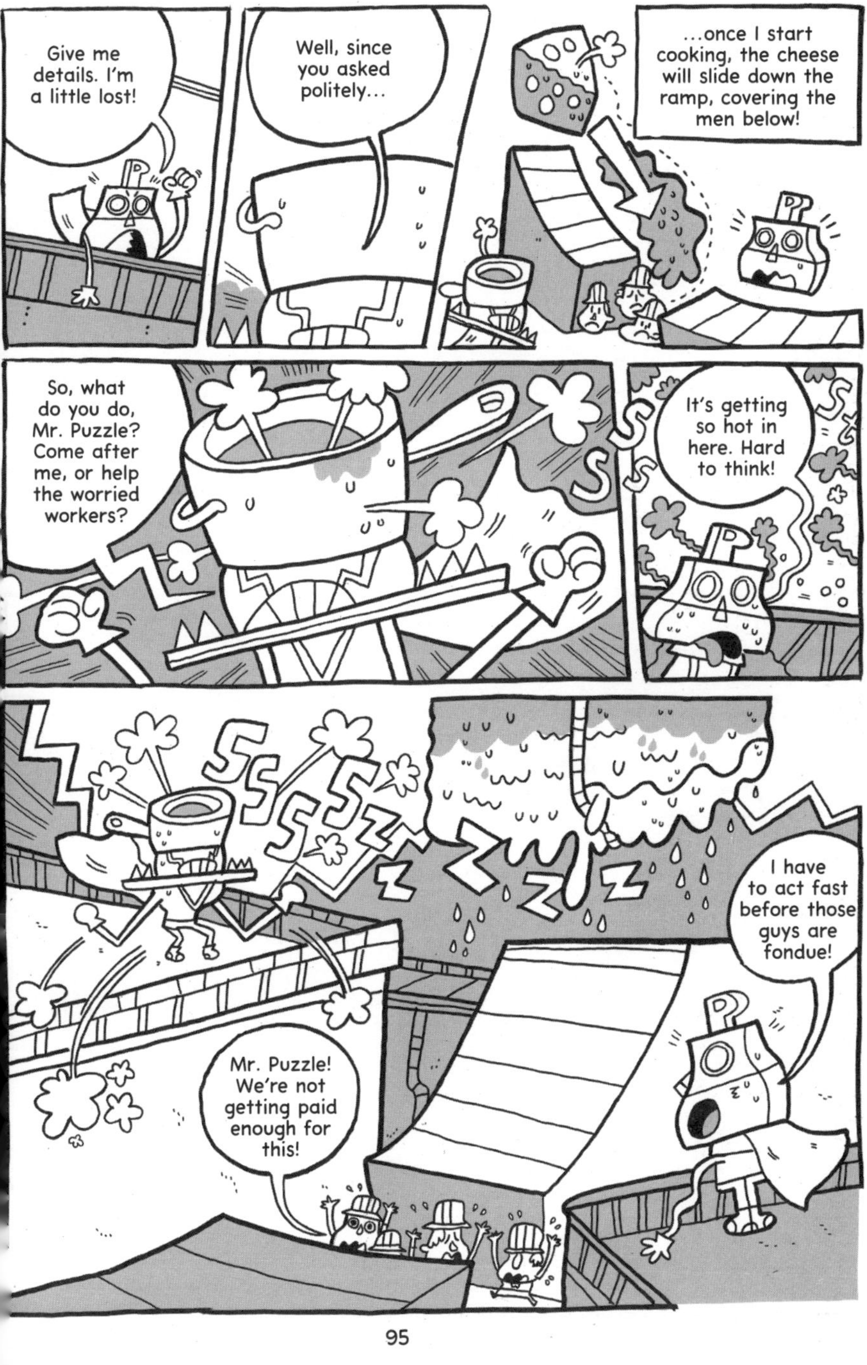
Give me details. I'm a little lost!
Well, since you asked politely...
...once I start cooking, the cheese will slide down the ramp, covering the men below!
So, what do you do, Mr. Puzzle? Come after me, or help the worried workers?
SSS
It's getting so hot in here. Hard to think!
SSSSSZZZZZZ
I have to act fast before those guys are fondue!
Mr. Puzzle! We're not getting paid enough for this!

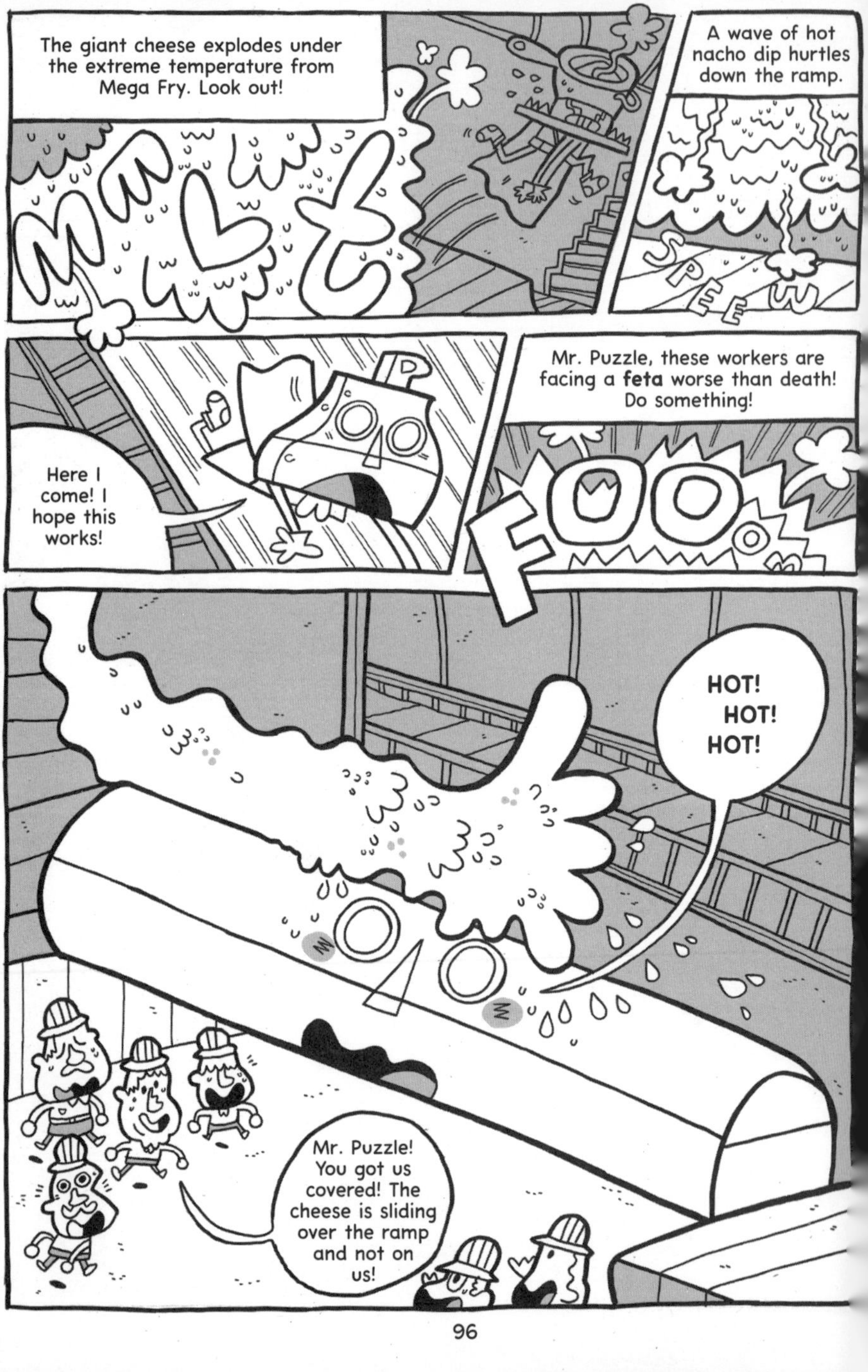
The giant cheese explodes under the extreme temperature from Mega Fry. Look out!
MELT
A wave of hot nacho dip hurtles down the ramp.
SPEEW
Here I come! I hope this works!
Mr. Puzzle, these workers are facing a **feta** worse than death! Do something!
FOOOOM
HOT! HOT! HOT!
Mr. Puzzle! You got us covered! The cheese is sliding over the ramp and not on us!

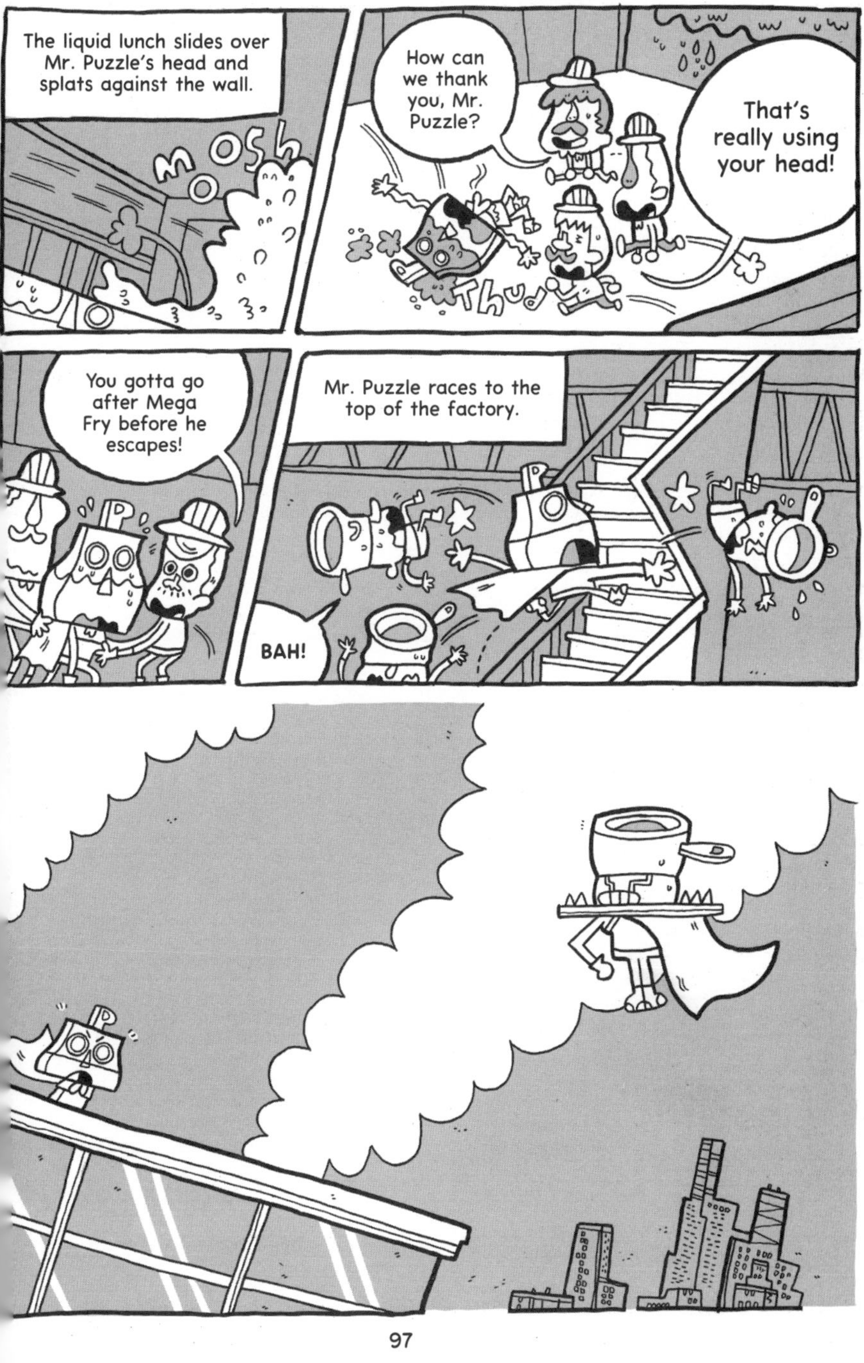

The liquid lunch slides over Mr. Puzzle's head and splats against the wall.
mOOSh
How can we thank you, Mr. Puzzle?
That's really using your head!
Thud
You gotta go after Mega Fry before he escapes!
Mr. Puzzle races to the top of the factory.
BAH!

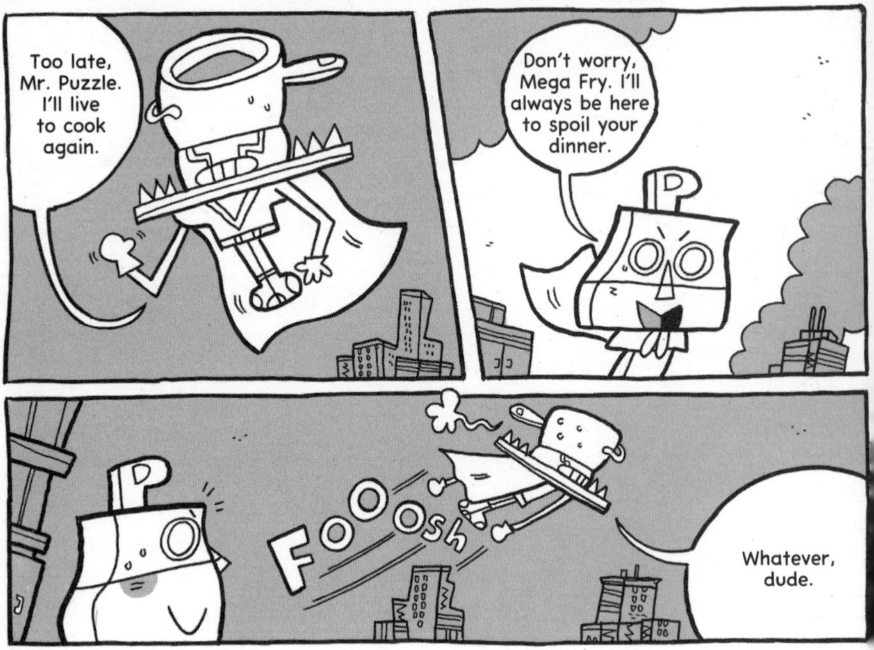
Too late, Mr. Puzzle. I'll live to cook again.
Don't worry, Mega Fry. I'll always be here to spoil your dinner.
FoOOsh
Whatever, dude.

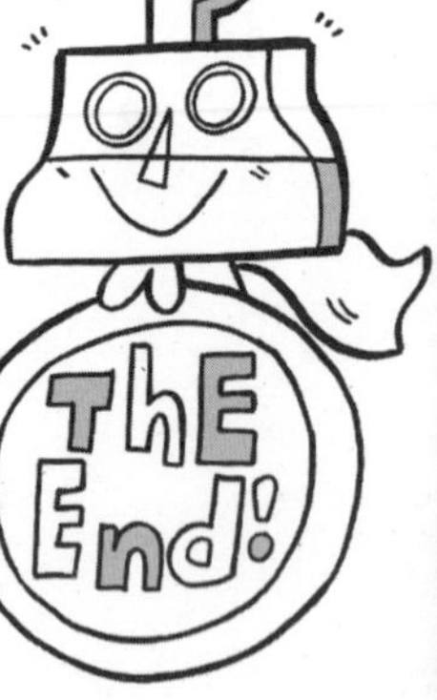
ThE End!

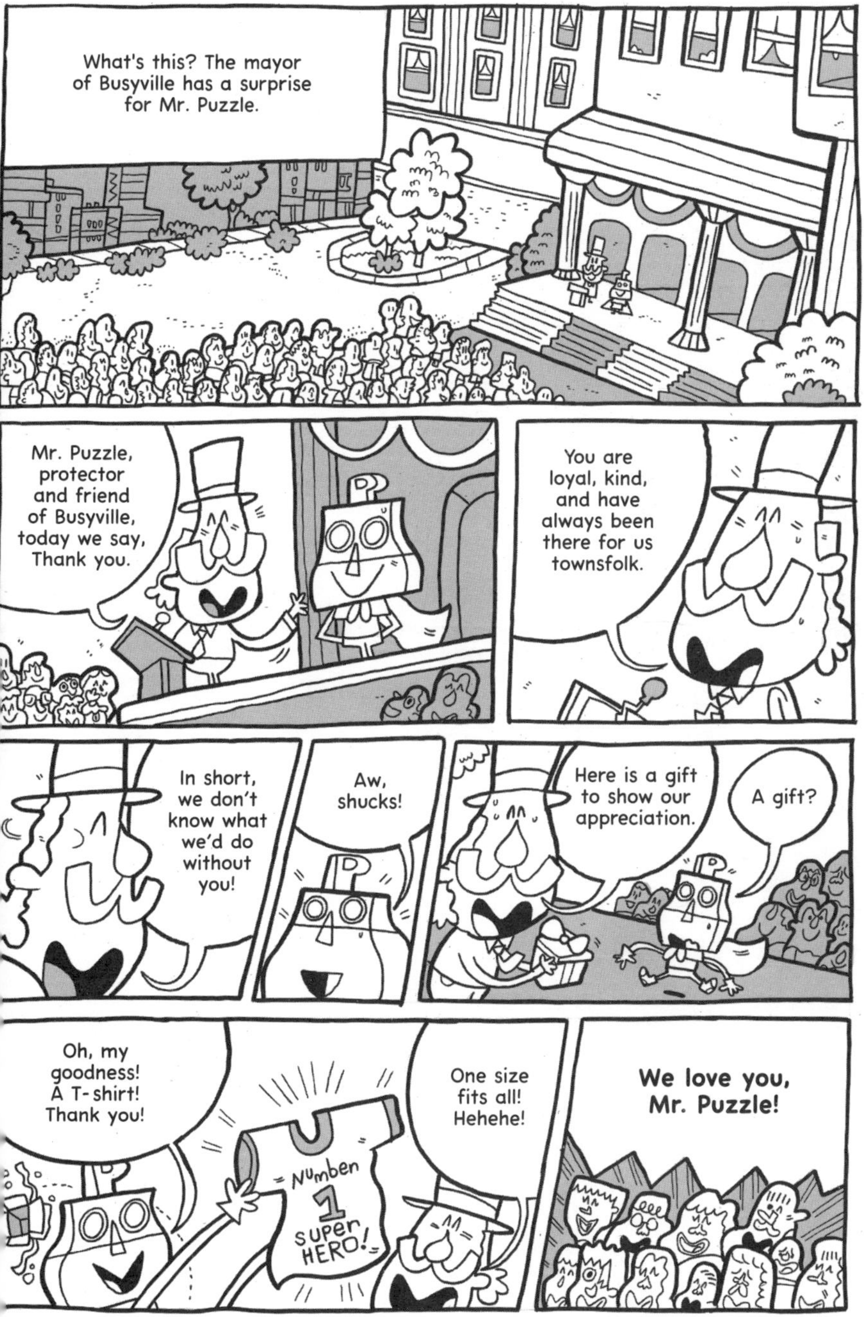
What's this? The mayor of Busyville has a surprise for Mr. Puzzle.
Mr. Puzzle, protector and friend of Busyville, today we say, Thank you.
You are loyal, kind, and have always been there for us townsfolk.
In short, we don't know what we'd do without you!
Aw, shucks!
Here is a gift to show our appreciation.
A gift?
Oh, my goodness! A T-shirt! Thank you!
Number 1 Super HERO!
One size fits all! Hehehe!
We love you, Mr. Puzzle!

MR. PUZZLE

Piece by Piece

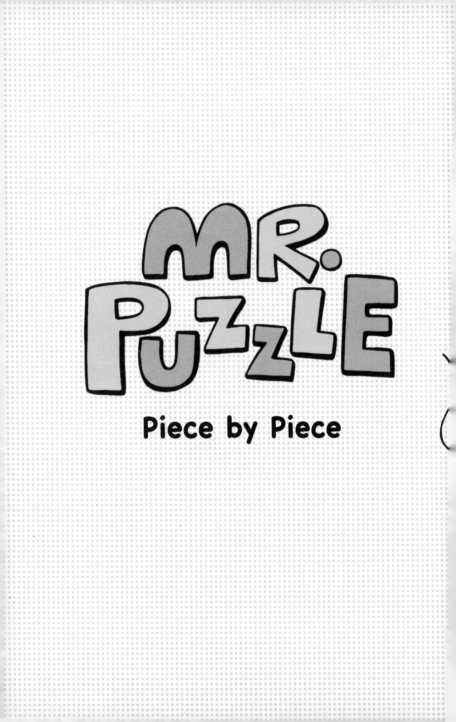

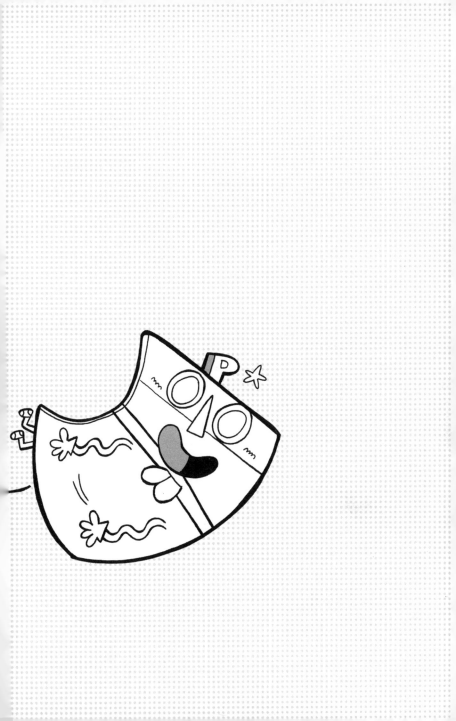

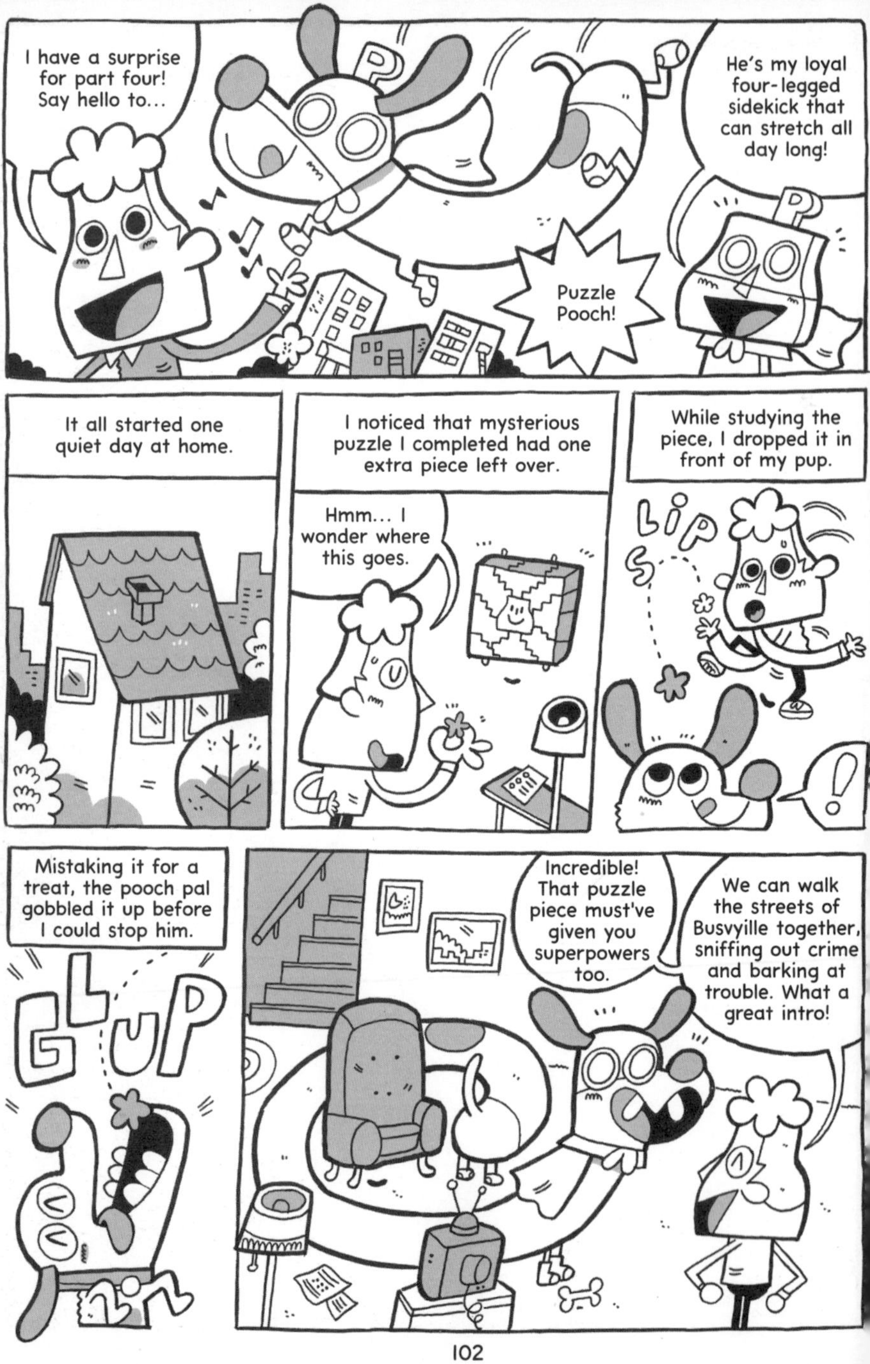

I have a surprise for part four! Say hello to...
Puzzle Pooch!
He's my loyal four-legged sidekick that can stretch all day long!
It all started one quiet day at home.
I noticed that mysterious puzzle I completed had one extra piece left over.
Hmm... I wonder where this goes.
While studying the piece, I dropped it in front of my pup.
SLIP
!
Mistaking it for a treat, the pooch pal gobbled it up before I could stop him.
GLUP
Incredible! That puzzle piece must've given you superpowers too.
We can walk the streets of Busvyille together, sniffing out crime and barking at trouble. What a great intro!

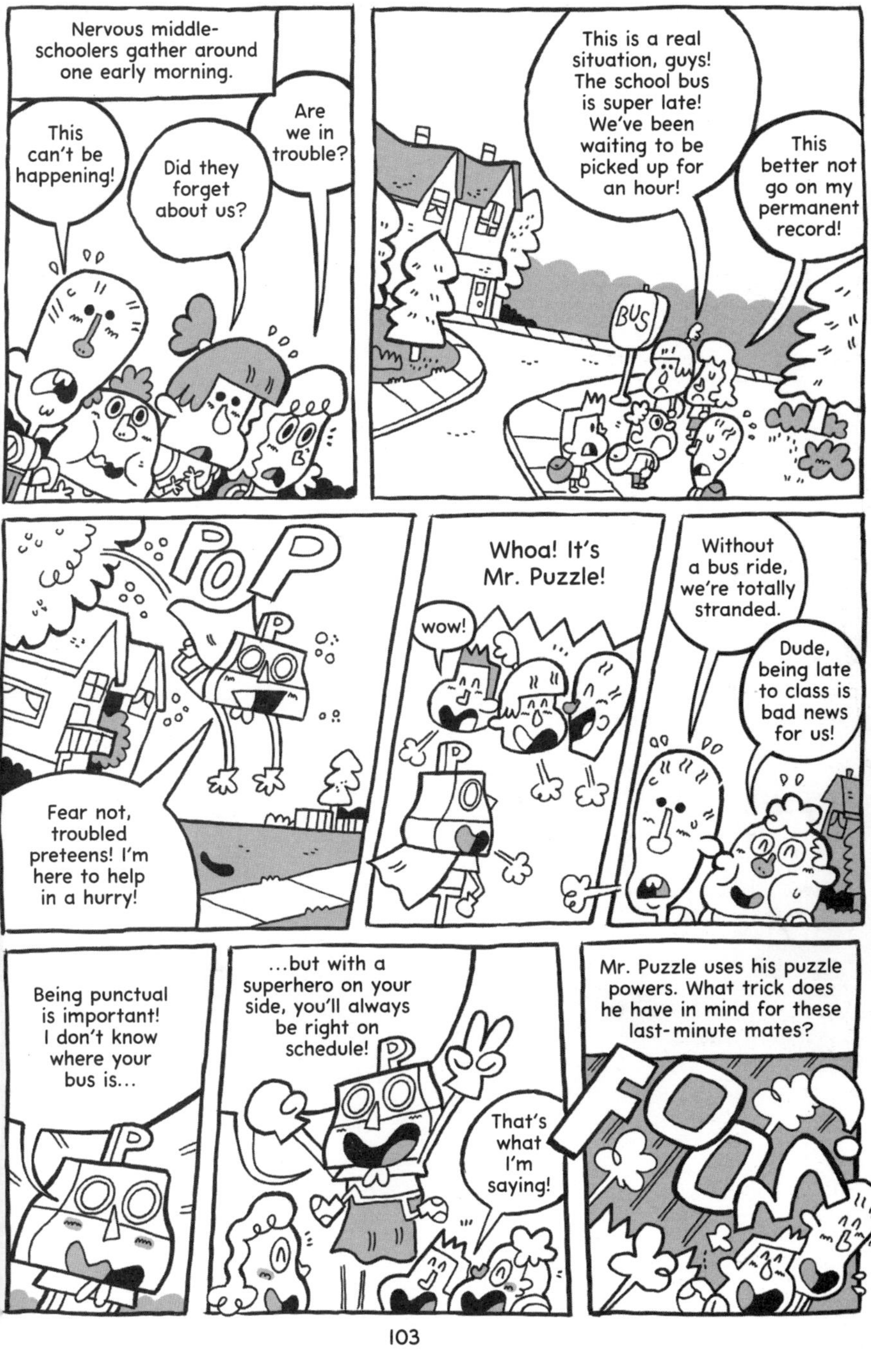
Nervous middle-schoolers gather around one early morning.
This can't be happening!
Did they forget about us?
Are we in trouble?
This is a real situation, guys! The school bus is super late! We've been waiting to be picked up for an hour!
This better not go on my permanent record!
BUS
POP
Fear not, troubled preteens! I'm here to help in a hurry!
Whoa! It's Mr. Puzzle!
WOW!
Without a bus ride, we're totally stranded.
Dude, being late to class is bad news for us!
Being punctual is important! I don't know where your bus is...
...but with a superhero on your side, you'll always be right on schedule!
That's what I'm saying!
Mr. Puzzle uses his puzzle powers. What trick does he have in mind for these last-minute mates?
FOOM!

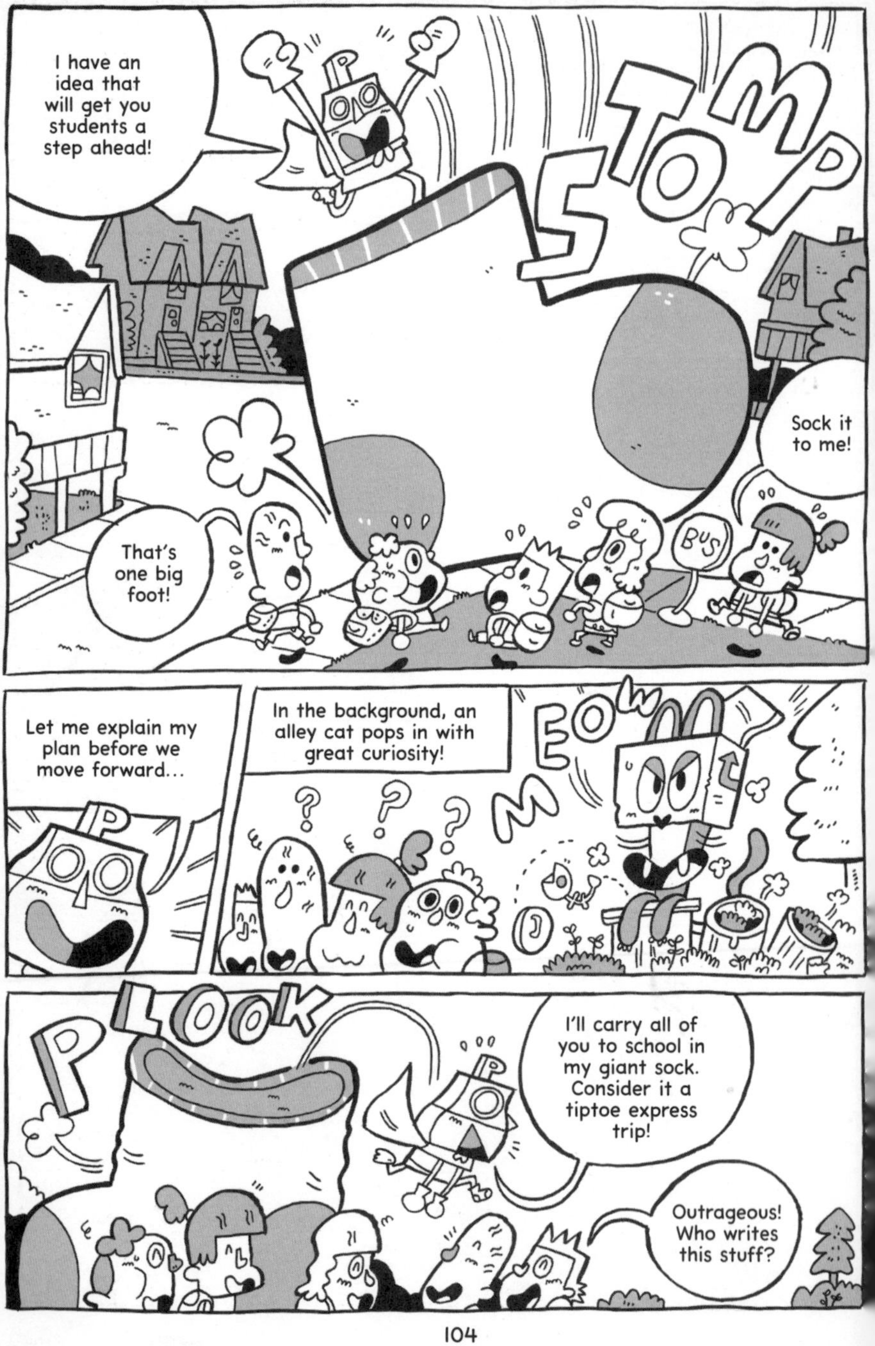
I have an idea that will get you students a step ahead!
STOMP
That's one big foot!
Sock it to me!
Let me explain my plan before we move forward...
In the background, an alley cat pops in with great curiosity!
MEOW
PLOOK
I'll carry all of you to school in my giant sock. Consider it a tiptoe express trip!
Outrageous! Who writes this stuff?

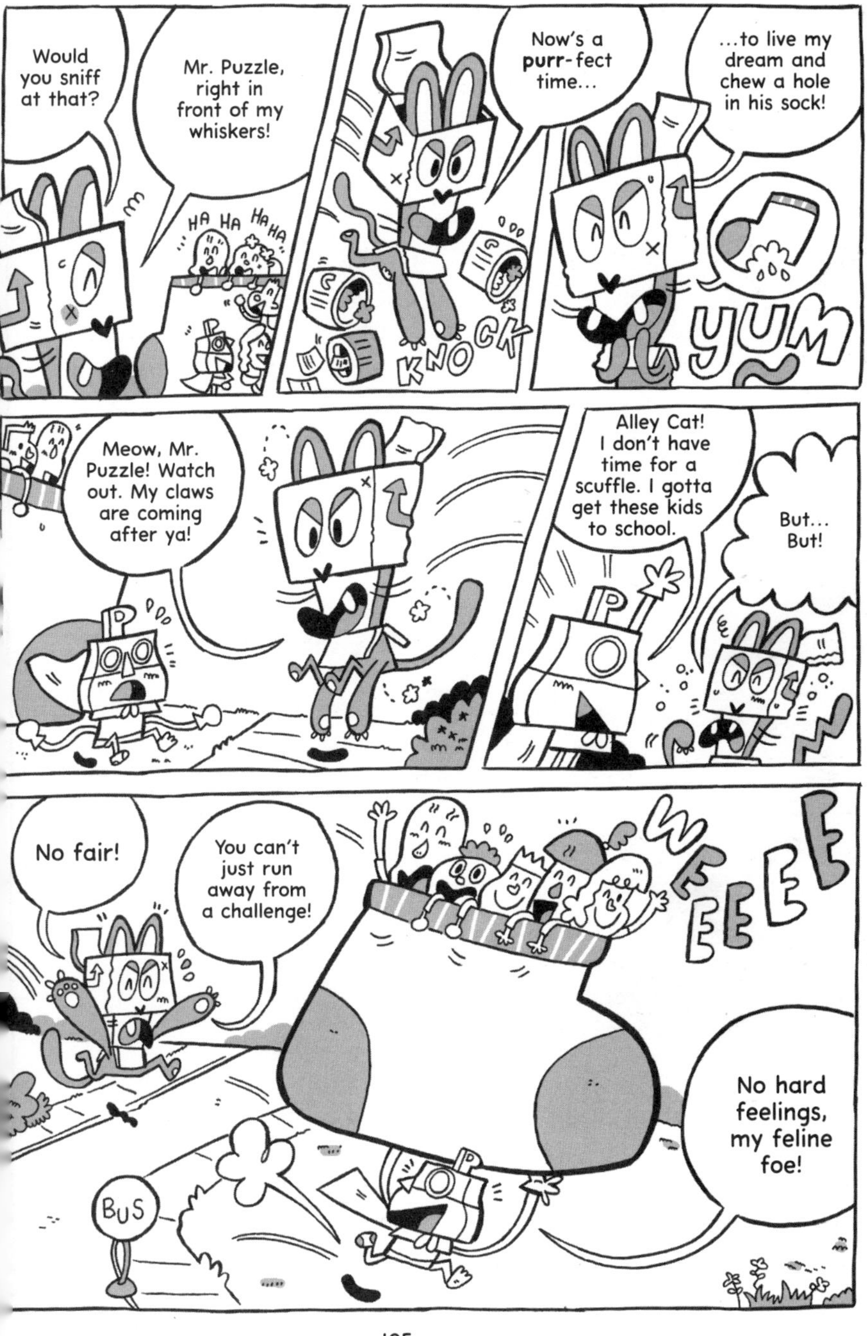

Would you sniff at that?
Mr. Puzzle, right in front of my whiskers!
HA HA HA HA
Now's a **purr**-fect time...
...to live my dream and chew a hole in his sock!
KNOCK
YUM
Meow, Mr. Puzzle! Watch out. My claws are coming after ya!
Alley Cat! I don't have time for a scuffle. I gotta get these kids to school.
But... But!
No fair!
You can't just run away from a challenge!
WEEEEE
No hard feelings, my feline foe!
BUS

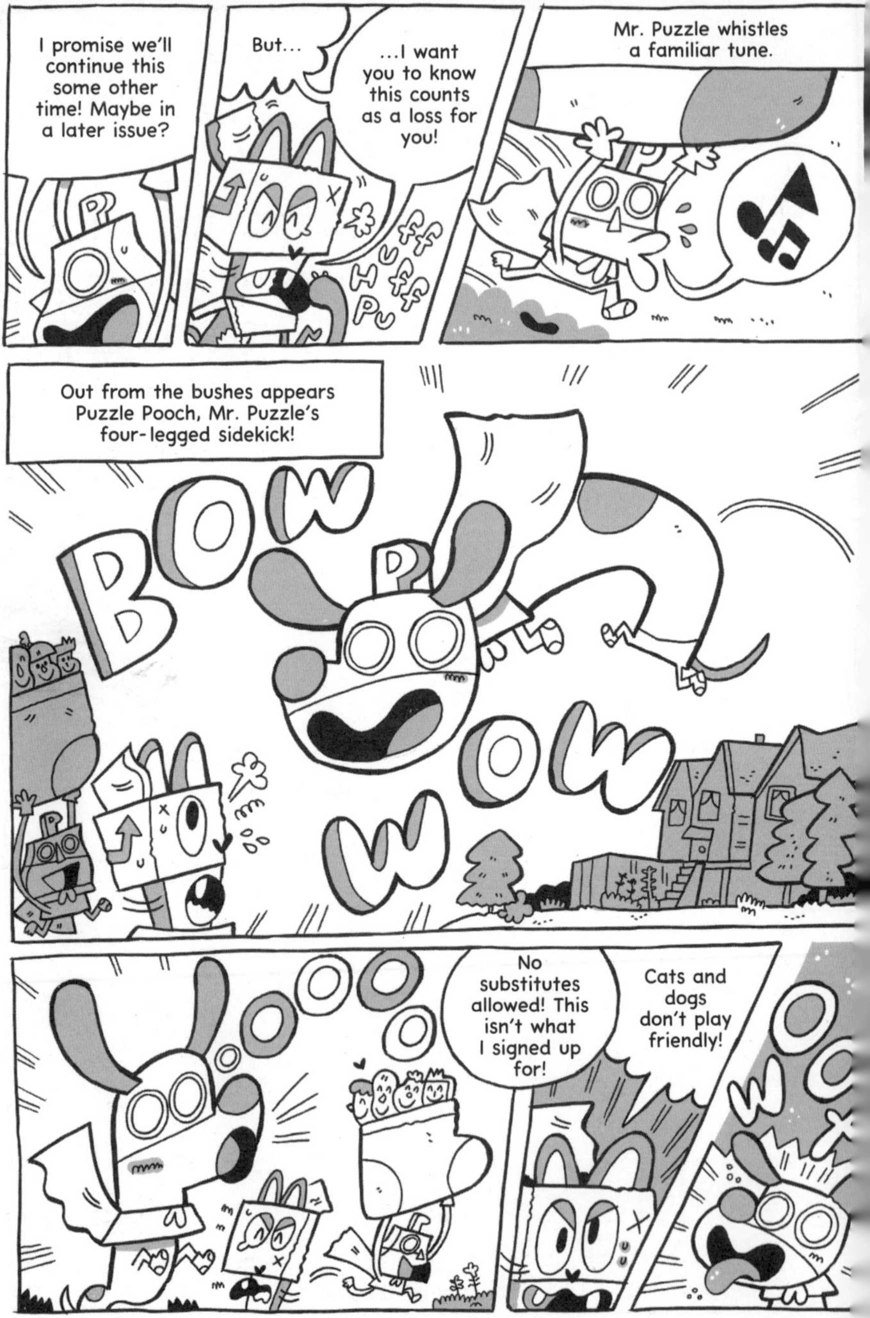
I promise we'll continue this some other time! Maybe in a later issue?
But…
…I want you to know this counts as a loss for you!
Huff Huff Puff
Mr. Puzzle whistles a familiar tune.
Out from the bushes appears Puzzle Pooch, Mr. Puzzle's four-legged sidekick!
BOW WOW
WOOOOO
No substitutes allowed! This isn't what I signed up for!
Cats and dogs don't play friendly!

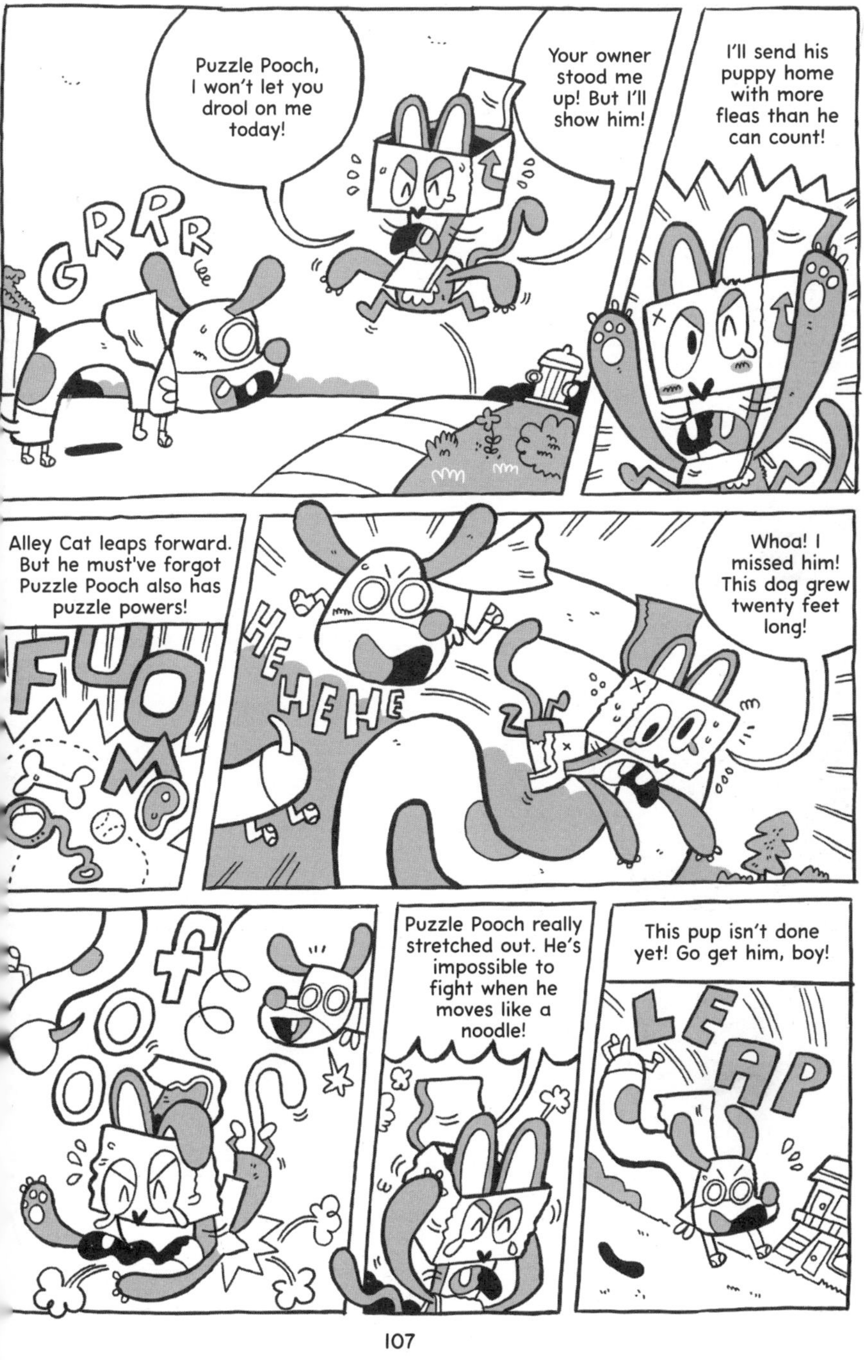
Puzzle Pooch, I won't let you drool on me today!
Your owner stood me up! But I'll show him!
I'll send his puppy home with more fleas than he can count!
GRRRR
Alley Cat leaps forward. But he must've forgot Puzzle Pooch also has puzzle powers!
FUOOM
HEHEHEHE
Whoa! I missed him! This dog grew twenty feet long!
fOOO
Puzzle Pooch really stretched out. He's impossible to fight when he moves like a noodle!
This pup isn't done yet! Go get him, boy!
LEAP

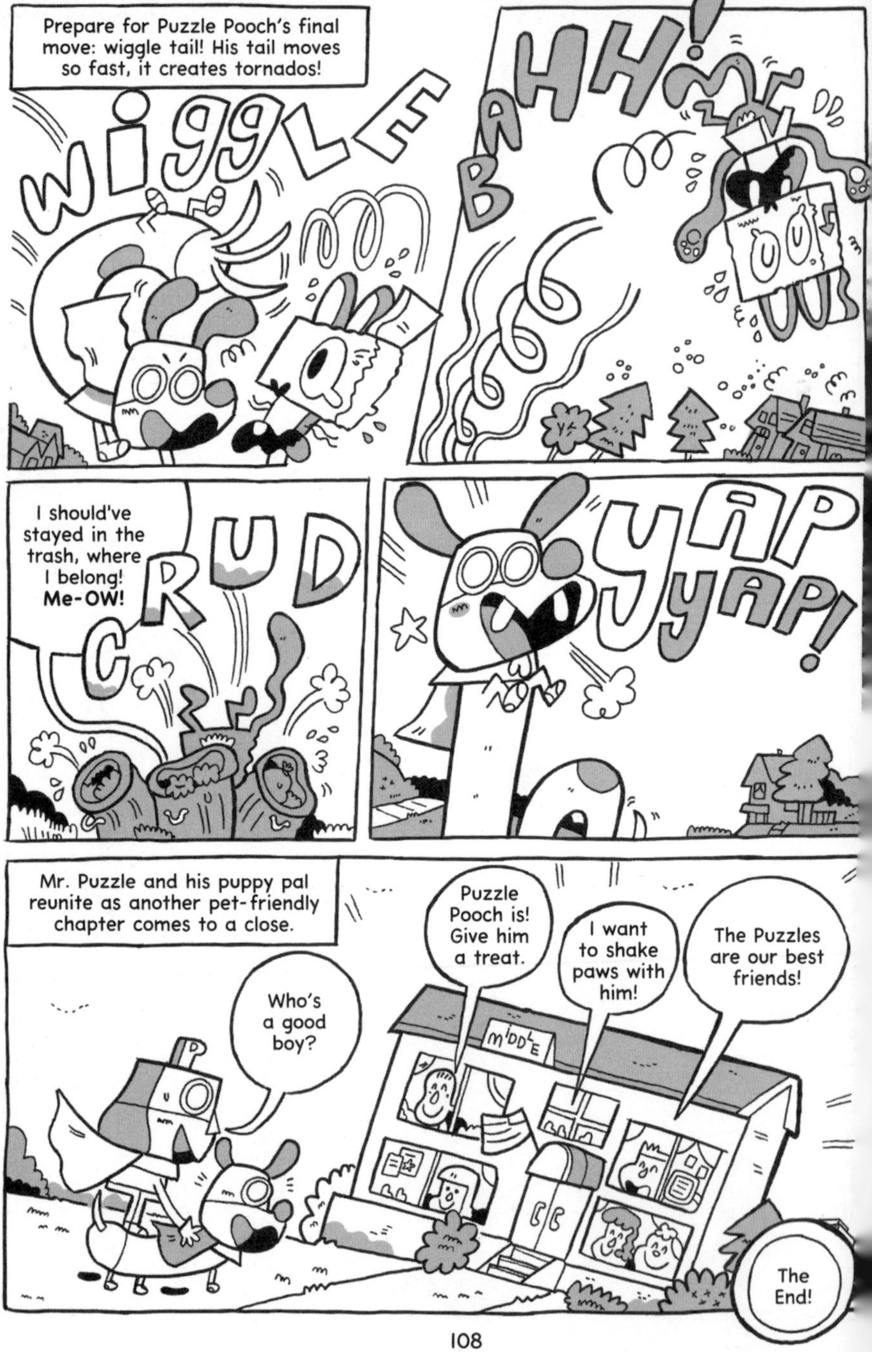

Prepare for Puzzle Pooch's final move: wiggle tail! His tail moves so fast, it creates tornados!
WIGGLE
BAHHH!
I should've stayed in the trash, where I belong! **Me-OW!**
CRUD
YAP YAP!
Mr. Puzzle and his puppy pal reunite as another pet-friendly chapter comes to a close.
Who's a good boy?
MIDDLE
Puzzle Pooch is! Give him a treat.
I want to shake paws with him!
The Puzzles are our best friends!
The End!

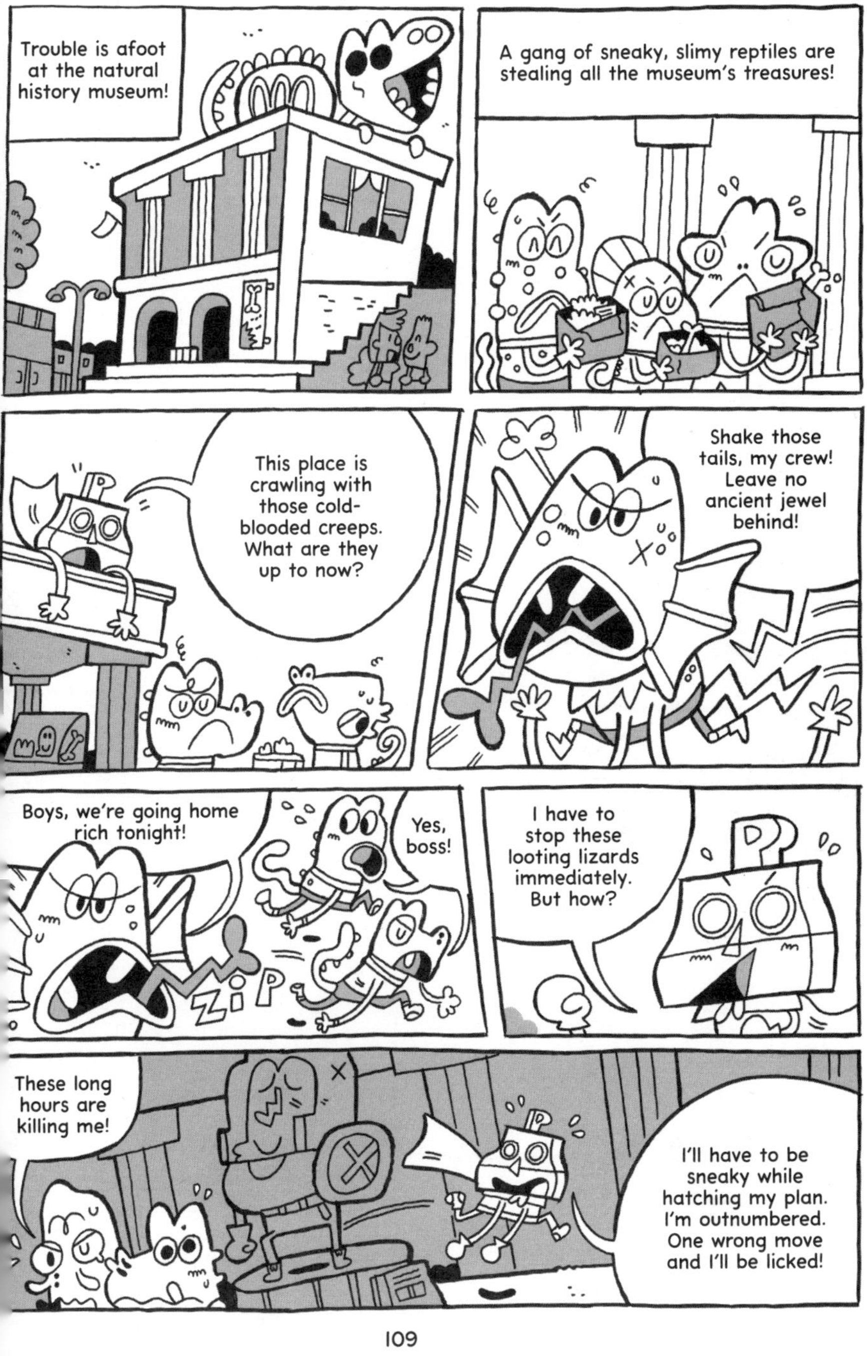

Trouble is afoot at the natural history museum!
A gang of sneaky, slimy reptiles are stealing all the museum's treasures!
This place is crawling with those cold-blooded creeps. What are they up to now?
Shake those tails, my crew! Leave no ancient jewel behind!
Boys, we're going home rich tonight!
Yes, boss!
ZiP
I have to stop these looting lizards immediately. But how?
These long hours are killing me!
I'll have to be sneaky while hatching my plan. I'm outnumbered. One wrong move and I'll be licked!

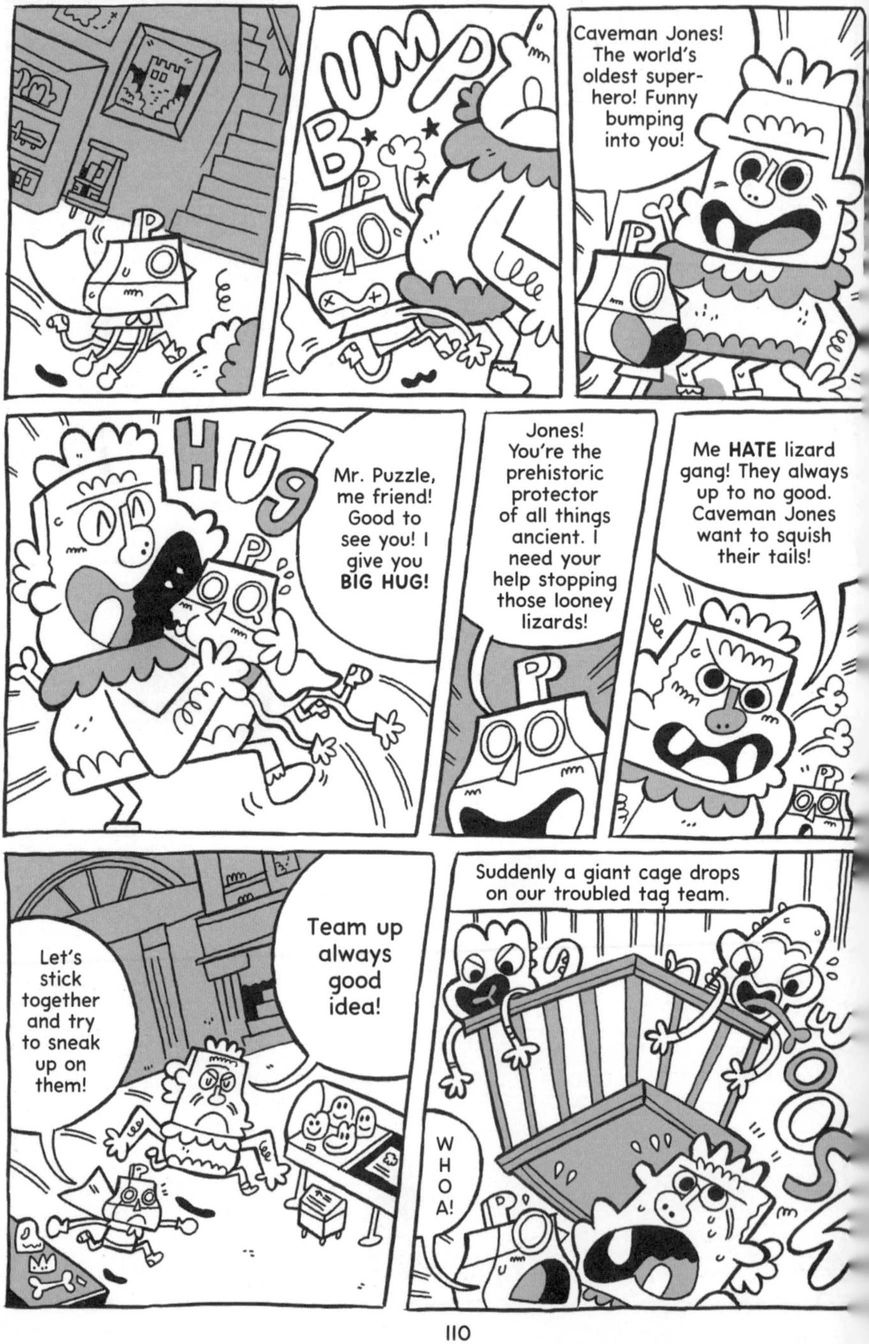

BUMP
Caveman Jones! The world's oldest super-hero! Funny bumping into you!
HUG
Mr. Puzzle, me friend! Good to see you! I give you **BIG HUG!**
Jones! You're the prehistoric protector of all things ancient. I need your help stopping those looney lizards!
Me **HATE** lizard gang! They always up to no good. Caveman Jones want to squish their tails!
Let's stick together and try to sneak up on them!
Team up always good idea!
Suddenly a giant cage drops on our troubled tag team.
WHOA!
WOOSH

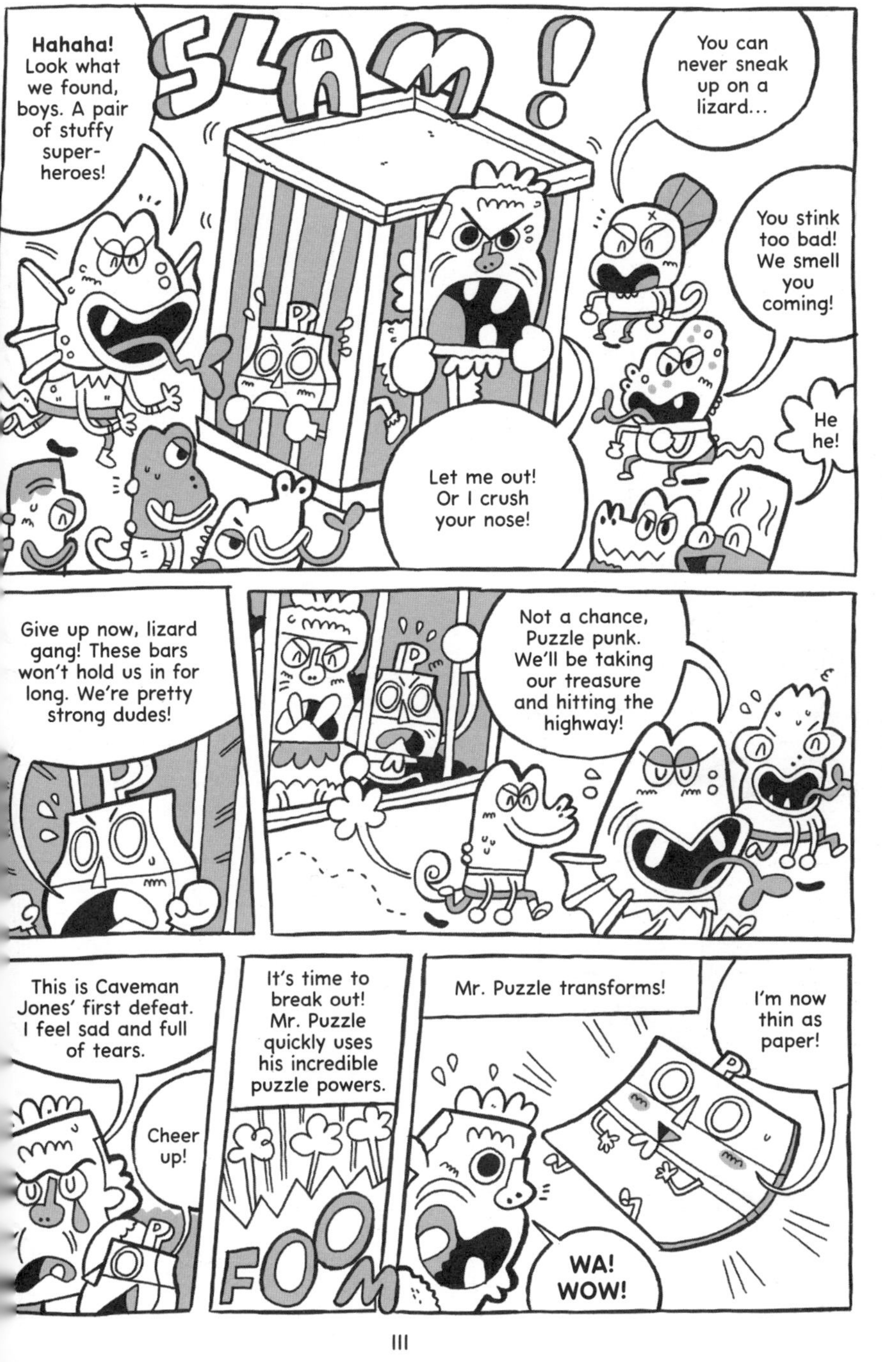
SLAM!
Hahaha! Look what we found, boys. A pair of stuffy super-heroes!
You can never sneak up on a lizard...
You stink too bad! We smell you coming!
He he!
Let me out! Or I crush your nose!
Give up now, lizard gang! These bars won't hold us in for long. We're pretty strong dudes!
Not a chance, Puzzle punk. We'll be taking our treasure and hitting the highway!
This is Caveman Jones' first defeat. I feel sad and full of tears.
Cheer up!
It's time to break out! Mr. Puzzle quickly uses his incredible puzzle powers.
FOOOM
Mr. Puzzle transforms!
I'm now thin as paper!
WA! WOW!

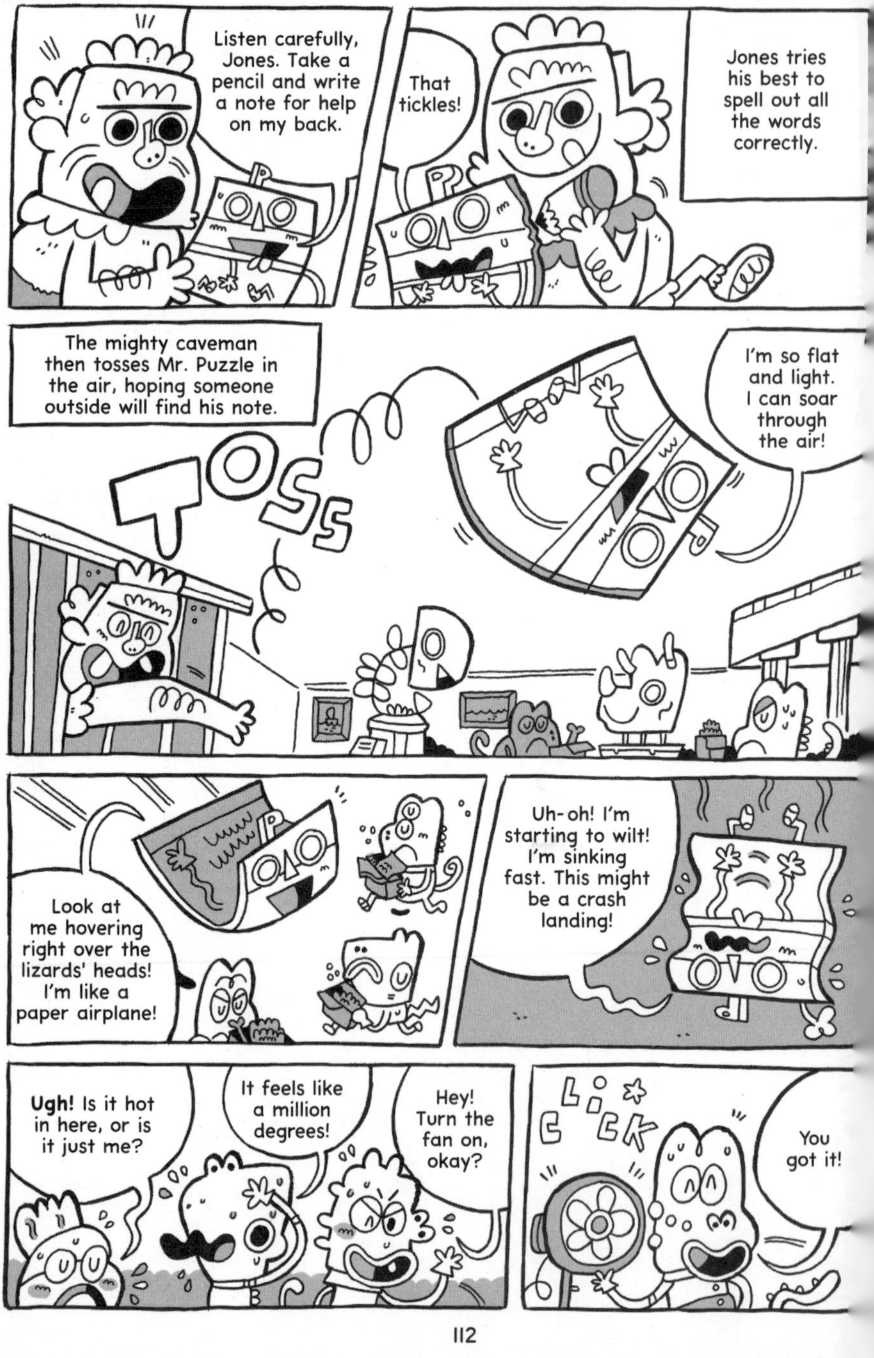
Listen carefully, Jones. Take a pencil and write a note for help on my back.
That tickles!
Jones tries his best to spell out all the words correctly.
The mighty caveman then tosses Mr. Puzzle in the air, hoping someone outside will find his note.
TOSS
I'm so flat and light. I can soar through the air!
Look at me hovering right over the lizards' heads! I'm like a paper airplane!
Uh-oh! I'm starting to wilt! I'm sinking fast. This might be a crash landing!
Ugh! Is it hot in here, or is it just me?
It feels like a million degrees!
Hey! Turn the fan on, okay?
CLICK
You got it!

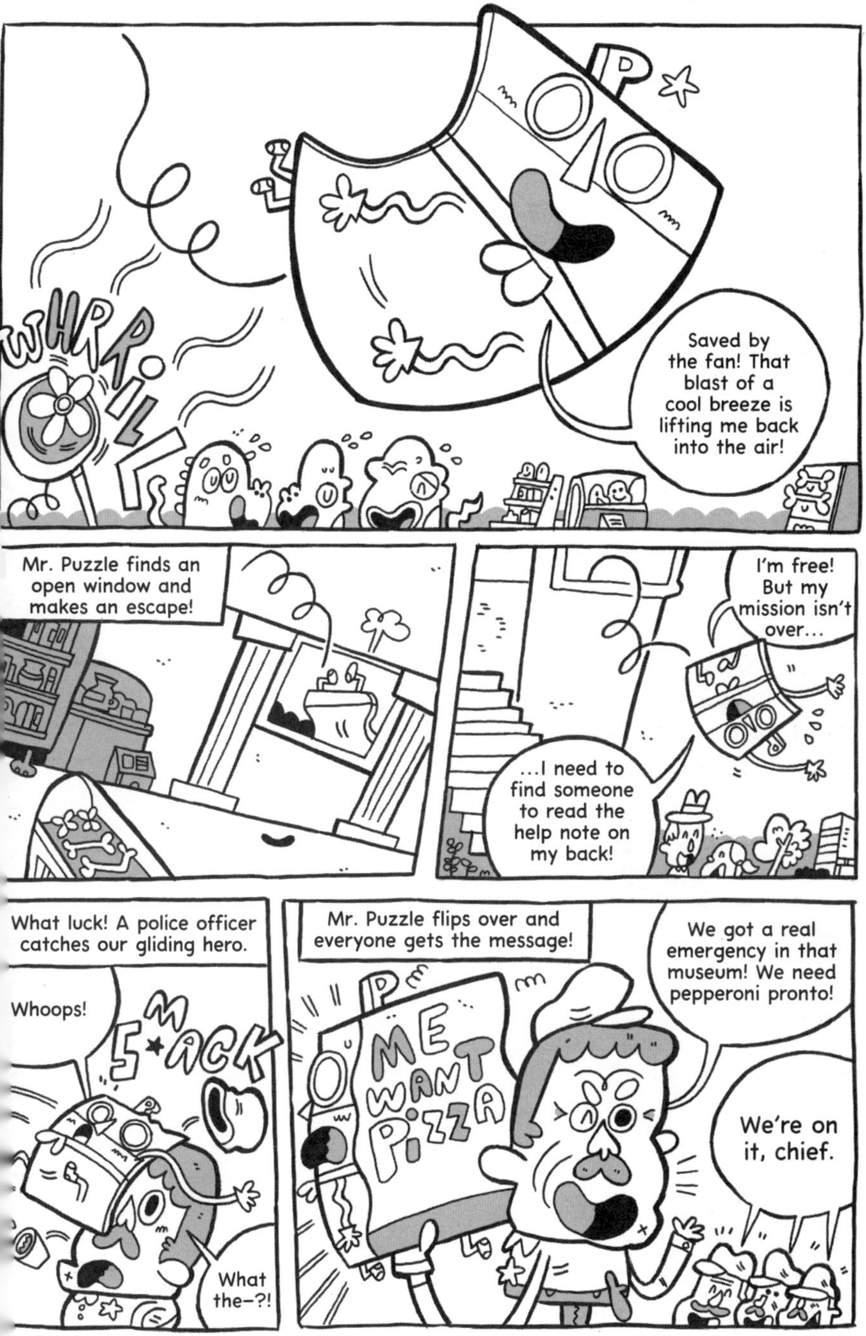
WHRRRIIIL
Saved by the fan! That blast of a cool breeze is lifting me back into the air!
Mr. Puzzle finds an open window and makes an escape!
I'm free! But my mission isn't over...
...I need to find someone to read the help note on my back!
What luck! A police officer catches our gliding hero.
Whoops!
SMACK
What the–?!
Mr. Puzzle flips over and everyone gets the message!
ME WANT PIZZA
We got a real emergency in that museum! We need pepperoni pronto!
We're on it, chief.

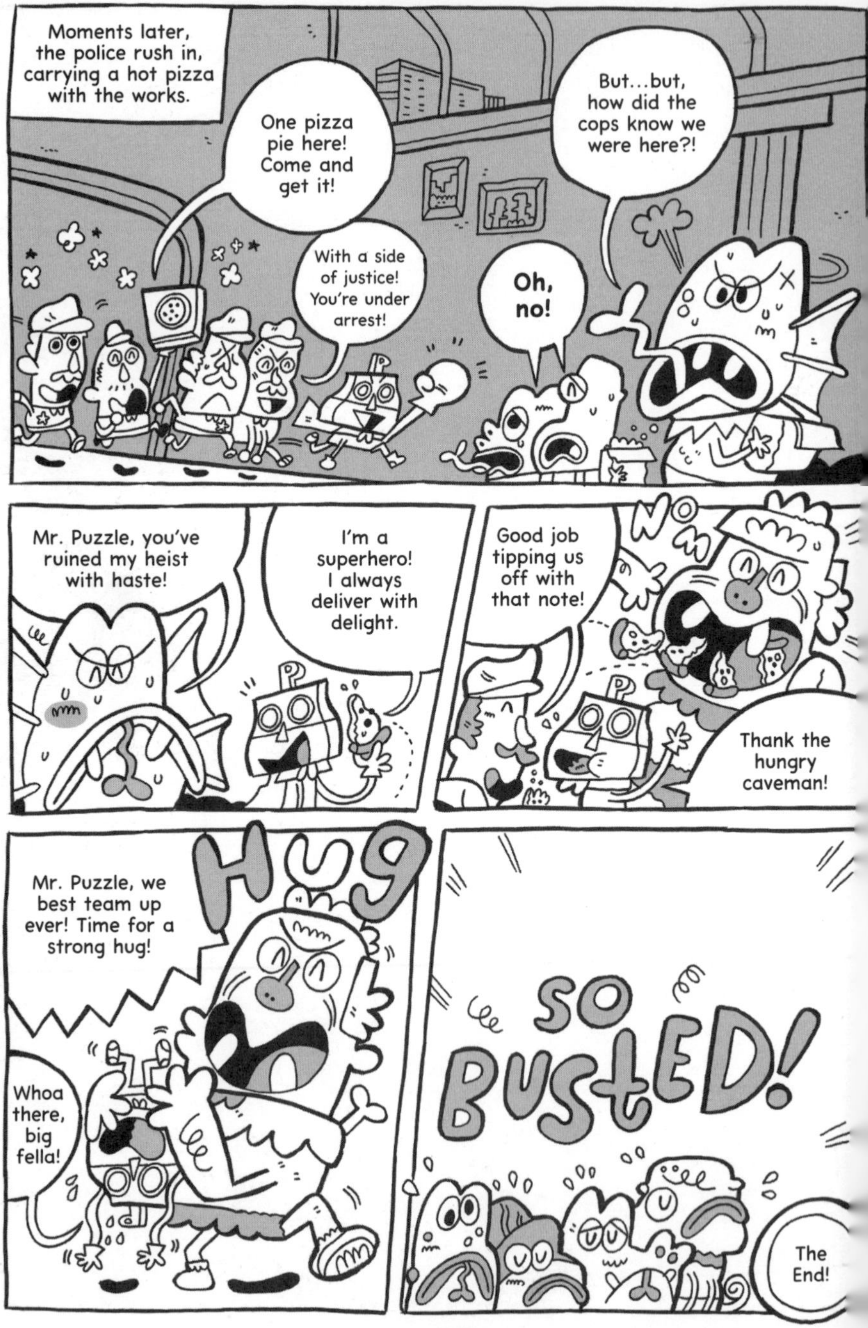

Moments later, the police rush in, carrying a hot pizza with the works.
One pizza pie here! Come and get it!
With a side of justice! You're under arrest!
Oh, no!
But...but, how did the cops know we were here?!
Mr. Puzzle, you've ruined my heist with haste!
I'm a superhero! I always deliver with delight.
Good job tipping us off with that note!
NOM
Thank the hungry caveman!
Mr. Puzzle, we best team up ever! Time for a strong hug!
Hug
Whoa there, big fella!
SO BUSTED!
The End!

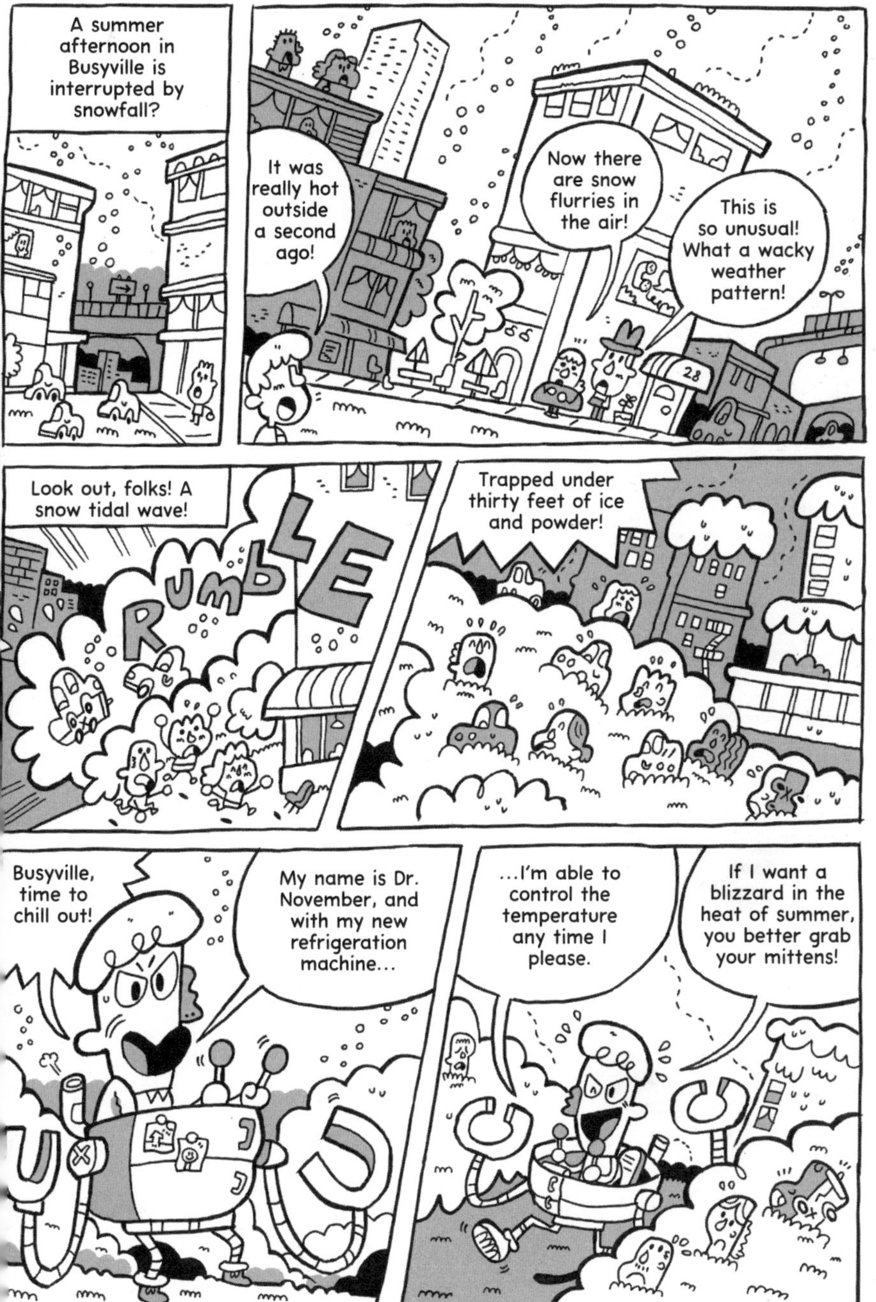
A summer afternoon in Busyville is interrupted by snowfall?
It was really hot outside a second ago!
Now there are snow flurries in the air!
This is so unusual! What a wacky weather pattern!
28
Look out, folks! A snow tidal wave!
RUMBLE
Trapped under thirty feet of ice and powder!
Busyville, time to chill out!
My name is Dr. November, and with my new refrigeration machine...
...I'm able to control the temperature any time I please.
If I want a blizzard in the heat of summer, you better grab your mittens!

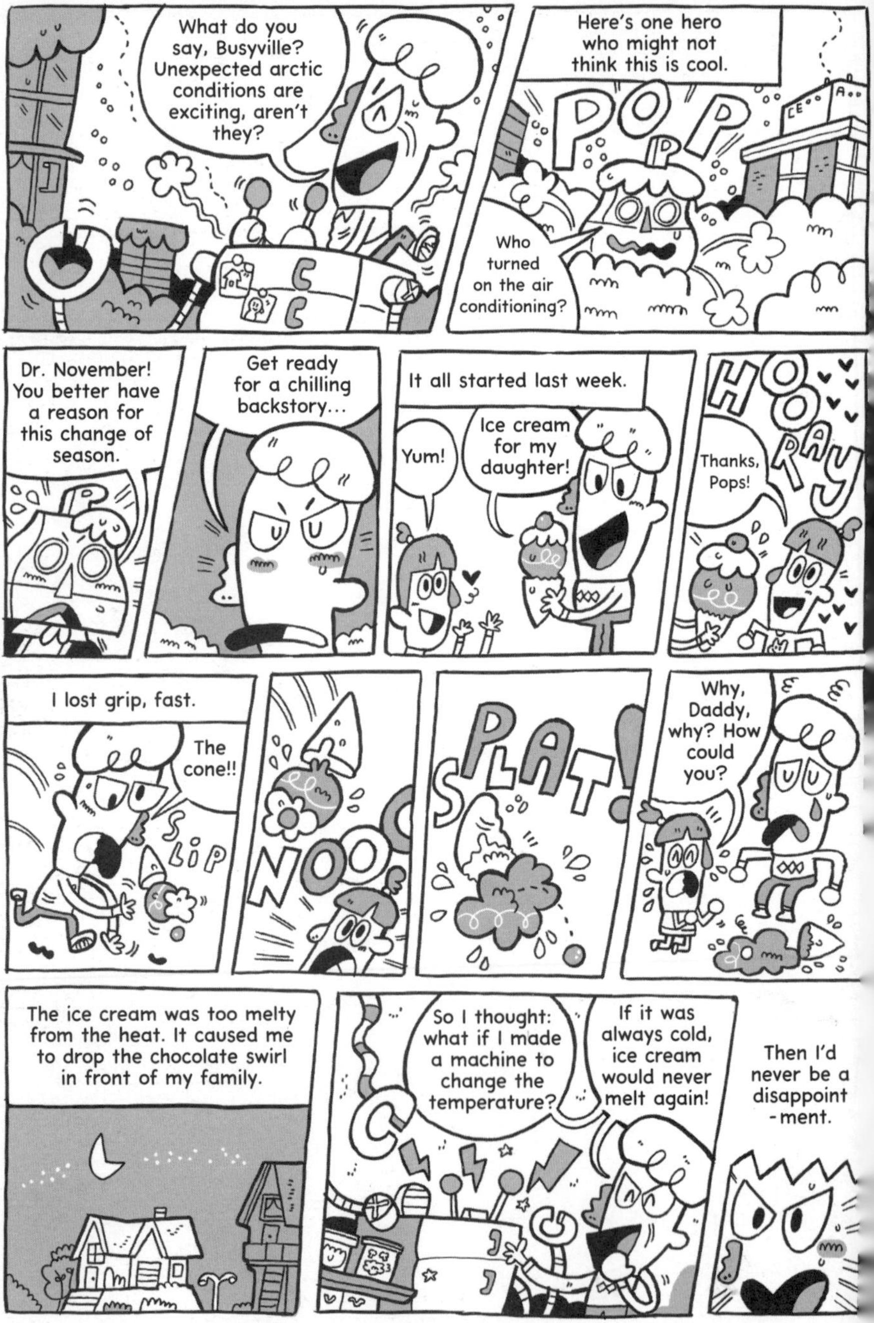

What do you say, Busyville? Unexpected arctic conditions are exciting, aren't they?
Here's one hero who might not think this is cool.
POP
Who turned on the air conditioning?
Dr. November! You better have a reason for this change of season.
Get ready for a chilling backstory...
It all started last week.
Ice cream for my daughter!
Yum!
HOORAY
Thanks, Pops!
I lost grip, fast.
The cone!!
SLIP
NOOO
SPLAT!
Why, Daddy, why? How could you?
The ice cream was too melty from the heat. It caused me to drop the chocolate swirl in front of my family.
So I thought: what if I made a machine to change the temperature?
If it was always cold, ice cream would never melt again!
Then I'd never be a disappoint-ment.

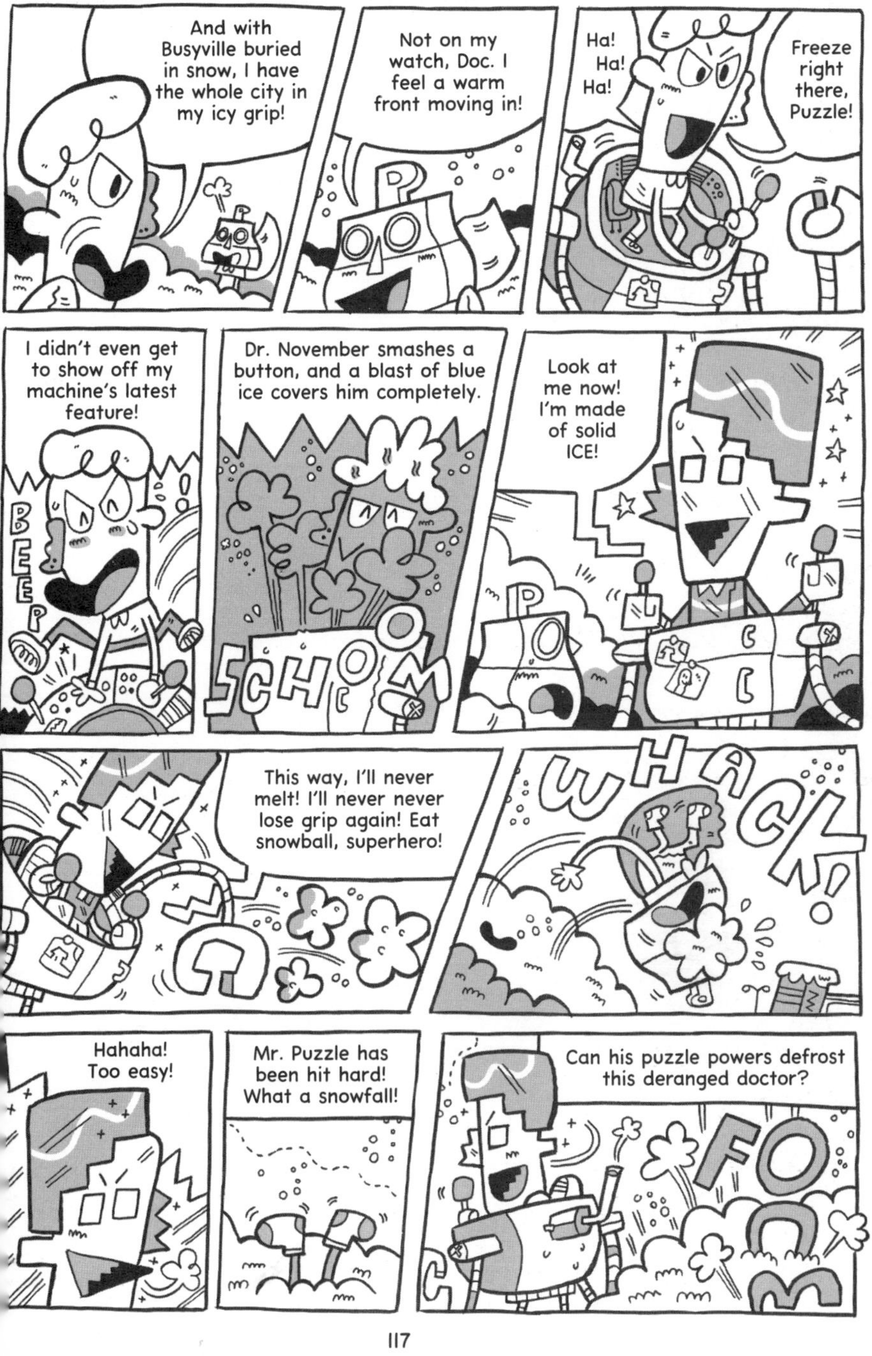
And with Busyville buried in snow, I have the whole city in my icy grip!
Not on my watch, Doc. I feel a warm front moving in!
Ha! Ha! Ha!
Freeze right there, Puzzle!
I didn't even get to show off my machine's latest feature!
BEEP
Dr. November smashes a button, and a blast of blue ice covers him completely.
SCHOOM
Look at me now! I'm made of solid ICE!
This way, I'll never melt! I'll never never lose grip again! Eat snowball, superhero!
WHACK!
Hahaha! Too easy!
Mr. Puzzle has been hit hard! What a snowfall!
Can his puzzle powers defrost this deranged doctor?
FOOM

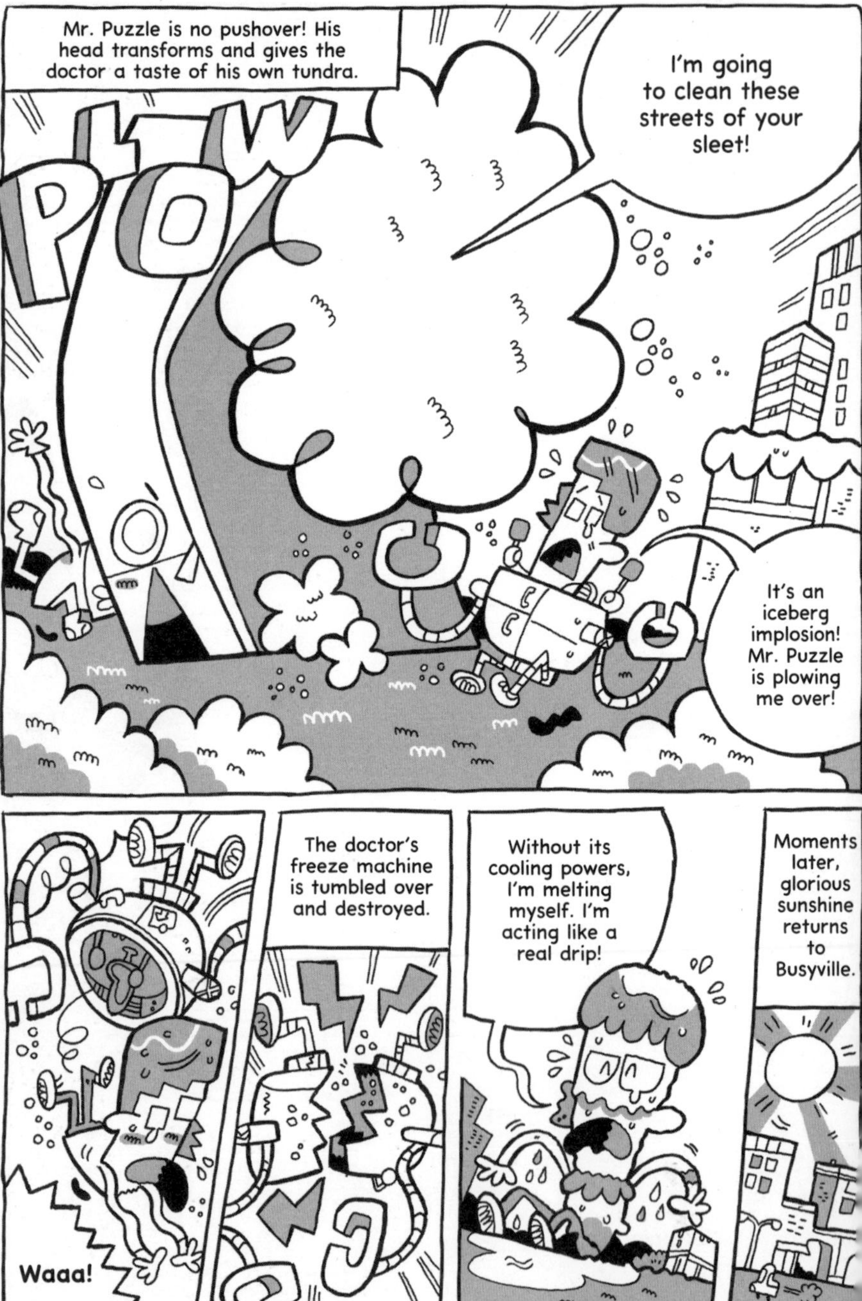
Mr. Puzzle is no pushover! His head transforms and gives the doctor a taste of his own tundra.
POW
I'm going to clean these streets of your sleet!
It's an iceberg implosion! Mr. Puzzle is plowing me over!
Waaa!
The doctor's freeze machine is tumbled over and destroyed.
Without its cooling powers, I'm melting myself. I'm acting like a real drip!
Moments later, glorious sunshine returns to Busyville.

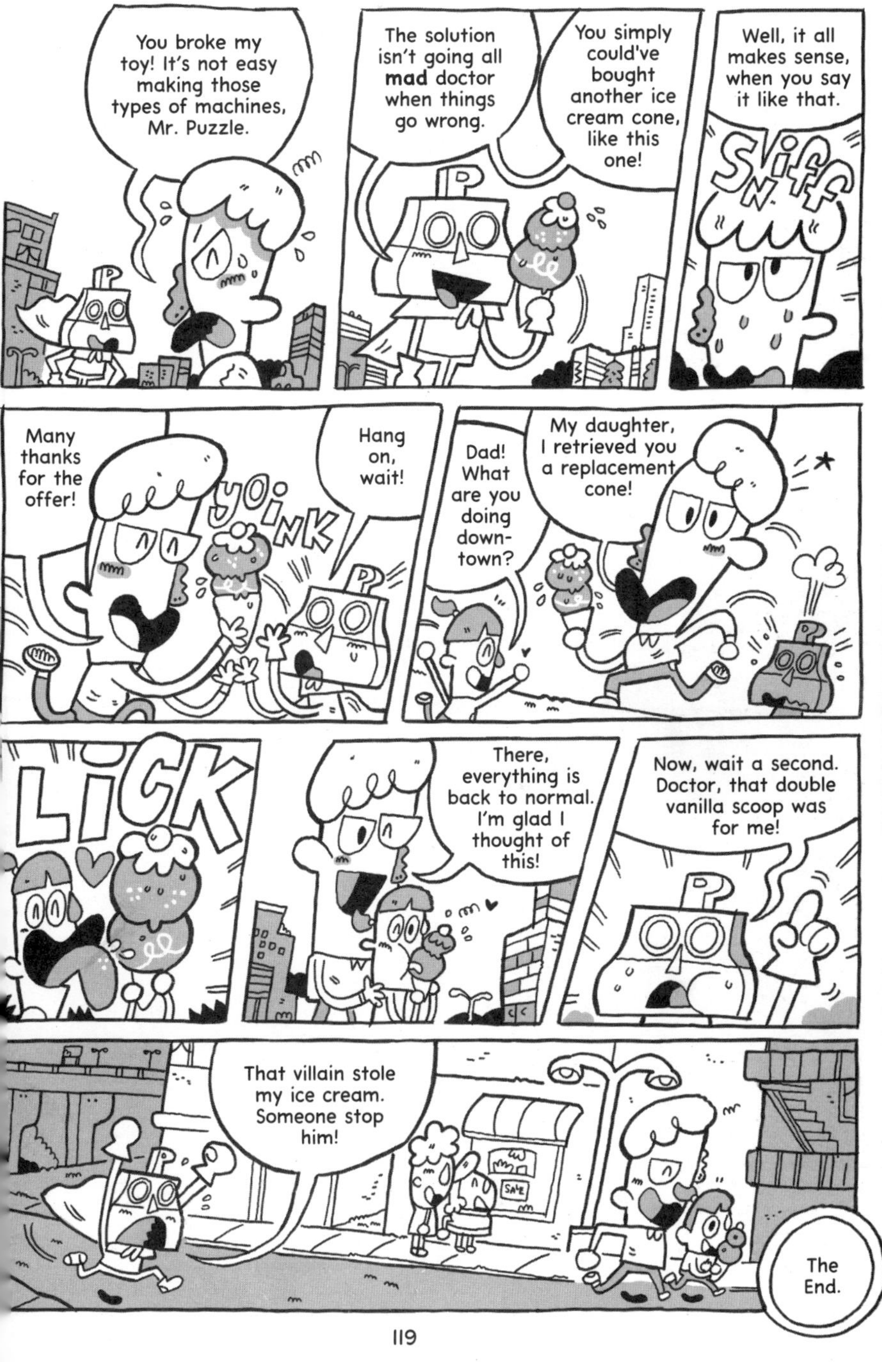
You broke my toy! It's not easy making those types of machines, Mr. Puzzle.
The solution isn't going all **mad** doctor when things go wrong.
You simply could've bought another ice cream cone, like this one!
Well, it all makes sense, when you say it like that.
SNIFF SNIFF
Many thanks for the offer!
YOINK
Hang on, wait!
Dad! What are you doing downtown?
My daughter, I retrieved you a replacement cone!
LICK
There, everything is back to normal. I'm glad I thought of this!
Now, wait a second. Doctor, that double vanilla scoop was for me!
That villain stole my ice cream. Someone stop him!
SALE
The End.

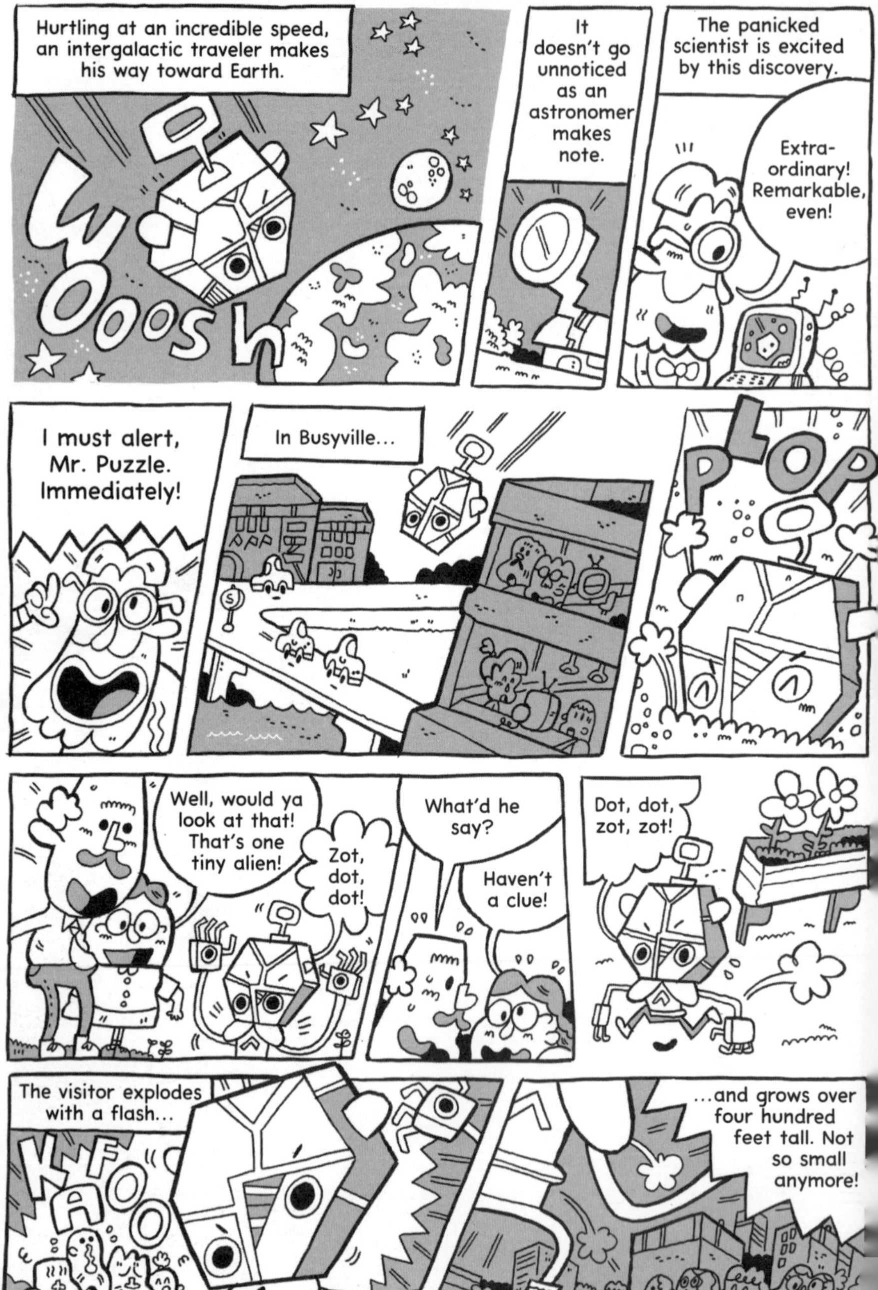
Hurtling at an incredible speed, an intergalactic traveler makes his way toward Earth.
WOOOSH
It doesn't go unnoticed as an astronomer makes note.
The panicked scientist is excited by this discovery.
Extra-ordinary! Remarkable, even!
I must alert, Mr. Puzzle. Immediately!
In Busyville...
PLOP
Well, would ya look at that! That's one tiny alien!
Zot, dot, dot!
What'd he say?
Haven't a clue!
Dot, dot, zot, zot!
The visitor explodes with a flash...
KAFOOO
...and grows over four hundred feet tall. Not so small anymore!

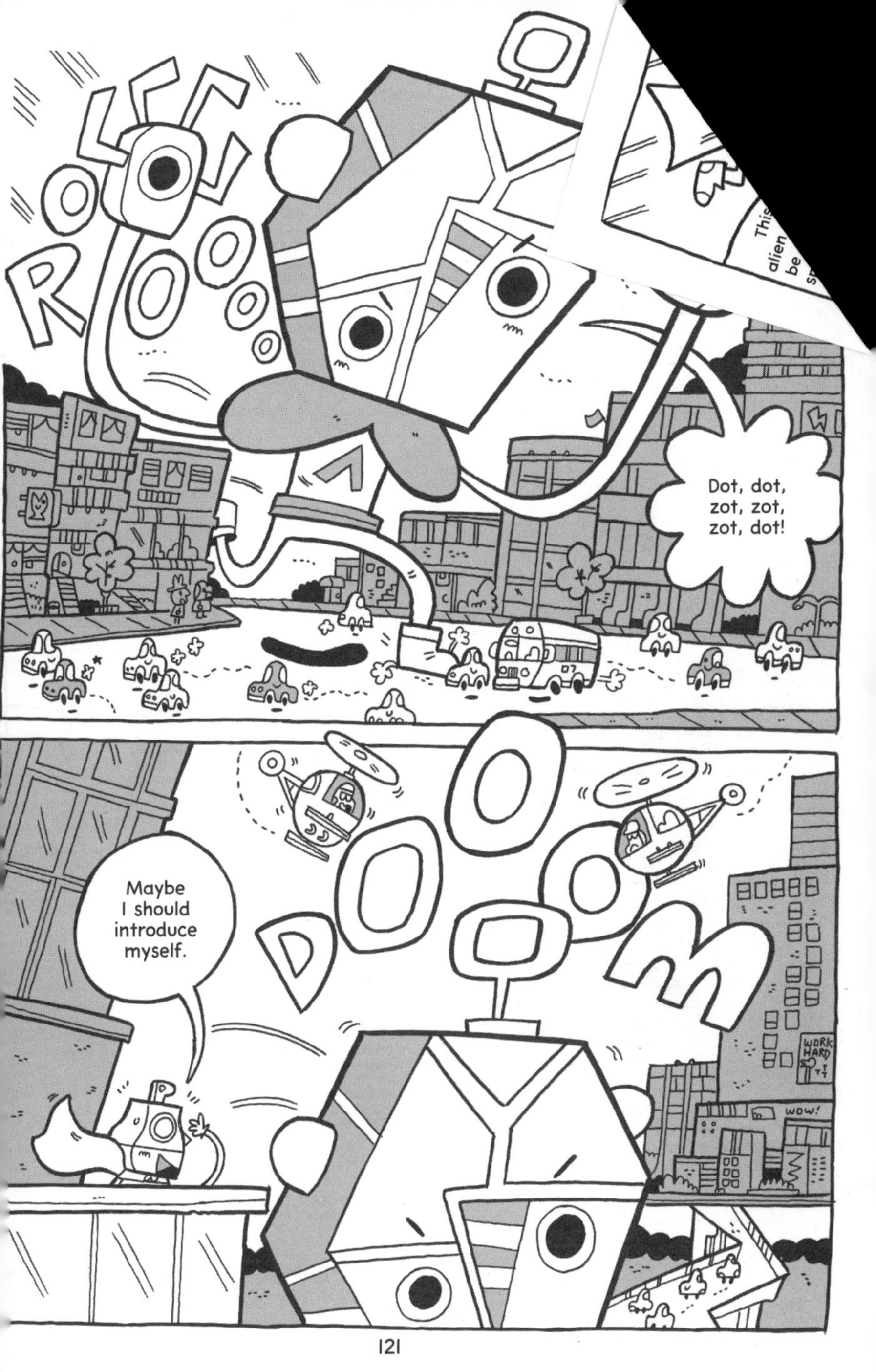
Dot, dot, zot, zot, zot, dot!
Maybe I should introduce myself.
WORK HARD
WOW!

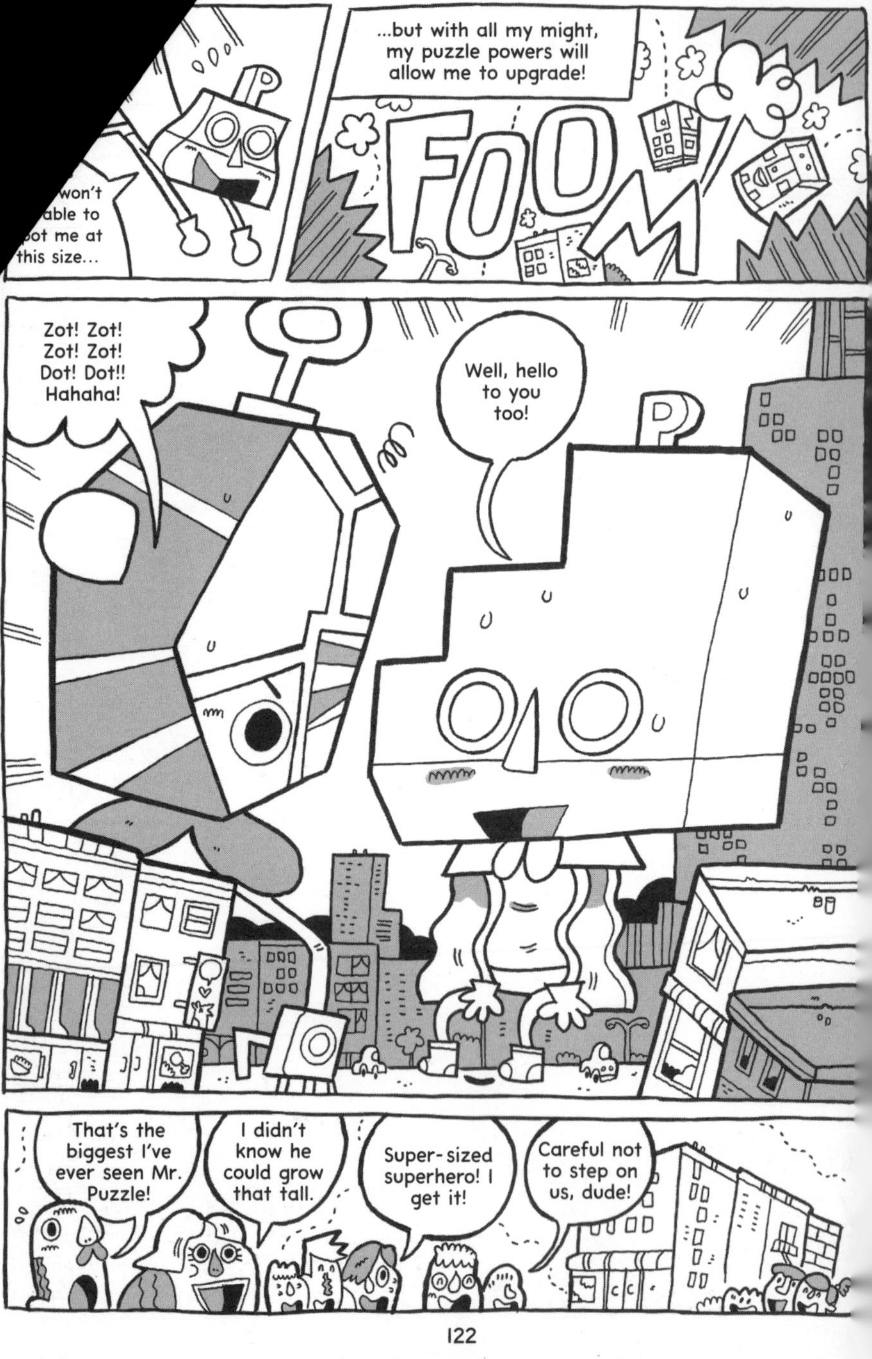
won't able to oot me at this size...
...but with all my might, my puzzle powers will allow me to upgrade!
FOOOM
Zot! Zot! Zot! Zot! Dot! Dot!! Hahaha!
Well, hello to you too!
That's the biggest I've ever seen Mr. Puzzle!
I didn't know he could grow that tall.
Super-sized superhero! I get it!
Careful not to step on us, dude!

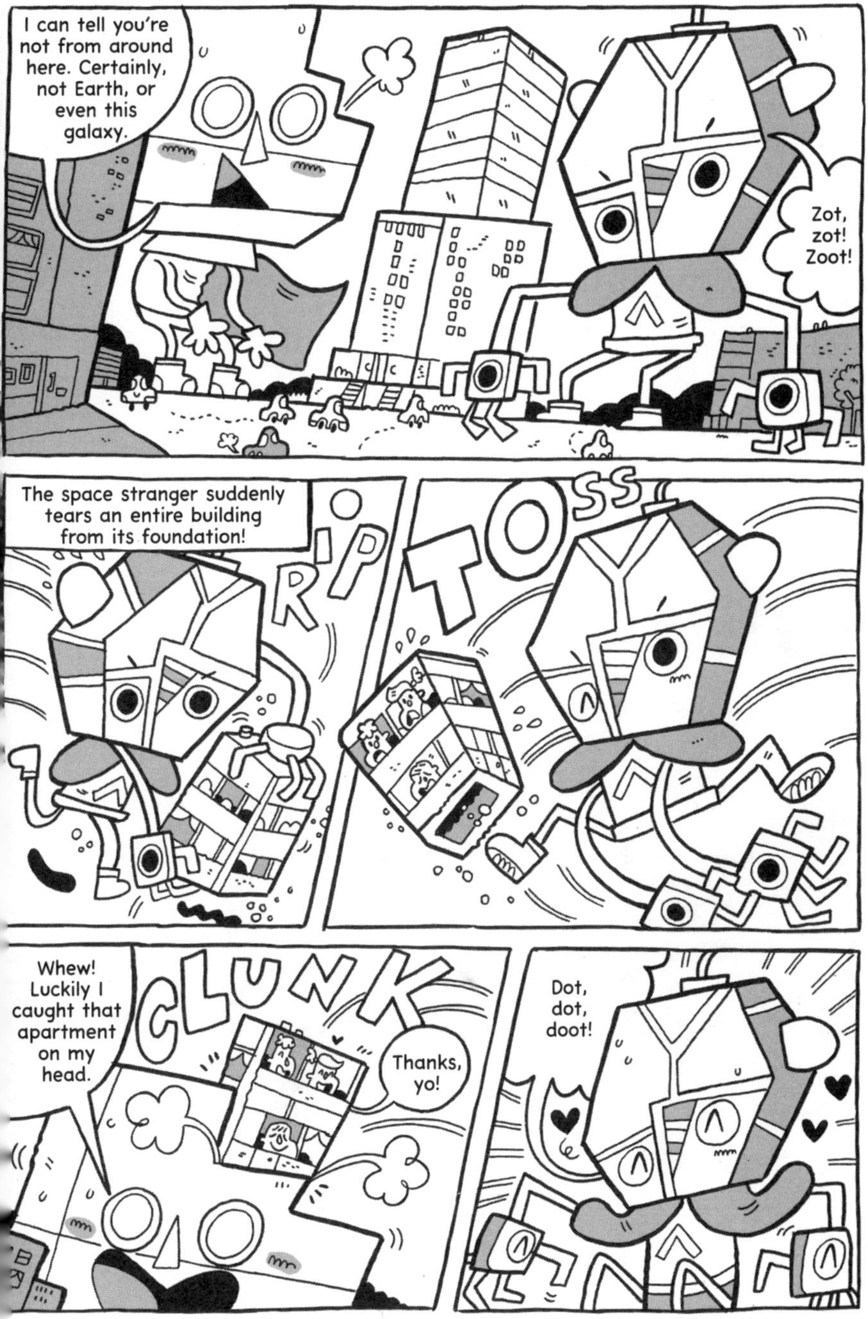
I can tell you're not from around here. Certainly, not Earth, or even this galaxy.
Zot, zot! Zoot!
The space stranger suddenly tears an entire building from its foundation!
RIP
TOSS
Whew! Luckily I caught that apartment on my head.
CLUNK
Thanks, yo!
Dot, dot, doot!

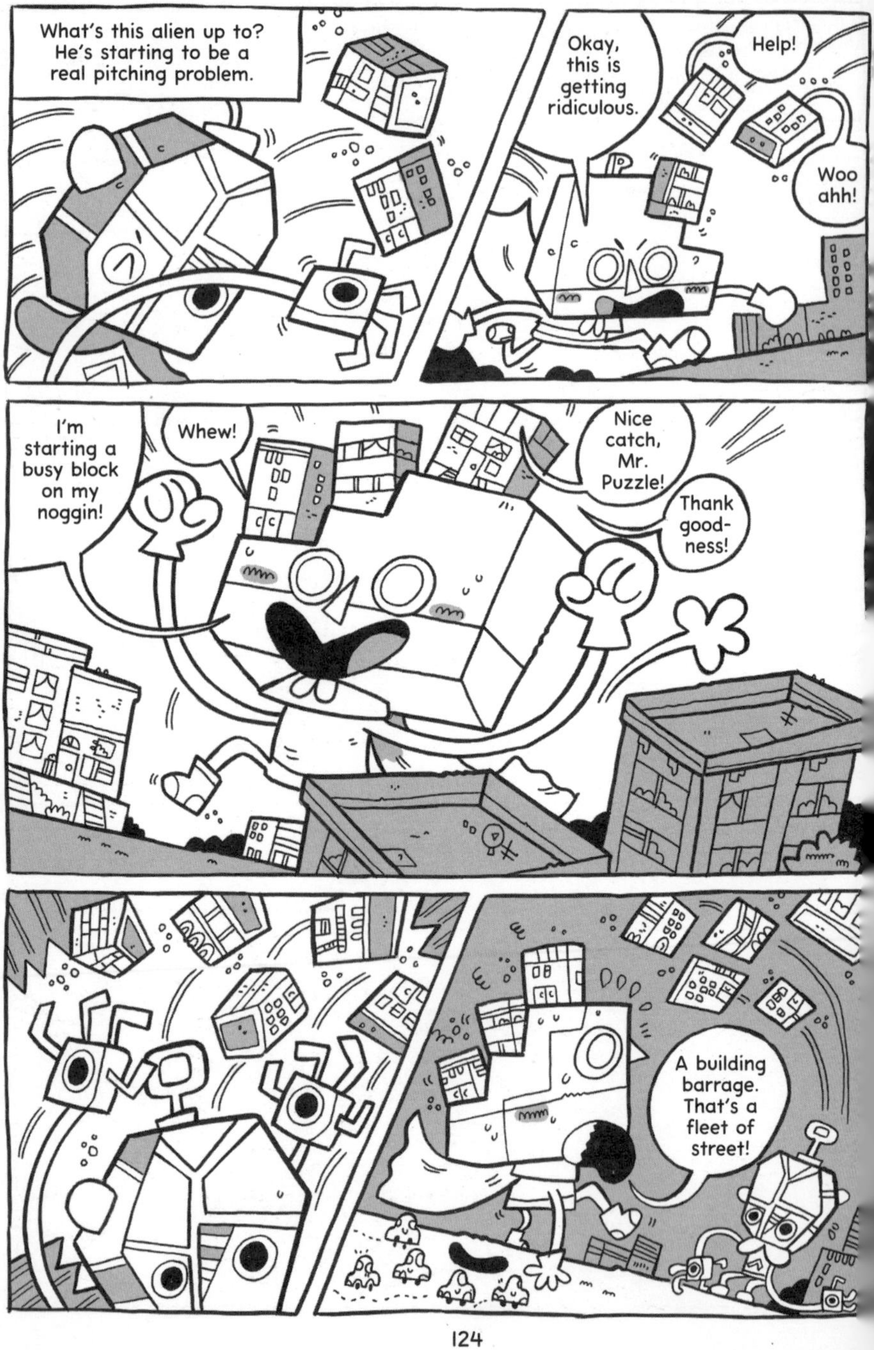
What's this alien up to? He's starting to be a real pitching problem.
Okay, this is getting ridiculous.
Help!
Woo ahh!
I'm starting a busy block on my noggin!
Whew!
Nice catch, Mr. Puzzle!
Thank goodness!
A building barrage. That's a fleet of street!

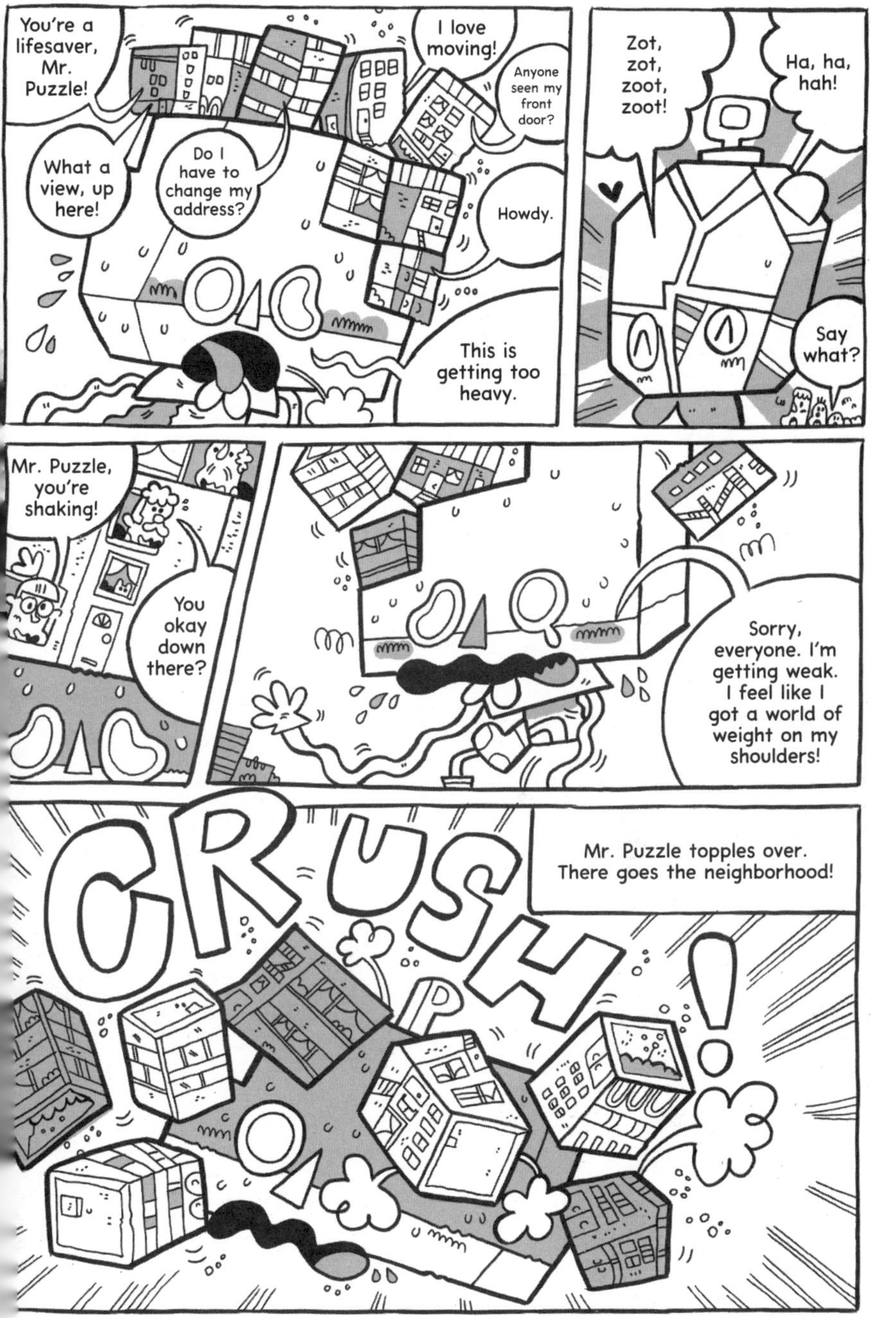
You're a lifesaver, Mr. Puzzle!
I love moving!
What a view, up here!
Do I have to change my address?
Anyone seen my front door?
Howdy.
This is getting too heavy.
Zot, zot, zoot, zoot!
Ha, ha, hah!
Say what?
Mr. Puzzle, you're shaking!
You okay down there?
Sorry, everyone. I'm getting weak. I feel like I got a world of weight on my shoulders!
CRUSH!
Mr. Puzzle topples over. There goes the neighborhood!

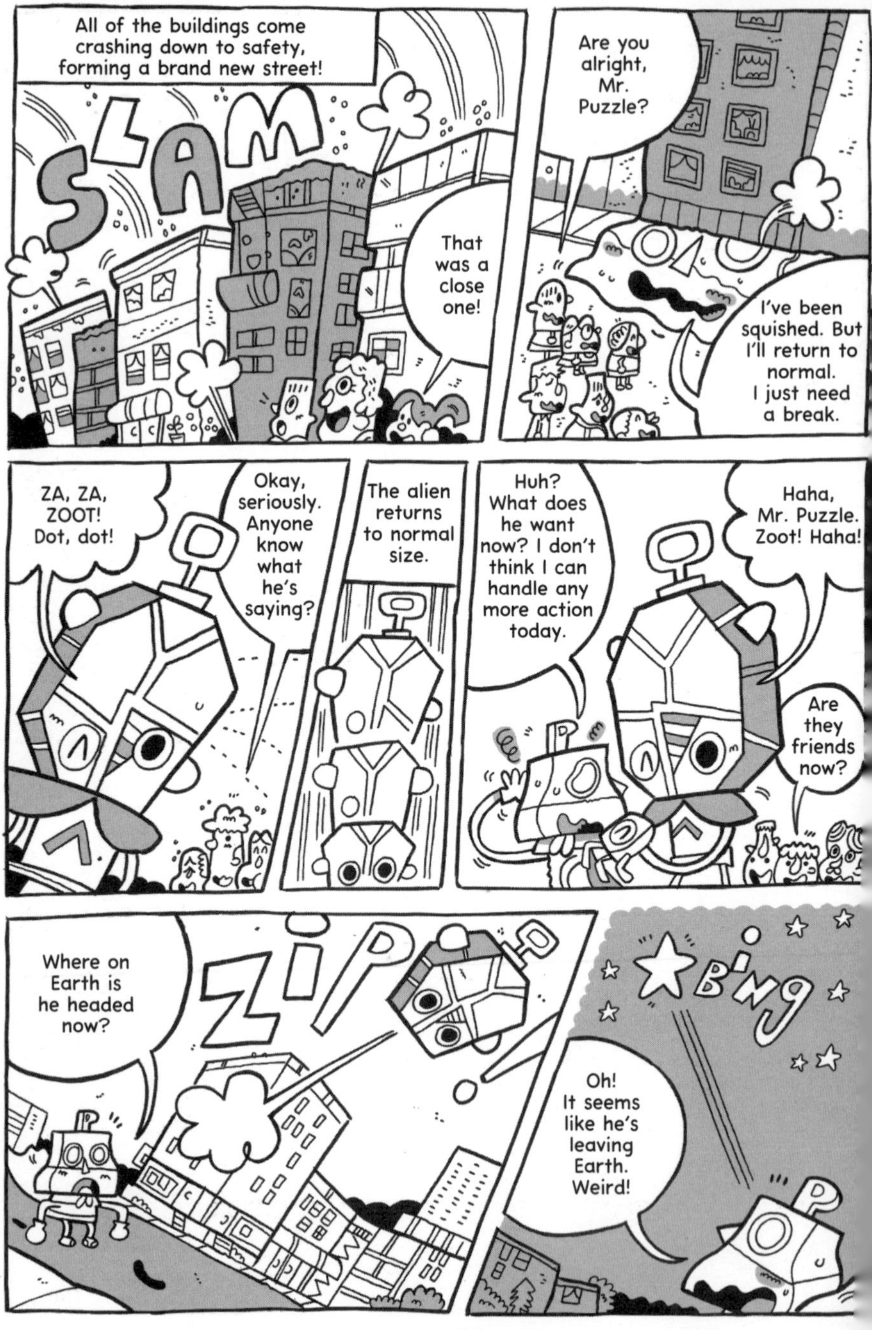
All of the buildings come crashing down to safety, forming a brand new street!
SLAM
That was a close one!
Are you alright, Mr. Puzzle?
I've been squished. But I'll return to normal. I just need a break.
ZA, ZA, ZOOT! Dot, dot!
Okay, seriously. Anyone know what he's saying?
The alien returns to normal size.
Huh? What does he want now? I don't think I can handle any more action today.
Haha, Mr. Puzzle. Zoot! Haha!
Are they friends now?
Where on Earth is he headed now?
ZIP
BING
Oh! It seems like he's leaving Earth. Weird!

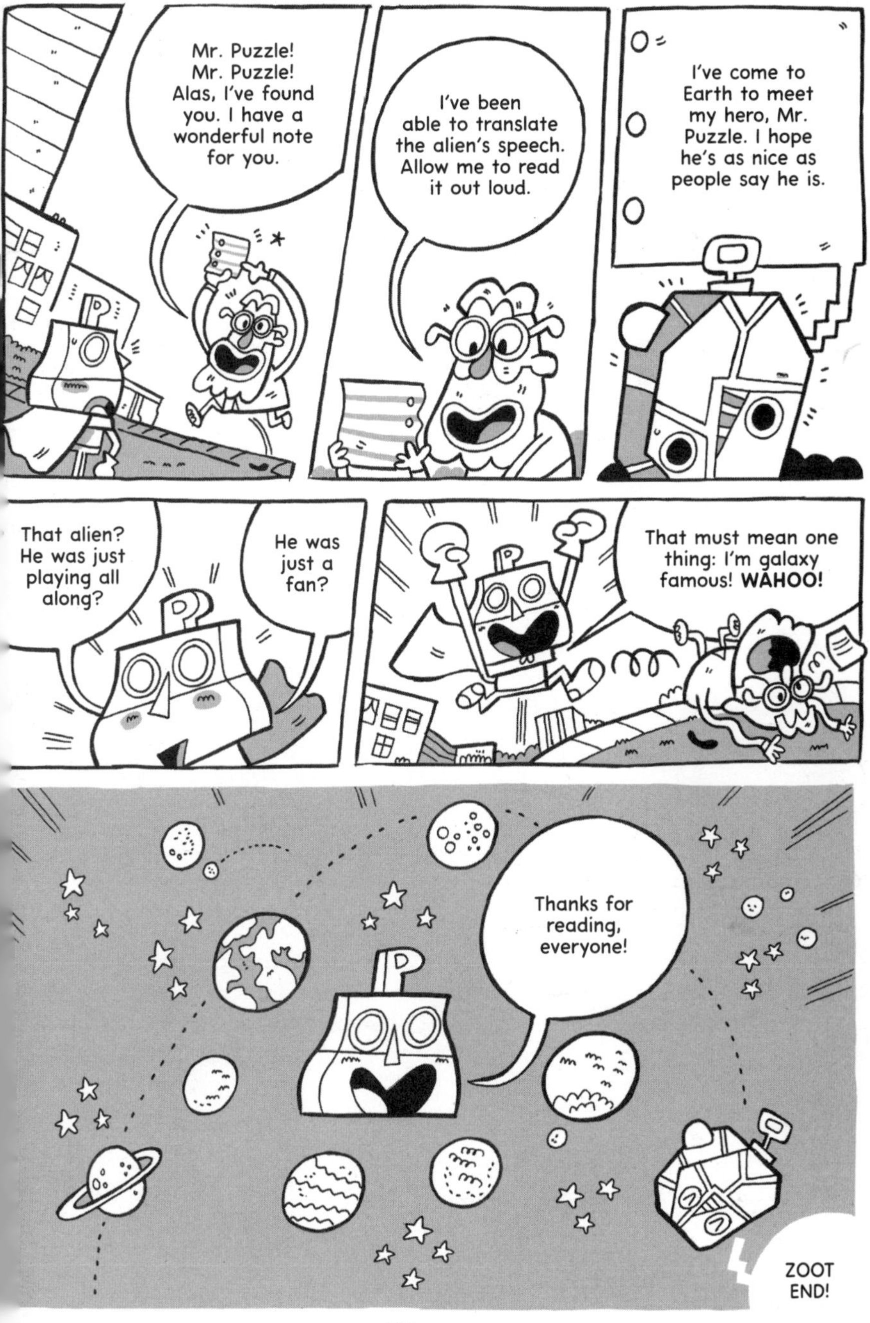
Mr. Puzzle! Mr. Puzzle! Alas, I've found you. I have a wonderful note for you.
I've been able to translate the alien's speech. Allow me to read it out loud.
I've come to Earth to meet my hero, Mr. Puzzle. I hope he's as nice as people say he is.
That alien? He was just playing all along?
He was just a fan?
That must mean one thing: I'm galaxy famous! **WAHOO!**
Thanks for reading, everyone!
ZOOT
END!

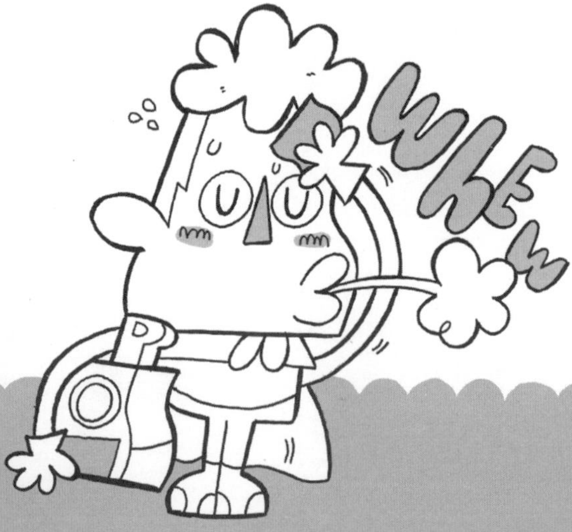
WHEW

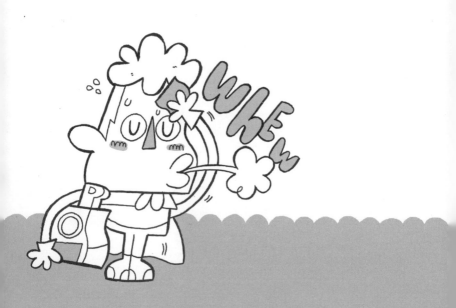

CHRIS ELIOPOULOS is a professional illustrator and cartoonist from Chicago! He is also an adjunct professor at Columbia College Chicago in the art and design department. He is the writer and artist of several all-ages graphic novels and series: *Okie Dokie Donuts* published by Top Shelf; *Gabba Ball!* published by Oni Press; and *Monster Party* published by Koyama Press. OTHER clients include Disney Animation Studios, Yo Gabba Gabba!, Nick Jr., Cloudkid, and Simon and Schuster.